A Georgian Love Story

London is made up of villages, once separate but now joined together as the vast city has expanded. One of the villages used to contain both a good area and a bad one, as Ernest Raymond dramatizes in this new novel.

The scene is set in the Edwardian and Georgian years, and it is likely that people with long enough memories will have little difficulty in recognizing Hollen Hill and Hollen Dene. Mr. Augustus O'Murry, chief editor of an old and failing publishing firm, lives in a large house in the respectable Hollen Hill. But his son, Stewart, being young, longs to know what goes on in the disreputable area of Hollen Dene, only a few streets away. In his search for the unknown here he finds himself following a seductive girl whom he suspects to be one of the very young prostitutes for whom the neighbourhood is notorious. He follows her into a small tobacconist's shop, and here the first of many great surprises awaits him. This chance acquaintance develops unexpectedly into a deep love. Stewart, who calls the girl by his own chosen name, Raney, introduces her to great literature and rejoices in educating her; Raney in return realizes that she has the chance to grow out of her environment and adores her mentor.

The parents of Raney and Stewart become resigned to what seemed an impossible marriage. But Fate has another trick to play, which must remain for the reader to discover. In the end Stewart accepts a commission in the Royal Naval Division and goes to war.

BOOKS BY ERNEST RAYMOND

NOVELS

A London Gallery *comprising*:

We, the Accused
The Marsh
Gentle Greaves
The Witness of Canon Welcome
A Chorus Ending
The Kilburn Tale
Child of Norman's End
For Them That Trespass

Was There Love Once?
The Corporal of the Guard
A Song of the Tide
The Chalice and the Sword
To the Wood No More
The Lord of Wensley
The Old June Weather
The City and the Dream

Other Novels

The Bethany Road
The Mountain Farm
The Tree of Heaven
One of Our Brethren
Late in the Day
Mr. Olim
The Chatelaine
The Visit of Brother Ives
The Quiet Shore
The Nameless Places
Tell England
A Family That Was
The Jesting Army

Mary Leith
Morris in the Dance
The Old Tree Blossomed
Don John's Mountain Home
The Five Sons of Le Faber
The Last to Rest
Newtimber Lane
The Miracle of Brean
Rossenal
Damascus Gate
Wanderlight
Daphne Bruno I
Daphne Bruno II

BIOGRAPHIES, ETC.

The Story of My Days (Autobiography I)
Please You, Draw Near (Autobiography II)
Good Morning, Good People (Autobiography III)
Paris, City of Enchantment
Two Gentlemen of Rome
(*The Story of Keats and Shelley*)
In the Steps of St. Francis
In the Steps of the Brontës

ESSAYS, ETC.

Through Literature to Life
The Shout of the King
Back to Humanity (with Patrick Raymond)

PLAYS

The Berg
The Multabello Road

A
GEORGIAN
LOVE
STORY

by

ERNEST RAYMOND

So it closed, and in these pages let it lie,
For who shall answer, if I ask him why?

CASSELL · LONDON

CASSELL & COMPANY LTD
35 RED LION SQUARE, LONDON WC1
Melbourne, Sydney, Toronto
Johannesburg, Auckland

First published 1971

I.S.B.N. 0 304 93716 9

Printed in Great Britain by
Cox & Wyman Ltd
London, Fakenham and Reading
F. 1070

for

GEORGE AND NANCY WOODS

with love

Contents

		page
1.	The Place	1
2.	The Hour	9
3.	Hollen Dene	13
4.	But the Next Year	19
5.	Peripeteia	35
6.	Conspiracy	51
7.	The Call Again	61
8.	Signing on and Walking out	72
9.	'Hadn't We the Gaiety'	95
10.	Between Old Swan and Southend Piers	115
11.	The Parents	123
12.	The Meeting House	147
13.	The Return Call	155
14.	Hadley Wood and Aldith's Garden	174
15.	'Theophrastus'	193
16.	'You Can Trust Her to Him'	200
17.	Fate Takes a Hand	217
18.	June, July	234
19.	Assignment with Truth	245
20.	It Remains like Yesterday	261
21.	St. Paschal's and St. Mary's	270
22.	Farewells	278

I

The Place

It was nearly sixty years ago; only a few more years to pass by, and it will be seventy years. And yet, ever and again, the urge comes upon me to wander back to those streets where it all happened, and, in dreamy mood, to recover the life we lived in Edwardian and Georgian days. Living now in my Sussex vales, I am far enough from what was then the Royal Borough of Kensington and from that strange area in its north where Prosperity and High Gentility stood shoulder-to-shoulder against a shadowed neighbourhood into which the law-breakers filtered, and where crimes were frequent, and which should have had no part in a Royal Borough. This part was a twilight and notorious district in my days; it is not so now; it has lost its Alsatian and therefore romantic character and is just a grey, unprosperous outmoded part of London: why, a policeman, all alone, can walk about it unafraid; and there is even a new and shining police station in its heart, with all the windows intact.

Yesterday I was lunching in my club during a day in town, and all the chatter at our centre table was about a landing on the moon. I listened with some sadness because it suddenly seemed to me that everything in my life had become antediluvian—or 'Ante-lunarian' as I put it to another old boy sitting opposite me. 'Ante-lunatic,' he grumbled; and I couldn't help hoping this was nearer the truth. Because the talk was making me think, 'I am old now; my children are nearing middle age and have full-grown children of their own.' I have often talked to them of Father, their grandfather or great-grandfather, because my memories amuse them, but how is it possible for them to know, or to feel anything, about happenings that struck so deep in my heart sixty years ago?

I have told them about Father, yes, but seldom, if ever, have I spoken of Raney.

Well, after lunching, and while still thinking these thoughts, my afternoon free, I found the old call of my childhood and youth dragging at me again, and I yielded to it. Wandering out of the club, I took the Twopenny Tube—I beg your pardon: I took at Tottenham Court Road the Central London Railway, which was the first of the 'Tubes' deep under London and in my childhood had only existed for a year or two, having been opened in 1900 by the Prince of Wales, soon to be King Edward. It was then the Central London Electric Railway, running from Shepherd's Bush to the Bank with one fare only, twopence, no matter at what station you alighted.

Alighting at Hollen Hill station, I found, in my present mood, that it was just the old station of my youth, its every passage, corridor and stairway a soiled white tube, with huge tubes above you and smaller pipes or tubes beside you. The only difference was that now, instead of heavy old engines and brown old coaches, lovely silver gleaming trains journeyed up and down through these scenes of the past—for surely this world where I was walking had died; or, anyhow, was dying fast. The exterior of the station was just as it used to be, except that someone had removed from the window:

FARE

2d

To Any Station

I turned up a broad residential road near the station to walk a few hundred yards into my past. The road still looked handsome and prosperous; its tall Victorian mansions, even though divided into maisonettes, were mostly white with new paint and looking as they were intended to look a hundred years ago. Only the listing piers of their gates, and the dwarf walls of their gardens seemed to enclose the sites of a dead world. It was a warm afternoon, and the trees that had been planted in these gardens—ashes, planes and limes, all very tall now—tall as forest trees—dropped their scent on the pavement, the warm scent of the limes prevailing over all.

Towards the top of this broad straight road I came upon my goal: the Crescents. The Crescents are four in number, and they wheel parallel with one another, each having private house-gardens behind it and a common garden between it and other back-gardens. Now, these parallel crescents form one of the strangest architectural compositions in London because they began in the first years of Victoria's reign as a fine attempt at town planning; all were designed to curve around the spired church of St. Jude's on the low summit of Hollen Hill—but then—well, they were never properly completed; they never fulfilled the admirable and elegant dream; they started well; they meant well; but the plan failed and stopped; so that now the easterly houses are classical and stately (according to Victorian ideas) with porticoes, pediments, pilasters and balustrades, but after about two-thirds of each crescent, all this stateliness stops—stops dead—and the houses become flat, unornamented and almost mean. No more pillared porticoes; no pedimented windows or balustraded cornices. In all London I think there is no more sudden change from a dream of prosperity to an acceptance of failure; from ambition to abandonment. Pomposity is abruptly left behind. The money, I suppose, gave out; or someone's heart gave out; the architects folded up their plans and went their way; and less ambitious men completed the Crescents with humbler homes for the less well-to-do.

But the failure of a fine plan may not have been due to money alone. Was it perhaps that as the low Hollen Hill sloped down to west and north it drew too near to the flat and squalid area of unenviable fame? Or was it that, as the houses in the Crescents sharply changed their handsome façades and became poor, the homes on the flats became poorer still and, as happened elsewhere in Victorian London, began to appeal to the bad lads and the wide boys as a suitable and amiable rabbitry or warren? Probably because this area of ill-repute lay on a flat plain under a hill it was known as Hollen Dene, but we always referred to it as 'The Dene', not wishing to have its name associated with our highly respectable homes on the upper slopes of Hollen Hill.

I walked into Dunkerry Crescent, past the great divide between pretentious and poor, and was now among the houses that were still pompous to look at, though this was now a faded and disconsolate London street. A few yards, and I stopped to stare at one of the houses. There it was: with all its old stucco ornament; five storeys of it if you count the semi-basement and an attic floor; but decayed now with the tumbled stucco unveiling coarse brickwork beneath, balusters cracked or falling, and separate bells for its separate maisonettes. In the narrow patch of grass between basement and dwarf-wall the ash-tree which in our day reached only a little higher than the first floor was now a mighty giant, taller than the house and half as broad.

To this house we had come when I was but four years old; behind those windows I had frolicked with my sisters, Aldith and Augusta, though they were eleven and ten years older than I; in that first-floor room our mother had died of heart-failure (though Aldith always declared that she had died of Father) and Augusta, then twenty-five, had assumed the management of the home, Aldith having long since married—quickly married, chiefly, as she would say, to escape from her beloved father.

As I stood on that pavement gazing at the old house, rebuilding the past, and dwelling less in the present hour than in the first years of this century, it was seldom Aldith or Augusta or myself whom I saw emerging from that front door and coming down those steps between the pillars of the portico, but always the figure of my father in frock coat and silk hat, his great height and breadth, and his wide drooping moustaches matching well with the pomposity of the portico. So big was my father, so did he seem to fill this not-small house that I was about to write of it as his 'forme' or his 'earth' but perceived at once that to mention the lairs of humble animals, whether the bed of a hare or the burrow of a fox, would be inappropriate to so self-important a man, and so impressive a figure. It would be less inapt, I decided, to suggest that he indwelt the house as the Almighty indwells the universe.

To penetrate the depth of my huge father's huge self-esteem

you should dwell upon our names. His first name was Augustus (as if his parents had foreseen what was coming), his second name Aylmer, and his surname O'Murry. Augustus Aylmer O'Murry. The Aylmer came from his mother and when he discovered that it was an old Saxon name, originally Æthelmere, compounded of words meaning 'noble' and 'famous'—adjectives wholly acceptable to him—but modified later by the Normans into Aylmer, he chose to believe that he was sprung from a family that had been here long before the Norman Conquest; and accordingly he selected for his first daughter the Saxon and indeed charming name, Aldith. This was when we were Saxons. I think we were still Saxons when Augusta was born and named, but if this name had no Saxon, it was a fine and imperial one like his own. I was born ten years after Augusta, and he gave me the name Stewart, because we were Scotch then. Father had long disliked the 'O' in his surname, because he declined to be an Irishman, and he was not well satisfied with the humble-sounding 'Murry', until he heard a powerful baritone sing 'The Bonny Earl o'Murray', squeezing every ounce of emotion and drama from the grand old ballard. With all his stops out he sang:

> He was a braw gallant,
>   And he rid at the ring;
> And the bonny Earl o' Murray
>   O, he might hae been a king.

> He was a braw gallant,
>   And he played at the ba';
> And the bonny Earl o' Murray
>   Was the flower among them a'.

> O, lang will his Lady
>   Look frae the Castle doon,
> Ere she see the Earl o' Murray
>   Come soonding through the toon.

Then we were Scotch.

The bonny earl, he learned, might more properly have been named James Stewart Moray, so we became a Highland family sprung from the hills of Moray and distantly related to this

5

romantic ancestor who had been a regent of Scotland and was shot by Hamilton of Bothwellhaugh. There was no evidence to support this pleasing fancy; it was hope, not history. All he would say was 'It's generally believed that we are a sept of the Clan Moray'. Thus I got my name Stewart, and Father his highland descent, his semi-royal blood, and a delight instead of a distress in his surname. He would tell us how he would like to change his name to Moray, but that his natural modesty forbade it. I suspect that it was only his fear of people's ridicule that inhibited such a step, but he did not admit this to us. He explained the inaction by saying only, 'A gentleman does not brag about his birth.'

There were factors in our fine-sounding names which he had not foreseen, and of which he much disapproved. From the first onset of his manhood, or perhaps I should say 'his first onset of chronic gentleman-hood', he had always been offended if someone unwisely addressed him as 'Gus'. And now he would loose the strong disapproval when Augusta's female friends called her 'Gussy' or, worse, 'Gusty'. 'Why not say "Disgusty" and be done with it,' he would bewail. And then, worst of all, my friends in school, in the street, or in our home, took to calling me 'Stew'. This was so bad that it usually drove him into a shocked silence rather than into speech. His mouth under the drooping moustaches pressed upward towards his big nose in total disapproval. If he could bring himself to speak, he would say, 'I so hate the vulgarity of it. I hate all vulgarity.'

It must be 1903 or thereabouts as I (still dreaming yesterday on the pavement of this tired street) see my father coming out of that doorway in silk hat and frock coat, followed by Aldith in large feathered hat and black veil, buttoning the last button of her long gloves, and by myself in Eton suit, starched collar, and smaller top-hat. This top-hat of mine shows that it is Sunday and that we are off to St. Jude's Church on the crown of our hill for Morning Prayer. Father held that an Anglican puritanism, like the frock coat, was the only proper wear for a gentleman, though I was soon to doubt if there was much more to it than this. He insisted that we went regularly to church; he was even for some years a sidesman at the church, and the most imposing of them all; for one year he was the People's Warden; but I was beginning to guess that he would often wonder, in the privacy of his study and behind his pipe, how Augusta, a simple soul, could swallow all that the Church taught.

I gathered something of this from his brother, my dear Uncle Douglas (of whom you shall hear much). Always making fun of his older and too pompous brother, Uncle Douglas would explain to me how poor Augusta was 'a great grief to your excellent father'. He so big, and she so thickly built and not even pretty! And all his life he had dreamed of a daughter, tall and beautiful, whom he could love and even worship. Aldith, though tall and pretty enough, didn't fulfil the life-long dream either. A much cleverer girl than her younger sister, she had her moments of mutiny and from an early age was overtly sceptical about religion (though attending church under orders) until, at twenty-one, she married a wholly irreligious solicitor, Jack Fellbright. Augusta, a 'born disciple', as I learned to call her, carried her churchmanship so far as to become a 'district visitor' and to teach in Sunday school, where she had some difficulty in keeping order among a large class of children who had come less for the truths of the Gospel than for the 'treats' in summer; and less because their parents desired them to be brought up in the fear and nurture of the Lord than because they desired a peaceful Sunday afternoon. I, as a gentleman's son, could not attend a Sunday school but had to attend a service at three in the afternoon, especially arranged for 'Children of the Congregation' who could not be expected to sit with the children of the poor.

This was a Sunday in June, and when Morning Prayer was over we came out of the church with the people whose carriages were waiting for them behind the plane-trees that encircled the church's green island; but we who were less than 'carriage folk' walked down St. Jude's Road to Hollen Hill High Street and took a green bus to Hyde Park for the Church Parade in Rotten Row. I was always allowed to ride on the top of the bus; if possible in the front seat by the driver's high perch, my father having given me my penny for the fare. If I secured that front seat I always noticed how loosely the driver held his reins, the horses, as he expounded, knowing their way by heart and understanding at once the meaning of the conductor's bell.

We found seats in the park by Rotten Row and watched the people promenading along the sidewalk in their fine Sunday clothes, or the riders on their sleek mounts, or the carriages of the fashionable with their high-stepping horses padding splendidly by. We recognized famous persons in the promenade or the calvacade, and hoped, but without success on this occasion, that one of the latter might be Queen Alexandra herself, or even the King, raising his grey topper in response to the straw boaters or silk hats that ascended all the way along his route, and the bowings or curtseyings of the ladies.

2

The Hour

1903, and just as the Crescents were a half-way point in London, with high gentility and decency on one side of them and the beginnings of something much lower on the other, so, standing in my old street, I thought of 1903, when my story begins, as a half-way point in time. But we did not discern this. Father sat by the Row, maintaining the mellow dignity of a silk-lapelled frock coat; and neither he nor anybody else promenading on foot or in carriage or on horseback foresaw what was shaping the world and would soon be upon us. Those who did discern a gathering darkness were little likely to be disporting themselves in Rotten Row. None of us in the Row that day understood the hour in which we sat.

Horses possessed the streets as well as the Row. Hansoms, broughams, buses, carts, and even in a few outskirts of London, trams were still drawn with grace by horses instead of by a series of explosions. Motor-buses were no longer an uncommon sight, but private motor-cars were still vehicles that could turn one's eyes to study them. And no one saw them as vehicles that would blaze the way to a new civilization. Not much longer would our St. Jude's be crowded for Morning Prayer; the week's end would belong no more to the Vicar and his Sunday, since many of his congregation would have sped away in their cars to green places or to sea beaches or to new week-end cottages.

The hansom has always been the symbol of Victorian–Edwardian London; and it was only the next year —or was it 1905?—that I witnessed what was really a parable of the hansom. Its horse, an animal of taste, shied away from a private motor-car passing it noisily and smelling abominably, and flung itself down across the ditch in disgust, so that the cab's upper part rested on the pavement's kerb. The driver in his midway throne behind the roof was lucky to escape with little hurt except to his feelings. These were so deeply wounded that he stood on the pavement and vented a brimming and plenary invective—continuous, repetitive, exhaustive, even at times inspired—against the goggled and ulstered driver of the car who had halted to help. His vehemence empurpled the atmosphere over a considerable area and before a considerable audience. I confess that with the rest of the fast-assembling crowd I enjoyed the excitement, and the language, but did not see the parable of it all. I did not see it as the beginning of an end, or the beginning of a beginning.

Change was beginning in our highly class-conscious Dunkerry Crescent. During the previous decade our neighbours, whether we knew them or not, had been persons of substance and, here and there, of distinction. Up the road lived a well-known dramatist, Mortimer Vale, and just across the road there was a Sir: Sir Aubrey Darte, high in the Civil Service, whom I always called Strawberry Tart, rather to Father's disapproval because he was not happy with the word 'tart'. ('I dislike all vulgarity.') Yet farther up the road was a beautiful woman with three young children who was of interest to us because it was whispered that she had been the great Lord Raintree's mistress and that these rosy children were the bonny fruits of his love. But now, slowly, the residents were changing. The richer, getting still richer in these prosperous years, went with their new cars to homes in the country or to more spacious houses near the parks; and the unprofessional classes, the shop-keepers and small merchants, having prospered likewise, rose from the lower ranks of the great Middle Class to take over our houses and commence to be gentlemen. 1906, 1907, and Dunkerry Crescent was at the start of its slide downhill. Father was now Editorial and Production Manager of a fine old-fashioned publishing house, Paul and Bembridge Ltd.— he generally spoke of himself as its 'Literary Director', which sounded well without implying that he had a seat on the board—and, considering himself very much one of the professional classes, he deplored this invasion of our neighbourhood by Trade. Publishing, even though it breathed and lived by manufacture, sale, and profit, was never in his view, or in anybody else's, so far as I know, Trade. Practitioners in this market were professional gentlemen. It was the same, and as far as I can see, still is, with the brewing gentlemen. And so it was to be with the makers and sellers of the new motor-cars. Gentlemen all.

Father, though perturbed by this advent of Trade among us, protested that his anxieties had nothing to do with snobbery. 'It's not that I'm class-conscious, Stewart,' he said to me one day. 'That's the last thing you could say about me. I get on magnificently with all tradespeople and with any working man who comes to do a job in my house or garden. Actually I would say I experience an outrush of goodwill towards them; and they respond; they enjoy my banter and my jokes. It's the same with the workers in our warehouse; the packers, for instance. They're just illiterate working men, but splendid fellows, most of them; and the office boy—he's a delightful youngster. I think it's hardly an exaggeration to say I literally love our workers; and I think they like and admire me. But there it is: if one's a gentleman one can't help wanting one's own class around one. You see what I mean? It's not snobbery to want persons of your own taste and culture about you. Be merry with tradespeople by all means—I get on splendidly with my tailor—but that's only for a passing moment. For permanent association give me gentlemen.'

So Father would say, but I don't think I ever heard anyone in whose voice and tone, when speaking with the lower orders, there rang a more palpable sense of social superiority and a greater happiness in condescension. Not that they seemed to apprehend this, but I did, from about twelve years old, and upward. So much so that, as my French improved I dubbed him to Aldith *Monsieur de Haut-en-bas*.

I could see that my big massive father was a mass of prides: pride in this geniality with common people; pride in his humour, though in fact it was of a limited order; pride in his ability to walk twenty miles and more in the country outside London, his sole companion being his big labrador, Hamish (we were Scotch when he acquired this animal); pride, vast pride, in Hamish, probably unjustified, though he was a big black handsome beast, well suited to his master; pride in his knowledge of French, and a disparaging of everyone else's 'accent', including his wife's and his children's—I never dared speak a French word in front of Father for fear of having its pronunciation amended; pride in his skills with any tool—this well justified, for he was a superb painter, decorator, carpenter, glazier, plumber and electrician—there was nothing about the house he couldn't do, or didn't love to do; and lastly, pride in his physical appearance, justified too, I suppose.

I remember a warm Saturday when he had put on the old trousers, stained with paint and threadbare at the hems, which he kept for house decoration or gardening; also an open-necked shirt but no braces ('no gentleman ever displays his braces, Stewart') and had gone out into this narrow front-garden (now beneath my eyes again) to repair the brick-work of its wall and renew the stucco on one of the gate's low piers (this one before me). Mother, who was still alive, came out of that front door and asked 'Do you think, Augustus, the neighbours ought to see you like that? You look rather like our crossing-sweeper.'

'That doesn't worry me,' declared my father. 'I've always said you can recognize a gentleman no matter how he's dressed.'

I overheard this and, though still only about thirteen, decided that it was remarkably untrue.

There was a day when one of our new and less desirable neighbours, a Mr. Wellington-Smith, suggested that they both pulled off some shady trick—I forget what—on their common landlord; Father refused; and very proud he was of this refusal. 'There are some things, Stewart, which a gentleman simply can't do. That's the difference between us and the lower classes. It would have paid me, of course, to do what he suggested but, well . . . I just couldn't bring myself to do it.' And he shrugged helplessly. 'It's the penalty of being a gentleman. Mr. Smith is emphatically not a gentleman. And "*Wellington-Smith*"! Such snobbery!'

3

Hollen Dene

Done with dreaming on a pavement before the old home, done with plucking faded memories from the past, I turned aside and, leaving house and Father behind, walked back past the meaner houses so as to visit again that shadowed and notorious neighbourhood to west and north of us. And as I walked I recalled the first time I ever dared to venture into these ill-favoured streets. I must have been still about thirteen, with Mother still alive, when, unknown to either parent, I stole guiltily, and not without fear, towards these wicked places. I had never attempted this secret adventure before because I had so often heard it said that they were of so dangerous a character that even policemen could patrol them only in pairs. It was a Saturday afternoon when I pretended to the family that I was going to watch a football match at school, but took the opposite direction. There was a good and dreadful reason why I should be drawn that way. Two days before, in the early morning, a prostitute had been found murdered in her lodging, with her throat slashed to the bone. Neither Father nor Mother would have mentioned this to me, but on the Saturday afternoon Elsa, our cook, Ada, our housemaid, and Elsa's husband, Josef Stauffen, a big fat German with some humble job in Brinsmead's, the piano people, exercised far less self-control. I was on the friendliest terms with these three in our basement; perhaps I had inherited Father's geniality with the working classes, but not, I hope, his spectacular delight in condescension; I just loved to be with them. Elsa was now a buxom and bustling woman of forty and Josef, six foot two, was nearly as big as my father—but not as big; I knew no one as big as he. Josef had already lived with us nine years, but I was never, so foreign and guttural was his English, able fully to understand what he was saying. I can give you only an approximation of his utterances.

'A teb-ble biz'ness it is,' he said on this Saturday. 'A girl only yung she vos, and in a pull (pool) of her own blood she was vound. Must'a bin dead for oors. Murdered in the middle of the night or in the small oors.'

'But who did it, d'you suppose?' I asked.

'Dat is not by anyone known. Some strange visitor, *vermutlich*.'

'But who would visit her in the middle of the night,' I objected.

'Ha! Might be any-vun of t'ousands and t'ousands.'

'It's something you wouldn't understand, Master Stewart,' Elsa hastily explained, though to my wide-open eyes, she was fascinated, passionately interested, in the facts it was her duty to hide from me. She was pleased to be hinting at them, if only covertly. 'Anything can happen in them parts. She's not the first person they done in since we been here.'

'And so close to us,' said the shocked Ada. 'Barely a mile away.'

Elsa improved on this. 'A shade more'n that, but not much. Oh, I wouldn't go along them streets for something.' And she turned and said to Ada, not for my hearing, her voice dropped: 'Some of them girls live in a you-know-what, with a lady looking after them.'

'*Ja*. Vot they call a Madame,' Josef supplied obligingly.

'And I'm told,' Elsa went on, with her eyes still away from me, 'that they jest loiter in the streets of a fine afternoon or evening because it's a recker-nised place for people up West to come and find 'em. Or they jest sit in their open doorways waiting. She's not the only one in that there street, not by a long chalk. Goley Street and St. Michael's Row are the two roads most famous for the you-know-whats.'

'Oh, I do think it's awful,' Ada bemoaned. 'I agree with you: I wouldn't go along one of them roads for nothing, I wouldn't.'

My ears were as open as my eyes. 'What's the name of the street where it happened?' I asked, feigning but a careless interest.

'Where *what* happened?'

'This murder.'

'Oh, *that*. St. Michael's Row. St. Michael's Row, of all unsuitable names.'

'*Ja*. St. Michael,' Josef echoed with a laugh. 'St. Michael and all Angels. But they're not all angels in *dat* street. It's a bad street. There are public houses there where the old criminals get together. Birds of a vether.'

'Yes, and caffs and doss-houses which the police know are their haunts, but they leave 'em be, because it suits 'em to know where they can put their hands on a suspect.'

A paper, the *Morning Chronicle*, lay on the kitchen table open at a headline which my eye now caught, 'The North Kensington Murder'. I picked it up but Josef put a hand on it to take it back, saying, 'Dat's no reading for you. *Nein*.'

Elsa, however, intervened. 'There's nothing there that can hurt no one. And nothing he don't know already. Do him good to see what decent people think about it.'

Josef shrugged and muttered something like '*Jawohl*' and '*Gut*'.

So I skimmed over a little of it. 'This shocking affair is a revelation of the dreadful conditions subsisting in an area of London proud to be called "The Royal Borough". Here at no distance from handsome houses where some of our most distinguished citizens can be found there are these purlieus largely inhabited by some of our least desirable denizens: people indifferent to all law and decency, with morals little better than—indeed probably inferior to—those of savages in an African kraal. . . .'

Now, as completely fascinated as Elsa, and filled with a hidden and half-ashamed craving, which has always lain in me and lies in most of us, I suspect, to savour the dirt of the world, I sauntered out of Elsa's kitchen, covering with a show of ease what I now had a mind to do. Father was in his study reading a manuscript submitted for publication and probably condemning its English, for he held that few people could write proper English but himself; Mother and Augusta were in their rooms dressing for some tea-party; so I slipped from the house

15

and walked quickly till the curve of our crescent took me out of their view; then fell into a slower pace, for I was not wholly unafraid of where I was going, and what I would find there. Or what might meet me there. I remembered Father telling me, as we passed one day the new Law Courts in the Strand, that these magnificent Gothic Halls of Justice (as he thought them) had been erected, most appropriately, over an area of courts and alleys 'largely inhabited by criminal elements'; and it was something like this that I expected to see.

Remarkable the deterioration from the ornate mansions in our part of Dunkerry Crescents, through the humbler but still genteel houses, and thence through narrow streets into a district of small grey-brick homes that plainly housed the 'workers', whether their work was within the Law or without it. Most of the little houses looked neat enough and clean enough and commonplace enough to disappoint my hunger for things strange and bad; but there was an aptness in the way the deterioration had marched exactly with the decline of our hill, this 'semi-slum' area lying on a bottom as flat as a marshland in the Fens. My heart palpitated a little as I walked past these small grey homes and I kept near the pavement's kerb or the gutter, fearing I knew not what—perhaps a sudden attack from one of these narrow doors, because Elsa had talked of strangers being 'coshed and robbed in the worst streets'. But here was this first street looking like any other street of the poor—long and quiet and nearly empty. There was a grey-brick board-school with sternly separate entries for 'Girls', 'Boys', and 'Infants', and I wondered who dared to come daily and teach here. Wandering on, I passed small dreary grey-brick warehouses, an unimpressive factory for making cardboard boxes, and a small sickly church with a spire much shorter than ours on St. Jude's, possibly because its aspirations were much lower in this neighbourhood. A dozen steps onward, and a surprise awaited me. Before a humble parish hall stood a crowd of children, many of them barefoot and nearly all in clothes too large or too small, either because they'd come down from older brothers and sisters or because they had been outgrown. These children seemed to be waiting for something

16

to emerge from the little hall. What it might be I could not imagine and was far too uneasy to ask, but after another step or two, one of four loitering men looked me up and down, to my alarm, and said either merrily or sourly—I knew not which: 'Yes, *you're* all right. You've *'ad* your dinner, and a good'un too, I daresay, but these poor little nippers are waiting for theirs. Parson gives it 'em as soon as the Army comes along to 'elp.'

'I see,' I said; which was quite untrue. Army? What on earth could he mean? Why should the army come marching into these parts? It didn't enter my head that he meant the Salvation Army. And dinner? Dinner, when it was already nearly three o'clock?

'You're not from these 'ere parts, sonny, are yer?' continued the man. And I realized, what had not occurred to me when I set out, that my blue serge school suit, starched Eton collar and coloured school cap would mark me as an odd unexpected visitor.

'No,' I said; and hurried on, wanting to be alone again.

So this was Hollen Dene. The infamous 'Dene', to which we were so unwilling to admit a relationship and accord the name 'Hollen'. The whole place, as I walked through it, was so different from our part of the Royal Borough, and from other parts east, west, south and north of it, that it looked like some different village which had been caught up and surrounded by prospering middle-class London as it marched east, west, south and north in the mid-Victorian years.

I did not dare to ask the way to St. Michael's Row, which was what I wanted to find so that I could look at houses one of which held the room where a woman had been found with her throat cut. It was by accident, and with a quick thrill, that I came upon its name at a street corner as I was returning home. St. Michael's Row: a long road, geometrically straight, of little houses, each with a separate gable but all joined together in a long terrace; both sides of the street the same; a public house at the far end. I walked the length of it but though there were people gossiping on doorsteps or in groups on the pavements, there was nothing to inform me which was the house of

17

the murder. 'She was not the only one in that there road,' Elsa had said with a strange relish. 'Not by a long chalk,' and I stared down the street, trying to guess at what these words meant.

And so home, fascinated, excited, but no wiser.

Such was my first venture, at thirteen years old, into our twilight area, so notorious sixty or seventy years ago, and such was its appearance then. But when yesterday I went wandering into it again I found it in every way improved, though still a neighbourhood with some grey parts that depressed the heart, but certainly no place to start fears; no place where police could walk only in pairs; indeed there was this shining new police station in the heart of it; there were cheery red-brick tenement buildings rising in sharp contrast with the old grey terraces; and the pubs from dingy taverns had become smart—or smart enough—hostelries. But St. Michael's Row was the same as ever, and a few other parts still looked to be homes of poverty which no Welfare State had been able to reach and overthrow. The little church hall before which the barefoot children had waited was clearly scheduled for demolition: corrugated iron sheets covered its smashed windows, and its padlocked doors were now a blackboard for the display of dirty words and drawings or the publication of the latest local news such as 'Alfie loves Molly J'.

For half an hour I wandered from street to street, gathering old memories as children used to gather little flocks of sheep's wool from thorny hedgerows. From my thorny hedgerows of memory I plucked many a vivid or shadowy picture of the past; faint recollections of the Rubin Vice Ring, of the murders in St. Michael's Row; pictures of the Wayburns' unlikely Meeting House and of hot-gospel services there; but most of all, of course, haunting every street, my memories of Raney.

4

But the Next Year

If as I have surmised, it was a Sunday in 1903, when in imagination I saw Father emerging out of 52 Dunkerry Crescent to attend Morning Prayer at St. Jude's with Augusta and a top-hatted Stewart in train, then it was three years later, 1906, that the unimaginable things happened.

The first of them was unimaginable only to Father; not to me who was then seventeen—fully imaginable to me: Augusta announced her engagement to the Rev. Abel Johns, a missionary on furlough from his church in India who had been giving Sunday help to Canon Plumworthy at St. Jude's.

Aldith, the older and far stronger of Father's two daughters, had often said to me when I was no more than ten years old that she'd marry the first man who asked her so as to escape as quickly as possible from Father's dominance and his hourly fault-finding; and in fact she was barely twenty-one when she gave herself to a solicitor, Jack Fellbright. When first she mentioned Jack to Father she spoke of him as her 'young man', a phrase which annoyed him since he declared it to be 'common'. It was the language of a housemaid, he said. 'You'll be talking of "walking out" with him soon, or saying that he's "courting" you'—which accordingly was what Aldith said for ever after. And it was only a month or two after her 'walking out with her young man' and his courting of her, that she married him at a register office without a word to Father. I was but eleven at the time so that this instant marriage implied no more to me than that Aldith, as she had foretold, had got herself out of 'Pa's' reach as quickly as possible; it required a year or two more before I discerned how completely Aldith must have rebelled against Father's professedly puritan standards. ('Personally,' he would say, 'I'm never ashamed when people call me a Puritan. I gladly accept the title.') Whether Father ever knew that they'd married suddenly and secretly because they'd anticipated the blessing of the Church I don't know; no grandchild arrived prematurely; but I have little doubt that he always suspected it. For a long time he was as chilly as a foggy day in November towards Jack Fellbright, who—all too probably—had dared seduce his daughter, though barely an acquaintance of the family, and he a solicitor too.

But Augusta! Augusta, the simple one, the *truly* pious one, the Sunday school teacher, the dutiful daughter, the 'born disciple', as I was to call her—that she in her own private and silent way should have wearied sufficiently of her too critical taskmaster and have rebelled to the extent of accepting the hand of an old parson twenty-six years older than she, and been ready to escape with him to India! It was wonderful. It was also magnificent. Aldith and I could have lifted our heads and assaulted Heaven with our laughter and cheers. It was not, of course—emphatically not—that the Rev. Father Abel Johns, like Jack Fellbright, had forestalled the legal sanctions of Church and State; it was only that he had to go back soon to Poona.

Aldith and I were, I think, manifestly Father's children, both of us tall and with features reminiscent of his, though less tall than he, I climbing to six foot, she about five foot ten, and both had slighter bodies and hair less black. Augusta was clearly our Mother's daughter, short, plump and fair. If magnificent and uproarious to us, this engagement was not so to Father. Just as Father could pretend to a Victorian puritanism, so he could pretend to an attractive sentimentality about a daughter; he was so far behind the clock of history that he did not know this kind of Victorian sentimentality was already out of fashion; and he would express his sorrow that Augusta lacked all beauty and was likely to remain a spinster all her life. Sometimes his eloquent phrasing of this grief affected him almost to tears, as once when he said to Uncle Douglas, 'I'd have so loved to have a beautiful daughter, Douglas, and to have seen her happily married to a good man with a baby at her breast.'

But now that there was every prospect of this beautiful

picture being granted him (at the double cost of losing a house-keeper and having to disburse large monies for a wedding breakfast) he professed a sad disapproval—ostensibly on the ground that the Rev. Abel was twenty-six years older than his bride. It was not quite nice, he said. 'I can't pretend that it is. Old enough to be her father. Older than I am. It's not that I'm losing a valuable housekeeper; don't think that. I hope I'm above that sort of selfishness. I would cheerfully have surrendered her to some young man of her own age. And then there's India. How do we know that the climate of India will suit her? Nowadays she's practically my only daughter.'

His other daughter, on the other hand, rejoiced in the twenty-six years' seniority. 'At any rate,' she said to me one Sunday when she'd come on a visit from her home in Ealing, 'we can't call Father Abel her "young man". That ought to please Papa. But I'm aching to tell him that Abel's been "walking out" with her for some time. "Courting", in fact. And that I've no doubt he'll do his stuff about the baby.'

'But *can* you at fifty-seven?' I asked.

'Can you *not*? Don't be so innocent, Stew.'

'I only thought it might be getting difficult.'

'Rubbish. It only gets difficult somewhere in the eighties, I believe. I'm sure that Jack . . . but never mind that. . . . Good for Augusta. She can have all the babies that Pa longs to see at her breast.'

'Are you going to say that to him? I don't think I should advise you to. It's no sort of talk for the bonny Earl o' Murray —coming from a delicately nurtured female. It wouldn't suit our Gustus at all.'

'No. Most unseemly. I'd better keep the delightful thought to myself. But, Stew, I hope you realize that, now Augusta's doing a bunk, you'll have to keep house for him.'

'I certainly won't. It's clearly your duty to come back and be a good daughter to him.'

'Me? *Me*? With Jack and the children? Have my children disciplined and corrected at every point and told that something they're doing is either unladylike or bad grammar or mis-pronounced French—not on your life. If my children are enjoy-

ing some freedom it's thanks to their grandpa. My children are
not going through what we went through. No, I tell you what,
Stew. The sooner you marry someone who'll come and look
after him, the better. Pa always liked you better than any of us
—or wanted to.'

This strangely pleased me, even if I replied only, 'He had
funny ways sometimes of showing his love.'

'Naturally. Because, as I say, he didn't manage to bring it
off. At least not as he wanted to. He tried hard, I think. At
first.'

Still, however Father might have been embarrassed by this
arrival in his family of the Rev. Abel Johns, and by this sudden compulsion to spend large sums of money, he played his
part better than Aldith and I had foreseen. Aldith had said
that he would have loved to love his children, and to be loved
by them; and it may be that in clear moments, as he smoked his
pipe, a lonely anchorite in a closed study, he half-perceived
that it was his hypertrophied and incurable self-esteem which
had forfeited the affection of them all. And in the end, though
with some sickness of heart as more and more guests were suggested, he did arrange a good wedding party for Augusta, and
gradually became not a little proud of this generosity. He pronounced before us all the proper sentimentalities. 'It's the
great day of her life, I know, and whether I approve of this
marriage or not, it's my duty to play a Father's Part. Besides
I'm going to lose her now, and this'll be the last thing I can do
for her.' Here there was a small break in his voice as he drove
back a suitable swelling in his throat. 'What it's going to cost
me God alone knows, but I'm not going to let that deter me,
and I can only hope that the presents you receive, Augusta, will
justify a very considerable outlay. But I'm glad to do it for you.
Only too glad.'

It shook him again when our brother-to-be, a devout High
Churchman serving the Anglo-Catholic 'Missions to India',
said he would like the wedding to be a Nuptial Mass. A Nuptial
Mass: Father's lips came together and stayed together, under
his moustache. He did not like to admit that he had no idea
what a Nuptial Mass might be, nor, if it was what he sus-

pected, to say that as a good Broad Churchman he disapproved of these High Church goings-on. But here again he behaved generously, saying with a laugh (and an appreciation of his humour), 'You must have whatever you think right. It's you that's marrying the girl, not me, ha, ha. Ha, ha, ha.'

Between the engagement and the wedding Augusta illustrated better than ever before how true was my description of her as a 'born disciple'. Hitherto quietly and unobtrusively 'Broad Church', she was now the happy disciple of her future husband and as extreme an Anglo-Catholic as he.

One day Father, Aldith and I walked into Augusta's bedroom to discuss the marriage. And there, above her bed, Father saw a crucifix hanging, and along her mantelshelf statuettes of the Blessed Virgin Mary, St. Teresa of Avila and St. Augustine of Hippo (her patron saint). There were pictures too of the Queen of Heaven, the Immaculate Conception and other holy but unidentified subjects.

Now Father, even if he was not sure that he believed all Canon Plumworthy taught, was very sure that he didn't hold with crucifixes and statuettes of the B.V.M. Indeed I always used to say that it was on the strength of having no settled convictions that he called himself Broad Church and condemned everything High Church.

'Goodness gracious!' he exclaimed as he saw this holy congregation. 'Who, pray, are all these?'

Augusta identified some of them, with pleasure and pride.

'But this one?' He pointed to a card-picture of an inordinately pretty maiden, round-faced, large-eyed, and haloed, her hair garlanded with pink roses.

'A sexy little piece,' Aldith commented.

'Really, Aldith!' he remonstrated. 'That's hardly the way to talk.'

'But it's so true,' she objected.

'Well, who is she, Augusta?'

'That's St. Philomena,' Augusta told him, proudly again.

'Fillum-who?'

'Philo-mena.'

'And who in Heaven's name was she?'

'She's a saint and martyr. She was made a saint by Pope Gregory XVII in 1837 and called the "Wonder Worker of the Nineteenth Century".'

'Goodness gracious.' Father picked up the pretty card and read on its back, '"Hail, O illustrious Philomena, who so courageously shed thy blood; I praise and glorify the Lord for the honour and power with which He has crowned thee, and I beg thee to obtain for me the graces I ask through thy intercession."'

'Heavens! Do you say this?'

'Of course I do. Regularly. Father Abel says——'

'"Father", is he? I thought *I* was your father. Please, where are we getting to? Who's your father now? Father Abel or Father Augustus?'

'Well, both, I suppose. In a sense.'

'Nonsense. A man who's your husband can't be your father, ha, ha.'

'Oh, yes, he can. In the eyes of Holy Church,' Aldith declared, though she knew little enough nowadays about any church.

Here I came in with, 'If that Augustine there is your patron saint, which Augustine is he?'

'What do you mean?'

'I mean, is he Augustine of Hippo or of Canterbury?'

'But aren't they the same?'

'Of course not. There's only about two hundred years and two thousand miles between them.'

Confused by this new information, Augusta paused and decided, 'Well, I think mine's of Hippo.'

'Good. That's fine,' I said. 'Then Augustine of Canterbury'll do for Father.'

'Thank you; I can manage very well without him,' Father promptly affirmed. 'And I may say that I'm not at all sure I want any room in my house turned into the Brompton Oratory.'

Aldith gave no heed to this; she was more interested in the business of patron saints. 'Who's your Abel's patron saint?' she asked. 'There's no St. Abel, is there?'

I don't know whether power had descended upon Augusta from her saints or whether it came from being suddenly a woman desired and betrothed, but of a certain she had now become more positive, self-assured and humorous. 'I haven't the faintest idea,' she said. 'But if there's no St. Abel, perhaps it's St. John.'

'But which St. John?' I inquired, continuing to be difficult. 'John the Baptist or John the Evangelist?'

'Oh, heavens, *I* don't know.'

'Obviously both,' Aldith offered. 'That's why his name is Johns. Plural, you see. If I were you, Gussy, I'd have——'

'*Must* you call her Gussy?' Father begged.

'I'd have both the Augustines and make Abel have both the Johns. Then you'd both be splendidly catered for.'

I looked at my watch. 'I think we'd better be getting down to the main business. It'll soon be twelve.'

'What's that got to do with anything?' demanded Aldith.

'Simply that Augusta's getting all this kind of thing in a big way, and that she says the Angelus at noon and at six p.m.'

'I certainly do,' said this new Augusta, defiantly.

All this scene in Augusta's room happened long before the archaeologists published their unanimous verdict that the bones discovered in the Catacombs were not those of anyone called Philomena or of any saint or martyr. And it was not till more than fifty years later that Rome removed the little virgin's feast from the calendar and ordered the dismantling of her holy shrine at Mugnano in Italy. Augusta was then a stout Anglo-Catholic still (a stout old lady too), and she declared that she owed no allegiance to any pope, and not for all the popes in Rome would she deny the wonders worked for her by Philomena, Virgin, Martyr, and Thaumaturga.

If our Canon Plumworthy, Vicar of St. Jude's, was no more than a Broad Churchman, he was broad enough and good-hearted enough to do all that a colleague asked; and a fine Nuptial Mass it was (though called only Holy Communion) with the Canon celebrating and a large congregation participating. Had not the bridegroom acted for a while as an assistant priest; had he not won the affection of all; and had

C

not the bride's father been at one time the most imposing of all the church's officers. Imposing he looked today in long frock coat with a white flower in its lapel—up there in the chancel—and standing many inches taller than the bride and several inches taller than either groom or best man on her further side.

Fortunately for his overstrained purse few carriages were needed because it was not four hundred yards from Church to Crescent, and all the tall toppers and feathered cartwheel hats went on their walkers' heads for the small journey. And here we all were in the large drawing-room at No. 52, a shouldering crowd before a well-furnished buffet. I, though seventeen now, and a pretentious and would-be witty seventeen, had still some of the unripened schoolboy in me, so I secured myself a good place at the buffet and spent an exceedingly profitable hour there, unnoticed by the noisy chattering throng. I mean, there were ices and sandwiches and éclairs and sweetmeats and soft drinks and wines red and white waiting there, and champagne to be drunk with the speeches. But there came a time when all these delicacies palled and I was not sure if I cared any more for the sight of them. Nor was I confident that I might not soon be sick. So I wound a way through the massed talkers, thinking it would be safer to be near the door and ready for any emergency. Near the door I saw Uncle Douglas in lively talk with Aldith and was glad of this, because I felt safer in the heart of the family while I was in this touch-and-go condition. I stayed talking with them, and gradually the menace within me settled down; it died and became no more than a ghost of its former self, in the midst of this uproarious conversazione.

My Uncle Douglas always seemed to me a ninety- or hundred-per-cent opposite of Father. Seven years younger than Father—there had been another brother between them who died as an infant—he was, I imagine, of a different composition from the cradle upwards. As boy, youth and man, he was as abreast—or ahead—of his times as Father was loyally—or blindly—behind them. He had no desire for a secure if stolid job with a stable income such as Father recommended, but he went out seeking adventure and large, if insecure, money. Just as my great-uncle had got Father as a youth into the counting house of Paul and Bembridge, Publishers, so Father, having risen in the firm, and proud of his 'influence', started his young brother there. But Douglas after only a few months refused to 'stay on an office stool'. Much to Father's disapproval he threw up the 'secure job' so as to go out and find life. 'No damned office stool for me,' he said to Father, who, though saying nothing, obviously recoiled from this ungentlemanly use of 'damned'. Recovering from this displeasure, he demanded how Douglas proposed to live. Uncle Douglas, having noticed Father's recoil from his 'damned' and thinking this too ridiculous, deliberately and mischievously went one better: he answered, 'I haven't a single bloody idea as yet. All I know is, I'm not going to spend half my life on a stool, adding up other people's money.'

The 'bloody' shocked Father out of his silent restraint. 'I don't know how you come to use such language,' he said. 'I wish you wouldn't. The fact remains that I can't approve of what you're doing. I was content to start humbly at a desk, and I worked my way up to my present position, which is one of some importance, I think.'

'Well, I'm not content to do that. Nor is there any assurance that the blokes above me will die and make room for me. I'm not going to wait for dead men's shoes.'

'Blokes' shook Father again, both because it was common, and because he was presumably one of the blokes. 'I don't know what you mean by "blokes". I hate all slang. I foresee you will regret what you're doing: throwing away secure employment with reasonable prospects in the future and a pension at the end.'

'You may be proved right, Gus, old boy, but we'll see; we'll see.'

No word of distaste from Father for the 'Gus' and the 'old boy'; only some silent pain.

Uncle Douglas had a gift for mischievous comedy and no small talent as a raconteur, so he turned at first to free-lance journalism, sending articles all over the newspaper world. He had a little success at first, but very little, because he still knew nothing of the market; nor had he refined his pen into a sharp enough rapier; but suddenly his thrusts went home. It was in the eighties, the Grant to Church Schools of 1862 and the Elementary Education Act of 1870 were twenty or a dozen years in the past, so there was now a new literate—or at least a new reading—generation in the market, all ready for very different newspapers and magazines from the solemn and heavy productions that had so far suited a privately educated public. Now, if Alfred Harmsworth had stumbled blindly into this fat harvest field with his *Tit-bits*, his *Daily Mail*, and his *Mirror*, Uncle Douglas had perceived at once what was coming; but it was not with the lucky Harmsworth that he found his home. Soon after Harmsworth had founded his Amalgamated Press, John Portwith, his eyes wide open, appreciated what was happening and created his 'Portwith Group', and never was the word 'group' more modest and inappropriate for the vast complex of illustrated newspapers, sporting magazines, women's journals and trade journals, that rapidly changed a group into a multitude—or a mob. Uncle Douglas, his style now at its sharpest, fired off two articles at Portwith papers, one to the *Daily World*, the other to the *Sporting World*, and they so pleased John Portwith himself that he summoned their author to an interview. The fruits of this interview, maturing slowly, were that by the time Uncle Douglas was standing with Aldith at Augusta's wedding feast, he was in exclusive contract to the Portwith Group, dramatic critic of the *Daily World*, 'feature writer' for other Portwith publications, London columnist for the *New York Star* and nominal editor of the *Sportsman's World*. In the *Daily World* at this time he was producing a popular column under the title, 'Bohemia, London' and over the mischievous nom-de-guerre, 'Wenceslas'—Wenceslas, who, according to the carol, had been a King of Bohemia and a man of such sanctity that his footsteps warmed the very snow wherever they trod. To gather his gleanings for this column he had to visit stage and music hall celebrities, frequent the Turf Club and Tattersall's, dine often at the Café Royal and attend very willingly the then fashionable supper clubs or the newsworthy night-clubs of the West End. He had certainly found life. As for John Portwith, in this year of Augusta's marriage, he was to become the first Baron Portwith.

'Hallo, our Stew.' Always Uncle Douglas's greeting of me rang with affection. And nearly always he called me 'Stew' because Father disliked the word. 'Quite a party. The Mandarin has surpassed himself. I take off my hat to him.'

'The Mandarin' was a favourite description of his elder brother for two reasons: the first, because Father's drooping moustaches reminded him of gentlemen in Chinese paintings or even of pigtails; the second because mandarins were of imperial birth or owed this honourable title to depths of knowledge and exceptional abilities.

'I think Pa's been rather splendid over this,' Aldith declared. 'I'm very pleased with him. And, I admit, surprised. Because he hasn't much money to spare and doesn't part with any of it easily. All this must have cost him no small spiritual effort, Uncle dear. He doesn't roll in money like you. Stew, d'you know what Uncle Douglas's present to Augusta was?'

'You shut up about that, Aldith, pet,' Uncle Douglas ordered.

'I'm not going to shut up. Augusta's told me all about it, and it does you great credit. I love you for it.'

'Then she shouldn't have told you. It was a secret between me and her. Good God, breathes there a woman on earth who can keep a confidence?'

Aldith left this query as unworthy of treatment. 'Uncle Douglas gave her a cheque for five hundred pounds, Stew, and said she wasn't to tell Pa because Pa couldn't compete with him in gifts like that and might feel humiliated. You see what a gentleman your Uncle Douglas is. Besides Pa had to meet all the expenses of this jamboree.'

'You've got it wrong, my dear,' said Uncle Douglas. 'I gave her two cheques: one for the slightly larger sum you mention, and one for twenty-five pounds. This last was the official present. I felt I could tell the Mandarin I'd given her twenty-five. I debated whether to make it half-a-grand, but decided that that might disturb him a little, so I kept it at a pony and told her that the monkey was to be an absolute secret, drat the girl.'

29

'"Pony"? "Monkey"? What language is this, Uncle?'

'Mainly thieves' language, darling. Twenty-five pounds and five hundred respectively. I told him I'd instructed her to spend the twenty-five on a really nice bed for herself and the Rev. Abel.'

'Didn't that shock him a little? I mean, mention of a bed?'

'I hope so. It was intended to. Between us, we must persuade him that it is now the nineteen-hundreds.'

'I love the Rev. Abel,' Aldith announced. 'I think he's adorable. My new and darling brother. Bobby and Lois are both in a state of hopeless confusion as to how someone older than their grandpa can marry his daughter. They're worried about it.'

'They seem to have released themselves from worry at the moment,' I said.

For Bobby and Lois, Aldith's two children of seven and six, were now doing what their Uncle Stewart had done before them; uninterested in the rest of this garrulous assembly, they had turned their backs on it and were giving themselves to the ices, the éclairs, the chocolates, and the lemon squash on the buffet counter.

'How old are you now, Stewart?' asked Uncle Douglas. 'I can never remember.'

'Seventeen.'

'Good Lord. And still at school. How much longer?'

'Till eighteen, I imagine.'

'Then?'

'I'll have to get a job.'

'You ought to go to the university.'

'Not a hope of that unless I get a scholarship. And I'm not on the scholarship level at all.'

'Well, for God's sake don't let him put you in the counting house at Paul and Bembridge, as he did me. Whatever you do, go out and live.'

'But Father always says he started work at seventeen, before he'd even matriculated, and it was only then that he realized he knew nothing, and he set to after office hours, working and working till he matriculated and could call himself "of London

30

University". He went on and on to get his Intermediate and his
B.A.'

'All quite true. The old boy has guts. And some humour—
not much, but some—because he told me he wanted "B.A."
put on his tombstone, since he'd nearly killed himself getting it.
At school he was magnificent at football but did no work.
Then the light broke on him, a blinding light, and he gave
himself to reading and studying, which he's gone on doing for
forty years in that study of his, with the unfortunate result that
he now thinks he knows more than anybody else and has the
truth on all points.'

'Yes, and that there's no justification now for anyone arguing
with him,' Aldith agreed.

'Exactly, but unfortunately while he's shut himself up in that
room, the world slipped past him, leaving him marooned
somewhere in 1888. Anything after 1888 is of no interest to
him; it's all modern and vulgar.'

'And what did you do?' I asked.

'I was never any good at games like him, and did no work
either. Nor did I ever dream of slaving for a degree, for which I
thank Heaven, since it's long been obvious to me that unless
your degree is a double-first, or something like that, it's of no
importance at all. In all my fifty years of life no one's ever
inquired about any exams I've passed. Which is just as well, as
I haven't passed any. So don't worry, Stew, dear boy; go out
and live.'

§

In Uncle Douglas's ridicule of Father it was not difficult to
perceive a tolerant affection; but even at fourteen I could perceive that Father's feelings about the success of a younger
brother whom he'd once patronized were tainted by a secret
disappointment—a distress which it would be unfair to call
envy or jealousy but was, let us say, a distant relative of
these. And I think that at the same age I saw how much easier
it was for a successful man to be generous than for one
who has achieved no such success, despite a powerful sense of
superiority. There was nothing for Father to do but to affect

disapproval of Douglas's ambitions and a disparagement of his prose style.

Uncle Douglas was shorter than Father; he was no small man—none of the O'Murrys, male or female, were small—but he was a few inches shorter, and his hair was much fairer; and I always suspected that Father's faint disparagements were not only because Uncle Douglas was younger than he but also—though this was probably unconscious—because he was shorter. And I couldn't be certain that the fairer, softer hair, when contrasted with Father's strong black hair and moustaches, was not a factor in the sum.

I remember a day when his hidden disappointment broke surface and revealed itself to me, though I was little more than fourteen: we were speaking of Uncle Douglas, he and I, and he couldn't keep the small vexation submerged. 'I must think it's a pity,' he said, 'that your uncle betrays his undoubted talent— I would be the first to admit he has talent—by writing such cheap stuff so frequently for the ha'penny press. It's a prostitution of his genius—though "genius" is hardly the word,' he added hastily. 'But a prostitution it is; I can't call it anything else; I can't pretend to consider much of it other than cheap and vulgar. It's not my idea of writing at all. For me the great essayists are such as Hazlitt, Pater, Ruskin, Emerson, Matthew Arnold. Theirs is great writing as *I* see it.'

Yes, I thought, and they all enjoy the distinction of being safely dead.

'I should have no desire to write for our modern ha'penny press,' Father proceeded. 'I know Douglas makes more money than I do—far more—but I hope one doesn't measure the quality of one's work by the money it yields.'

Anxious to defend Uncle Douglas whom I loved and preferred to believe in rather than in my father, I submitted— cleverly, as I thought: 'But isn't it possible that Uncle regards some of his articles as a barrister regards a brief given to him, to which it's his duty to plead? Isn't it his job to make the best show he can for the stuff his Chief requires of him?'

'What? Whether he agrees with it or not?'

'Yes, of course. Just like a barrister does.'

'"*As* a barrister does",' said Father, instantly correcting my grammar. 'You can't use "like" as a conjunction. It's what the illiterate do.'

'All right: *as* a barrister does. Doing his best for his client.'

'No, Stewart; the cases aren't parallel. I can only say that if a journalist deliberately advocates some cause in which he doesn't believe, because he's paid to do so, that, in my view, is the sin against the Holy Ghost.'

'Golly!' I just breathed.

If in this exalted judgment there was glimpse of a truth, there was no truth whatever in his conviction that he wrote English of a higher quality than his successful brother's—and, for that matter, of a far higher quality than the shocking prose of most people. Father's conception of 'good English' was full-brother to his ideal of a 'true gentleman's' behaviour; this must have a puritan and consistent dignity about it; not to say a loftiness; and most certainly it should have little truck with loose and slangy colloquialisms. But as Uncle Douglas would point out to me this notion applied to good English was more often than not the opposite of the truth. 'The more rotund, resounding and polysyllabic the letters of our Mr. Augustus O'Murry, the better he imagines them to be. In solemn and purely expository writing, my dear Stew, there may be some truth in this, but in ninety cases out of a hundred, the smaller, the simpler, the homelier the words, the better. It's monosyllables that stir us, and polysyllables that put us to sleep. The homely monosyllables of our language are loaded with emotional power, but Mr. O'Murry's grandiose polysyllables are loaded only with bromide. God help the poor writers who are beginning to see how to write and have their manuscripts submitted to his judgment at Paul and Bembridge's.'

Uncle Douglas was much in demand as an after-dinner speaker; and usually his speech was a great success; sometimes an uproarious success. But he confessed to me often that he was no natural spontaneous orator but simply a writer-cum-actor. He had to compose his speeches, commit them to memory, and then, most deceptively, deliver them, after much rehearsal at home, with every grace and technical 'trick' of the born

33

platform orator. I was his guest once at such a dinner, and I think that in the brief twenty minutes of his speech I learned almost the whole art of public speaking. I noted with delight the deliberate varying of his voice's pitch from higher to lower, the varying of his speech's *tempo*, now quick, now suddenly slow; the dramatic pauses when he fiddled with the stem of a wine-glass before him so that the words just uttered might sink in; and the clever intrusion ever and again among more dignified words of some popular colloquialism or current slang. What he could do with a line of great poetry as he quoted it was wonderful. He led up to it; paused for it; spoke it with a voice slightly lower and slower than anything before; then waited a few seconds as if he wanted to remember it and love it; then resumed his louder and livelier tones, with a smile.

The people were hypnotized into a silence for it.

I saw too on that night how all these skills belonging to the orator's art, had much in common with the art of the essayist, since the business of both orator and essayist is a communicating with the hearts of the people.

I can't believe my father would ever have perceived this at all, or conceded any of it.

5

Peripeteia

It was a day late in August when Abel and Augusta went out of that house in Dunkerry Crescent, followed by confetti, blessings, rice and cheers; and it was less than three months later, at October's end, when the next unimaginable thing happened. This one was unimaginable to all of us.

Until this year of 1906 Messrs. Paul and Bembridge had been moving along in an old-fashioned but comfortable way, not the most prosperous of publishers, but content with their turnover and untroubled by anxieties. The costs of book production were still low because the wages of compositors, machinists and binders were still small, and so was the bookseller's discount. The cost of authors, unfortunately, was not as low as it had been because an extraordinary phenomenon had appeared in the land, the literary agent, who seemed as ready, on behalf of his authors, to drive as hard a bargain as any publisher. But up till now these unnecessary and uncouth arrivals in the literary field had been held in check, several publishers refusing to have any truck at all with such vulgar tradesmen. Paul and Bembridge were among these recusants, with the instant agreement of Father, who said that 'he didn't know what the honourable profession of publishing would come to, if the worth of authors was going to be determined, not by the publishers, but by this type of hard-bargaining business man calling himself a literary agent'. Such adventures were indeed a threat on the horizon; they could be seen as dirty weather in the offing; but so far Messrs. Paul and Bembridge had gone sailing on gently and peacefully, not as fast as some nor as slow as others.

But now! Now in 1906, in the very first month of the year, the Liberal Party, after ten years in opposition, had come to power in outrageous numbers, sweeping the Conservatives off half the earth, hurling them not only from urban and industrial constituencies, but, unbelievably, from rural seats hitherto conceived to be as impregnable by radicals as stout medieval castles by the arrows of the peasantry. Never in the history of Parliament had there been such a reversal of fortunes. And embattled in power, the Liberals at once showed their teeth. Father—I need hardly write it—was a natural conservative; to be sure, he would have made a very tolerable fascist, had such beings been invented then; and his indignations at the Liberals' new policies were so frequent and so convinced as to be hotly inhospitable to opposing arguments from anyone—certainly from a boy of seventeen. There was this Trades Disputes Bill which would set the Trade Unions above the Law of the Land by lifting the law of conspiracy from them and enabling strikers to adopt methods of 'picketing and peaceful persuasion'—or, in other words, to bully and persecute men who were content to be loyal to their employers. There were these proposals for National Insurance and Old Age Pensions—five shillings at seventy, and doles for the unemployed to which the employer must add every week half as much again as his workman's contribution. Could one imagine anything more certain to discourage thrift and self-help and a sense of personal responsibility? It was to make spongers and dependants of them all.

He allowed that the high unemployment in the country was 'an unsatisfactory business' and he felt a real sympathy with the 'genuine' unemployed; but he maintained that 'most of them were unemployed because they were unemployable'. He had nothing but reprobation for those who marched with banners to Trafalgar Square in the interests of the workless or organized mass demonstrations in Hyde Park. As a conventional, if not fully convinced, church-goer, he was stern in his condemnation of those who attended divine service in St. Paul's or Westminster Abbey so that they could shout 'What about the unemployed?' at the Dean in the pulpit or a canon at the lectern.

So the good old rolling stock of Paul and Bembridge, Ltd., went trailing and tup-tupping along its familiar tracks, through a comparatively peaceful landscape, with never a fear of sudden derailment and overthrow. And Father who found it so difficult to believe he wasn't always right, naturally found it nearly as difficult to believe that a firm with which he had been associated for thirty-odd years had been less than excellent in its habits and methods. Often when he was discoursing to one of us on the ways in which women were inferior to men—and there were many such ways—he would deplore their tendency to panic at the first breath of danger. 'A man, thank God,' he would say, 'keeps calm and collected.' This was a favourite phrase of his; but there was plainly some disarrangement of his calm and collection when he learned that Paul and Bembridge, after sixty years of reasonable success, were proposing to amalgamate with—or, more truthfully, to be absorbed in—Saunders and Winfield, a much larger house which could be called 'book publishers' certainly, but had other vast interests in the production of magazines, popular weeklies, and provincial newspapers, with a syndicate for dispersing stories and articles all over the local papers of Britain, and, moreover, with their own printing works in Farringdon Yard.

Father, though styling himself 'Literary Director' was not on his firm's board, so he knew nothing at first of this proposal. He did not know that it was either this step for his house or the crash.

§

The first blossoming of this new merger was a new board of directors, some of them stockholders in Saunders and Winfield, with Sir Wilfrid Gunn, chairman of that house, now Chairman and Managing Director of Paul and Bembridge. Father was summoned to a private audience with Sir Wilfrid.

It was only long years afterwards that Father told me all that happened at this interview. At the time a sickening shame struck him dumb before his children, and he suffered alone.

From his office at the top of the building he went down to the Board Room, a proud chamber on the first floor, furnished like most board rooms with a long handsome table down its centre and old-fashioned portraits of Mr. Paul and Mr. Bembridge, and of other early directors, hanging, large and bearded and stately, on the walls.

To Father it looked very empty today with only Sir Wilfrid sitting in the big elbow chair at the table's top; usually he pictured it with the weekly staff-meeting in progress, and all the heads of departments seated left and right of the Chairman.

Sir Wilfrid looked almost as if he had stepped down from one of the gold-framed portraits and come to large and bulky life in the elbow chair, because he still wore drooping grey side-whiskers less well likened to 'mutton chops' than, perhaps, to long rashers of bacon. Between the whiskers there was a plump red face, a benign smile, and an extensive cigar. And the words issuing from this face, and from the vicinity of the tossing cigar, strove by means of the smile to be as friendly as they were ruthless.

For a time he said nothing because he was preoccupied with a letter on his blotting-pad. He just looked up and said, 'Oh, good morning, Mr. O'Murry. Mr. Augustus O'Murry, isn't it? Do just sit down . . . I won't be . . . just sit down. . . .'

Father sat on his left while Sir Wilfrid, momentarily removing the cigar with his left hand, put the point of his pencil on his tongue and wrote marginal notes on the letter.

'Yes, just sit there one moment. I. . .'

Father suspected that he had some reluctance to start, but at length he pushed the whole blotting-pad aside and began. 'Yes, Mr. . . . Mr. O'Murry . . . well, I fear you will not like what I shall have to tell you, but —' the 'but' was succeeded by a shrug as of one who would say, 'But, alas, there's nothing else for it.' Then he managed to add, 'Things of late have not been too good for P. and B., as you must know.' Throughout the interview he spoke of 'P. and B.' while giving his own firm at least the dignity of 'Saunders', half of its name.

'Yes, I know they have not been at their best,' Father said, 'but we've had our ups and downs before.' And proudly he added, 'I've been nearly forty years with the firm now and seen plenty of this;' which was just about the unwisest contribution he could have made to the morning's talk.

'Of course, of course . . . ups and downs,' Sir Wilfrid agreed

38

most genially; 'always ups and downs . . . but this is a time of quite exceptional change and—oh, do have a cigar, won't you?' He pushed a cedar-wood box of large Havanas towards Father. 'No? You only smoke a pipe? Wise man. Do smoke it now, if you'd like to.' Father, years later, was able to say with a smile that this suggestion that he smoked was rather like an acknowledgment that a pipe, as an old friend, could be a comfort to him in the shocks that were about to ensue. 'Yes, in the present disturbed state of the book market we've decided that we'll have to make some elaborate changes. I want to be completely frank: we think some of the methods at P. and B. are . . . rather antiquated. I mean, I mean, the whole face of the publishing field has changed in the last few years. As never before. As never before. And we can't feel that P. and B. have changed sufficiently with it. Not sufficiently.' He emphasized 'sufficiently' to soften the indictment. 'Yes, changes. We . . .' He paused; the pause plainly springing from a desire to speak of an unpleasantness coming to persons outside this room before he came to the one sitting before him. It showed that he was stumbling; and Father, beginning to wonder if a wholly unforeseen, hitherto inconceivable, and—oh, God—insufferable blow was about to fall upon him, was not ready to offer a word in his help.

So the parole remained with Sir Wilfrid. 'Yes, we're aiming at a total reorganization. Or to put it simply—I must be frank —we need younger blood in the firm . . . er . . . shall I say new sap in the old tree?' And he smiled as if both of them would think this a rather charming metaphor. 'It will mean great changes . . . great changes. . . .'

Father shot at him, 'Such as?'

Sir Wilfrid's silence was almost the answer. And Father spoke first. Terror rising within him, and wrath rising behind it, he spoke. 'Sir Wilfrid, I do not know why I have been summoned here this morning, nor do I know what all this is leading up to. May I please know without further prevarication? Is it that I am a subject for one of these changes?'

Sir Wilfrid looked relieved by this invitation to speak clearly. 'Well, yes, it is. I'm sorry, but so it is. You must

39

understand—you probably do—that if Saunders hadn't come to the rescue, P. and B. would have . . . well . . . slowly disappeared. I hope you appreciate that.'

Father, intolerant of being lectured by anyone, unwilling to be told by anyone that he was wrong, was now possessed by wrath. He was a vessel in which wrath was at the boil. He rose to his feet as if ready to receive an answer and then leave this man for ever. 'Please tell me, Sir Wilfrid, what you intend.'

'Younger men are naturally more resilient——'

'Please, may I have an answer? And may I point out that there is no great difference in our ages; what difference there is probably lies in my favour. If you're resilient enough to be Managing Director, why——'

This being a question extremely difficult to answer, since one couldn't very well say, 'Because, you see, I happen to consider myself a very different sort of chap from you,' Sir Wilfrid left the question on the table. 'Our Mr. Crowther will take on your department. He is a young man of great ability. We have taken him on the board—you were never on the board, I think. He is an Oxford graduate with an honours degree——'

'I am a graduate too.'

'London, I think?'

'Yes, and a London degree is considered one of the highest.'

Sir Wilfrid shrugged, and left London somewhere in a wilderness, unvisited. 'He is highly amenable to new ideas . . . new standards. Young, he has a mind of great flexibility.'

'And I have not?'

'Well, Mr. O'Murry, you are fifty-seven, aren't you?'

'No. It's you that's fifty-seven, Sir Wilfrid. I am fifty-six.' I know what Father was longing to say: 'Fifty-six, but that is only an arithmetical measurement. Biologically I believe I'm very much younger. I can walk my twenty miles a day, and can still scull with the best.' (This was true: it was still his joy on a Saturday to get to the Mall, Hammersmith, hire an outrigger there, and scull up all the tideway to Teddington, rowing as professionally and perfectly as he decorated a room or built a cupboard.) 'I flatter myself that my flexibility of mind is at least as great as that of my body. And if it comes to knowing

what is good writing and good English, and what is fitting
material for publication by an old and reputable house, then I
consider myself infinitely more to be trusted than some youth
thirty years younger than myself.' But he said none of this.
Amazement and fury left him standing there dumb.

And again Sir Wilfrid had the floor to himself. 'You see,
what it amounts to is that Saunders have only taken over the
goodwill of an old firm and could, as a matter of fact, do without most of its staff. You see that, don't you?'

'I certainly see that.'

'And so many of your P. and B. staff, in whatever department, have thirty or forty years' service behind them.'

'They certainly have, and we take pride in it.'

'Of course. Of course.'

'And I would hope that full account will be taken of
this.'

'It will. It will,' said Sir Wilfrid, but he did not say how.

'It has always been our belief that we should treat old
servants well.'

'Assuredly. Assuredly.' The cigar danced twice around this
'assuredly' and stood still. 'But the first duty of any company
is to stay afloat—you will agree. We cannot be too senti-
mental. A younger staff will not only be more resilient but will,
in the nature of things, cost us—I mean, will be a smaller
drain on available resources.'

'The second of those observations is obvious. Not, in my
view, the first.'

'We don't want to be too hard. We shall naturally strive to
compensate those whom, alas, we shall have to—well—say
good-bye to.'

Father had now brought all his six foot five very erect, so
that he looked like a guardsman at attention, except that one
hand was fingering the other's thumb. 'And all this means,
plainly enough, that I am one of those you propose to dis-
charge. To throw out.'

'But, Mr. O'Murry, you must remember that in any case you
would be retiring in a few years——'

'Not, I had imagined, for nine or ten——'

'—and all we are really asking you to do is to accept a pension a little early. That is all. A *small* pension,' he hastily improved.

Still unable to speak adequately to this tremendous occasion, Father just heard himself asking, 'And what is the pension you propose?'

'Well, you earn, it seems, £650 a year. We think £250 would be the reasonable offer. Very reasonable.'

This was staggeringly less than Father, in his confusion, had dared hope; and it produced in him such an emotional chaos that he could only blurt out, almost humbly, 'But I cannot live on that.'

And as Sir Wilfrid was not ready with a comment on this simple statement, Father elaborated it. 'I have a family.'

Which helped Sir Wilfrid. 'But that's all to the good, isn't it? A family can always be of help.'

'I have a son still at school.'

'Of what age?'

Father couldn't remember in these chaotic circumstances. 'Seventeen, I think.'

'Well, that means he'll soon be in a position to help.'

Here, at last, Father found something to say which matched his erect and dignified stance. 'Sir Wilfrid, I still feel myself in the prime of life, and I do not throw myself on my children.'

'Oh, come, Mr. O'Murry, it's hardly as bad as that.'

Not listening, Father continued, 'I have always preferred to provide for my children; not to expect them to provide for me.'

'You have no savings? No capital?'

'Only a little. On a few hundreds a year, and with three children, large savings have not been possible. I am happy to think I have spent my earnings on those dependent on me.'

'Well, Mr. O'Murry, we don't want to part on unfriendly terms. We want to be of all possible help to old and faithful servants. I will see if I can induce the board to suggest perhaps —shall we say—' but he mentioned no figure, not willing to say the unpleasant words £300. 'I will at least speak to them.'

It was at this point that Father, with all the irrationality of fury-at-the-boil, said something which seemed to him magnificent—and which for ever after he persisted in thinking magnificent. He said, 'You need not worry them, sir. I shall not, in these circumstances, accept from you any pension at all. You say you are seeking economies; I will save you the cost of this. I shall seek employment elsewhere, and I have no doubt that with my long and wide experience I shall easily find it. I would remind you that I have served many years in our Accounting and Production departments and that, while in Production, I have been considered something of a specialist in exports.' All this was being listed to reassure himself and to lay an intolerable doubt at rest. 'With such experience it is not going to be difficult for me to find employment—probably in some position better paid than anything Paul and Bembridge have been able to give me. I will, if you agree, hand over everything in good order to my successor and then withdraw. The sooner, the better.'

'Oh, but come, come, Mr. O'Murry. This is not a time for false pride. I hope you will reconsider what you have just said. We want to do our duty by you. We are an honourable firm. I have to go now. A luncheon appointment.' He drew from his waistcoat pocket a massive gold watch on a massive gold chain, hung with seals. Thrusting it back, he rose. 'Don't hurry out. Rest a bit. You look shaken. I trust you will soon think more kindly of all we have discussed.'

'There is no hope of that, Sir Wilfrid. I shall continue to think what I think.'

He allowed this new Chief to precede him through the door and followed behind him. In his office, high aloft, he began to put things in order for his successor, but then, at the mercy of a wild resentment and a stunning dismay, he suddenly left everything as it was, muttering to himself, 'They'll never see me again. Let them dig themselves out of their own mess,' and he came down three flights of stairs without saying a good-bye to any of his colleagues or to the packers and warehousemen, towards whom he had always prided himself on being so admirably affable and humorous. He walked out of the

43

building and, unable to endure companions in a bus, walked all the long way home, one of the unemployed.

§

He arrived at his door in Dunkerry Crescent, and I have often wondered what his thoughts were as, shaken and fumbling, he turned his key in the lock. This was the house of which he had been so proud, painting it, carpentering shelves for it, fixing ever new ornaments to its walls, rejoicing in pieces of its furniture and imagining them much more valuable than they were. Wanting to be alone, he went upstairs to his study followed by Hamish, the labrador, who was barking and leaping up at him, in a delighted, if inappropriate, welcome at this early hour of the day. I was the only person in the house to whom he could have told his story; but never a word. Nor in subsequent days to any human being.

Usually, when he returned to Hamish's noisy welcome, he would play with the big black animal like a boy, pretending to shut a door on it and then peeping round a corner at it, or dashing into the dining-room, slamming its door and, while the dog barked and leapt and demanded entry, passing quietly through the folding doors so as to emerge out of the morning-room behind the petitioning animal, who thereupon, enjoying the joke, leapt towards his shoulders as if to embrace so well-loved and humorous a master, only to be picked up bodily, rolled on the floor, and tickled here, there, and everywhere.

None of this now behind the closed study door. Only a frequent stroking of the dog's silky black shoulders, a fondling of the velvety ears, or a sad smile and shake of the head at those gazing and adoring eyes which were so palpably pleading for greater activities: say a new game of hide-and-seek or, best of all, an adventurous journey through the streets.

Never in all his long years of impatience with his children had he been so easily irritated as now with me. There was anger shouted from his study window if he saw me treading on the turf-edges of his back-garden; anger indoors if I left a gas-lamp burning in my room or the gas-fire alight in the dining-room; if I dragged out one of his books by the top of its spine; if I sat on the arm of an upholstered chair instead of on its seat; if I pushed at the long window-curtains so that they didn't hang in proper parallel folds; if I came in from the street with boots unwiped.

So much of this that I, ignorant of what he was suffering, would tell myself that soon, very soon, I would escape from his endless corrections and irritable rebukes as Aldith and Augusta had done.

But all this while, behind his closed door, he was writing letter after letter, letter after letter, each applying for some vacancy and setting forth his many qualifications in his studiously orotund 'English'. 'I have work to do at home' was all the explanation he gave me for this absence from the office. Sometimes he went out of the house, unspeaking—probably to the Public Library to study the advertisements of vacant jobs.

So for several weeks; but the day came when his pride broke down, and he had to share his swelling and inflamed anxieties with a confidant. At last they had to break forth. And sometimes I think it strange that the confidant he turned to was Uncle Douglas, the young brother whose work, however prosperous, he'd always pretended to think of lower quality than his own. To him at last he confessed his humiliation, and from him he sought consolation and advice. And not only this: the breaking of his pride enabled him one day to accept the presence—and perhaps the comfort—of his young son.

One day at luncheon (even with ruin threatening him Father would not tolerate the vulgar abbreviation, 'lunch'; furthermore, I believe that even in these days of despair he would have been upset if I had spoken of our luncheon as our dinner. Only the lower classes ate a dinner in the middle of the day; we dined, however modestly, at the gentleman's hour of half-past-seven)—at 'luncheon' then, after a long silence, he said, 'Stewart, your Uncle Douglas is coming to see me this evening, and I think you'd better be there. I shall have important things to tell him, and you'd best know of them because they're bound to affect you. You are eighteen now, and thank God

45

you're a man. No woman would understand these things properly. They have no brains for business.'

So there we all were that evening in his study: Father, Uncle Douglas, myself, Hamish and Uncle Douglas's little border terrier, Parkhurst—'Parkhurst' because of his criminal tendencies. Uncle Douglas sat with legs crossed in the one big upholstered chair; I sat on a stiff upright chair, a silent listener; Father either paced the carpet back and forth or sat through uneasy minutes in the revolving chair before his desk. This solemn assembly did not begin too well, because the happy little terrier wanted to wrestle and riot with a very willing Hamish twice his size, and once when he was up on Hamish's hinder parts, gripping him around the waist, Uncle Douglas enjoined, 'Keep it clean now, Parkhurst.'

Father couldn't have approved of this, but it was no time tonight in which to rebuke his brother, so he suffered it to pass.

'Over a hundred and thirty letters I've written,' he said, slowly pacing. 'Hundred and thirty-six to date. And would you like to know what they have produced? For heaven's sake keep those dogs still. Seventy-six "No's"—and the rest—the other sixty—a grossly insulting silence. No answers at all. My application chucked into the waste-paper basket. No, wait: three people did concede me an interview—perhaps I'd omitted to state my age—three out of a hundred and thirty. And what did they all say? All of them. When I'd stated my qualifications, it was "Thank you, Mr. O'Murry, but I'm afraid your experience is not quite in line with what we're looking for. Good morning. Thank you for calling." So they all said, but it was nothing to do with my experience, which was all and more than they could possibly want, it was merely age . . . age. One is an old man at fifty now, if not at forty. You'll be fifty in a year, Douglas.'

Did he, unconsciously, need to say this for his comfort? Listening, I could imagine Father, well aware of his fine height and presence, walking to these interviews with some hope, but coming away from them into the sunlight, where the glare of an intolerable truth awaited him.

'You have tried employment agencies?' Uncle phrased this

as a confident assertion rather than a doubting question; he knew his brother.

'Have I not? What do you suppose? I am not a fool. And they all in the kindest terms say the same thing. Say it almost before I've finished speaking. Say, "I'm afraid it's your age that's against you."' He mimicked their manner and tone. Mimicked them excellently, since a burning wrath, when it breaks into flame, can make for a moment an artist of any man. '"It's your age, Mr. O'Murry. I can assure you, Mr. O'Murry, that we're constantly trying to persuade employers to base their selection of staff on experience and ability rather than years. You mention your London degree and your French, Mr. O'Murry. We could tell you of graduates of Cambridge with honours in Modern Languages for whom, despite all our efforts, we could find no place." But it's all pretty talk, Douglas. It's obvious their policy is not to bother with us older ones since they can never place us, but to take our registration fees and concentrate on the young ones who'll get them the employers' commissions.'

'There are those panel advertisements in the best papers,' Uncle suggested, his sympathy resting in his voice, since there was little help in the words.

'My dear boy, I've read my eyeballs raw in the Public Library, searching for likely vacancies, and some of my letters were in answer to them. Answers that got no answer. I suppose I'd been honest enough to state my age.'

Maintaining the sounds of sympathy, since as yet he had little else to contribute, Uncle protested, 'You mean no single job has been offered you?'

Probably Father would have liked to answer 'Yes' and make his case as shocking as possible, but he had, unwillingly, to concede the truth. 'I was offered one job at a ridiculous salary which I decided it was beneath my dignity even to consider. And another which was little more than that of a temporary clerk with the payment of a typist; naturally I refused to listen to it. But those were some time ago, and I begin to wish now that I'd accepted either of them. But no, I don't. I'm glad I showed some people I was not going to be humiliated that far.

47

Whatever I may yet have to do or take, I have at least flung two people's insults back in their faces.'

'And how are you managing now?'

'Well, naturally—what do you think?—I'm—' incurably Father addressed a younger (and shorter) brother as if he'd spoken like a fool—'naturally I'm using up what little capital I have. I tell you, Douglas, I've had to live over fifty years before I realized what this world is like. I've been a blind fool. Hitherto I've always been a conservative but I'm not sure I'm not a socialist now; and I begin to see what these Liberals are up to with their National Insurance and Old Age Pensions and so on. Look; look. Here am I, a man of great experience and considerable abilities—as I think you'll allow—I ought surely to be of some value to the nation, but no: I'm to be tossed out on to the dust-pit, an unwanted nuisance. I should have thought this would be a loss to the nation; but nothing of the sort: no one, whether employers or agencies, has any interest in my abilities but only in my birth certificate. Instead of being someone of great service to the community, it looks as though the country will have to keep me, if only on the bread-line.'

Much of this was true enough, as Uncle knew, and he was hard put to it to find words of comfort, so, well knowing his brother's nature, he turned for the present to flattery. 'It's too early to despair yet. With your truly splendid—your quite exceptional—height and presence, Gus—I mean Augustus— you will get a job of some sort.'

'A hundred and forty letters, old boy'—the number had swollen by four—'and all to no purpose.'

'But sooner or later.'

'Oh yes, as a commissionaire on the pavement outside Harrods or a hall-porter in the Piccadilly Hotel or a chucker-out at a public house.' ('Pub' was one of the many vulgar abbreviations that he condemned.) 'Or as a top-hatted bank messenger. Some employers, I believe, like old gentlemen as messengers because they can get them at a low wage and they are too old to have a share in expensive superannuation schemes. They even use them as office boys. There are ancient office boys all over the place—old gentlemen in temporary jobs because they're pleased to have any sort of pay. . . . Then there's this house which I've almost built around me by redecorating it from top to bottom so that it's like my shell now. And there's Stewart.' I don't think I minded coming after the house. This after all, was Father. 'I have a son to consider.'

'Yes, what do we do with Stew?'

Neither looked at me, sitting there. I might have been an insentient object in the room.

'He'll have to go out and work. *He'll* get something all right. Eighteen years of age and total inexperience are the coins to offer. Get down, Hamish, get down; I can't deal with you now. One thing is certain: neither Stewart nor Aldith nor Augusta is going to have to keep me. I've kept my children for these fifty years and I'm not going to be kept by them now. God, no! I think I've managed to keep them in decency and comfort, and in a home to be proud of. . . .'

At last Uncle found something to say that might hint at comfort. 'But, look, Gussy'—Father shivered—'the world's a wicked place, I know, but there *are* jobs for men of any age— jobs which depend, not on what you know, but who you know.'

'*Whom* you know'—by force of habit, but probably unconsciously in this dark hour, Father corrected the grammar. 'Unfortunately, Douglas, I know very few people. I've always been something of a solitary, preferring my books and my work to worthless social activities. Something of a hermit, you might say.'

'Exactly. And my nature's the opposite. Come away, Parkhurst. Can't you see the gentleman's busy? Come here. Lie down. I *do* know heaps of people, and there's no reason for you to be ashamed if I use my influence on your behalf.'

Father hesitated, as if not sure of this; then said a little sadly, 'I don't think I mind accepting help from a brother.' And he proceeded with a sentence that left me, as I sat silent on my chair, amazed. Never till this day of mortification could he have spoken it. 'You've done better in the world than I have, Douglas.'

I began to think it time I contributed something to the

discussion. So far even the dogs had been noticed more than I had. So I ventured diffidently, 'I should think there are probably ways in which we could help, Father.'

My words perished on the air; unregarded by Father; unregarded even by Uncle Douglas. Father, instead of heeding me went on to demonstrate, once again, how fury and pain can invest many an ordinary man with wit. He said, 'I've learned my lesson. It's simple. I've committed infamous conduct in a professional respect by living to be fifty. So they've struck me off the register. Told me to go and rot. Really it's a wonder that employers and employment agencies don't send us, instead of application forms, a few packets of euthanasiac drugs, ha, ha, ha.'

§

When Uncle Douglas and I went out of that room, Uncle took hold of my elbow and said, 'I didn't enjoy that, Stew, old boy. It's no fun seeing a man who's always been by nature a Lord High-and-Mighty so hurt and humiliated. "You've done better in the world than I have." To *me*! To his younger brother whose work he's always looked down upon. It was rather like the fall of Nelson's column. We must get together on a work of repair, you and I.'

6

Conspiracy

'I've given deep thought to this,' said Uncle Douglas as we sat together. This was many days after he'd said, 'We must get together, you and I'—so many that I had begun to wonder if these were little more than sympathetic words soon forgotten. Was not Father still upstairs writing his letters; still turning the advertisement pages in the Public Library; still going every morning, as the postman's knocks were heard in Dunkerry Crescent, to the front door to see if any hope would fall on the mat? But in this suspicion I had been unjust to my Uncle. Here we were in his comfortable chambers—or flat—in Chapel Buildings, Lincoln's Inn. How he, who had nothing to do with the Law, had acquired these convenient chambers in this eighteenth-century block, I don't know, but there was his name on a stone jamb of one of the arched doorways: '3rd Pair, Douglas O'Murry, Esq.', while on the opposite jamb it said 'Ringwood and Craven' under 'Gottberg and Stein, Solicitors'. His flat was on the third floor, overlooking a Dickensian green. The sitting-room was very much a bachelor's room, with deep leather chairs and a few good pieces of antique furniture. Uncle Douglas was unmarried, but not, at this time, uncomforted, up there in his high chambers. A charming French widow came regularly to cook meals for him, clean his rooms, make his bed, and, on occasions, lie in it. He did not confess this to me till I was some years older, when he explained his silence on a delicate subject with a laughing eye and with Juvenal's axiom, *Maxima debetur puero reverentia*, translating the next lines, 'If you are about to be guilty of some turpitude, Stew, do not despise a youth's tender years.'

'Keep your glass filled, old son, and help yourself to fags. To a cigar, if you like it, but you've not got as far as that yet. You want to hear my conclusions?'

'Of course, Uncle.' I felt happy sitting there as a fellow conspirator.

'Well, the first and basic one is that I can't believe your father'll get any job at fifty-seven in his old field—at least no job that wouldn't humiliate him. And it's funny since he's never inspired much affection in me, but I don't like to see the old boy hurt. He should, of course, have accepted that pension which Sir Wilfrid Gunn offered him, but the trouble is that Augustus is blinded by a view of himself that's altogether too bright. Now listen: I know Wilfrid Gunn, and his Saunders and Winfield well enough—he's a lunching pal of my old Portwith. I don't know if you've noticed it—if you have, for heaven's sake don't point it out to Gustus—but it's my up-and-coming world that's overthrown his old and peaceful one. So, dammit, I feel a duty to do something. And I'm going to see to it—over good drinks—that Wilfrid contrives to persuade your father to take that pension. I'm sure I can work this. You see I don't want him to have to lose that house which has always had so much of his heart—most of it, in fact. That means we'll have to find him some work that won't injure his pride too much, and in the meantime get you a job at once. I can easily do that in Portwith's. At eighteen it won't be well paid—a quid a week, perhaps—or it may be a bit more since you are Douglas O'Murry's nephew. Little enough, in any case, but here is where I come in. I'm your godfather, aren't I?'

'I didn't know it.'

'One of them, surely?'

'I don't think so.'

'Gracious, aren't I? Well, I ought to be. Who *is* your godfather?'

'God knows.'

'Shameful how godfathers neglect their duties. I'm godfather to Aldith's second brat, and I take it seriously. Well, fairly seriously. She gets a quid at Christmas.'

'Yes, but do you bring her up in the fear and nurture of the Lord?'

'Is that what I ought to do? No, I'm afraid I'm not much

good at that. But about *you*. I see no reason why I shouldn't
appoint you my godson, which I do here and now. You're not
to be as proud as your old man. Be a little proud by all means
but, in the name of pity, not as proud as that. It doesn't make
for happiness. He could never bring himself to take money
from me but you bloody well can and shall—and don't tell your
father I taught you to say "bloody". He's got troubles enough.
You'll pay him for your board and lodging in that house and
pretend that it's come out of your screw at Portwith's. Lies are
sometimes admirable things, if not overdone. I can never see
how you can get through life without a few. You'll give him,
say, twenty-five bob a week out of the hundred pounds I'm
going to add to your screw——'

'Oh, *no*, Uncle!'

'Oh, yes, godson. Oh yes, and shut up. Twenty-five bob a
week'll leave you another twenty-five for pocket money. One's
got to *live*, dammit, and am I not your godfather, so don't do a
Gustus on me. You've got to hear more yet. I'm not leaving
you on a stool at Portwith's. I'm sure you can do more or less
what I did, with a little training from me. I'll make you a free-
lance journalist earning good money in a year or two. You'll
write for "the ha'penny press", much to your father's disapproval. I've seen always that you're as clear-eyed as Augustus
isn't. You've surprised me sometimes with your instant perceptions—so odd in your father's son. You'll write for me
essays and feature articles and witty middles, and I'll go
through them with a tooth-comb pointing out what's good and
what isn't good enough yet; and you'll probably end up
cleverer than I am.'

It was wonderful to sit in that room, surrounded with
leathery comfort and objects in good taste, and to think that
one day I might have one like it. But I had to protest, 'I can't
take up your time like that.'

'Shut up, godson. I'm not arguing with you; I'm telling you.
Nobody's going to argue with me. I'm quite as big a bully as
your father. Runs in the family. So you're looked after. Now
we come to Papa.'

'Yes?'

'I've got the job for him.'

'*No?* What? Where?'

'There won't be big money in it, but I think it solves his real problem—which is to find him a job that'll enable him to hold on to his pride and continue looking down upon less high-principled men like his young brother.'

'But I think it's wonderful of you to do it, Uncle.'

'No sense in doing anything else, Stew. And I find it fun to accept people just as they are and enjoy them.'

'*I* find it damned difficult. So far from enjoying the Bonny Earl, I live with a dream, like Aldith and Augusta, of doing a guy.'

'I beg your pardon,' demanded Uncle, pretending to no knowledge of this low phrase.

'Doing a bunk when I can afford to. I'm sick of being hauled over the coals five times a day for my grammar or my choice of words or my clothes.'

'I agree with him about your choice of words. I sympathize.'

'No, you don't. But what's this noble job?'

'It's not really noble, but he'll be able to think it is. You remember that when our father's business began to go downhill he was unable to send Gussy to Wellington, as he wanted to, but had to send him to a private school, Oxford Court, in South Kensington. It was a typical privately owned school for the sons of people who couldn't afford the great boarding schools but wanted them to be at schools "For the Sons of Gentlemen". Seven years later I went there and learned nothing but remained a gentleman's son. There was no hope of Gus going to Oxford or Cambridge and he had to leave school at seventeen and go to that counting house job. It was then that he worked himself sick getting his Matriculation and Intermediate and B.A., as we've heard a hundred times——'

'Have we not?'

'——while I, a vulgarer type, set out to find the places where the money was. The school is still there in Trevanion Gardens, run now by our old headmaster's son, Bob Gatehouse. I see him often because, believe it or not, he's rather proud of me as what he calls a "Famous Old Boy".'

'I can well believe it.' It was always pleasant to please Uncle Douglas.

'Thank you—and long ago he asked me to come and talk to the boys as "a distinguished old Oxfordian." This was flattering, so I repaid him by getting him into my club. His old man, grooming him as his successor, had sent him to Oxford—hence "Oxford Court"—and after about ten years of deep consideration the Reform Club felt equal to electing him. Never was a man more bucked or more pleased with me. Consequently I meet him there at dinner sometimes, and the other day we got talking about this disgusting too-old-at-forty business, which had sent to the bottom a perfectly seaworthy old tub like your father. He was shocked—and went silent—and in his silence the great idea came to me. I know my Bob Gatehouse. He has his M.A. but the school won't support other Oxford and Cambridge graduates: apart from him the staff are young chaps of nineteen and twenty whose parents can't afford universities——'

'Like me.'

'Just so. Just so. And for a little I thought of sending you there to teach something—but it's a blind alley for non-graduates, so I decided differently.'

'Thank you so much,' I said satirically. But affectionately.

'Don't mention it. Non-graduates don't look well on a prospectus, so Bob doesn't print them, but he'd like to add a man with a B.A. after his own name. Never mind where the B.A. came from or whether it's merely a pass degree—parents don't probe into these things. So I came out with my idea. What about my elder brother joining him as his second-in-command? I stipulated that it would have to be second-in-command; my brother couldn't accept anything less. Bob stayed quiet, but yesterday I heard that he'd like to have Gussy if he'd come for what little the school could afford. Perhaps £350 a year or so. Gus must know now that he won't do better than this at fifty-seven, so I think he'll end by accepting with alacrity. He'll hide the alacrity, but he'll accept. The only unsatisfactory aspect of it is my terrible feeling of guilt at having sacrificed all those nice boys to whom he'll teach English. God help them all.'

'They'll grow out of it.'

'Oh, no, they won't—most of them; only the brighter ones like you and me. It sticks. The ghastly indoctrination sticks. Mustn't end a sentence with a preposition, so alter "We are such stuff as dreams are made on" into "We are such stuff as that on which dreams are made". Or "A man's reach should exceed his grasp or what's a heaven for?" Try messing about with that. God, I could weep at what I've done. But now sit down and smoke'—he shot his cigar box towards me—'or go and weigh yourself in the bathroom or something, while I put together a letter to Augustus, because I'll want your estimate of it. A distinguished journalist like you.'

Here was the difference between Father and Uncle Douglas: Uncle Douglas suggested that my opinion would be valuable; Father usually suggested that, because of my youthfulness, it was either ill-informed or idiotic.

I sat and smoked, not one of his cigars but one of his Turkish cigarettes, and I read some of his articles in pictured journals on the table while he composed the letter, chewing his pencil, letting his cigar go out again and again (an unpardonable lapse to the epicure in him), wasting match after match on it; and sometimes getting up to walk about, as he raked his mind for the safest words.

At last he said, 'Okay. Here it is. And I hope it's in English he can tolerate. "Dear Augustus, I chanced to meet Bob Gatehouse at the Reform the other day. You will remember that he is now headmaster of our old school in succession to his old man"—no, I'd better alter that to "in succession to his father".' He altered it with his pencil. '"I just mentioned that you'd resigned from P. and B. since the merger"— "resigned" is good, I think—"and that you had not yet found work to your liking, and, if I may so put it, worthy of you. Bob then, to my surprise, made an extraordinary proposition. . . ." Here follows Bob's surprising idea, and I go on: "I quite see that the income would inevitably be less than you desire and deserve but at least it's an honourable and creative job, such as I've often heard you say is the only kind you want." That's rather good again, isn't it? "Anyhow I told Bob I would pass it on to you for you to take or leave. I met Stewart the other day and was glad to hear that he had got a job at Portwith's. This means that he will be able to contribute for his upkeep and you and he should be able to stay in your present home to which, after all the endless labours you have given to it, you are naturally attached. But of course"—oh, dear, he won't like that opening "But"—mustn't begin a sentence with "but"— "But of course it's for you to say. Maybe it's just a silly idea of Bob's that has little appeal to you."'

'Absolutely splendid,' I said. 'Perfect in every line.'

'I think so. I think so. Nothing there that can upset him.'

And of course Father, taught now by a hundred disappointments that nowhere was there honourable and well-paid work for him, accepted this proposal with no more than a preliminary display of doubts and questions. Let him pretend as he liked to a doubt or two I could see that the offer excited and pleased him. Ever underestimating the sharp perceptions of youth, he let fall before me, with a show of laughter, his eagerness that the story could be got through to Sir Wilfrid Gunn ('old Swill-pot', as he called him)—this news that the man who was no longer of any use to him had 'more or less promptly' secured a distinguished job as 'Deputy Headmaster' (thus he described it) of a famous school where he might have been useful to publishers like Saunders and Winfield who had a strong list of educational text-books. He even turned the matter of his diminished income into a cloak of honour, repeating to me what he'd said so often before, when contrasting his earnings with those of a younger brother, 'It's only the vulgar, Stewart, who measure the quality of their work by the money it earns. What better work can there be than teaching the young, in Matthew Arnold's words, "the best that has been thought and said in the world"?'

Meanwhile Elsa and Josef Stauffen were given all our basement rooms free on the understanding that she would still cook a breakfast and dinner for us and clean the few rooms above which we hadn't closed. I gave Father, as Uncle Douglas had suggested, my twenty-five shillings for board and bed, and—again at Uncle's request—abandoned my idea that

E   57 when I was earning fair money I'd 'do my guy' and live by myself.

§

I longed to get a glimpse of Father at work in his new and wholly unforeseen character as a 'Deputy Headmaster', and on one occasion I contrived to do so. That morning I was at home from the office in Portwith House, after being feverish the day before, and soon after eleven came the dramatic double-knock of a telegraph boy. I opened to him: the telegram was from India. Excited, as one always was, by the envelope of a telegram, and then (after some mental arithmetic) guessing it was from Augusta and might announce what Father had professed his longing to see, namely 'a baby at her breast', I lost all sense of a temperature and told the boy that I could give him no answer but would take the telegram at once to my father. Hurrying along Parkside towards South Kensington, I came quickly to Trevanion Gardens and 'Oxford Court School'. On being admitted by a maid I saw the Headmaster himself, a little plump man in an M.A. gown, standing at a table in the hall, and I told him that I had a telegram for my father. As with many a little and plump man, his face was benign, and his eyes told me that he was one of those in whom there's a surge of goodwill and benevolence directly they speak to anyone young. He greeted me genially. 'So you're Mr. O'Murry's boy. Yes, I think I can see you are. Though you're not quite so tall as he is, but who could be? Of course it shall be sent into him at once. He's in his class-room.'

Respectfully I asked, 'Might I take it into him personally, sir, in case there's an answer to be sent?'

'Why, certainly, my dear boy. Quite the best thing to do. It's the Third Hour so he'll be taking the Lower Sixth in French. Come, I'll show you the way myself.'

And he led me along a broad and lofty corridor, typical of these mid-Victorian Kensington houses, to a handsome panelled door. He opened and entered, and instantly twenty boys shot themselves erect from twenty desks. And there stood Father, looking monumental in his flowing gown. He was walking up and down with a book in his hand as Mr. Gatehouse said, 'Visitor to see you, Mr. O'Murry. Gentleman of the same name as you. You'll probably recognize him. Bringing an important message. Hope it's good news. Sit down, all of you.' And with a parting smile for me he left me there with Father.

'Hal-*lo*!' Father exclaimed. 'What's brought you, Stewart? I thought you were ill. You should never leave the house on a day after a temperature. It's the unwisest thing to do. Most unwise. I've often told you so.' Even in this public room he couldn't control his habit of rebuking youth for its foolishness.

'I thought it might be important and you would want an answer sent.'

'Still, it's foolish to go out with a temperature hanging about you. The last thing we want is to have you ill on our hands.'

He took the telegram, tore it open, grimaced and showed it to me. It said, as far as I remember: 'Daughter born early this morning Augusta and Abel.'

'Golly!' I exclaimed. 'That's rather fun. Fancy Augusta——'

But Father lifted a hand to stop me, almost as if mention of a daughter giving birth was unsuitable before a gathering of six-teen-year-old boys. *Maxima debetur pueris reverentia.*

'I shouldn't publish what it says. Good news, I suppose, but I must confess that at my age I'm glad it's happening ten thousand miles away. Not the sort of thing I ought to say, I suppose, but I've always been one who believes in speaking the truth. You can show it to the Headmaster if he's still there. Now I must get on with my work. Partridge, begin again. Right from the beginning.'

One boy rose and as I went out I heard him reciting something in French.

That evening Father, wanting my admiration for his knowledge of French Literature, told me that it was one of Ronsard's Odes, and he quoted some of it, manifestly displaying the perfection of his French accent.

> *Dieu vous gard', messagers fidelles*
> *Du Printemps, visites Arondelles,*
> *Huppes, cocus, Rossignoles. . . .*

59

I have always thought that this picture of my father standing in a class-room, after his dark night of the soul, and trying to distil into the young 'some of the best that has been thought and said in the world' was one of the best and happiest creations in all Uncle Douglas's lively career.

You can be sure I described the scene to Uncle. And delighted he was to have become overnight a great-uncle again. 'But what do I do about this new grand-niece, Stew? Do I send it a hell of a gift or something? For its first birthday—though it's not her first birthday, that's the next one. This is her first-birthday-minus-one. Tell me what to do. You know all about these things.'

'I know nothing whatever about them.'

'Yes, you do. You know all about the fear and nurture of the Lord.'

'A gift is always acceptable.'

'Yes, but this is a highly religious grand-niece. I tell you what: I'll send her old man a hundred quid to be spent on her. Most parsons are poverty-stricken, and I don't want him to have to sell his boots. Besides, remember that, though he's eight years older than I am, he's my nephew. It'll be pleasant to be able to do something really avuncular for him. You know, I suppose, that her grand-pa is quite a success at Oxford Court; and I don't wonder; he's always taken his work seriously, considering it to be—unlike mine—an important service to humanity. And, between you and me, I suspect his recent experience of not being wanted anywhere has mellowed him a bit, so that he's careful not to argue too dogmatically with Bob, wanting to hold on to this job. Sad that he should have had to be humiliated, but there it is. And Bob's got a graduate master on the cheap, so both are on the best of terms. Almost a couple of love-birds.'

7

The Call Again

A foreshortening in the long panorama of memory makes it seem but a year or so after these events that our Crescents, and indeed the whole country, was shocked by another murder in our grey neighbourhood, the Dene; but as I search again along the misted paths of memory I perceive, from related incidents suddenly recalled, that it must have been four years and more. It must have been 1911. The coronation of King George was just behind us.

This murder was oddly similar to that of eight years before: a harlot found naked and murdered on her bed in that same long ill-famed street, St. Michael's Row. The only differences were that this girl was much younger than the previous victim, little more than nineteen, and that she lay, not with her throat slashed, but strangled, and with her legs wide apart, each tied by its ankle to an upright post of her brass bed. Her hands hung free with the finger-nails empty, as if she had offered no resistance at first but perhaps enjoyed some process—and later it was too late.

Once again, as eight years before, it was down in Elsa and Josef's kitchen that I discussed this terrible but all too fascinating story. Once again the local paper was on the table with its headline, 'Murder in the Dene'.

'Will you only believe it, a child of nineteen,' said Elsa, peeling potatoes over a basin, because it was evening and would be supper-time soon—yes, we called it 'supper' now. 'Only nineteen, they say, and a whole-time professional, as you might put it—you're old enough now, Master Stewart, to hear these things put plainly before you. And in the same street, that there awful St. Michael's Row'—(she pronounced it 'Smikel's Row'). 'They say no one knows where her parents are, or if she had any. More'n likely she was a love child, out on her own, who turned to doing what so many others were doing around her. Bringing the men home.'

'Boor child,' said the big and gentle Josef, from over his long, drooping German pipe. He sat polishing cutlery for his wife. 'It's not always their vault.'

So ignorant, so innocent, and so interested was I, that I sought further information from Elsa on this 'bringing the men home'.

Pretending some diffidence, she paused before explaining, 'Them St. Michael's Row girls . . . you see . . . go prowling in any part of London at any time of the day; they foller likely strangers even in the West End and bring them back to the Dene where their flats or rooms are all that cheaper. Or the men, knowing it's a notorious place come and find 'em lolling at their doors. Probably this girl was lolling there—or just walking up and down the street when the murderer found her.'

'A berry terrible story it is,' said Josef, shaking his head over his cutlery.

I, rather in Father's fashion, was pacing back and forth, as Elsa continued, not listening to Josef, 'And so near to us—like that last time. Almost next door to us, as you might say; next door to a real ladies and gentlemen's neighbour-wood.' She could never get this word right. 'One neighbour-wood of real ladies and gentlemen, with famous people among them—sirs and all—and then right up against it, these awful streets, summa' the worst in London. And it's not only bad women that's to be found there, but plenty of bad men too.'

'Birds of a vether vlock together,' said Josef, repeating— proudly perhaps—words he'd used eight years before.

'Thet's right, but I mean something worse than mere burglars and pickpockets and such like,' Elsa explained in a significant tone, plainly wanting to be asked what she meant.

So I asked her, and not only for her pleasure; even more for mine. 'Meaning what, Elsa?'

'Things I daresay you hardly know about.'

'Oh, come, Elsa! I'm not ten years old now. I've had my twenty-first birthday.'

'*Ja*, that is *richtig*,' Josef kindly obliged, mixing German and English. 'He's come of age, *nicht wahr*?'

'But I don't know if your father'd like me to be talking to you about these things. He's that strict, in't he? If he thought I was telling you things you didn't ought to know, he mightn't half create—if you ask me.'

'Father isn't going to decide for me what I hear and don't hear. I decide these things for myself. So come along, Elsa. You must. You've stirred my interest, and if you don't tell me, I shall find it all out from someone else.'

So Elsa, relieved to have this justification for continuing, began, 'Well, there's the Rubin Vice Ring, for a start.'

'The *what*?'

'No, I don't like to talk about it,' she parried, almost coyly, as if it was a subject far too rude. 'I don't, ree'ly.'

'Well, then, I shouldn't,' suggested Josef.

But she didn't want to be denied this opportunity to speak of a subject so engrossing. 'There are . . . you see . . . well . . . men prostitutes as well as women.'

'Perverts, you mean,' I interrupted, to show I was fully abreast of her subject.

'Eh, what?' This was not a word she knew, so she continued in her own ways. 'The police know all about 'em and all about their favourite pub, that there St. Michael's Arms. But they're not so much prostitutes themselves, of course, as the providers of—no, I can't go on with it. I don't like to.' Elsa was buxom and fifty now, but her coyness at this point was almost maidenly.

'Procurers,' I suggested, to show further that she was speaking to a man-of-the-world.

'Procurers?' This again was not one of her words.

'Yes. Procurers of young men for those who want them,' explained the man-of-the-world.

'Well, yes,' she allowed, not unwillingly. 'And it's said they have a secret sign and a kind of password for anyone who looks a likely customer.'

'Now that's really interesting,' I laughed. 'What are they?'

'They kind of accidentally tread on the foot of any loitering

63

stranger and then apologize, saying, "I'm that sorry, but I was thinking of other things." And if the stranger's a possible customer he says "What things?" And he's told what things.'

'*Ja*. He's told all right,' Josef agreed.

'But if the police know all about them and where they foregather, why don't they go and pinch them? And why doesn't the pub lose its licence?'

'*Ja*, vy?' asked Josef, breathing on a spoon back and front, before polishing it. 'Vy? That's what I always want to know.'

'And I've told you why again and again,' Elsa protested impatiently. 'It's either because they ain't got enough evidence or because they like them to get together in a favourite place so that they can know where to collect their man when they want him. It's quite simple.'

'It's not simple to me,' Josef objected. '*Nein*.'

'And they like to know,' Elsa pursued, indifferent to his objections, 'where they can find informers when the time comes. There are generally one or two who'll grass.'

'*Grass?*' I might try to display my worldly knowledge, but this was not a word which so far had found a place there.

'Yes, turn copper's nark. The splits know which of 'em'll talk if they oil his palm well enough.'

'*Splits?*' My worldly knowledge was failing badly.

'Tecs. Detectives.'

'Oh, I see. Tomorrow I'll go and take a look at this pub.'

'Don't you do nothing of the sort, Master Stewart. You keep away.'

'Why? Are you afraid they'll enlist my services?'

'Don't talk like that. Oh, I shouldn't ought to of spoken. Why didn't you stop me, Josef?'

'Because it'd take a cleverer man than vot I am.'

She pretended to slap his hand. 'You're a rude old man; that's what you are.'

'And I am not certain that any man cleverer enough exists. Not vunce you are really begun.'

'Did you ever? Did you ever hear anything like it, Master Stewart? Did you ever know such a man?'

Reasserting my independence I declared only, 'Tomorrow I

go there,' and I left them to their playfulness; mumbling, 'Tomorrow I go and study this St. Michael's Row and this tavern.'

Tomorrow was a Sunday, and I had the day to myself. For some months past I had refused to go to church with Father. He still worshipped at St. Jude's—or, rather he had renewed his attendance at Morning Prayer there after many weeks of displeasure with God. He went again to his old pew in his frock coat, high wing-collar, broad black cravat, and with a silk hat to lay on the floor—all vestures which, unobserved by him, were passing out of date.

There was a notable row when I informed him that I was now an agnostic. This assertion one Sunday morning was not only an act of rebellion against an authoritarian Government, an Unilateral Declaration of Independence within the walls of 52 Dunkerry Crescent; it was partly that I was now delighting in books of deeply serious intent, Lecky's *History* and Herbert Spencer's *First Principles*; and several of them had raised in me a genuine difficulty to believe. None the less, it was with some pleasure that I told Father I was an agnostic.

His impatience with this announcement was rooted, I am sure, less in his own firm faith, which had never been strong, than in revulsion against a young man's conceit—and that young man a son who but yesterday was a child.

'Agnostic? I never heard such nonsense. What are you talking about? A boy of your age! Do you really think you're qualified to dismiss things that——'

'Yes, I do.' I was ready for battle. 'I certainly do.'

'Let me finish. Things that have been believed by some of the wisest of men for two thousand years?'

'And disbelieved by some of the wisest. For the same period.'

He did not choose to hear this perfectly valid answer—possibly because he could not think of an answer to it; instead he poured out the old invalid argument, which left me seated more firmly than ever on my fine pedestal of agnosticism.

'You're ready to think that you, just out of school, know better than——'

'Four years out of school——'

65

'Do let me finish—but the fact that, unfortunately, you had to leave school at seventeen only strengthens my argument. You're ready to think you know better than hundreds of men of the highest learning like Lord Halifax, like . . .' but here I could see that for a moment he could think of no other layman than Lord Halifax, very prominent just then. He was urgently summoning memory to come to his aid, but memory sat stubbornly impotent, in spite of the fact that he was far from satisfied with Halifax, an extreme High Churchman. There was Halifax and . . . but nowhere any other name. So after a moment's hesitation—and he didn't want to hesitate—he fell back upon the clergy. '. . . like Keble and Pusey and Newman and Manning—God knows I'm not a Catholic but at least these men were Christians—and Kingsley and F. D. Maurice and——'

'Professional parsons, all of them,' I countered, pleased with this comment and happily unaware that it was no more watertight than his. 'All with a vested interest in their Church.'

'Well, what about men like'—and for the present, call on memory as he might, only the untidy and somewhat scruffy figure of Doctor Johnson had wandered into his mind—'like the great Doctor Johnson, a scholar if ever there was one?'

'And what about your Matthew Arnold?'

'What about Matthew Arnold?' He repeated my question, facing it with a bewildered frown.

'His "Dover Beach"?'

'"Dover Beach"?'

'"Dover Beach". Doesn't he talk about the sea of faith retreating from the world "with a long melancholy withdrawing roar"?'

'A long melancholy what?'

'Withdrawing roar.'

'Withdrawing roar?'

'Just so.' I was proud to have remembered something he hadn't read—or had forgotten. I had recently succumbed to Matthew Arnold's poems. 'A wonderful line. You can simply *hear* the sea of faith dragging away down the pebbly beach. I forget how it goes on.'

Again Father had no instant answer, and I felt a victor on the field. So while Father was rallying his forces I attacked again, since one should always attack the enemy while he is in disorder. 'And what about Huxley? Didn't he invent the word "agnostic" to describe his own position?'

But here I'd left a flank open. 'Of course he did. I knew that. You don't have to teach me that.' My words had left him able to lecture me again. 'He was alluding to that "altar to the Unknown God" which St. Paul saw in Athens. *Agnosto theo.*' He came out proudly with the actual Greek. 'And St. Paul expounded to them who their "Unknown God" was. And I may say I happen to be on St. Paul's side in this argument.'

'And I happen to be on Huxley's.'

Father's indignation at this rendered him almost speechless. He spluttered, 'You're on the same side as his! You put yourself on a level with Professor Huxley.'

'No more than you do with St. Paul. And I should have thought it was slightly less cocky to equate oneself with Huxley than with St. Paul.'

'Don't talk to me like that. Don't you dare to call me cocky. I don't like that tone.' And in the heat of argument he said something he would never have admitted to a child of his, had he been only a few degrees cooler. But he had to make his point; he had to win. He said, 'I know what I'm talking about. Let me tell you that when I was beginning to despair of getting employment I prayed to God for help, and within days came that quite inexplicable offer from Mr. Gatehouse.'

So that was why he was back in his place at church. An hour later I was able to feel a pity for Father, a proud man so wounded that he fell to his knees; but not till this fight was over. I too was heated, and it was only my loyalty to Uncle Douglas which saved me from explaining that the offer was not at all inexplicable; that in fact it had come from Uncle Douglas, and whether the Almighty was involved in it, who could say? All I answered was, 'I have as much right to be Huxley's disciple as you have to be St. Paul's.'

'I happen to be forty years older than you.'

'Granted,' I conceded impudently. 'But does that mean

you're bound to be right? So's Josef Stauffen, and Elsa too—getting on that way. Are they therefore always right, and me wrong?'

'Good God!' was all that Father could now say; and 'Pah!' as, refusing to deal further with youthful insolence, he walked from the room.

Infuriated by this contempt, I fired after him, 'And Grandfather Purvis? He must be twenty years older than you. Is he therefore twenty times more likely to be right?'

I don't know how much he heard; most, I suppose, since I shouted enough for him to hear all.

So on the Sunday morning after my discussion of the new murder with Elsa and Josef I waited till Father had left the house alone for Morning Service; waited till he was out of sight round the curve of the Crescent, for I was ashamed in secret of my present purpose; then slipped from the house and, taking the opposite direction from him, walked quickly towards our grey and rascally streets.

As I picture myself walking that way on a Sunday morning I see myself as a young man at an adventurous age, hemmed in by the unending bricks and pavements of suburban London, unable as yet to find adventure in foreign lands, on high seas, or amid Himalayan crags, and so seeking this poor adventure in the dusky realms of wrong. He walks quickly, that young man, longing to look at a house where murder has been done and terrible emotions known; longing to see its windows behind one of which the victim had sold her wares—for he is as prurient as any other young man of twenty. But prurience is not his strongest urge; a relish for drama is stronger; and compassion is not absent.

Anyway, I had heard a call from the old Dene to come again.

And here I was—in the Dene again. Eight years had made little or no difference in it; and this time I walked with none of my fears of eight years ago. Youthfully vain of my height (four inches shorter than Father), my broad shoulders, and my muscles, I was confident that I could deal adequately with any ruffian who tried an assault on me—should any such be abroad on a Sunday at noon. Indeed I rather looked forward to such a competition. Eight years had not erased my memory of the approaches to St. Michael's Row. I walked through the low-built streets, all so plainly the habitats of the poor but none of them obviously those of criminal types; and so I came to that corner which looked down the unusually long artery which was St. Michael's Row. There ran its rows of gabled houses all joined in terraces, with each side of the wide road matching the other. Barely three people were to be seen in all its length; presumably most of the men were enjoying their Sunday 'lay-in' with their goatish Sunday newspapers, while their women were in the kitchens preparing the Sunday spread. I had expected that the house of the murder would be identified for me by a cluster of gapers before it or a policeman on its threshold, but no: two days had passed since the discovery of the murder, and apparently what might be a nine days' wonder in the Crescents was less than a two days' excitement in the Dene. And, in any case, would it have been safe for one policeman to stand alone in St. Michael's Row?

I was disappointed because it seemed I would never know which was the house; and so it happened; I never did. One or two people passed me as I walked down the road, but I dared not ask them anything; a small buried shame prevented this. Still, at the end of the road was the St. Michael's Arms, and I had the satisfaction of gazing at that and wondering if members of the Rubin Vice Ring were drinking within. I heard no voices within; the doors looked grimly shut, and I hadn't the courage to push at them lest they opened. If they opened, I should have to go in, and I had no desire for someone to stand significantly on my boot and apologize. The place seemed deserted, and I remembered that the Liberal Party had brought in Licensing Acts to limit the hours of drinking—Acts strongly supported by Father who endorsed anything that kept the lower classes in order.

The sepulchral silence of the whole road defeated me, and I turned homeward, walking slowly because of my disappointment.

Then it was that I heard footsteps behind me. Footsteps a little faster than mine. Turning, I saw that they were the steps of a girl who, even as I looked at her, passed me. But I had seen a face so rounded and fresh and pretty that it was certain to capture the interest of a young man of twenty-one, still virginal. The face of a girl who might have been any age from sixteen to twenty. Her hair was more amber than auburn, and it was partly hidden by a cream tam-o'shanter set aslant— perhaps a little coyly. Her dress was demure, fitting close to a slender waist but the skirt flaring out below to reveal slim ankles that suggested slender limbs. Though she had passed me, she was not really walking fast; rather she was sauntering as if lost in dreams; but hearing my steps which had slightly quickened, she turned, saw me, and gave me a smile. It was a smile which set my heart quivering. It was like the smile of a friendly child.

Then suddenly I wondered. . . . I remembered the street I was in. I remembered Elsa saying, 'They prowl about in that road at any time of the day.' And 'Their dress is often as demure as it can be because that excites men more.' I remembered that this was Sunday, and men were free. My mind pulsed quickly and roughly like a caged bird fighting its bars, as I imagined this girl available for me, drawn close against me, and avidly possessed. It raced, as I thought of those lips below mine and at my mercy; those slender limbs enfolding me—even if all this had been bought (as they told me) for a sovereign or less.

I kept my distance behind her. At the second corner out of St. Michael's Row she turned into a side-street, and I, still captured for a moment, turned the corner too, though it was no part of my way home. Once again she looked round at me because of my following steps, but this time without a smile. Her curiosity satisfied, she walked on. In my innocence I wondered if this was all part of the technique when you were 'bringing men home'. Towards the end of this side-street there was a small shop, a newsagent's which dealt also in sweets, tobacco, small stationery and cheap toys. It had double glazed doors opening into the shop and a narrow, unwelcoming side-door leading, no doubt, to a staircase and bedrooms above. Its newspaper bill-boards—surprisingly all of them Saturday's rather than Sunday's—stood like an array of aprons under the shop windows. Sunday—noon—the shop doors were closed. The girl went to the side-door, pushed a bell, and turned yet again towards my following steps. I, of course, walked straight past her, eyes ahead as if uninterested in anyone but myself; but as soon as it was safe I turned round to learn what had happened. She was no longer to be seen. The side-door was shut. Somebody must have let her in; and at first I was almost disappointed because this seemed to show that she was only the newsagent's daughter. I considered the shop again and decided, with the same shameful touch of disappointment, that the house, being only two storeys, was surely too small for both the newsagent's family and other hostesses upstairs. But then I recalled Elsa's talk about girls and women who had 'cheap flats' in the Dene; and I didn't know what to think. Only I was surprised to find myself suddenly relieved because I was thinking the opposite thought from the shameful one and hoping she *was* only the newsagent's daughter. I am not certain now, after all these years, why I troubled to learn the name on the shop's fascia, which was 'N. D. Wayburn' and the name of this little side-street, which was 'Mortress Lane'.

This closes the story of that Sunday morning. Except for the sight of one pretty girl walking home and giving me a smile on her way, my shamefaced exploration had yielded nothing; I felt rather cheap and silly as I came back along Dunkerry Crescent.

8

Signing on and Walking out

However I might rebel against my father's despotisms and oppose his religion, I stayed the son of a Victorian home and still believed without question in the sexual morality which he and my mother had paraded before us children as the only tolerable one. Whatever Aldith may have done with Jack Fellbright before marrying him, I had no doubt that sexual intercourse before marriage, or outside it afterwards, was highly sinful, and that one-night affairs with women of the streets were misdemeanours, practised perhaps, but quite unspeakable.

But this is not to say that I would never commit such a sin. Young and twenty, I let my thoughts stray often to just such a sin, though always with guilt following close behind them. And often these guilty thoughts flung on to the screen of my mind the streets of the Dene and that attractive young figure in St. Michael's Row who might be traced again and found available.

So there came a day when I wandered back there, hoping I knew not what, except that it was a Saturday afternoon when women of the Dene might be on the prowl for customers, and that it was just possible I might see again the girl who had smiled at me. So down the narrowing streets I went, heart slightly irregular, a young man leading his hidden life and blindly craving some sort of adventure within the prison of London. Soon I was back in St. Michael's Row, and once again it looked no different from any other poor street in a working-class area. A few groups of men gossiped on the pavements; a few women stood gossiping between their front doors; but nowhere in the long uniform street were there strolling or loitering women such as our over-enthusiastic Elsa had described to me. Whatever my purpose on these pavements might be, I was relieved by this; I should have been dismayed if accosted by a soliciting woman as I passed. I kept my steps brisk so as to appear no loiterer myself. Naturally I turned round the corner of that little side-street, Mortress Lane, where a stationer's shop had swallowed up the girl who was drawing me.

It was empty, and I slowed my steps as I drew near the shop while I wondered what I was going to do. Then an idea was quickened in me by two legends along the top of the shop's windows: 'Player's Navy Cut' and 'Ogden's Guinea Gold'. In these first days of my manly independence I flew a standard of freedom from my lips—a large pendent meerschaum pipe, in shape like an inverted question-mark, with a deep yellow bowl which, in common with many other young men, I aspired to 'colour', by hard smoking, a fine chestnut-brown. It was not at its mast-head today, because I still believed with Father that no gentleman smoked in the street; but from its distant home in a pipe-rack in my bedroom it whispered to me, 'Go in and buy tobacco. Yes, I know you've plenty in your pouch and plenty in the jar on the mantelpiece, but you'll need more in due course so buy it now, and who knows what you'll learn?'

Nervously I pushed open the door of the shop—and there, between a counter laden with newspapers and magazines and a wall of shelves holding cartons or tins of cigarettes and packets of tobacco, stood the girl. She offered me the same smile, not arch or sly, but just friendly and welcoming.

I thought her even prettier now that she was without the cream tam-o'shanter aslant on her hair. The eyes were wide apart in the round face and bright with goodwill; the amber hair was manifestly abundant because, though parted in the middle and allowed to loop over the ears, it was rolled into a projecting chignon at the nape—a chignon like a small cottage loaf.

Knocked off balance by this sudden sight of her, I could not speak at once, and it was she who opened our encounter. 'Can I help you, sir?'

'Indeed you can,' I said, trying to be funny, now that I had recovered from my derangement. 'Have you got'—and I mentioned a tobacco much advertised just then because Sir James

F

Barrie had confessed that it was the glorious leaf extolled in his *My Lady Nicotine*.

'Oh yes, sir. Of course I have.' I noticed that like a practised counter-hand she said 'I' and not 'We'.

I paid its price, and then, not wanting to go, said, 'No, I'll have another packet while I'm about it.'

'Yes, sir.'

It was not only the charm of her face which was tethering me to her counter; there was also an uprush of gladness that she was no harlot of the streets. Almost certainly, since this was too small a shop to employ outside labour, she was the newsagent's daughter.

As an excuse for staying, I said, 'Surely I've seen you before somewhere?'

'I don't think so, sir.' But she said it with the same smile.

'Then I suppose I must have seen you in the street. I'm sure I have.'

'Not to speak to, I don't think.'

'Oh no; I didn't mean that. It's just that I live fairly close in Dunkerry Crescent.'

'Dunkerry Crescent? Where's that? "Dunkerry", did you say?'

So these people in the Dene had no such interest in our highly reputable Crescents as we in their ill-behaved streets.

'Yes, Dunkerry Crescent is only a few streets away from here. Are you the daughter of the shop?'

She frowned, bewildered by this fanciful expression. (The frown suited her, I thought.) 'Daughter of the *shop*?'

'Yes, I mean: are you your father's daughter? I mean: is this your father's shop?'

'Yes, of course it is.'

'I see.' How was I to go on staying here? 'Are you—do you regularly serve here?'

'That's right. I've helped Dad almost ever since I left school.'

'That can't be very long ago.' (Flattering, I hoped.)

'Five years. I didn't work for him at first, but I do now. You see, I stayed at school till I was nearly fourteen.'

That she was proud of this I found pathetic. 'Which school was that?'

'Stubb Lane,' was all she answered, but I remembered it: the dingy grey board school I had passed on my first visit years before.

'I know it.'

'I was in the fifth standard, you see, and could of got a certificate at thirteen to start working, but Dad and Mum let me stay on.'

All these board-school terms, 'standards' and 'certificates to start work' described methods and customs of which I knew nothing. But I lied for her comfort. 'I see. And what did you do between leaving school and starting work here?'

'Well, I got a situation at Patterson and Morley's.' I knew this for a large laundry on the western edge of the Dene, and 'situation' seemed a grandiose word for a child's first employment there. 'But after a year or so Dad and Mum kep' me at home to help in the shop. They'd heard things, and didn't like the kind'a girl I met there.'

The kind'a girl! These unexpected words stirred a wonder whether I was 'the kind'a young man' her parents would wish her to meet. Was I from the Crescents trustworthy enough to associate with a girl from the Dene? For a second the whole Dene seemed to turn upside-down.

I escaped into facetiousness. 'Then if you're your father's daughter you must be Miss Wayburn—unless you're married.'

'Oh, don't be absurd. Me married! Of course I'm Miss Wayburn, but nobody calls me that, not yet.'

'Well, what do they call you?'

'"Ireen". Just "Ireen".'

'"Ireen"? Is that short for Irene?'

'No. It's my name.'

To save her from distress I forebore to point out that this was a mispronouncing of the beautiful Greek name, Irene, or to air my classical learning by telling her that it was the Greek word for 'peace'. I went, however, so far as to pronounce the pleasing syllables, 'Irene Wayburn' in my own way, and aloud. Then, still making conversation instead of sensibly smiling and going,

75

I asked, 'What do the initials "N.D." stand for in your father's name over the shop?'

'Nelson Darby.'

Could there have been two more unexpected Christian names in a district like this? But I hid my surprise, merely exclaiming, 'Wonderful names. "Nelson Darby Wayburn".' And here I came to a stop. Lacking the wit to pursue these somewhat impertinent and altogether too facetious questions across a small shop-counter, I said feebly, 'Well, I suppose I must be going now, but I hope we shall meet again. I think I'll come always and get my tobacco here.'

No 'I hope so' or 'Please do', but at least a smile which was the opposite of a discouragement.

'Good-bye, Ireen,' I said, seeking to please her by the use of her Christian name.

'Good-bye, sir.'

Commonplace syllables, but spoken in a tone friendly enough, interested enough, to send me out into the street with a sense of pleasure, and a sense of something achieved. Was something strange, interesting, exciting going to happen to me; something that acquired an added attraction because it would be so extremely irregular as to be no small shock to Father: a son of his 'starting an affair' with a working-class girl in, of all places, the Dene? Aldith had gone off without so much as a by-your-leave, and at a dubious speed, to marry a young Mr. Fellbright, almost a stranger; Augusta had gone off to the other side of the globe with an old parson; and here was Stewart 'taking up with'—as he would probably put it—'a girl who was not only not out of a top drawer, but, believe it or not, out of the bottom drawer of all.'

§

With my meerschaum pipe drooping from its mast (for I had looked around and cast aside Father's out-of-date notion that gentlemen didn't smoke in the street) I returned the next Saturday into the Dene's grey streets. I walked past the open doors of Wayburn's the newsagent's, and a quick side-glance showed me a short middle-aged man behind the counter chatting with a woman customer over his magazines. Mr. Nelson Darby, no doubt. So for a while I walked on, strolling lazily around the streets and wondering sometimes which among the small homes housed a famous burglar, or a recidivist temporarily at home, or—more interesting—a harlot in her flat. In one street I saw two policemen ahead of me, sauntering casually enough, but the sight seemed to lend some truth to—or to remove some of the exaggeration from—the story so current in our parts—that 'no copper dared walk alone in the Dene'.

I allowed thirty minutes or more to pass before I came walking slowly back to the shop with the hope that its master had withdrawn. I had no desire to buy tobacco from him. The hope was fulfilled; passing again I saw Irene behind the counter—but the sight was a broken pleasure because she was serving with much laughter a young man. A young man in a labourer's clothes of whom I felt an instant jealousy. My mind framed an instant address to him: 'Get away. She's for me; not for you.' This after two sights of her and one conversation. The young labourer's pleased smile as he came out on to the pavement was an offence to me; and it enlarged whatever might be the nameless feeling I was indulging about this girl. Ludicrous to call it love at this stage, but, remembering how she had passed me and smiled I found myself quoting, after years of forgetfulness, two lines from a poem given me at school to render into Latin verse: 'I did but see her passing by,' and the next line which is surely the ultimate in exaggeration—but there it is; and a little hyperbole is allowed to lover or poet: 'And yet I love her till I die.'

A pleasing thought in a street of the Dene.

Annoyed by that glimpse of a likely and smiling supplanter I gave him thirty seconds to be gone, and then walked into the shop. Fortunately the door leading into the back parts of the house was closed and curtained. Probably Mr. Wayburn was taking his tea. Might he enjoy it, and partake of it idly. Irene, seeing me, showed immediate recognition and welcomed me with a bright-eyed and amused smile. As if to please me, she put her hand on the shelf behind her and laid in front of me the tobacco I had bought before. This so encouraged me that I spoke out boldly—so boldly that the detached watcher, the independent *alter ego*, who sits in all our heads, observing our behaviour, whether it is extravagant or properly disciplined, was not only surprised but admiring. I said—outright I said it, as I picked up the tobacco—'Do you think I might see more of you sometimes?'

'Why?' She stared at me, bewildered—or pretending bewilderment.

'*Why?* What a silly question. Isn't the answer obvious?'

'No. I don't know what you mean, ree'ly.' A plain but, I suppose, maidenly lie. 'Why should you want to see me?'

'Well, my dear child'—and at this point I heard myself translating that school poem into less hyperbolical terms; into the modesty of prose—'because I liked you the first moment I saw you.'

'But that's silly. That's impossible.'

'It's not at all silly. It's most enormously possible. When I came in last week, it was not the first time I'd seen you. I pretended I couldn't remember where I'd seen you before, but I knew perfectly well. I came in on purpose because a few days before I'd seen you passing by.' (Damn the poem.) 'Couldn't you come out with me some evening? '

A blush, not to be controlled, broke over her cheeks. She looked down and up again. 'My Mum and Dad are terribly strict.'

'Strict? How do you mean?' I hid my surprise. That there should be strictness in the Dene! 'Strict about what?'

'About who I go out with.'

I laughed. 'But I think I'm quite respectable. I'm a journalist of sorts. With the Portwith Press.' I pointed to the array of magazines on the counter. 'Your father'll know all about Portwith's. Several of these are our magazines.'

'Oh, it's not that,' she compromised, lest I should be offended. 'It's just that—it's just that this is not a very good neighbourhood—in some ways.'

'No, I rather knew that. But I don't belong to it. I live up on the hill. Where we're all hugely respectable.' As I thought of her neighbourhood, the jealousy stirred again. 'Do you go out with many . . . friends?'

'Sometimes with school friends.'

'Girls or boys?'

'Well, both, naturally. But Mum and Dad aren't so keen on me going out with boys, not ree'ly.'

'I could take you to some shows sometimes. My uncle is high up in Portwith's and he gives me tickets for theatres and music halls.'

'Oh, Mum and Dad don't hold with theatres. At least Mum don't. Dad isn't so down on them. But as for music halls, Mum'd have a fit.'

'Is your mother very religious?'

'Oh, yes,' she answered, as if it was the most natural thing for a mother to be. 'She and Dad go to the Meeting here.'

'Meeting?'

'Yes. Of the Brethren.'

'Brethren? And they meet. Where do they meet?'

'At the Room.'

'What is that? A chapel?'

'Kind of, I suppose. But we never call it that, we call it the Room. It's just a room like.'

'Just a bare room?'

She nodded, smiling.

I didn't want to show that all this was defeating me, but I stood there more and more bemused by what I had stumbled upon in the Dene. Brethren? A Meeting? Prayers and preachings, no doubt; good works. . . .

Picking up the tobacco, I said, 'Forgetting Pa and Ma for a minute, would you yourself *like* to come out with me sometimes and perhaps have a little meal together somewhere? And occasionally see a show?'

'Oh, *yes*.' I had surprised her into disclosing an enthusiasm. 'Of course I should love it if it was possible, like.'

'Well, you're about—what—eighteen?' This was younger than I truly thought her but I imagined that, as a woman, she would wish to be thought younger.

In this I was wrong. 'I'm nineteen,' she assured me proudly.

'Then, good gracious, surely you can persuade Pa and Ma that you can look after yourself.'

'I might persuade Pa all right, but Ma's the one; not Pa.'

I was pleased that she should have fun enough (whoever the Brethren might be) to substitute my would-be-jocose titles, 'Pa and Ma', for her 'Mum and Dad'.

'Well, stand on your own rights. To go out with whomever you want to.'

'You don't know my Mum,' she parried with a significant grimace.

'Well, you needn't mention any theatres or music halls——'

'—good *heavens*, no! Not music halls!'

'—until we get them used to the idea. The idea of a theatre, at any rate. We needn't speak of music halls.'

'I shouldn't like to do anything to deceive Mum and Dad.'

'No. I understand. You're not to do anything you don't want to do.' I was assuming an incipient proprietorship and control. 'Look. I'll give you a week. You're generally here on a Saturday, aren't you?'

'Oh, yes. Saturday is a busy day. Especially Saturday afternoon. I always help Dad on Sats. It gives him a rest.'

'Then I'll be here next Sat. And remember you've got to have good news for me. *Please*.'

§

So it all began. In that week of waiting I carefully sought instruction from Elsa about the habits of the highly respectable poor, she herself being sprung from the midst of them. And much I learned from her kitchen chatter one evening after tea. So did her Josef. Much that surprised us. Of course I made no reference to my activities in the Dene which would have certainly 'put her about a lot'. I employed the easy stratagem of a writer, pretending I'd promised to do an article about the customs of strictly brought up and still well conducted young women of the working classes in their after-school and first working years.

Needless to say Elsa delighted in telling me all she knew—and in telling Josef her husband—as she bustled from table to

dresser or stove in her large Victorian kitchen. Josef and I sat—
out of her way, please—I smoking my yellow meerschaum and
sometimes rubbing its bowl between my nostril and my right
cheek, which was the accepted way of putting a bright sheen on
each browning side of it; Josef smoking an even longer and
more drooping pipe which had a bowl of white porcelain, a
stem eight inches long, and a mouth-piece of white bone. This
so-typical German pipe seemed to bring all Mittel-Europa
into our kitchen.

'It usually begins,' said Elsa, carrying a saucepan to the
range, 'with what they call the "signing on"—that's to say if
both parties are of the decent sort——'

'Vot usually pegins?' asked Josef.

'Why the "walking out", silly. Isn't that what we're talking
about?'

'But what under heaven is a "signing on"?' I asked in my
turn. (Would I have to sign a document before Mr. Nelson
Darby Wayburn?)

'Oh, it's not writing down nothing; it's no more'n a phrase,
ree'ly'—here was the same language as Irene's—'it jest means
that each has kind-of accepted the other as the one he or she is
going to walk out with. Not necessarily courting, mind you;
they ain't got as far as that yet. They're jest walking out, you
see.'

For a moment I felt a relief. 'I see,' I agreed.

'It's usually like this: the young man's walking about the
streets of an evening probably hoping to see and get off with a
pretty girl—you know what young men are—and he passes
one at last who ree'ly attracts him, you see——'

'I do.'

'—and he guesses at once, p'raps from no more'n a turn of
her eyes that she knows and is pleased she's attracted him——'

'You pet she is!' Josef endorsed.

'—so he jest walks on rather more slowly and then turns
about and sees that she's also walking more slowly, or p'raps
pretending to gaze into a shop window——'

'Vot? In the dark?' queried Josef.

'Oh, don't be a silly old man. You know what I mean. P'raps

the blind ain't down and she can pretend she's interested in something. So the young man walks back and makes some daft remark like "surely we've met before", or——'

But she couldn't think of any alternative daft remark, so I provided, 'Where are you going to, my pretty maid?'

'No, he wouldn't come out with nothing like that. That'd be a shade too clever for him. That'd be all right for you, Master Stewart, I dessay—though for anyone it'd be a shade too up-and-coming at this commencement, like. If he said that, she'd probably answer "Nowhere in pertickerler" and he'd say, if he's not too shy and nervous, being as how he's a nice young man, and if he's a bit of a comic like you, Master Stewart, "Well, can I go there with you?" and she'll say, "I don't mind if you do," like enough without a smile, because it's not the time to smile too easily yet; jest "I don't mind if you do"; and there you are: they've signed on.'

'*Mein Gott!*' Josef exclaimed.

'A real pick-up,' I said.

'Oh, no.' Elsa wouldn't allow this. 'If he's a real nice properly brought-up boy, this is no invite to come into some back alley and start hugging and kissing and taking liberties; it can be no more'n——'

Josef rephrased the situation for me. 'Zo der's no getting vresh mit her, you see. Boor lad.'

'Don't keep on int'rupting, Josef, if you've nothing better to say than that. And if that's all you feel about it, you're a naughty old man. It can be no more, Master Stewart, than an agreement to walk together for that night only, and always in the girl's direction, or wherever she has a fancy to go. It's possible they may kiss at the end, but it's not very likely, as you might say, as yet. And they may say nothing at all about seeing one another again. The girl can have no chaperone, you see, not being in your class and having no nice home for——'

'Canoodling,' I supplied, since she lacked a suitable word.

'Pilling und cooing,' was Josef's suggestion. '*Ja.*'

'No, you see, she's only got the London streets, like. But if that first meeting ain't the end, and they feel they ree'ly like each other, they'll arrange to meet again. And when the signing on has turned into a habit, as you might say, well then, it's a walking out. They're courting; ree'ly courting.'

'But, Elsa, if all this happens in the street, doesn't he ever enter the girl's home?'

'Not at first. Oh, no.' She was emphatic about this. 'That only happens when the walking out has become a ree'ly serious thing, with the parents knowing all about it; and then, sooner or later, they'll invite you to tea; a very special tea, with everything laid on; lettuce and cream buns and doughnuts and celery and all; and there you are!'

'*Ja*. Der he is,' echoed Josef. 'She's god him. *Ja*, the vly is safely in the veb.'

'Not me,' I laughed hastily, for this began to sound as if they were relating all of it to me.

'No, you know what I mean. The young man in the story you're writing. He's kind-of accepted by the girl's parents.'

'You mean they're engaged?'

'Well. . . .' Elsa pursed up her lips as one who hesitates to be precise. 'It don't necessarily mean things'a got as far as that, but it *does* mean he's now her young man. Definitely her young man. Let him cross her doorstep and come to tea, and he's her young man. Definitely.'

'I see.' But God save my poor father from hearing such words and knowing the thoughts of his only son.

Next Saturday, at three in the afternoon, I was before Irene's door, and if I did not cross the door-step that led into her family's private rooms, I did cross the threshold of their shop, for she was there behind the counter and alone. I asked my question by simply lifting my eyebrows; and she, understanding it, answered, 'Dad says I may, but Mum's not so happy about it. She says she hopes you're a godly young man. Are you?'

'Oh, lord!' I worried. 'I don't think so. I'm afraid not. But wait: my father used to be a sidesman up at St. Jude's and he goes there regularly. Will that do?'

'That's Church of England, isn't it? Mum don't hold with the Church of England. Not altogether.'

'Oh dear!'

But then I suddenly thought of an even better qualification. 'And my sister's married to a missionary in India. She's ever so godly.'

'Oh, that'll suit Mum all right. Mum's great on converting the heathen.'

'Yes, my sister's godly in the extreme,' I promised her— omitting, however, that she was also High Church in the extreme because I suspected that this would be no recommend- ation to Mrs. Wayburn of the Brethren. Wanting to keep some link with the truth I did admit, apologetically, 'But she's Church of England, of course.'

'*I* can't see anything wrong with the Church of England,' Irene avowed obligingly.

'Well then you must be the only person in England who can't,' I submitted; then feeling that this witticism didn't improve my position at all, I added the fatuous remark, 'Ah well, the old C. of E. isn't perfect, perhaps, but who is?'

'I'm sure Mum thinks the Brethren are.'

This remark pleased me because it showed she had fun, clear eyes, and the readiness to criticize a formidable mother. All these ecclesiastical exchanges—across a shop counter— passed between us before it was half-past three on that Satur- day, and they closed with her telling me that her father liked her to help him on Saturdays 'till about five or so', after which she could go out with me; whereat I demanded, 'Well, what about tonight? What's wrong with tonight?'

'Nothing . . . particularly,' she said.

'Well, will you come this evening? Say at half-past five.'

'I shouldn't mind.' Almost the words that Elsa had provided for her imaginary heroine.

'Fine. I'll be waiting in the street round about five.'

I had to wait from five till a quarter to six, having before this sat over a tea-cup and two buns at a Lockhart's in the Dene; but when at last she came out from the narrow side-door, I was made happy and touched to see that she had been studi- ously dressing herself for this occasion with me. So unexpected was this that it remains the only time, after all these years, that I can remember the clothes she wore. She was wearing a large hat that supported a white ostrich feather and was somewhat cheekily tilted; the whole of it seeming a little too adult for the round, simple, almost childish face below. Her long-skirted black dress, fitting close in to her small waist, had a white-bordered V opening in the blouse which showed her throat and suggested the small young breasts beneath; its black sleeves finished above the elbow, and, as she came out, she was buttoning the long elbow-length black gloves. Such distinction in the Dene! My dark lounge suit and straw boater seemed unworthy of this finery, and I wished I was wearing my bowler.

Another thing I recall is that, no matter how studied her finery, the young face among it showed not a trace of make-up. This I found strange because even Father allowed Augusta—and Augusta, the most pious of us all, allowed herself—to touch up her skin with *papiers poudrés*, her cheeks with a flush of rouge, and her lips with lip-salve—as the only permissible confection was called in the genteel years before these blazing scarlet lipstick days.

Where to take Irene had been exercising my thoughts all day. I was no natural working-class walker-out, who would be content to stroll with his girl through the gas-lit evening for mile upon mile, lingering once or twice perhaps under the spread of a roadside tree or within the dim golden halo flung on to the night pavement by a lamp-post's whispering jet.

I had learned from Elsa that if the nightly companionship had become a true walking out it was then incumbent on the girl's young man to see her to her door but not, as I have told you, to cross the door-step into the privacies of her home. In the first days there should be no embraces, but after a suitable time there might come a linking of hands and a swinging up and down of the same; and if this happened it was an advance towards larger issues. And when at last it was followed regularly by a kiss before the family's door sternly closed, why—this was to be approaching the brink.

I am speaking of course of customs that ruled once among the strictly respectable poor—and may do still, for all I know—but these were a majority then—in their outward behaviour at least—and manifestly Irene's parents, even though they lived in one of the lowest of neighbourhoods, were among the top-most cream of these.

By the time she joined me in her feathered hat and ladylike gloves I had determined where to take her. A theatre was out of the question for the present, but I had conceived a compromise.

I said, 'How lovely you look,' and without heeding her necessarily arch denial, hurried on with, 'Come along. I know where we're going to. I've the whole course mapped out. We're going to see Life.'

'See *Life*?' Her tone like mine implied the capital letter. 'What sort of life?'

'Noisy and rowdy and delightful. You'll see. And after that I'm going to take you to Earl's Court Exhibition. Nothing your mama can object to there.'

'Oh, that'll be lovely. I've been to the Ex. once before. But I'm not going up in the Big Wheel. I'd die first.' (The Big Wheel, towering hundreds of feet in the air, was a mighty creation, picked out in electric lights, its iron circumference strong enough to carry swaying coaches like Pullman cars. In this year its electric lights, visible from any eminence in West London, advertised, between its outer and inner illuminated rims, 'Horlick's Malted Milk'; a year or two later it all perished in an East London yard as old iron.) 'Daddy didn't mind my going there but Mummy wasn't too happy about it. She thought it a bit ungodly.'

'Few godlier places anywhere,' I assured her. 'But Life first. Horse bus or motor bus?'

Horse buses and motor buses were now sharing the London streets with the motor buses fast winning their larger share.

'Oh, the motor bus! Every time! *Please*,' she said.

I regretted this because I still liked to sit if possible on the front seat of a horse bus's top deck so that I could speak with the driver on his elevated throne.

We got ourselves on to the top deck of a green Oxford Street motor bus and under the black waterproof rug ostensibly lest it should rain, but really to increase our togetherness. Travelling west, this bus would take us to the Goldhawk Road and the top of the Hammersmith 'Grove'. And it was while we were seated here on a bench at the back that she answered all my questions about the Brethren and their Meeting. Though attending the Meeting with her parents, and being sometimes known as 'Sister Ireen', her descriptions of her brethren and sisters didn't lack a sprinkle of satirical salt. They were a break-away branch of the Plymouth Brethren, calling themselves 'The Exclusive Brethren' and still referring to each other, if they were older members, as 'the saints'. Her father was the son of two Exclusives so devoted that they had embarrassed him (and certainly Irene) with the Christian names 'Nelson' and 'Darby' after the Brethren's founder, Nelson Darby, an Irish protestant clergyman who became dissatisfied with every form of Christianity except his own. And just as George Fox with his very real saintliness gathered around him followers who became the Quakers, so John Nelson Darby, after establishing himself at Plymouth drew many 'saints' around him; and thus the name, 'Plymouth Brethren', descended unsought upon them. Perhaps because 'Dad' was born into the community he, though loyal to it, was far less strict an adherent than 'Mum'—'he admits he's no saint, and I'm sure I'm not'—but her mother was a convert and after the manner of many converts was as eager as John Nelson Darby himself for the extremes of piety and the companionship of saints.

From Goldhawk Road we walked down The Grove, a long grey residential road, straight as a taut rope. Sparsely lit by gas-lamps alternating from side to side, it was as little like a grove as any street in London. It debouched on to Hammersmith's King Street, and today, it being seven o'clock p.m. of a Saturday, on to 'King Street's Saturday Night'.

King Street was then as narrow a high road as you could find in London, but nevertheless on Saturday nights market stall after market stall, barrow after barrow, stood ranged along its southern pavement, all of them with their naphtha flambeaux flaring like cressets in worship of Good Business and Saturday Night. Before each stood its prophet and priest bellowing its wares, whether old clothes, new clothes, second-hand books, butcher's meat, greengrocery, cheap jewellery, or cheap sheets of music for the pianos of the poor. These barkers had to roar in merry competition, not only with the stall holders on either side of them but with the spielers of the wide-open shops in front of them, across the narrow pavement.

'Come along. Come along. Twopenn'orth of pot-herbs, enough for the whole family, for Granny, Mums, Dad, the nippers and all—even the baby—yurse, don't forget the baby' —holding out a large onion. Here and there between the stalls a gutter merchant stood offering 'Loverly vi'lets; penny a bunch. Loverly vi'lets, lady. Give her a bunch, guv. Be a gent to her now; be a gent;' or a man with a tray of mechanical toys which he put through their paces on the pavement; or an organ grinder turning the handle of his piano-organ to produce a tinkling Merry Widow waltz. Here was a singer defying the din with 'Just a song at twilight' and then 'Jerusalem, Jerusalem, sing for the night is o'er.' We passed a man crying his cockles and whelks—'Cockles and whelks, all alive-o'. His barrow was the humblest of all: it was but a wide board supported on an old perambulator, but it was gay with shellfish set forth in little saucers for immediate eating; with dishes of shrimps and prawns and one magnificent crab to be the centre and king of a festive display.

The people streamed past the stalls, not only on the pavement but on the camber of the road behind the stalls so that the electric trams in that narrow street could only make headway and evade disasters or deaths by persistent clanging of their bells. Some of the people between stalls and shops were poor women with men's caps on their tattered hair and shawls about their shoulders, all on a slow prowl to find cheap garments or cheaper cuts of meat—which got steadily cheaper as the night wore on.

Irene and I kept to the pavement, but so slow was the wandering procession that more than once I had to put a hand under her shoulder or even right round her back (but always gently) so as to guide and help her who was so much smaller than I—gentle courtesies which not only gave me pleasure but stirred something more, some excitement and desire.

It was in this first 'walk out' amid the uproar of a street

market that I crowned her with a new name. No one could have been more surprised than I at this prowess—was it that in this din, so largely composed of banter, fun and ribaldry, all things seemed possible? Anyway I knew, after Elsa's expositions, that I was going much too fast and infringing the protocols of signing on and walking out. I had now told Irene to hold on to my arm, and occasionally she had clutched my arm against her side in her delight or amusement; this was encouraging. We passed a melancholy street singer who from his stance in the gutter was singing, 'Pale hands I loved beside the Shalimar' and this had so diverted Irene with the incongruity between his dilapidated figure and his little lost Indian maiden beside the Shalimar, that she drew my arm tighter than ever against herself as she laughed; and I knew that we were close enough (in both senses) for me to be a little bold.

I said, 'I cannot and will not call you Ireen. You have one of the loveliest names in the language. Strictly it's Irene and the Greek for "peace". I imagine it's equally beautiful in French where I suppose they pronounce it "Irène". Your parents can call you what they like. I'm going to have my own name for you. May I?'

'If you like.' Hardly encouraging words, but I could see that they masked, as modesty demanded, a surprise and pleasure which could not be spoken.

'I like the sound "Irène" and I'm going to call you "Raney".'

'Oh, I like that! I wish everybody'd call me that.'

'I don't. Nobody else is going to call you it. Nobody at all. It's my name for you and mine only. Raney, have you seen enough here? Shall we go on to the Ex.?'

'Oh, yes. But don't go spending too much money.'

'I needn't. I have a season ticket to the Ex—' but at this, fearing I was bragging, I explained, 'It costs only ten shillings for the whole season. Do we go now?'

'Yes, *yes. Let's*,' and as she said this, the clutching of my arm against her was not only a matter of delight and laughter but a first touch of affection.

'Come then.' And we struggled back through the streams of people to Hammersmith Broadway so as to take the District

G

Railway train to West Kensington. From the West Kensington station you could climb a slope and reach a side entrance into the Exhibition; we clicked through its turnstile; and grey gas-lit London died behind us; we were in a Dream City of white palaces, illuminated gardens, wonder side-shows, with fairy-lamps outlining all, including the rims of the Big Wheel circling high in the night sky. Galaxies gleamed in heaven and on earth; Ursa Major, Polaris, and the Pleiades shared the sapphire night with the haloed Wheel and 'Horlick's Malted Milk'. Did ever a lovelier evening overhang with its blessing this strange ornamental play-city than on this Saturday when Raney and I wandered together into it? A moon, waning but brilliant, sidled slowly through drifts of thin white cloud, and its company of stars competed almost equally with the fairy lamps garlanding all.

Since it was now late in the evening the visitors were mainly massed in the central area and parading round and round the bandstand, crowned and garlanded with lights, where a red-coated Guards band was playing tunes from *The Geisha* and the happier lads, inspired by the music, and almost as lit up as the bandstand, were obliging the crowd, ever and again, with the 'cake walk', just imported from the Negroes of America.

On the eastern side of this ambulating area was the fashionable Welcome Club with its chain of vine-hung alcoves where the moneyed and the privileged could dine in private parties, and its flower-bedded lawns where these same expensive people could loll in wicker chairs, smoking long cigars or, if ladies, fanning themselves under their picture hats, as they watched commoner people in circulation round the bandstand.

The Welcome Club was not for such as Raney and me (it might well have been for Uncle Douglas) so we trailed round with the common people and the cake walkers. To keep close to me where the crowding was thick, Raney kept her hand within my arm; outwardly this was no more than a necessary precaution but I could feel already that it was declaring an advance in our friendship, and, knowing this, I often, in my turn, pressed it against me.

Far to the left of the circulating throng there was a 'Continental Café', and to this after a time I took Raney for refreshments, suggesting to her as we sat ourselves at a table under the open sky as we might in Paris, Vienna or Rome, that she'd best avoid mentioning the word 'continental' to her mother who probably thought the whole Continent a wilderness of vice—even though—and perhaps because—she herself lived in one of the most vicious areas of London.

Raney pleased me by being ready to make fun of her mother's excessive puritanism, but pleased me less by calling this place a 'caff'. I think it was that night under the stars and amid all the artificial brilliance of Earl's Court that I decided I would make a pupil of Raney, correcting her grammar and teaching her much of the poems and literature that I loved. It was remarkable in Raney that, while her grammar was all over the place, with double negatives, missing auxiliary verbs and erratic sequences, her pronunciation of misused words and her 'accent' were only a little different from that of any girl in Dunkerry Crescent. Later I was to know the explanation of this: her mother, before her marriage, had been for years a lady's maid to a baronet's wife, 'a *real* "lady"', and had learned to copy her accent. Thus Raney had lived from birth with this new accent; and I, a true son of my father, was glad of this, for grammar could be easily amended, but an accent was irremediable. For the present, however, I left her grammar where it was, and ordered a lager for myself, a safe and uncontinental ginger beer for her, and sliced French bread embracing salami sausage for us both. That we might linger under the starred and moonlit sky I persuaded her to take more and more of the French-bread sandwiches, even though their slant-wise slicing and the Italian salami lying within the slices seemed to partake in a small way of continental wickedness. Any such dubious quality in them I diluted for her with a further draught of English ginger beer, honest and pure.

At last, the night deepening, I thought of her mother and said, 'Raney, we must be going now.'

'Oh, no,' she protested. 'Not just yet. I'm happy.'

'Yes, now,' I insisted, picking up her fingers where she sat. 'Come along. Mum waits.' Already the master, you see.

And she saw this at once, for she said, 'I see. The whistle's gone, has it?' Which pleased me because it seemed evidence of a ready wit. 'Oh, all right.' Grudgingly.

'Yes, whistle's gone. Close of play. I'll take you back as far as your home.'

She had risen and was drawing on the long lady-like gloves which had rested on the table in lady-like fashion, little suited to the Dene, beside a salami sandwich. 'I don't want to go a bit. It's been that lovely. All of it. Lovely.'

'What? Even the King Street Saturday Night?'

'Yes, with you to make it all that exciting and funny. I been often to the market in the Portobello Road, but I never seen it as you made me see it. It was just ordinary to me, but you made it seem wonderful.'

'So it is, and we must go and see a lot more things, but now it's home, and home quickly, or your mother'll never let you go out with me again.'

'I shall do it if I want to.'

So then: she was ready to defy her mother for my sake. A happy thought. but I was now delighting enough in her to want her parents to tolerate me as a suitable walker out, so I recommended caution. 'No, but listen, darling'—this word slipped from my lips of its own accord, uninstructed by me— 'listen: I shall want your mother to think well of me.'

'Oh, I'll make her do that.'

'You want to?'

'Well . . . naturally. . . .' But lest this word should suggest too much or sound too forward, she wrapped it up with 'I mean, why shouldn't I . . . I mean . . . I like . . . sometimes . . .'

I helped her with prompt words out of the swamp into which she had got herself. 'Home then it is. Home like a good girl.'

And we walked over a covered bridge with its arcade of bazaar stalls on either side, served by houris, acclaimed by raucous spielers, and some of them exuding oriental smells of joss sticks or incense—and neither of us knew that it spanned the cinder-black wastelands and dark, cheerless waggon-tracks of a London, Midland and Scottish coal depot; or that the white Byzantine palaces of golden lights hid and covered the dreary route of the West London Railway in its cutting between Addison Road and West Brompton stations.

As we made our way through a palace and drew near the Exhibition's main entrance, Raney bewailed, 'Oh, I don't want to leave it. It's been so lovely.'

'You shall come again,' I promised. 'It lasts till October.'

'What happens to it then?'

I answered dramatically, for the idea appealed to me, 'It lies, I imagine, like a city of the dead for six whole months, all silent and dark in the very heart of London, and then springs back to life in May—with all its ten thousand lights. And its bazaars and its bands.'

'You do explain things so wonderfully,' she said.

And with that we left the white and bejewelled lake-side city behind us, emerging into the murky gas-lit darkness of Warwick Road.

'Bus?' I asked. 'Or walk?'

'Oh, walk. Let's walk. I like walking. With you.'

'It's all of a mile and more.'

'I don't mind. I wish it was two miles. Or three. I'm happy.'

These were the words which encouraged me to pick up her hand and intertwine my fingers between hers, so that we could walk homeward linked. She responded with a slight, very slight, pressure on my fingers as if she welcomed them. Soon we were swinging the linked hands and I suddenly realized that, if Elsa's rulings and time-tables were right, I had advanced in some two hundred and fifty minutes to a point which should have required several evenings of 'walking out' to attain. I had arrived at the linking and swinging of hands. And when at last, having walked our mile and more, we arrived at the threshold of her father's house I did not immediately let her hand go but, observing something like affection in her eyes looking up into mine as we said good-byes, led her towards a lamp-post six yards ahead and there within the wavering cone of yellow light flung by a gas-jet shuddering in a breeze, I drew her against me and kissed her. Which amounts to saying that in less than four hours of a summer evening I had covered the whole of Elsa's first course to the first post. The next

93

course could only begin when I crossed that stony threshold and enjoyed that fine ceremonial tea with its lettuce, celery, cakes and doughnuts. In my first humility I kissed her only on the cheek once and again, but, uplifted by her quiet acceptance of this, I grew bold and kissed her on the lips, holding the kiss for a long time and feeling a response from her lips that, if shy and perhaps doubting, was yet happy and mutual. 'Where are we going to?' I wondered as I held that kiss. 'Where are we going to? What will this lead to?' And yet, when at length I lifted my lips from hers, I whispered, I could but whisper, my heart demanding the words, 'You're beautiful. *So* beautiful.'

Old syllables gently breathed in a dark and ill-favoured London street but first spoken, I imagine, in the beginnings of the world.

She answered nothing, but her eyes looking up at me were two stars in the lamp-post's small tent of light; and that some love had lit up in them no man could doubt. This was the moment when I knew I was in love. For the first time in my life I was truly in love; but as I let her go, the only words I could say, 'I hope I see you again . . . soon.' And hers, as she looked up at me without reproach, were only 'I hope so too.'

But these were declaration enough and I walked home, out of our disreputable Dene, up the meaner streets of the hill, past the poorer houses of Dunkerry Crescent and into the midst of our pretentious homes, caring not a damn that I was in love with a girl from a degraded neighbourhood and of a board-school class, such as would plunge my poor father into Tartarean depths; nay, rather, rejoicing in both these thoughts, and with an aura of defiance and ecstasy encompassing me all the way.

9

'Hadn't We the Gaiety'

This may have been a record lap, run in three hundred minutes, but there would have to be many more laps before I covered enough ground to justify my crossing that threshold and entering as a welcome guest a parlour where the tea would be spread out for me, in the family's best tea-service, and all bright and inviting with its greengrocery and cakes and buns. Till then I had no homely, covered, private place where I could sit with Raney in my embrace, and apart from a few more visits to the bright lights and fairy gardens of the Exhibition, and some brief hours in cheap restaurants, we had to enjoy our happiness together in populous streets and our embraces in quiet and dark corners. And so things would have stayed if there had been no Uncle Douglas in Chapel Buildings, Lincoln's Inn.

Not daring as yet to speak of Raney to Father, I had taken Uncle Douglas into my confidence, and I have to relate that for all his high liberality and tolerance he was yet somewhat shocked at my having 'picked up a purely working-class girl from that festering sore, the Dene'. There had always been a rebel in him, but nonetheless he was of the same blood as my father, and it took him all of twenty minutes to adjust himself to this idea. But then the rebel was in full command again, and he began to rejoice in my story, especially when he wondered what 'the Mandarin' would think about it. And since he was often given free tickets for theatres and music halls he would frequently hand them to us. 'You can't just wander the streets with her, old boy,' he had protested at first. 'Take the poor child to the Gaiety or the Tivoli or the Alhambra or somewhere.'

'Yes, Uncle, but I'm not a man of wealth. I——'

'I know; I know all about that; but I can help. That's what

uncles are for. To say nothing of godfathers. And by God—don't tell the Mandarin I said that—by God, if the worst comes to the worst, you shall have this room for a little reasonable spooning when I'm out. Damn it all: one's only young once. But first we'll see what we can do about theatres and music halls. Just wait.'

All this I told to Raney, and we both agreed that we'd avoid all mention of music halls to the parents and speak only of theatres: this she insisted on; there was no open rebellion in her but only a loyalty and devotion to both of them, undisturbed by her laughter at them. Indeed it remains a wonder to me that all our early love-making stayed wholly bound up by the morality prescribed by our parents. Just as I was the willing prisoner of my parents' system of morality, so Raney, whatever fun she might make of her mother's puritanism, accepted without debate the morals taught her.

And the moment came, but only after weeks, when, Uncle Douglas having offered me two passes to the Gaiety Theatre, Raney came running out to me on the pavement before her door, seized hold of both my hands excitedly, and said, 'I told Mum! I said "He wants to take me to a theatre", and when she didn't answer, Dad said, "If it's a decent show, Mother, let the poor kid go;" and I said it was the decentest show—ever so—just music and songs—I nearly said "dances" but left that out; and Mum, though obviously put about at first, said, "Well, I dunno; I can't say I hold with theatres, but if your father says"—and at that point I rushed up and kissed him before he could say anything else, so Mum just sighed and said, "Well, he seems on the whole a godly young man." That's *you*. *You*. The godly young man.'

'Oh, lord,' I wondered. 'I've doubts about that.'

'So've I. But I didn't say so. I said, "Oh yes" and kissed her and dashed up to dress before she could change her mind. And here I am. Thank you so much. Oh, isn't it all lovely?'

And to the Gaiety we went in its new domed home at the corner of Aldwych and the Strand; and this was but the first of many visits, thanks to Uncle's friendship with George Edwardes, 'the Guv'nor'. Since our tickets fell from the throne itself it was in stalls that we sat. I look back and know for certain that nothing in a long life has given me more happiness than to sit beside Raney, child of a dubious street in the Dene, and watch her delight in these gay shows, all so new to her, and her leaping pride that she should be sitting in these, the top seats of all. I am certain too that, while I enjoyed the shows as much as she did, my enjoyment in the performances was less than my joy in her sparkling happiness. Slyly watching her at my side, and thinking my secret thoughts, as she laughed and clapped and sometimes hugged my arm as if to squeeze her pleasure into it, I found myself more and more possessed by an ambition to make her my pupil, educating her taste till she should be ready to come with me and enjoy with an equal fervour fine 'straight' plays, such as those lately produced at the Court Theatre, and this year at the Duke of York's, by Granville Barker; plays by Hauptmann, Ibsen, Shaw and Galsworthy. It was thus early in our love that I was surprised, even bewildered, but certainly pleased, to find that, for the first time in my life, I was truly caring more for someone else's happiness and advancement than my own. This, then, must really be love; and love of a kind far better than I had conceived. So I would now set about striving to give her much of the education she'd been denied and to make of her all that she had it in her power to be. In brief, I was now, with no small enthusiasm, casting myself in a role like those of King Cophetua with his beggar-maid, and Pygmalion with his Galatea.

Meantime these Gaiety and Daly's musicals were enough to entertain us both, and even though all this 'real love' was for Raney, I got plenty of joy from the beauty of the Gaiety girls; I was capable of a simultaneous 'crush on such stunners' (our contemporary language) as Marie Studholme, Constance Collier, Mabel Love, Evie Greene—but, queen of them all in my heart, just as she was now acknowledged 'Queen of the Gaiety', was that exquisite little trifle, Gertie Millar. Picture postcards of these smiling lovelies were in the windows of every stationer's in London (except N. D. Wayburn's in Mortress Lane), and I was no different from a million other young men who had these portraits paraded along their mantelpieces. I had as full a gallery of them as any, but in the centre of them all, queen of them all, was Gertie Millar—Gertie Millar with an enormous up-ended hat rising like the sun in its strength behind that lovely little face with its gay little smile. I have the picture still, a bit stained and wrinkled with time, and I sometimes look at it, and the old days with Raney return.

It captured the hour when, though low in the programme and merely the 'First Bridesmaid', Gertie Millar won the world. Her right hand points saucily away to the right, her left hand lifts one corner of her ground-length skirt to allow us a strictly incorrect peep at a petticoat's hem. It shows her as she was when singing the song that lifted her at once to great lights blazing over the Strand:

Cora! Cora! Captivating Cora,
   Just a little bridesmaid, that is all.
With a smile, a-walking up the aisle
   Captivating Cora makes the bride look small.

It was to her last performance at the Gaiety in *Our Miss Gibbs* (though she went on to play at Daly's and the Adelphi) that I took Raney to see her; and we were seated there when she brought down the house, and brought down a few tears too, with her last song, *Moonstruck*:

I'm such a silly when the moon comes out,
I hardly seem to know what I'm about,
   Skipping, hopping,
   Never, never stopping,
I can't keep still, although I try.
I'm all a-quiver when the moonbeams glance,
That's the moment when I long to dance;
I can never close a sleeping eye
When the moon comes creeping up the sky.

It was the next evening after this hearty and emotional occasion that Father came into my bedroom and saw my picture parade. He studied the lovely smiles, walking from the first to the last.

'Good lord,' he sighed, after the last, and 'Good lord' again. 'I go into Augusta's room and see along her mantelpiece nothing but pictures of the Blessed Virgin Mary and The Immaculate Conception and St. Augustine of This, That or the Other and Saint Fillum-Somebody——'

'Saint Philomena,' I supplied. 'The sexy little piece' (remembering Aldith's comment, and that it had suitably disturbed him).

'*Please*, Stewart!' he reproved me, as he had reproved her. 'And now, instead of the Blessed Virgin I see nothing but actresses. All of them are Gaiety girls, aren't they?'

'Most of them.'

'And this is Gertie Millar, isn't it?' Even Father knew the fame and face of Gertie Millar.

'Yes, indeed. My beloved Gertie Millar. Talk about a sexy little piece! Don't you think she's adorable?'

'I can't say I'm the sort of person that adores Gaiety girls. Most of them are peeresses now, aren't they?'

'Rosie Boote, Sylvia Storey, Denise Orme,' I rattled off the names, happy to instruct him.

'And this Miss Millar?'

'Good heavens, does anybody call her Miss Millar? No, *she* isn't yet. But she will be one day, bet your life.' (And so she was, many years after this, when she married the 2nd Earl of Dudley.)

'Well, I don't know,' murmured Father, musingly. 'I'm all for having an aristocracy, but I like it to *be* an aristocracy.'

'And not an actress-ocracy,' I suggested, having heard this joke somewhere.

'A what?'

I repeated the word, but he didn't laugh. He didn't laugh easily at other people's jokes, though he had a good 'ha, ha' for his own. He just said, 'Yes, I certainly think that. And is it the Gaiety that you go to every night?'

'Not every night, alas. Only occasionally.'

'What, alone?'

'No, with a friend.'

'Do I know him?'

(*Him!* So blind he was to the fact that I was now older than I had been for so long.) 'No, I don't think you do.'

'I understand there are crowds of young fools who wait at the stage door of the Gaiety to pick up these girls.'

'Oh yes,' I agreed cheerfully. 'Crowds. And they like to go off in hansoms.'

'Well, I suppose it's all right as long as *you* are content with pictures of them. I hope sincerely that you'd never pick up a girl at a stage door.'

'Gracious, no,' I assured him, though not without memories of a shop door.

After a time Raney and I went together, not only to the Gaiety and Daly's, but to the more famous music halls, justifying this deviation to her parents by calling them 'harmless musicals' for which my journalist uncle was often given passes. Father, who knew better what they were, was effusive in his condemnation of my visits to such vulgar resorts. 'How you can bring yourself to go to these places,' he said to me, 'I simply don't understand. I should have hoped a son of mine would be above that sort of thing. From what I hear of the best known music hall artists they seem to be, in the main, purveyors of the cheap and the dirty. Most of it's drivel for the half-educated.'

'Oh no; not only that,' I countered impatiently. 'Ribald they may be, but some of them are very great artists in their way. You should at least see them before you condemn them.'

'I wouldn't be seen dead in one of those places.'

'Well, I think that's grossly unfair. I think it's just prejudice to pass judgment before you've seen any of the evidence.'

This blow reached its mark, so that he could only fire at me, 'Think what you like. I know what *I* think.'

'And I know what I think too.' Warming to a quarrel, I selected the name most likely to offend him. 'You should come and see Marie Lloyd if you want to see real artistry.'

'Marie Lloyd! Thank you, no! I gather she's Vulgarity Personified.'

'Maybe she is. But she's also Goodwill and Humanity and Gorgeous Mockery Personified.'

'Well, if that's your taste, keep it; and I'll keep mine, if you've no objection.'

Even in those days, though yet in my twenties, and as cock-
sure and opinionated as I was unwise, I suspected that he was
blind in this conventional and contemporary vision as he was in
so many other things; and today, more than half a century
later, I am sure of it. There were other factors than ribaldry and
vulgarity to be seen in the contribution of these famous comedians and comediennes to the needs of their hour. These were the
last days of the old music halls; something was coming down
upon the world that no one, on stage or in stall, in pit or in
gallery, foresaw; it waited for us but forty months away; and I
see now that these old Variety artists, by their very ribaldry,
taught their audiences, so largely composed of the poor and the
unprivileged, to dissolve most of their troubles in a potent
mixture of cynicism, mockery and fun; they played a part in
enabling our country's poor, for whom the country had done so
little, to stand and endure when the storm broke. By making
fun of all possible mischances they prepared unwittingly the
people of Britain for what was coming. Whether in their
poor streets or in the lowest ranks of the army, the people
stood. They stood; bitterly laughing and mocking themselves
as well as everyone else, when the citizens of a neighbouring
country collapsed. So it was in the year 1917 and in the year
1940.

Something of this gift to the poor by these laughing old
comics I would expound to Raney, and she agreed enthusiastic-
ally, though perhaps, as a child who'd left school at fourteen,
only half understanding. This educating of Raney was now my
happiest hobby; I pursued it with relish and self-satisfaction,
but with real love as well. Not only did I laughingly amend her
grammar and her ways of speech, but I strove to enrich her
knowledge and enlarge her tastes. I made her read all the
poems I loved in the books I lent her: Matthew Arnold's
Scholar Gipsy, Kipling's *St. Helena Lullaby* and even Omar
Khayyam's *Rubaiyat*, explaining that the gloriously atheistic
hedonism of this last needn't worry her, because great poetry
was simply the most felicitous statement of beliefs sincerely
held, whether they were your beliefs or not. 'Oh, I see!' she
said. 'Yes, of course.' And I echoed 'Of course, but I think it

would be wiser not to show old Omar to Mums.' We had some fun too with, 'There is a lady sweet and kind, Was never face so pleased my mind; I did but see her passing by'—but when I followed with the last line, 'And yet I love her till I die,' she objected, 'Oh, come!' Now this was no natural phrase for Raney of the Dene, and it pleased me secretly because it meant she was modelling her language on mine; this was an habitual phrase of mine. 'Oh, come.... Isn't that a bit thick?' to which I retorted, 'Perhaps it is. I don't know. But that's what the gentleman said. Either Mr. Thomas Ford or Mr. Robert Herrick. Nobody quite knows which.'

I know I did all this gently enough, so that she took no offence but, rather, was exhilarated by it. Once I apologized for a correction of her grammar, and all that happened was that she flung her arms around me and exclaimed (with interjection marks), 'But I love it! I love it! I love every bit of it! I'm not only *mad* to learn everything I don't know and you do know, but you see—you see—I so adore Teacher.'

Naturally Teacher had to kiss her for this, and when at last the kissing was over, she submitted with an unconscious pathos, 'You see you went to a school where your parents paid.'

'Not one of the best schools,' I hastily reminded her, so as to lessen the chasm at which she was staring.

'And you were in the top standard, weren't you?'

'Only at the very end. But we didn't call it a "standard".'

'Well, what on earth did you call it?'

'We called it a "form". Or more usually nothing at all. Just the Upper Sixth.'

I hoped 'Upper Sixth' wouldn't frighten her because she had been in the 'Fifth Standard' at Stubb Lane, but she did lament, 'Oh dear, oh dear! I wish I knew more. You will go on teaching me everything, won't you? *Please*, Teacher!'

Impossible to answer this with other than a reassuring smile.

'I know I know absolutely nothing that I really should ought to know.'

'"*Should* know",' I corrected, maintaining the smile. '"*Should* know", sweetheart. Not "should ought".'

'Well, there you are. You see? I'm hopeless. Please tell me

always when I say things like that. Don't let me, will you? *Please.*'

If you can only believe it, I promised her a surprise reward when she had properly read three of my books, the title of the thickest being *The Well-springs of Civilization*, and its sub-title, *Jerusalem, Athens and Rome*. She read it, leaning her arms on her shop counter whenever no customer entered for a copy of *Tit-Bits, Home Chat*, or a packet of Gold Flake. She read on and on; and I imagine that if her mother looked over her shoulder and saw 'Jerusalem', she was satisfied. She read it with no great difficulty because her intelligence, hitherto but sparsely nourished, was so good that at times it astonished me. 'I'm loving it,' she would tell me. 'Loving it. Golly, I'm getting clever.'

By now she was on fire for education and improvement. All three books she read. And after she had closed the third and last book, her task completed, she told me, 'I'm feeling just as I'm sure someone must when he's climbed to the top of a mountain where the air's absolutely terrific and he's seeing a whole new world for the first time. I'm educated. Like you. Isn't it gorgeous?'

The surprise award for this achievement was a stall at the Tivoli in the Strand and (again I say, 'If you can believe it') an after-theatre supper in the majestic Piccadilly Hotel. But you must understand that the stalls tickets had been only four shillings each, the supper five shillings each, with liqueurs to follow at sixpence a time, and my festal cigar at a shilling. When it was all over—and we had to rise quickly lest her parents should be angry with us—she just looked round the stately room and at the table we were leaving and said, 'Oh, it was too gorgeous. I've never known anything like it before, and never imagined I should.' She held my arm tight against her in a surge of affection as we walked out of that imposing hotel; and all the way homeward, on top of a red Hammersmith bus, her hand gripped mine under the waterproof apron, ever and again pressing it almost to the point of pain in her gratitude.

§

'Dreams, impossible dreams.' So I used to say to myself in these first months of our love story. Son of Victorian parents, my youth and schooldays spent in the Edwardian end of their class-ridden era, I could see the high seas of snobbery that would race between us, if ever I went so far as to ask a shop-keeper's daughter from our notorious Dene—not to say a laundry-girl emeritus—to be my wife. Just think of Father: I had only to picture him in his black frock coat collecting the dues of the well-dressed at St. Jude's and coming out of the church in his silk hat, to abandon all prognosis as to what he would think and say—and perhaps even suffer, which I didn't desire—when I opened before him my story.

But I had no doubt now that I truly loved Raney; I told myself that I was not just a young infatuated fool, I was giving too much reasoned thought to the problem for that. I seemed to have advanced somewhere beyond the ordinary fields of self-seeking and desire; in Raney's response to me—let her background be what it was—there was something that met and fulfilled a longing that had been part of me all my days—the immortal longing that aches, I suppose, in all of us, seldom finding its satisfaction in this life, but sometimes, for the lucky ones, largely, if never wholly, fulfilled. Never mind the little shop in Mortress Lane, never mind its wicked surroundings, again and again when Raney's lips were on mine and she forced herself close to my breast as if longing to blend her being with mine, or as if, in her vehement love she would absorb me into herself, I would think, 'This is what I have been wanting all my days. It never seemed possible that it would come to me, but here it is.' Raney had an enchanting way—enchanting for me—of turning her face from mine when she was in my arms but we were not lip to lip, and then of a sudden giving me a quick look and as quickly drawing her escaping eyes away; a habit which somehow—I cannot explain how—so inflamed my passion that it was a need intolerable till I too had crushed her against me and within my limbs and could hold her there, feeling that we were, as nearly as possible, one being. Did other young men in love feel this sudden fading of their individuality and its change, its loss, into oneness with another? Perhaps

many never did. But I was now possessed by an ecstatic sense
of unity, and one evening, as I paced my room back and forth,
with hands joined behind my back, I decided, 'Not yet; not
at once; but let people say what they like, and think what they
like, let them laugh and sneer how they like, I'm going to drive
on to the time when I'm sure she's ready, and then I ask her to
marry me.'

It was—for the time being—a fervour of decision.

§

Meanwhile we went to the Pav, the Tiv, and the Pal—which I
need hardly translate for you into 'The London Pavilion','The
Tivoli Theatre of Varieties', and 'The London Opera House',
later called 'The Palace of Varieties', and today just 'The
Palace', in Cambridge Circus.

It was the Tiv that we learned to love best and attended
most often, because sooner or later all the great names shone
out upon the Strand from the canopy of its colonnade, and
because we soon had a free pass. Uncle Douglas, having
resolved to bless our strange affair, said to me one evening,
'Look, listen, and learn: next Saturday both of you are going to
meet my very great friend, the manager of the Tiv'; and next
Saturday he was presenting us in the theatre's vestibule to a
large plump man in full evening dress, with a red carnation in
his button-hole. 'This,' he said, 'is my very dear nephew, and'
—drawing Raney forward —'friend. Mr. Stewart O'Murry
and friend. Miss Raney—no, Miss Irene—Wayburn.' The
large plump man looked at us both, and, I have not the least
doubt, loved us both; you could see he was a round and rosy
mass of jovial sentimentality; and one of us was exceedingly
pretty and the other young. 'You like my little theatre, do you,
ducks?' He asked this of Raney since it was she who was
exciting him the more. 'Then you come to it whenever you
like. And your friend.' Plainly the friend was no more than
ancillary. 'Any friend of my dear old friend, Dug, is a friend of
mine'; and, plunging his hand into a pocket, he produced his
professional card, scrawled his initials on it, and put it into
Raney's hand. 'Just produce that whenever you feel like it,

my dear, and any available seats in my little theatre will be yours.'

After we'd thanked him and left him he said to Uncle Douglas (so Uncle told me later): 'That's a nice boy, your nephew. A real nice boy; but who was the really lovely young thing with him?'

'That,' said Uncle Douglas, probably thinking of Father, 'is his young lady.' And said no more.

The large plump manager said a good deal more. 'Well, I admire his taste, Dug. Ah-ha! he gets his taste from you, I fancy,' poking Uncle in the ribs. 'She was just about the sweetest bit of work I've seen for ages. I couldn't take my eyes off her. They say a woman's as old as she looks, and a man's only old when he stops looking; and if that's so, well, you and I are about two years old, eh, what? That was as lovely and blooming a kid as I've seen for many a long day.'

So it is that now, fifty years after my days with Raney, the old Tivoli is the theatre in which she and I seem to be sitting together, watching the great ones, often shouting with laughter, and sometimes singing with the rest of the audience the chorus of one of their songs. I remember Raney leaning against me in her delight, and my putting an arm around her to hold her there, as we helped roar the words of Katie Lawrence's song, still famous today the world over, 'Daisy, Daisy, give me your answer true, I'm half crazy, all for the love of you.'

The Tivoli! We would come away from it, swinging each other's hands and demanding—in a favourite quotation, stemming from our Gaiety days—'Hadn't we the gaiety?'; but, as I rebuild the old place in my mind's eye, it holds one memory that was not gay at all.

It was a Friday evening, and I had arranged to meet her in the vestibule half an hour before the show began; but, liable to day-dreaming at this time about love and its consequences, I sat thinking the day was only Thursday. It was not till half-an-hour after I'd promised to meet her that, sitting in our dining-room, the certainty came flooding into me that it was Friday. I had blindly missed an appointment with Raney. Incredible. I rushed out, my heart racing madly like a machine that has broken from the governor that controls its velocity; the Tivoli was no short distance from our Crescents; and Raney would have been waiting an hour in the vestibule when I ran into it.

I ran into it apologizing, 'Oh, my darling, Raney darling, I forgot it was Friday. I thought it was Thursday.'

'Well, it happens to be Friday.' She said it coldly, rising from her chair.

Instantly her tone offended me. Her reception of me was going to be sour, was it? 'All right,' I objected. 'I've said I was sorry. We can all make mistakes. *You* forget things sometimes. I've seen you day-dreaming often enough.'

She did not choose to hear this. 'It's not all that pleasant to be absolutely forgotten and left sitting here for an hour. I don't see how you can care for me the way you say you do, if you can forget all about me and forget an engagement like this, I don't ree'ly.'

This refusal instantly to forgive blew my resentment into a flame. So unstable was my imagined conquest of self-love and self-regard. Unreasonably, too, the flame was enlarged by that 'ree'ly', a lapse into the language of her streets which I thought I had long corrected in her. 'All right!' I said again. 'If you want to have a row in spite of my apology, have it. I know there are few more pleasant things than having a grievance. I know how much *I* can enjoy one. So don't let me deprive you of it.'

Again no notice of this commentary, though I thought it singularly true to life, and apt to the occasion, and was proud of it. She only grumbled, 'Some of the best turns are all over now. I've just sat here listening to them in the distance.'

'Don't be absurd. You may have waited an hour but the show's only been going for half an hour, and you know the best turns don't come on at first. It's just that you want to have a quarrel. All right: if you want one, that's okay by me. I'll oblige.'

'The manager came and offered to let me go in anywhere I liked without any tickets.'

'Well, why the hell didn't you go in?'

'I *like* that! After I'd decided for your sake to wait here because you wouldn't know where I was. I've just sat here for an hour, and it's not a place for a girl to be seen loitering about in.'

'Oh, please don't go on and on. And don't be so damned pious and superior. It's a perfectly respectable place. Women will go on and on——'

And Raney went on. 'It's not very nice to be pitied by the manager who, after nearly an hour came up and said "Sigh no more, lady. Men were deceivers ever." You might at least——'

'Please don't start lecturing me. I'm not going to be lectured to by anyone.' (I could hear my father speaking.) 'The manager was only having a joke. Can't you see a joke? I always thought you were one who could see and enjoy a joke at once, but apparently I was wrong. The essence of a joke is that it's ridiculous. Can't you even see that? Or, more likely'—now *I* was going on and on, and could hear myself doing so—'you can see it perfectly well, but just seized on this remark as a stick to beat me with.'

Fortunately a drum-fire of applause, with some cheers, sounded from the auditorium as a woman's voice ended on surely its top note, and the orchestra with a fortissimo chord.

'Well, for God's sake come in now,' I broke off to suggest hotly. 'It's not very serious to have missed some screaming woman. Probably the other turns were no better.'

I had collected our tickets that morning, and with them in my hand I led the way, she following with her grievance still around her like a cloak retained for a room that will be cold.

We found our stalls and sat there side by side, the plush tip-up seats forcing us close together, but not so near that there was no room for a stern frontier of mutual displeasure, and even dislike, firmly between us. Usually when the house lights were down her fingers would search for mine, or mine for hers, so that we could sit in the darkness with hands joined and gently stroking, but there were no such hidden explorations tonight. The hands of each rested unlovingly, uncommitted, lonely, each pair fingering its own fingers on its own lap.

As we sat thus, each of us, in an unforgiving isolation, the next artist appeared. On to the stage from the wings walked Mark Sheridan with his famous swagger, his ludicrous dress of ragged frock-coat and wrinkled bell-bottomed trousers, and his fully anticipated clown's greeting, 'Here we are again,' which the whole audience—except for two in the stalls—welcomed with cheers.

What song Mark Sheridan sang that night I forget; but not the song of the artist who succeeded him, for its tune was—and still is—probably the most haunting melody ever born of the old music-hall stage. Long and lithe, his eyes large and round in a coal-black face, for he was the most famous coon from the Mohawk Minstrels, came Eugene Stratton, the limelight following him on to the centre of the stage; and as the orchestra began the lovely air, the audience broke into universal applause welcoming 'Lily of Laguna':

> She's ma lady love,
> She is ma dove, ma baby-love.
> She ain't no gal for settin' down to dream
> She's the only rose Laguna knows
> And Ah knows she likes me,
> Ah knows she likes me
> Kase she says so. . . .

We had heard him before in other theatres and could easily have joined with the audience in the well-loved chorus. But not tonight; we did not sing tonight.

His song finished, the orchestra, according to custom, repeated softly the bewitching air for him to boot-dance to it in the limelight, while the audience, in association with the orchestra, hummed the accompaniment too. Raney did not hum; nor I.

Other artists followed Eugene Stratton, of whom T. E. Dunville was one, a champion of poker-faced nonsense, who barked out at us with never a smile, but rather with a sick indifference as if he disliked us all, and even with a contempt for our intelligences, for he would pause at the end of every simple line as if to let it sink into the minds of the subnormal.

> Little Billie Bates . . .
> Fastened on his skates . . .
> Skated where the ice was thin . . .
> Suddenly a crack . . .
> Laid him on his back . . .
> Little Billie Bates went in . . .
>
> And the verdict was. . . .
>
> Little boy . . .
> Pair of skates . . .
> Hole in ice . . .
> Heaven's gates.

Only two in the packed audience who didn't laugh, or, at least, smile.

I seem to remember that artists who appeared on that night after Eugene Stratton and T. E. Dunville were Harry Fragson with his songs at the piano, G. H. Elliott, 'the chocolate-coloured coon', and Little Tich with his elongated boots; but who shall trust a memory after fifty years? There remains no doubt, however, about the flamboyant lady who brought the evening to a triumphant close, Marie Lloyd, that full-blown rose of vulgarity, impossible not to love and rejoice in, as she made outrageous fun of all the mischances that had befallen her audience or herself; Marie Lloyd, singing:

> You can bet your life there isn't a doubt of it,
> Outside the Oliver Cromwell, last Saturday night,
> I was one of the ruins that Cromwell knocked about a bit.

This was the last song she sang before she died; and Raney and I sat there in our unhappiness, listening to it.

With this song, and the cheers and whistles that acclaimed it, ringing in our ears, we all went crowding out from the gay lights into the darkness of the Strand. Not one word had Raney and I accorded each other since we first took our seats in the stalls.

She was the first to speak now. After a score of steps which brought us to the front of Charing Cross Station and a crossing between the night's traffic in the Strand, so that we were in

Duncannon Street, she opened hostilities again. 'I don't much like the way you treated me in there.'

'Well, that's a pity, isn't it?' This further enraged her, as it was intended to do; its implication being that my attitude to her belabouring of me was not going to change, so she'd better get used to it.

'I think you're being utterly beastly. Never once speaking to me for nearly two hours.'

'Well, I didn't notice that you said much to me. Perhaps I may be allowed to say that I'm not in love with the way you're treating me. Isn't it six of one and half a dozen of the other?'

'No, it isn't. Because it was your fault to begin with. It wasn't you was kept waiting an hour.'

'Anyone can have a failure of memory. And it isn't "you was", it's "you were".' This second grammatical lapse was a welcome addition to my springs of irritation, even though, as I spoke, I heard again my father speaking. 'The actual sequence is "I was, thou wast, he was, we were, you were, they were"; didn't they teach you this in your fifth standard?' So much for caring more for another's happiness than one's own.

'What's all that got to do with anything?'

'Quite a lot. It's just as well to speak English even in a quarrel. Personally I think that if ever there's a time when it's best to avoid all solecisms and facile colloquialisms it's when one's trying to be intolerably rude to someone.'

'Oh, you're hateful. You know I don't know what you mean by your "solis-isems", and words like that. You're just trying to hurt me. I think you're hateful. I hate you.'

'If you feel like that——'

'I certainly feel like that.'

'So? Do you? Very good: then I go. It's nice to know where we stand. If I'm hateful, I go. I willingly relieve you of my presence. I don't inflict my presence on anyone who doesn't want me.' And then and there, cruelly, sharply, exulting in anger and punishment, I crossed the road to the other side and left her alone on her pavement.

So surprised was she by this instant desertion, so maddened by it, that she had to cry out at me while there was time; while

I was still within hearing. She shouted after me, 'Why did you ever come near me? Why didn't you leave me alone? I didn't ask you to come.'

And the people on the two pavements ahead of me turned to look at a shrieking girl and at me.

Without acknowledging her shouted words by a turn of the head I walked quickly onward, leaving her to her punishment and pain. The convenient corner by the steps of St. Martin's-in-the-Fields enabled me to walk out of her sight.

And home I walked—all the way because I was too shaken and sick for any such commonplace action as mounting a bus; was I not, all the way, fuelling my grievance to keep it aflame? Both exulting in my wrath and poignantly wretched in it, I was resolving to continue her punishment for shouting after me like a Billingsgate fishwife, and yet dreaming, oh, dreaming, of a reconciliation, and peace and love again one day.

But day followed day and I could not force myself to be kind and put an end to a child's pain far away from me in Mortress Lane. An iron resistance stopped my hand a dozen times from writing the gentle letter which would admit my larger share of the blame and beg that we might meet and love again. More than once I was on the verge of doing this, but chose to recall, 'Why did you ever come near me? Why didn't you leave me alone?' and the wound fermented. It is a grief to have to write that Dunkerry Crescent and Mortress Lane played their part in my contumacy: was not I the one who had stepped down from my upper class level to hers; was not I the king who had descended the steps of his throne to pick up the hand of the beggar-maid? I could see now that those shouted words, 'Why didn't you leave me alone,' were no vulgar invective yelled by a fishwife but one desperate cry from a wounded love; I saw this, and understood, and still could not move. 'Why did you ever come near me?'

Of course it was she who, after long silent days, wrote her pitiful letter. Is it always the woman who must plead first? She wrote saying she was sorry she had lost her temper and, without mention of my cruelty, asked that we might be happy together again. 'Please may we? I was so terribly happy till that night. In all my life I've never been so happy; I never knew it was possible to be so happy. Do come and see me, not to take me out but just to tell me all is right again. Please please come. I am sorry.' It was a Monday morning; probably she had written after Sunday Meeting with her parents in the bare Room. And of course, within minutes of opening her letter, I was at her door; I seized her hand as she came out on to the pavement and drew her out of sight of her father's shop—into St. Michael's Row, of all wicked places, where I took her into my arms and pressed all my contrition on to her lips; pressed a firm denial there, when she tried to say it was largely her fault; only stopping the kisses to tell her, 'Chicken, you were absolutely right when you called me an unutterable beast; you didn't exaggerate one little bit;' only lifting my lips once more to beg sadly, reminding her of happier 'treats', 'Hadn't we the gaiety?'; then back to the kissing again.

And then, since I could not stay, hurrying home, laden with all the peace and joy of reconciliation, and with the swelling assurance—ever a sweet fruit of reconciliation—that we were now loving one another more than ever before.

§

The Tivoli. To think of it is to remember all the great ones we saw there and to wonder, or to remember, what became of them all in the end. Some of them, I know, went down in tragedy. Dan Leno, who lives among my childish memories as always the Dame in Drury Lane pantomimes, lost all grip of his art and died insane, believing himself a great actor-manager like Beerbohm Tree and offering long contracts to leading actresses who exercised all their most delicate art in declining them, and wept as they left him. T. E. Dunville, having lost his public and all engagements with them, walked one day into a Leicester Square café, where he overheard someone say, 'There, if you like, is a fallen star'; at which, after telling them he'd heard, he withdrew from the café, took train to Reading and the Thames, so that he could end a failing life in 'The Suicide's Lock'. Mark Sheridan, failing too, was one evening 'given the bird' by a merciless Glasgow audience, and went out and shot himself in a Glasgow park. Katie Lawrence—who thinks of this when he sings her 'Daisy, Daisy'?—died in poverty and forgotten. So did Maggie Duggan. Some of them, thank God, seem to have lived happily ever after. Little Tich with his long-booted sand-dance, Harry Tate with his 'Motoring' and Eugene Stratton with his 'Lily of Laguna' and 'Little Dolly Daydream, Pride of Idaho' were idols of the halls till their end.

And the Tivoli. The story of the Tivoli contains within itself the brief life-history of Vaudeville's greater days. Doomed like so many of the young men who sat roaring its choruses, it was closed in 1914 with a view to converting it into a finer building, but the War made a desolate wreck of it, and in 1916 it was pulled down and its site, then a wasteland, given over to temporary wartime buildings, one a recruiting office for Kitchener's Army. Thus, like the youths who had loved it, the War stopped its career in the pride of its promise, used its site for war work, and left it to die. Peter Robinson's palatial store now stands on its grave by Adam Street in the Strand, and if you know where to look in those majestic premises, you can find a plaque recording that it was here Marie Lloyd, 'a brilliant artiste and great-hearted woman', once sang.

10

Between Old Swan and Southend Piers

This excellent and enthusiastic pupil of mine received a further award after she'd read no less a book than Matthew Arnold's *Culture and Anarchy*, for I myself had belatedly discovered my much loved poet, Matthew Arnold, as critic and essayist, and longed to share my discovery with her.

But it was not only an award. Raney completed her reading of the book within days of our reconciliation, as if by so doing she would make full amends and win me back more firmly than ever. And I too, longing to purge my cruelty by some generous giving, seized upon this so-called award to make of it something unexpected, large, and memorable for her. The so-called award, accordingly, became a pleasure trip down the Thames on a Saturday afternoon all the way from London Bridge to Southend Pier, and a dinner at Southend's Palace Hotel before the journey home. At the Old Swan Pier on the Southwark side we boarded the *Golden Eagle*—where is she now, that popular, elegant graceful ship, if a little broad in the beam, like an ageing beauty, because of her high paddle-wheels? She was crowded today with Saturday holiday makers, and in their midst a band of four musicians—all of whose instruments I have forgotten except the cornet which asserted a powerful supremacy over its colleagues, and over all the din of talk and laughter, with 'I do like to be beside the sea', as the ship broke from its moorage and slid into the open stream. It dipped its funnel to pass under London Bridge, and there before us was the Tower with its turreted Keep encircled by walls and bastions—the eleventh century strong and alive amid the hideous creations—factories, wharves, warehouses and giant chimneys—of eight hundred years later. And there at its foot was this prosperous nineteenth century at its most pompous and uninspired in the twin Gothic Towers, pinnacled and helmeted, of Tower Bridge, standing in the water like the west towers of a cathedral, with the tide swirling between them for aisles and nave.

To our pride the *Golden Eagle* loosed its loud siren, and this enormous cathedral-entrance responded to us by lifting its bascules left and right, and halting all the traffic from the North of Britain and the South that we might pass with dignity along its watery nave. Once we had passed, the bascules bowed down behind us, and the nation's traffic was suffered to proceed. We were in the Pool—London's Pool, ready to pass and wave to great ships come from all over our watery globe, bringing the produce of the world to the capital of the world.

Covertly, masking it as happy chatter, I taught my eager pupil great packets of history and geography as these ships loomed in the distant haze, and passed us by, flying their national flags. We recognized flags from Turkey, Greece, Scandinavia, Finland, and Russia. Inevitably I told her the old story of a proud Londoner's answer to a proud American's contemptuous question, 'D'you mean to say this dirty wet ditch is the famous river Thames?'

'This, sir, is not a river. It is liquid history.'

Raney, unacquainted with the immortal story, was delighted with it. 'Liquid history,' she kept repeating as we sailed on, 'liquid history.' And, proud of the history, we saw in imagination together Roman triremes, high-bowed Viking galleys, Flemish carracks and Spanish caravels. At one point we saw the body of Nelson coming in slow state to Whitehall Steps from the capes of Trafalgar.

So much for history and geography; we were well into architecture as we came down the slate-grey waters of Limehouse Reach and rounded the Isle of Dogs, for now we saw before us Wren's magnificent imprint stamped upon a crowded bank of dreary nineteenth-century terraces, factories, and power-houses—his Greenwich Hospital with its classical façade embracing spacious courts which swept the eye towards the lovely 'Queen's House' at the vista's end.

As we left all this behind us, sailing down the Blackwall and Bugsby reaches—as unlovely in their riparian buildings as Wren's brief moment was beautiful—as we passed through villages that are now London, I talked learnedly of Inigo Jones and Wren, of the classical 'orders', Doric, Ionic, Corinthian and Composite, of colonnades, entablatures and pediments, 'showing off' not a little, but more, I know, for her help than for my glory.

And so we came to the widening of the tideway, with London far behind us, and the smells of smoke and tar yielding, or so we fancied, to a clean, fresh, salty breath from the sea. Certainly a wind from the sea was breaking up the surface of the tide and freckling it with foamy wavelets; and it was here among those green and windy desolations withdrawing from either side of us, the Erith Marshes and the Barking Levels, that, by way of Wren and the façade of St. Paul's Cathedral we came to the discussion of religion. How far, I asked, was she in agreement with the unbending puritanism of her mother and the lesser strictness of her father. The answer she gave me, after a pause for thought, pleased me because it seemed to reveal seeds of intelligence and wit that lay unfed and un-tended within her; and a new readiness to use this intelligence, evading conventions and speaking the truths of her heart.

'I'd put it like this,' she said. 'Mum in her way is a real saint; she's the whole thing as she sees it, whether other people think it right or wrong; Dad's a good half of it, and I'm naturally, being thirty years younger, a little less than he. Or, if you like, Mum's a whole sovereign, Dad's a half-sovereign, and I'm about six-and-eightpence.'

'My angel, what an admirable metaphor! But I don't feel it's quite true. After all, you're the same coin as they are, and it doesn't mean that because you believe in more freedom than they do, you're not in every way as good as they.'

Another pause, during which she stared first at the empty marshes with their feathery reeds bowing before the wind, and then ahead of us at the white-flecked water. 'Oh yes it does,' she said at last. 'I don't agree with that. Mum's a lot better than me; and Dad, I know, is better too. I don't think you can call us the same coin; not really. You see, a sovereign's gold, and so's a half-sovereign; but six-and-eightpence is only silver and coppers.'

'Darling, you're surpassing yourself,' I said, and indeed I was experiencing a curiously excited joy in her answer; it was as if some doubts still hidden deep in me had been healed. 'One of these days I shall come along to one of your Meetings. You needn't worry. I'll wander in *incognito* and sit at the back.'

This I said because her metaphor of the sovereign had thrown on to my mind a memory of that day when she first passed me by in St. Michael's shameful Row. I had dared then to presume she might be one of those young girls who could be bought and enjoyed, in Elsa's words, 'for a sovereign or less'. That had been a Sunday at mid-day, and in this moment I perceived that, instead of loitering in a street for custom, she had probably been returning from a Meeting of holy Brethren. With a pretence of laughter I reminded her, 'The first time I ever saw you was on a Sunday as you walked home. I suppose now you were returning from one of your Meetings.'

'I expect that was it. What time was it?'

'About a quarter to one.'

'Oh, then, we'd probably had a Breaking of Bread and Prayers and Scripture afterwards. I've been made a full communicant now and I'm allowed to break bread with the adults.'

'Oh dear, oh dear!' I sighed, since this seemed to open wider the chasm between us, and deepen it. 'But why were you alone? Where were your parents?'

'I expect Dad, and Mum who's the real power there, had stayed behind to shake hands with all the saints as they departed.'

'*Saints?*'

'That's right,' she laughed. 'I've told you that before. That's their old name, and Mum sometimes drops into it when she's leading Prayers. Dad says he can't bring himself to use it. He says it makes him laugh.'

'I like the sound of your father. So officially *you're* a saint.'

'Don't make *me* laugh. If I'm a saint, God help all the sinners. I prefer Mum when she's calling us all the chief of sinners, and half the people agree with her, saying "Amen, Amen."'

'Which isn't very appropriate,' I submitted, 'because it means "So be it. So let it be".'

'Does it? I always thought it meant "that's me every time".'

'But is it you, my heart? Do you really believe everything they believe?'

'I dunno.' Often she would drop back into this cockney pronunciation. 'Much of it, I suppose. Yes, I think I love much of it. I love the quiet and simplicity of it all. But I'm a shade embarrassed when Mum, even at Meeting sometimes, explains to everybody in a prayer that she's given me to the Lord.'

Given her to the Lord! And that first day I had imagined . . .

'One day when I was ill, really quite ill, she knelt at my bedside and prayed aloud that "if this illness was the Lord's hand extended in chastisement of me for my sins, or of her and Dad for their sins, it might be revealed to us what the sins were so that we could all repent and lay hold on Jesus again"—those were her words—and I must confess that a lot of it seemed a little unfair.'

To me it seemed a little ridiculous, but I didn't say so, because I didn't want to damage in any way her love for her mother, or to spoil her beliefs, so I just said laughingly, 'I'm beginning to wonder that you have anything to do with me. I'm sure your mamma must think I'm still in the bonds of iniquity. And of course it could be that she's right.'

All this time, as we thus discussed religion, and our sanctity or lack of it, the sailing barges were passing us by as they came up with the wind, their sails brown or red; the little tugs were fussing along with their trains of blackened barges, and sometimes a great ship, flying an alien flag, trailed such a wash as it passed that it rocked even our large broad pleasure-steamer, whose more facetious passengers thereupon leaned over the side and pretended to be sick. Or called, 'Steward! Steward! Basins, please.' The river banks were retiring farther and farther from any interest in us, so that now, save for these occasional passers-by we seemed to be alone on a wide sea. The sea wind was stronger in these open spaces, whipping up waves against our prow and slapping them indignantly against our paddles; otherwise the expanse was grey and silent under an enormous sky. Our band was silent too, because the cornet player was coming round with a bag to collect the offerings of the musical before some of us were lost to him. There was a prospect of this now, for there, in the haze ahead of us, was the longest pier we had ever seen (and, in fact, the longest pier in the world) reaching out to find deep water in the wide estuary at any state of the tide, and so to allow steamers of any and every size to berth. And now our siren was addressing it with two loud blasts which could well have been two heart-broken hysterical groans. Southend pier; where the *Golden Eagle* would make its first call before crossing the estuary from Southend to Margate. With much clever manoeuvring and much ringing of the engine-room bell she drew alongside the pier's landing-stage and tied up. Raney and I and many others disembarked, the band, well encouraged by coppers and tanners, sending us ashore with 'Good-bye, Dolly, I must leave you, Though it breaks my heart to go'.

Just behind the promenade deck the electric tramcar waited which would take us the entire length of the pier, nearly a mile and a quarter of it, in a few minutes, to the pier's foot. High above the kiosks at the pier's entrance, so that its many windows commanded the estuary and the panorama of passing ships, stood the huge Palace Hotel staring whitely at us. Raney and I found our way into its Terrace Restaurant, a many-windowed palm-court stretching, I imagine, the whole width of this great white building. So far the diners were few, but the orchestra was already playing under its palms, and gradually more and more diners came to fill up the tables, as Raney and I sat in privileged state against a deep plate-glass window, lazing over our meal and watching the ships.

'The proper thing at Southend for mere trippers like us,' I said, 'is to eat cockles and whelks, or fried potatoes out of a page of the *Daily Mail*; but not, I think, in this lovely place.'

She stretched forth the palm of her hand and laid it over my knuckles.

'You're that good to me,' she said with a lapse into the idiom of her streets, as often happened when she spoke from her heart instead of from her head where the new grammar lay. 'Bringing me to this lovely place. I could never have believed that I'd come to such places as this. With the band and all. And all these truly beautiful waiters. I'm not quite sure that I'm here now. Supposing it's all a dream, really. Suppose I'm dreaming *you*! Oh, gosh, wouldn't it be awful to wake up!'

'You're not dreaming, my dear.'

Dreams, impossible dreams? How could I suffer all this to be only a dream for her? For a Raney like this? I gathered the hand that she'd laid on mine. 'We're safely here, my child. Together.'

(Later we were to see together this 'lovely place' with a very different company in it; not a crowd of cheerful diners smothering the orchestra with their laughter and chatter; but a silent and suffering company, with quiet orderlies moving among them.)

After our dinner together—never a happier one—we had to get into one of the pier's tramcars again so as to meet and rejoin the *Eagle* on its homeward journey. Most of its original passengers were still aboard, and the waggish ones greeted all of us who had earlier deserted them with a broadside of wisecracks and badinage. 'Nice to see you again.' 'How you've grown since we saw you last.' 'Any more for the *Skylark*?' 'Did-joo enjoy your winkles?' 'I got an aunt at Sath'end. Didn't meet her, did-joo?' 'All aboard for London.' 'Have your tickets ready, please.' 'Next stop, London.'

The *Golden Eagle* put to sea again, its bows towards London. It was the hour of sunset, and we went westward into a late summer sunset of startling glory: a shallow ridge of darkling cloud was aflame along its jagged bases with a phoenix-fire of scarlet and gold, while above it long ribbons of white cloud, in a sky of luminous blue, were flushed into a salmon pink. The river beneath, tranced by the quiet evening, was a long silver mirror reflecting fire. That apt sentimentalist, the cornet player,

I

led his musicians in 'Abide with me; fast falls the eventide'; and there were few on the ship who didn't feel compelled to sing the words, for the most part gently.

Just as I cannot think nowadays of the old Tivoli and the doomed youths who sat with us singing choruses; so I cannot recall this journey into the sunset over London, and the soft starred evening which welcomed us through the city's gates, without wondering that so few of these happy and boisterous passengers on that summer night of 1911—1911 as far as I can conjecture now, because it's all so far in the past—were aware of what was drawing to us nearer and nearer.

II

The Parents

Not for ever could I hide from Father that in my frequent visits to theatres and music halls I was accompanied by a girl. All I could do to ease his reception of this disturbing news was to refrain from calling her my 'young lady'. Nor could I withhold the interesting fact that she was a working-class girl from a little shop in the Dene. The Dene, of all places.

In a sense, though I postponed and postponed this disclosure, I was spoiling for the moment when I should uncover it. A need smouldered in me after twenty years of sharp rebukes, learned corrections, and well-meant but overbearing parental snubbings, to show him that I was now ordering my own life, and that, moreover, many of my values were now the opposite of his. This rebellion and defiance played their powerful part in preparing me to tell the truth, so much so that I began almost to look forward to the great moment. But I decided that, at least in the court of first instance, I would 'submit all the facts of the case' as nicely as I could, over some meal of roast mutton and Yorkshire pudding, or curry and rice, or whatever was before us at the time.

I had already told Aldith; deciding to tell her, I'd made a point of going to her prosperous home in Ealing when her solicitor husband, Jack Fellbright, was away at his offices in Gray's Inn. I didn't want to destroy two people at once; one casualty at a time would be enough. Happily there was no immediate need or occasion to tell Augusta, far away in another hemisphere, and busy at good works—perhaps with the help of St. Philomena—at her Bunderlore Mission in India. Aldith's shock was more than a little, but it was unenduring. She hardly deserved the name of 'casualty'; just one of the 'walking wounded', shall we say? Uncle Douglas's shock had been noticeable, if covert, and he recovered from it in twenty minutes. Aldith took longer to travel through the same course but she arrived at the same goal, which was to forget all shock in the luxurious relish and piquancy of considering its effect upon Father. Then I think it was all joy. 'But Stew, Stew, what about Augustus O'Murry? What about when you tell him? Won't the Bonny Earl o' Murray come soonding through the toon?'

'It'll certainly be an interesting episode,' I agreed. And then more coarsely, 'Not half he won't.'

I see now that I owe a debt to my father in that my resistances to his despotism and dogmatism were redoubtable allies in any eccentric adventures I might have in mind.

I told him over a meal of roast duck and chopped shallots which Elsa always prepared excellently, which was always enjoyed by him, and which therefore might lighten the atmosphere around the deplorable news.

But this last notion was altogether too sanguine. Father came down to the dining-room from his lonely study upstairs, followed, as always, by the pattering but happy feet, the occasional encouraging barks, and, when possible, the friendly leap of Hamish, his inseparable companion. Had Father not been so tall and heavy, these leaps might have disturbed his balance; but not Father's. Father sat himself at the table's head, and Hamish sat himself on the floor on Father's right-hand side looking up at him with his big moist eyes full of his habitual love and (since this was dinner-time) his wistful hopes. But Hamish's hopes, like mine, were too sanguine for such an evening as this. As soon as Elsa had spread the food and retired, I broke my news. It was a bomb, and from its first detonation Father, I am sure, had no idea what he was eating, or even that he had a fork in his hand and was occasionally addressing its freight to his mouth. Nor had he any sense that there was a dog called Hamish at his side, gazing up with a dream in his eyes.

'Good God! A shop girl? From a tiny stationer's?' A small slice of duck with an accompanying morsel of potato went into the mouth. 'And, what's more, a girl from one of the most disreputable areas in London? Is that what you're saying?'

'I'm afraid so.' I suspected he was seeing some girl of milk-and-water prettiness, hearing her utter 'ain'ts' and 'blimeys' in a Cockney accent 'you could cut with a knife' and all in a grammar that doubled its negatives, mislaid its aspirates, and split its infinitives—which last, unfortunately, was often true of Raney.

'And you imagine you're in love with her?'

The word 'imagine' lit a bomb-fuse inside *me*.

'I don't imagine it. I know it. I know it as I've never known anything in my life before.'

'But that's what every foolish young man thinks. A girl with little education, I suppose, who doesn't even speak our language. And you think you're going to marry her? Is that so?'

'I dream of little else.' Whether this was finally true at this stage of our 'walking out' I am not sure, but during a conflict with a father one softens no punches. 'I think she's the loveliest thing I've discovered in London, Dene or no damned Dene——'

'Let's have no swearing, please.'

'All right: I'll cut out the swear words so long as you don't tell me I'm "imagining". I'm not a damned—I'm not a fool; and after plenty of thought, I don't care what anyone else says or thinks; I know what *I* think. I think she's lovely in form and figure, and sweet in character. She's simply overflowing with tenderness and laughter'—naturally I was piling on the superlatives—'and she loves me, strange as it may seem, as I've always wanted to be loved. Her figure always makes me think of a Greek nymph on an Athenian frieze—an oread or a dryad.' As well to introduce a little culture into this altercation since, in part, it was my literary taste that he was calling in question. 'A naiad, if you like. I think, if you saw her, you'd have to admire her. I can't imagine any man, however old, not being moved by——'

'I'm not all that old.'

'No . . . but the fat old manager of the Tivoli fell for Raney absolutely at once——'

'"Raney"?'

'Yes, her name's Irene, but I always call her Raney because her parents call her Ireen.'

'Good God!'

'Let's have no blasphemies,' I advocated.

'Don't talk to me in that manner. Does no one nowadays treat their parents with respect?'

'Well, it's what you said to me, more or less.'

Since it was, he couldn't very well pursue the point. So he continued, '"I-reen". I suspected as much.' His tone was one of enlarged despair.

'The fat old Tivoli manager took one look at her and gave her a free pass into his theatre for the rest of her life, as far as I can make out.'

'Well, I'm not the manager of the Tivoli. My tastes, I imagine, are different from his. And I'm not one who looks only at the outside of a girl. I want to know what's within. I take some account of their minds, their intellects. She's a board-school girl, I suppose?'

'Oh, yes. Yes.' I said it ruthlessly. And added, angrily now, so as to make a real dum-dum bullet of it. 'Stubb Lane School, Hollen Dene.'

He said nothing aloud, but his silence and his face said all that words could say.

Talk having temporarily ceased, Hamish decided that this was a chance to draw attention to himself and his dreams, so he lifted a black paw and laid it on Father's thigh. Usually Father would have responded to this appealing gesture with a morsel from his plate; but today he merely thrust the paw impatiently away. And Hamish could only sit there, looking up at him, with forgiveness in his eyes and hope springing eternal.

While they were both waiting I followed my first dum-dum bullet with another. 'After school she did a period at a laundry. Patterson and Morley's in the Dene.'

'And this is what you hope to marry? A board-school girl out of a laundry.' He made the words sound the ultimate in lowness. 'May I ask when?'

'Just as soon as I can afford to.'

'And do you never think of me? I'm to have an uneducated

laundry-girl for a daughter and a small backstreet shopkeeper for my brother-in-law—or whatever it is he becomes? And the mother? What was the mother?'

'She was a lady's maid.'

'Oh, my lord!'

I shrugged, as one who would say, 'Sorry, but there it is. We can do nothing about it.'

'Well, don't you ever think about your sisters? What about Aldith and Augusta? Augusta is married to a clergyman.'

'Oh, Raney's all right there. More than all right. She comes from a deeply religious family. Frightfully religious. Meetings every Sunday. Bible reading every day. Family prayers.'

'A religious family in the Dene!'

'Most assuredly. And it's religion of the strictest sort. You often say you're proud to be a puritan, but you're not in the same street with them, as far as puritanism goes.'

'Not in the same street—what on earth do you mean?' By now Father was unaware that he was no longer eating; unaware that his plate lay before him with portions of duck and shallots and potatoes sitting cold upon it.

Hamish, meanwhile, was not unaware.

'Why are they more puritan than me? What do you mean?'

I went on eating, not at all unhappily. 'They're Plymouth Brethren.'

'Oh heavens! Plymouth Brethren! The most bigoted, exclusive, intolerant sect in the world.'

'Yes, that's them,' I assented cheerfully. 'At least, that's Raney's parents. Or anyhow her mamma. They're called "The Exclusives".'

'And in this interesting marriage are you going to change your religion like royalty? I thought you were an agnostic.'

'So I may be, but that at least means I'm tolerant. I have the utmost admiration for their devotion. I only wish I could find something like it for myself.'

'God, God, God. . . . One of my children marries someone who's practically a papist, another goes to the other extreme and marries a man who's an out-and-out atheist, and now you want to marry a Plymouth Brother. Or is it a Plymouth Sister?'

'That's it,' I endorsed unsparingly. 'Sister Irene—or, rather' —let him have it in full—'Sister Ireen, they call her.'

He sighed heavily over his abandoned meal. 'I haven't been into your room lately. What about all that show of grinning actresses on your mantelpiece? Are they going to remain there? Or are you going to substitute for your Gaiety girls pictures of Calvin and John Knox and General Booth—or perhaps Ridley and Latimer and John Bunyan? I remember the Blessed Virgins and Immaculate Conceptions on Augusta's mantel-piece——'

'Oh, no,' I interrupted to reassure him. 'No change. The ladies will still be there. I still worship them. Especially Gertie Millar. There are different kinds of worship, you know.'

'Thank you. I know how many kinds of worship there are——'

'Of course I might put John Nelson Darby among the girls.'

'Who's John Nelson Darby?'

'The founder of the Plymouth Brethren. As a matter of fact, Raney's father's named after him. Yes. Mr. Nelson Darby Wayburn.'

He sighed even more heavily. 'Do you want me to meet this girl?'

'I think we can manage without that. For some time at least. I haven't met her parents yet. So far we've managed very nicely on our own—just walking out.'

'For pity's sake don't use that awful phrase.'

'It seems quite a good phrase to me. We do walk, and it's out in the air. There's really nowhere else for us to go—except into a theatre sometimes. You see, in their particular social stratum the ethical system'—culture again?—'says that once the parents have invited you in to tea you're as near as dammit engaged.'

'Well, I pray God they'll postpone this denouement as long as possible. That'll do, Hamish. Do leave me alone, can't you?' (And not one tit-bit from Father's plates did Hamish get that evening. He just sat permanently at Father's side, ever looking up imploringly, and now and again presenting a paw to remind him of his dog's existence. Here was the one creature in the world who loved him with a completeness that forgave all.)

'Does this ethical system,' he asked, 'mean that if I invite her to tea here I practically accept her as a future daughter-in-law?'

'That, I confess, I don't know. I must find out.' (Always anxious to play fair with a father.) 'I'll certainly find out.' I nearly continued, 'I must ask Elsa,' but decided against this and said only, 'I'll dig it out from somewhere. On the whole, I should think the answer's No. After all, it's the girl and her family who accept you, isn't it? Not t'other way round.'

'The girl and her family choose to accept *you*, do they? *My* son?' He shrugged helplessly, as if all his understanding was defeated by a sudden aspect of life that had never entered his imagination before. 'Well, all I can say is, For mercy's sake go slowly about this. A boy barely twenty-two. A girl of nineteen. For God's sake wait and see what happens. I beg it of you. Plymouth Brethren! Well, at least there's one comfort: they'll hardly ask for a Nuptial Mass.'

§

The day of acceptance came: I was invited across the threshold in Mortress Lane and into the parlour of Raney's parents; receiving thus, like an accolade, their recognition of me as their daughter's 'young man'. Through all the long weeks of our 'walking out' Raney had naturally spoken of me in glowing terms and probably exaggerated my ecclesiastical associations: my father a pillar of St. Jude's, up on the hill, and my brother-in-law a 'minister' wielding the sword of the spirit in India. I had only described Father Abel as a 'High Churchman', so there was no danger of her mentioning that his sword was a very fair copy of the Holy Father's in Rome.

These 'godly' connections of mine had, I gathered, satisfied her mother, while her father, less demanding, had said only, 'I want the child to be happy, so long as he seems a thoroughly decent young man.' And Raney, whose powers of social criticism had developed under the spell of Matthew Arnold, Lecky, and John Stuart Mill, told me that she could see her father was socially impressed by the fact that my father had been a publisher and my uncle was a famous journalist whose articles he had often seen—and sometimes read—in the many Portwith journals on his shop counter.

The day was of course a Sunday when the shop doors were sternly shut. I rang the bell on the side door, and it was Raney who rushed to welcome me, drawing me in with both hands holding mine.

'They're in the parlour,' she said. 'So smile and look ever so nice.'

'Yes, but how do I look godly when I'm not?'

'Just keep off any bad language, which you do drop into sometimes, and try to look interested when Mum gets on to religion.'

'I shall be truly interested. No doubt about that.'

She touched a lapel of my jacket. 'And you look properly smart. I'm proud. Ever so proud of you. So come along.'

'But don't we kiss here? It would be pleasant.'

'No, no, no. Not yet.' And, taking me by the hand, she led me into the parlour.

The parlour was the first-floor front. The house being small, shop, office and kitchen occupied all the ground floor; Raney's bedroom was but an attic under the roof with a square dormer-window, high up and so small that it needed only two glazing bars, crossed.

In the parlour father and mother were seated in easy chairs on either side of the fireplace. Both were in their black Sunday best; the father bald and plumpish; the mother slim and graceful. Her hair was grey and her face worn, but in figure she was obviously Raney's mother. Both rose as I came in, and this small movement marked for me the difference between their social customs and ours up on the hill; where the lady would have remained seated and bowed.

I approached the mother first. 'Pleased to meet you,' she said. 'We've heard so much of you from Ireen.'

'Nothing too awful, I hope,' was my answer in a feeble effort at being witty.

As wit it failed entirely, neither winning a laugh nor getting a reply.

The father's welcome was more emphatic. 'Ever so pleased to meet yer at last,' he said. 'Do sit down. Mother, give him that there chair. I always say easy chairs are wasted on ladies because, instead of leaning backwards in 'em and sitting more or less on their shoulder-blades as every sensible man does, they sit bolt upright on—they sit bolt upright, like.'

His quick evasion of a word defining what part of themselves women preferred to sit on showed me in a flash a difference between him and his wife. I had no doubt that if he and I had been alone he'd have preferred precision.

'No, no,' I protested to Mrs. Wayburn. 'Please don't move.'

But she said, 'Yes, I quite agree with Mr. Wayburn. Sit here and be comfortable.'

'That's the idea,' acclaimed her husband, as Raney brought up dining-table chairs for herself and her mother. 'Only men ree'ly understand comfort. Ladies don't sit down for comfort but for a non-stop talky-talk—eh, Mother?'

'Don't be silly, Nelson. He talks every bit as much as I do, Mr. . . . Mr. . . .'

'Stewart, Stewart, Stewart,' supplied Raney. 'Call him Stewart. It's one of the nicest things about him, his name.'

'Yeah, call 'im Stoo'rt, do,' said Mr. Wayburn. 'He don't want no Mister.'

They might be able to accept me, but it was only the fact which I now knew to be a bewilderingly happy truth that I had grown to love Raney better than myself which enabled me to accept this parlour. In its centre was a square table covered by a red cloth fringed with furry red pom-poms. On the mantel-piece under many china ornaments and 'presents from Mar-gate' or 'from Southend' was a valance of the same red material with the same hanging pom-poms. Set diagonally on the red table-cloth was a lacy white cloth and a tea-service plainly the one reserved for 'company'. Between tea-tray and plates there were dishes of sandwiches and shrimps and sea-food with its attendant bottle of vinegar; also a large coffee-brown Mocha cake to honour the occasion. Against the wall opposite the window was a cheap upright piano with pink pleated silk behind its fretwork panels. Gas lamps projected from either side of the overmantel, and it seemed typical of the Dene that they had not yet been adapted to the white light of incandescent mantles.

Is it reprehensible that, if Raney's parents had been seated in some aristocratic chamber, or in some professorial library where I knew that my academic attainments were sadly smaller than the parental scholarship, I should have been embarrassed, shy, and labouring in my talk, whereas here, in this simple parlour of the poor, my sense of social superiority liberated me from all such fetters and my talk soon ran fluently and at ease—though I am sure I never allowed this inevitable consciousness to appear above ground to their hurt. If any difficulty showed itself anywhere it was rather in the parents themselves; and there was a tiny note of anxiety in Raney's manner lest they should use too many wrong words or pronounce them too wrongly.

The contrast between Mrs. Wayburn, the ex-lady's-maid's pronunciation, which was almost too 'refined', and that of her husband, and between her idioms and his idioms, was instantly apparent.

At first commonplace exchanges passed between us, like Mrs. Wayburn's repetition of 'It's so nice to get to know you,' and Mr. Wayburn's endorsement, 'Thet's right. Anyone who likes our Ireen is going to be liked by us, I reckon. That's so, ain't it, Ma?' but then, determined that he wasn't going to be overawed by anyone, and least of all by a stripling in his twenties, he suddenly broke in with the jovial proposition, 'Well, what I say is, now we've got our young gentleman here, what about settin' down to tea, Mother?'

'If Mr. O'Murry . . . if Stewart is ready for it, I'm sure——'

'I'm perfectly ready,' I encouraged.

'Good,' said the father. 'Righty-o. Well, I'm sure the kettle's boilin' its 'ead off, so go and 'elp your Mum, Ireen, and we'll set down. Come along, sir. Sit you down at the table wherever you like, except 'ere by the tray where Mrs. Wayburn'll want to pour out.'

So we two sat ourselves opposite each other with the lacy cloth and all its festival dainties between us; and it was while the women were gone that I learned much about Mr. Wayburn. It was plain to me that, ashamed of his neighbourhood, he was resolved to mention early his Brethren and their Meeting as a counter-balance to St. Michael's Row and St. Michael's Arms, and to suggest too that he and his family were not without culture. For instance, one of the first things he said was, 'I don't altogether like our Ireen having to serve in the shop sometimes. She's fit for better jobs than that. I did try once to get a lad to come and live with us and learn the business so as to set 'er free but his Dad wouldn't come up with the ten bob a week I arst for his board—which surely wasn't much, being as how this is a nice cultured home.'

I agreed that it was little enough for a nice cultured home.

'Yeah.' And he nodded sagely. 'I mean, Ireen done ever so well at 'er school—mind you: I kep' her at school till she was rising fourteen—and Mrs. Wayburn is a ree'ly well-read woman. I've read a tidy lot too in me time, which, *law*, I should ought to 'ave done, being as how I have all them magazines and books in the shop.'

It was almost as if he was justifying himself to me, instead of I to him.

'You live on 'Ollen 'Ill, Ireen tells me, so you'll know all about us down 'ere. Well, what I say is, if there's a place in London where the Brethren ought'a work, it's here. There's plenty to fight against here, and I'm pleased to be in the van, if I may put it so. It's the same with the Army.' I realized that he meant the Salvation Army. 'They got their barracks 'ere, and a proper nice place it is too. We work alongside 'em sometimes, but it's heavy going; it needs 'ope and trust. I could tell you a lot about this neighbourhood, a terrible lot.'

This was the moment when I saw deepest into him. I saw that his loyalty to the Brethren was sincere and his morals of the best, but, being a good, simple man with no self-perception, he could indulge the prurience of an ordinary man—or of Elsa in her kitchen—by talking very soon about the prostitutes in St. Michael's Row, only just round the corner from his Mortress Lane.

'A newsagent knows all that is to be known about what goes on,' he explained. 'Would you believe it, there are newsagents 'ere what'll put the prostitutes' cards in their windows for a quid a week——'

'You mean?' I pleaded, bewildered. 'Cards?'

'Yeah. Thet's right. Cards. I mean they describe theirselves as "Miss So-and-So, dress-maker's model" or "artist's model" or some such barney, but the men know what's what and who's who, and if the lady's address isn't on the card in the shop's window it'll probably have "Enquire within" on it. Think of it. The p'leece know all about it but it's very difficult to act against newsagents—I mean, what's wrong with a business card in a window? Then I know there are cops who're not above being kep' sweet by a nicker in their palms now and again. Not all, by no means, but a few of 'em. I been told, and I can believe it's true that in some of these case-houses there are long mirrors set at angles so that for a tanner or two you can watch what's— well what's going on in the next room. The girls are told by their case-keepers to leave their doors ajar.'

'Case-keepers?'

'Thet's right. Keepers of case-houses. St. Michael's Row's well-known for 'em like Gerrard Street in Soho or Judd Street. Why, cabbies up West know it and get their commission from the bosses, if the West End places are "House Full", so to speak. And some of the touts at the worst places in Soho have copies of these 'ere cards and get their commission for introducing gentlemen.'

I murmured the required shock. 'Good lord. . . .'

'Yes, I been arst in my time to take one of these cards but whoever it was that offered it to me—the poor girl herself or her tout—was out on the pavement before he knew what 'it him. And the funny thing is my business ain't suffered by my taking a stern line. 'Uman nature's funny stuff. They know they won't find none of our real bad goings-on in my shop or in my window, and yet some of the worst like to deal here. P'raps they like a change. I dunno. It's the same with the Army. The bad lots *like* 'em—actually *like*—'em. It's said the p'leece have to patrol in couples here, but what's certain is that a Salvation lassie in her bonnet is safe, day or night, wherever she goes. Same with a nurse from that there St. Paschal's 'Ospital up your way. She may be about eighteen and as pretty as they make' em, but nobody'd dare touch her. The burglars and the case-keepers and the toughest boys of the Trenter Gang'd fair murder anyone who hurt a Salvation lassie or one of the "little sisters" from St. Pasky's. She might be going to some woman in her pains, you see.'

At this point Raney came in with a big earthenware tea-pot, followed by her mother, and announced joyously, 'Here's us.'

'Ah!' Mr. Wayburn quickly dropped his subject. 'Here's the missus; here's the tea. Come in, Mum; come in, Ireen; let's set about it. Me and this young gentleman of yours are hungry.'

We set about the tea. And just as at some dinner with the wealthy I might have had furtively to watch my neighbours so as to learn which was the right fork to use, so now I had to watch when, along with the bread-and-butter slices, we dealt with the cockles and winkles. The cockles were easy enough, eaten from saucers with a dressing of vinegar, but the winkles had to be extracted from their shells by a thin pointed stick. All very different from the Terrace Restaurant in Southend's Palace Hotel, with the palms, the band and the white-coated waiters balancing their dishes high. I had never eaten a winkle before and I enjoyed the experience.

During and after tea the fluent talk passed to Mrs. Wayburn and more or less remained there. As in many homes the wife was the ceaseless talker, the husband being afforded but little chance to comment, though when he did speak it was often with a humorous but tolerant criticism. Her dominance of the talk soon suggested to me that there was more here than a woman's garrulity; she was the dominant partner, however chatty her husband might be in her absence. She exuded a power which all obeyed. Answering her (when I could get an answer in) I was often thinking that if, in due course, she and her husband had to meet my father, she with her massive and masterful loquacity, her husband with his insecure aspirates and rocking grammar, there would be a scene worth watching. But a scene less than comfortable.

When the tea had been all cleared away, chiefly by Raney—'No, leave all that to me, Mum'—we two men were back in the easy chairs, and Mrs. Wayburn sat on a hard chair between us with her crochet. Quickly she contrived to crochet herself into her besetting topic, religion: she was telling us—or me especially—about her days in the 'mis-named Church of England' when 'she was a stranger to salvation'. No doubt she held it her duty, as enjoined by St. Paul, to be instant in preaching, whether in season or out of season.

Gently, so as not to embarrass Raney, I submitted that I'd no doubt the Brethren possessed the basic essence of all religion, namely a surrender to God and a trust in his guidance; but that as a humble member of the Anglican Church I found it difficult to believe that we in our Church didn't possess this too, even if we'd added other things which she couldn't accept: bishops and priests and sacraments and ceremonials—thinking (with a blend of amusement and misgiving) of my good brother-in-law standing in full eucharistic vestments before his altar with a thurible swinging behind him, and the incense rising to the roof, and the tapers being lifted high, as he elevated the Host. 'Are we then, in your view, all strangers to salvation?' I asked, deliberately smiling. 'Damned, as you might say?'

Before replying, Mrs. Wayburn went on and on with her crocheting, as if needling her way through it to an answer; and, being a kindly woman, no more ready to hurt me than I to hurt her, she said at last, 'I don't think it's for me to answer that.' (In other words she wasn't ready to deny that I was still a stranger to salvation. And damned.) 'Obviously I don't believe in much of the things the misnamed church of our country does, because I accept nothing that cannot be justified in the pages of God's Holy Word, but I would not say for certain that all who practise these things are damned. I wouldn't go so far as to say that, though there are those of us who would——'

'Not me,' her husband put in. 'Not once in a life-time.'

'Let me finish, Nelson dear. No, I wouldn't go so far as to

say that there may not be mercies granted by God which are not anywhere written in his Word.'

Of a truth I felt relieved. Such power emanated from this woman that for a moment I'd been frightened by her dark religion, even though with all my heart, mind and soul I recoiled from it; even though I was thinking 'How in the name of Sense and Charity can the only saving truth have been vouchsafed to a few pious chaps in Plymouth and denied to all the thousand millions worshipping devoutly in other Churches all over the world?' But for Raney's sake I said only, 'I see. I see what you mean,' and was ready to leave it all there—so pious as it was, and so unpitying.

But she was not of the kind to let me off the hook easily. Fearing that she had admitted too much, she proceeded, 'Though, honestly, I find it impossible to believe that the so-called "priests" of the Roman Corruption and the poor misguided people who follow them won't find themselves subject to God's wrath hereafter.'

'Even if they've been wholly sincere in their beliefs?'

'Yes, even so.' She said it with a conviction deliberately stern.

'Oh, *no*, Mummy,' came a protest just breathed by Raney; and I confess it came like a distant sound of hope to me; almost, say, like that distant sound of a Highland bagpipe that came to the British, besieged and near despair, in the City of Lucknow. Then Raney was not like this. Raney was capable of being saved from this.

Mrs. Wayburn was not one to listen to a nineteen-year-old daughter.

'Sincerity won't save anyone if it's given to beliefs that are utterly contrary to God's Word, a desertion of it, a desecration of it——'

'Not even if their lives are holy? Not even if some were undoubted saints like'—but, of course, I couldn't think of the name of a single suitable saint. Only Augusta's pretty little St. Philomena came to my mind, and she didn't seem of much use in this room.

Mrs. Wayburn saved me from the necessity of enumerating saints, by completing what she'd been about to say. 'Works are nothing. No one is saved by works, only by faith. And by the true faith.'

I did not pursue this further because the ground seemed to be getting more and more mine-strewn; I did not force her by demanding 'So you believe that all other Christians than you, in their millions and millions, past and present, are destined to God's wrath and everlasting torment'; I just thought, 'There into the fire go Augusta and Abel and Father'—and even though I was so often in hot disagreement with Father, I was annoyed; I didn't want this for the poor old boy. It was easy to be jealous for Augusta and her good Abel, but here was I actually being jealous for Father.

Appropriately—or not appropriately—perhaps for the sake of speaking, or to ease any discomfort on my part, Mr. Wayburn pointed to a framed photograph on the wall, showing a tall, slim beautiful girl in the tight-waisted bodice and richly flounced skirt of the 1880's, and said jokingly, 'That was Mother in her unconverted days.'

'Yes,' she agreed. 'That was taken when I was twenty and before I really found the Lord. You know, I expect, that it was at one of Nelson's Meetings, to which I'd come at his suggestion, that I really found salvation. I always think it's nice to know I owe my state of grace to him.'

'Yeah,' he said, 'but it wa'nt me what was preaching. It wa'nt me that done the trick. It was Brother Saunders, a mighty powerful preacher.'

'Yes, if ever a man knew how to win souls, he did.' Mrs. Wayburn nodded fervently. 'But it was not only his sermon; it was also one of Moody and Sankey's hymns that we sung afterwards. I suddenly felt flooded with grace; I felt alight with it. I think, Mr. O'Murry—Stewart, I mean—I think there's some answer to your question here. I was a regular member of your Church then, and we believe that before you're converted you can be "in a gracious state" but not yet "in a state of grace"—if you see what I mean.'

Once again I felt relieved; it vexed me to be feeling relieved; but there it was: I felt relieved from the full force of this woman's power. Perhaps I could now think of my poor old

father as 'in a gracious state' if no more. Curiously I wasn't
worrying much about myself. I got up to look at the picture of
Mrs. Wayburn when she was only in a gracious state, and a
sweet-looking girl she was: slim and bright-eyed and smiling.
There, for certain, was Raney's mother.

I moved from this to another on the wall: a bald man with a
full moustache and side-whiskers, sitting in the midst of a large
group of men, young and old. A caption under the photograph
said, 'Ira David Sankey, Revivalist and Hymn Writer, with his
Famous Choir'.

'So this is the great Sankey himself?' I said.

They agreed.

I pointed to the men. 'And all these, then, are Sankey's
Hims?'

I have never thought this one of my best jokes, but Mr. Wayburn roared with laughter and slapped a plump leg. 'That's
good,' he said. 'I must remember that.' Raney laughed too;
but I quickly suspected I'd dropped a ringing clanger before
Mrs. Wayburn and her crochet. One should not jest about holy
things. I remembered too Father saying 'A pun is the lowest
form of humour,' though, as ever, I was ready to disagree with
him, considering a pun quite good fun, if it was a good pun.
And sometimes, in fact, the worse the pun, the better the fun.
But 'Sankey's Hims'?

Supportable or not? Even good? I'm still unsure.

Mrs. Wayburn said nothing to rebuke me for this unholy
remark. All she did—or so it seemed to me—was to divert the
talk to seemlier things, among which was a palpable desire to
lead me towards the Light. For her sake, and for Raney's, I
played the part of a deeply interested listener; I sat there pos-
ing as one not at all averse to being saved and made an inheri-
tor of glory. I said, for example, 'I'd so much love to come to
one of your Meetings. Could I?'

'Of course you could. We love to welcome any'—I don't
know what was the word before which she hesitated—'sinners',
perhaps; what she finally said was 'any seekers after the truth'.
Her husband in his easier way, echoed her warmly, 'Of course
come along. Any ole time. You've only to say you're a friend of

139

mine—I'm an elder, you see; jest mention Brother Wayburn, and you'll get a real welcome; no mistake.'

'Come by all means,' Mrs. Wayburn repeated—but had not a new note of irresolution entered her voice as if she thought her husband's words a little too easy-going? 'But, Nelson, I don't think he ought to approach the matter without a certain amount of thought. I think he should seek guidance first.'

'How exactly?' I asked.

'Well, by your prayers'—as if these were in constant use!— 'and by some study of his Word with this visit in mind. Do you read it regularly?'

'I'm afraid not.'

'Then I must say that if you are to profit from our Meeting, you should read carefully what is his offer to us all, and what he asks from us before he will grant us the benefits of redemption; what are his stated and irreducible terms.'

Upon my soul, it sounded at first as if in this business of salvation, I, like a good business man, should consider the Lord's prospectus before deciding to close with it, and as if she, talking on and on, exhorting in season and out of season as the apostle prescribed, was a broker urging me to invest in a good proposition quickly.

The preliminary outcome of this brokerage was that I, chiefly because I was anxious to sit well in her view, but also out of a real curiosity, said again that I would truly like to attend one of their Meetings, and where was their church?

'Church?' She disliked the word. 'We have no church.'

'Oh, no, I remember that. Raney told me.'

'We have only the Room.'

'Yes, yes, I remember.' I was stumbling weakly. 'The Room is where?'

'It's in Wilton Place. We were lucky to get it. It used to be the Army's first shelter before they built their present citadel, and they gave it to us. Before that, we were only a few and had to meet in each other's rooms.'

'The Army and you are more or less allies?' I inquired, trying to maintain my show of deep interest.

She shrugged. 'Hardly that. I'd agree there's really no

difference in our teaching, but we are certainly not organized as an army with colonels and captains, all vowing total obedience to the officers above them, and they to a single general. Oh, no; none of that. We have no popes. One or two elders——'

'Of whom I am one,' Mr. Wayburn reminded me.

'——but we try to be just brothers and sisters worshipping together.'

'Everything you say makes me long to come,' I declared, still seeking their good opinion, but speaking truth as well.

'Then look,' began Mr. Wayburn, as one who would like to bring this talk to a practical point. 'Wouldn't it be best if Mr. O'Murry——'

'Stewart, Stewart,' Raney interposed.

'——if Mr. Stewart came 'ere in the morning—say next Sunday—and we all went to Meeting together. I reckon you could be 'ere by hah-parse-ten?'

'Easily I could. I'm only about half a mile away.'

'Oh, yes, yes!' cried Raney. 'And we'll all go together. Next Sunday. Oh, that'll be gorgeous.'

'Hardly "gorgeous", darling,' corrected her mother. 'Next Sunday then.'

All this time neither Mr. Wayburn nor I had smoked. I had pipe and pouch in my pocket and often fingered them longingly, but I did not feel happy about introducing them to this company. At one point I did ask Mrs. Wayburn how it was that if Mr. Wayburn didn't approve of smoking he was willing to sell tobacco and cigarettes to his customers; and she answered, 'We'—not 'Mr. Wayburn'—'we hold that it's between them and the Lord.' So much for my meerschaum pipe.

We talked till the little clock on their mantel struck six, when Mrs. Wayburn explained, 'We usually go to Evening Service at six, and to the Believers' Prayer Meeting afterwards, which can last a long time, so today we've made an exception, staying at home since you were coming.'

'That was most kind of you,' I said, feeling flattered and pleased, but was somewhat shaken as she proceeded, 'Still, there's no reason why we shouldn't all have Family Prayers together. When possible we have morning and evening worship. We'll begin with a few hymns, shall we?'

'Oh, yes,' I said. And hoped it sounded enthusiastic.

'Yes, thet's the idea.' Mr. Wayburn was undoubtedly enthusiastic. 'Come along all. Hymns first and Prayers afterwards.'

Mrs. Wayburn went to the upright piano against the wall, sat there and lifted its lid, disclosing keys yellow and chipped.

'So you're a pianist,' I ventured, in a kind of social flattery.

'A very poor one. I just made it my business to learn enough to accompany the hymns when our usual pianist is away. I felt it was my duty to. A small work for the Lord.' There was a large hymn book with music on the piano's music stand. 'Now what hymn would you like?' she asked, turning its pages. 'Have you any favourites?'

I tried to think of a favourite; I ransacked my mind; but of all the hymns that I'd sung in my twenty years, only 'Onward, Christian Soldiers' would come and stand firmly in my mind (like a solitary Christian soldier). This moment of vast amnesia was just like my father's when, seeking a devout Christian layman to set before me as an exemplar, he could only think of Lord Halifax. I was about to say (untruthfully) since I must say something, 'I love "Onward, Christian Soldiers",' when I recalled that extreme Protestants objected to its 'ritualistic' couplet, 'With the Cross of Jesus Going on before', and that its author, learning this, had offered as an alternative, 'With the Cross of Jesus Left behind the door.' 'Onward, Christian Soldiers' then was unsuitable; and, much as I should have liked to tell them this comic story, I decided that I had better not—not after 'Sankey's Hims'. So I just stood there behind the waiting pianist without a single hymn available, and was only able to stutter, 'I am sure I shall like whatever you choose.' It had not yet occurred to me that the Brethren's hymn book would be any different from *Hymns Ancient and Modern* which we used at St. Jude's.

Luckily, considering the boundless hymnological desert which my mind had now become, Mrs. Wayburn stopped at one of her pages and said, 'What about "For ever with the Lord"? Do you know that?'

'Oh yes; oh, good *gracious*, yes,' I emphasized, almost as if hurt that she should question my knowledge of it. 'I *love* that.' And I even spoke its opening lines proudly, 'For ever with the Lord. Amen! So let it be.'

'Good,' said Mrs. Wayburn. And she began to strum—one could call it nothing else—the accompaniment. We all sang the hymn together; and it was now I learned that the Brethren sang their hymns with (to me) a drear and monotonous slowness, in reverence, no doubt, for sacred words. Yet, even so, it was good to hear Raney singing in her girl's voice, small and thin though it was, at my side.

The hymn sung, Mrs. Wayburn, turning her pages again, asked, 'Do you know "I heard the voice of Jesus say"?'

'Oh, yes,' I said, happy that once again I was not found wanting. 'Indeed I do. "I heard the voice of Jesus say Come unto me and rest".'

So she strummed this accompaniment, and we sang together slowly and sombrely the opening verse, but here, alas, came a great surprise, for instead of the slowly measured accompaniment Mrs. Wayburn suddenly hammered the piano for a resounding chorus. It was a chorus quite unfamiliar to me, so that I was left standing there dumb while they sang it *fortissimo* to the heartily drummed piano.

> Oh, the Voice to me so dear,
> Breathing gently on my ear,
> Happy soul, look up and see—
> 'Tis thy Saviour speaks to thee.

After each of the verses which I knew well they sang without me this loud and lively—indeed I can only call it this jolly and uproarious—chorus.

By this time, because of these choruses, they seemed to have forgotten me, standing there in my ignorance, and were ready to sing only hymns beloved by themselves. The next one, new to me on this evening, was destined to become a haunting memory in my thoughts to this day. It was 'Will you be there, and I?'

I know there's a bright and glorious land
Away in the Heavens high,
Where all the redeemed shall with Jesus dwell;
Will you be there, and I?

nd with what a chorus!

Will you be there, and I?
Will you be there, and I?
Where all the redeemed with Jesus dwell;
Will you be there, and I?

Now it was that Raney saw I was standing lost and left out, and she came closer to take my hand and press it. 'Mum, Mum, you're leaving Stewart out. Find one that he knows.'

'Oh, I'm sorry,' her mother said. 'Of course we're leaving him out. Tell me what you'd like.'

I was in no difficulty now for in these periods of solitary idleness I had remembered another hymn than 'Onward, Christian Soldiers'. It had been recalled to me by their hymns, and I was happy to be able to say confidently, 'Do you know "Take my life, and let it be"?'

'Of course, of course,' cried Raney, glad to have me in action again. 'Do we not! Who doesn't?'

And, thank heaven, their words for this hymn, and their tune, were the same as I had known at school and at St. Jude's. So Raney and I, hands linked, were able to sing it in unison together.

That was our last hymn. Mrs. Wayburn shut her hymn book and said, 'That'll do for hymns. Now for prayers.'

With some apprehension I fell to praying with them. Or, rather, much as I had watched their movements to learn what to do with the shell-fish and vinegar at tea, so now I copied them as they knelt around the dining-table, elbows resting on it and hands clasped; each was at one side of the table and I knelt at the fourth side worrying lest I too should be expected to pray alone, aloud, and impromptu.

Mrs. Wayburn might be the power in that room, but she was a woman loyal to convention and allowed her husband, an elder, to pray first.

Mr. Wayburn's spontaneous praying, I was to observe, was in marked contrast to his wife's; it was formal, uninspired, and merely the words of a dutiful elder performing his task. No power or passion, no personal or original words, rose upward from his properly upturned face. He delivered his words in the properly sanctimonious sing-song, and his prayer, as custom demanded, was full and long; but to me it seemed all too like a one-sided chat, unctuous in voice but familiar and even matey in language, with the Almighty, the Absolute. While he prayed and prayed, I had time to delve for words which, if so required, I in my turn could offer as impromptu worship; some words, perhaps, about my sins and my desires for amendment, but—yet again—just as I had been unable to think of any hymn but 'Onward, Christian Soldiers', so I could think now of nothing, nothing, no prayer at all, except 'Almighty and everlasting God who alone workest great marvels, send down upon our Bishops and Curates . . . the healthful Spirit of thy grace', which I'd heard so often at St. Jude's and always with amusement. But since in all the Book of Common Prayer there was hardly one prayer less likely to be welcomed by Mr. and Mrs. Wayburn, my mind remained nothing but a low-visibility fog. Of course the Lord's Prayer loomed in the mist but I was vain enough to decide that this would be much too simple and imitative to compete with the prolonged and conspicuously home-made efforts which would come from my hosts—these 'do-it-yourself' efforts, as we should say today. In my apprehension I found myself perspiring, and had to wipe my forehead and the nape of my neck. Well, if pray I must, I would pray. Mustn't let Raney down. Or myself.

I need not have suffered so. Mrs. Wayburn, going in next, prayed with power enough for us all, and surely there would be little need to say more—or indeed anything left to say—after she had done. She dealt fully and faithfully with our sins, our needs, and our difficulties, even reporting to the Lord the substance of our discussion after tea. 'We pray to thee, our gracious Father in Heaven, for this young man who has just come among us this day; we beseech thee that light may be vouchsafed to him and that he may lay hold on the Lord Jesus.

With all our hearts and souls we ask that in the fulness of thy time he may know his election sure and give his life to his sole and only Saviour. May he be brought to see that whatever his sins may have been, and whatever his good deeds, which I am confident have been many, all, all, are as nothing before thee, but only his faith in the redemption, salvation, and forgiveness earned for him by the blood of thy dear son. It may be that thy hand will be extended in chastisement and that it is by his stripes that he will be healed and brought to thy feet'—I was not sure that I liked this, as I knelt there, wondering what the stripes, so earnestly pleaded for, would be, and not looking forward to them at all; but I was mollified as she went on: 'We greatly desire this for a new and dear young friend in the morning of his life, even as we ask it always for ourselves, beseeching thee that we may learn to praise thee for our afflictions and to beg that they may be sanctified for us.'

'Ay-men,' Mr. Wayburn interjected, as an elder.

Then she was praying with a like magniloquence for Raney, obviously seeking guidance from the Almighty in the difficult problem (though mentioning no name) posed by the arrival of a dear young man in their midst. 'We ask thee, of thy love and mercy to watch always over our beloved Ireen, this sapling in thy vineyard'—which I thought a pleasant description of Raney—'and to guide her steps into paths that are meet for her, leading her by the hand and surrounding her always with the protection of thy great love.'

Adequate protection from me kneeling there?

I remember no more; evidently the children were not obliged to pray, for after this not inconsiderable orison we all rose from our knees; the adults refreshed, and I relieved. Was Raney relieved too? Perhaps. I suspected so.

12

The Meeting House

So it came about that one Sunday morning I went to the little house in Mortress Lane, prepared to join its family in a Meeting of the Brethren.

Raney opened the door to me, leapt up to kiss me, and led me by the fingers into the parlour. The same parlour, but with Mr. and Mrs. Wayburn in their Sunday black seated at the table on severely upright chairs and maintaining a Sabbath silence. Mrs. Wayburn was reading in a Bible open before her; Mr. Wayburn, unlike most of the men in the Dene who were probably in shirt sleeves, reading their Sunday papers, alert for salacious stories, was drumming his fingers on a closed Bible and hymn book before him. A chair at the table waited for me with a similar Bible and hymn book before it.

Mother and Father, looking up, gave me a smile but no words. Raney went to her chair and read in a book which I had given her; a book no doubt approved by her mother for Sunday reading because of its title 'Songs of Innocence'; but Raney, I knew, was reading it less for its Sabbath suitability than because I had lately fallen in love with William Blake's poetry and had infected her with a like adulation. Now, as I sat down, she caught my sidelong glance at this book and gave me a smile, of which the character seemed slightly unSabbatical. Raney's eyes always lit up with a quick new brightness when she smiled; they did so now; their corners wrinkled fanwise; and I doubted if this sudden radiance, in part mischievous, accorded with the solemnity in the room.

While we waited I, seeking to enact my part fittingly, opened the hymn book and, turning its pages, was diverted by its (so to say) noisy and gushing difference from our staid and temperate *Hymns Ancient and Modern*.

At about half-past ten Mr. Wayburn spoke. He said, 'Well,

Mother, better be getting ready. 'Op it, Ireen, and get yer 'at.'

The women gone from the room, he changed his whole attitude; he pushed back his chair, crossed one plump leg over the other, and prepared for a good masculine chit-chat.

'I 'spect you'll find it all different from what you been used to. Personally I think it's a bit too solemn, like; I could always do with something a tot more lively. The Army does it better, I reckon: their meetings can get real jolly sometimes, and I like a spot of jollity meself. The 'ymns are all right. We get going then a bit.'

I murmured that I realized it'd be a bit different.

'Yeah; and there'll be the Breaking of the Bread but you can't take no part in that. That's only for those who been accepted.'

'Accepted?'

'Yepp. Been properly baptized.'

I laughed and suggested that I'd been properly baptized.

'Yepp; but not after our fashion. Not what we think's being properly baptized.'

'What fashion's that?'

'Why—you know—total immersion—over your 'ead and all.'

'Good lord!' I almost said, but managed to change it to 'Oh, I see.'

'Yepp; and not all that'll be there this morning'll have been accepted. It takes time. You got to prove your worth, like. You got to prove, more or less, your calling and election sure.'

Mercifully I was saved from sliding into the argument that 'election' involved its opposite, the intolerable doctrine of 'reprobation', by the return of Raney and her mother.

We rose, in silence, to go.

And in Sunday silence, the shadow of Dread Omnipotence falling before our feet, we walked along a couple of streets to the Room. It was on the ground-floor of a three-storeyed building, and a monogram composed of the letters S and A over its pedimented doorway showed that it had once belonged to the Salvation Army. A square bare room, it had benches, row behind row in the middle of the floor, and another bench along

each side-wall. At the far end stood a plain deal table, little
more than a kitchen table, with a piano in the corner near it;
and this was all the furniture. Some brethren and sisters sat
here and there on the benches but not many. All were silent.
Mr. Wayburn went to a chair behind the deal table; we three
to a bench near the back, still empty.

A few more worshippers came in, and then somewhere in the
Dene a clock chimed eleven. Mr. Wayburn immediately knelt
down to offer prayer, and we all knelt down to listen to him.
Once again I observed the merely formal and uninspired quality of his prayer, embracing only the dutiful words expected of
an elder; and this morning it was soon over, as if he was tired,
and his imagination exhausted. Rising, he announced a hymn,
for which we all rose; and a woman walked to the piano. It was
no hymn I knew, so I stood among them at a loss. The congregation sang the first verse loudly, but all too slowly and sol-
emnly, considering the vivacity of the words:

> Come thou Fount of every blessing,
>   Tune my heart to sing thy grace.
> Streams of mercy, never ceasing,
>   Call for songs of loudest praise.

But then the piano was banged and hammered for the chorus,
and loudly we got it.

> Glory, glory, Jesus saves me!
>   Glory, glory to the Lamb!
> Oh! the cleansing blood has reached me,
>   Glory, glory to the Lamb!

The voices slowed and quietened for the next verse:

> Here I raise my Ebenezer–

(Ebenezer? Later explained to me as a meeting house.)

> Hither by thy help I come
> And I hope, by thy good pleasure,
>   Safely to arrive at home.

After the hymn Mr. Wayburn preached, and again a very
simple sermon it was, touching upon no intellectual subtleties

or scepticisms, as if the preacher were unaware that such ungodly things were to be found among men; just a short pious
exhortation which at school we should have dismissed as a
'pi-jaw'.

Then another hymn:

> Who are these arrayed in white
> Brighter than the noonday sun,
> Foremost of the sons of Light
> Nearest the eternal throne—

and I found myself contrasting these souls in Heaven, so gloriously arrayed, with these sad people around me in their dismal
black; and comparing the difference between the golden and
resplendent Heaven they foresaw for themselves hereafter and
their grey and dreary tabernacle in this world of sin. Why a
room so bleak, so dry, so drained of all poetry?

There followed the Breaking of the Bread on the plain deal
table. Only a few went up to take communion, so that I wondered if the others had not been 'accepted'. The whole cere-
mony I thought tender and touching, and not less so when I
was contrasting it with the magnificent rituals which would
surround my good brother-in-law, Father Abel, when he celebrated a High Mass.

After the Breaking of the Bread there was a rumble of all
kneeling down; the time had come for the spontaneous praying
of the separate saints in their pews. I don't know if in those days
preaching was denied to the women, but this didn't seem to
matter because Mrs. Wayburn, who inevitably led off, got all
the sermon she may have wanted to preach into a long talk
with her Creator wherein, as a means of instructing the people
around her in the ways of salvation, she told him, at length and
in some detail, all about his purpose for men, which he knew
already and must have known since the beginning of the world.
A much finer sermon it was, even if disguised as communion
with God, than her husband's; far more pungent and passionate for her purpose of saving the saints. Some of it offended me
because it leaned too heavily towards God's wrath rather than
towards his love; towards his damnation awaiting the faithless

or the apostate rather than towards his bewildering patience
with the worst of us and his breathtaking mercy that stands
and waits. But other parts of this sermon-prayer were beautiful. Glancing in her parlour at the Bible she was reading, I had
seen that she was studying the eleventh chapter of 'Hebrews',
doubtless in preparation for a worthy prayer; and no one can
reproduce that chapter without reproducing beauty. 'May we
not serve thee less, dear Lord, than those who died in faith,
not having received the promises, but having seen them afar off
and were persuaded of them, and embraced them, and confessed that they were strangers and pilgrims on the earth. But
now they know a better country; that is, an heavenly; wherefore thou art not ashamed to be called their God, for thou hast
prepared for them a city. . . .'

Dear and good Mrs. Wayburn: so limited in her outlook, but
from her prison window seeing so great a light.

When our worship was over, there was hand-shaking with
Mr. and Mrs. Wayburn, and the general management of these
courtesies by Mrs. Wayburn showed me again the prepon-
derance of her power over that of her husband, the elder. Some
of the departing congregation waved to Raney, and one even
called her 'Sister Ireen'. All gone, we four came back to Mortress Lane for dinner, which was the customary Sunday meal of
their class, rich and heavy: a round of beef with its attendant
Yorkshire pudding, followed by apple and cranberry tart. It
has always been a mystery to me how Mrs. Wayburn, though
apparently occupied throughout the morning with the advancement of God's kingdom, had contrived to have the joint standing in the oven at the right state of cooking when we returned
from prayer and praise.

After dinner on this holy day—what? A long doze in his
easy chair appeared legitimate for Mr. Wayburn; while his
wife read in some saintly book and even nodded over it without
sin. A sun of early July blazed down on the streets, and Raney
and I had been told that we might take a walk along the High
Street to Kensington Gardens. In this decision it was revealed
to me that while Mrs. Wayburn might be the more dominant
power in the Brethren's Room, her husband was an equal power

in the home—if only just. She had been in doubt as to whether the Gardens with their irreligious Sunday crowds were a suitable goal for Raney, a child of grace; but her husband was untroubled by any such qualm. 'Oh, come, Mother, jest look at that there sun; young people like them ought to be out in it; ain't that what God put it there for? And ain't that why he grew a place like Kensington Gardens? T'ain't as if Ireen had to go to Sunday School any more.'

'I always think she ought to be taking a class there.'

'Oh, give the poor child a chan'st—after working for her ole man all the week. It's a day in a thousand. If I 'adn't eaten a shade too evv'ly of that there beef of yourn I'd be out in the sun meself and taking you along of me. And 'oo's fool enough to stay on the pavements when he can get on the grass and among the trees? If Mr. O'Murry—I mean, Stoo'rt—had brought his bike, I'd suggest their going to Kew or somewhere. You got a bike, 'aven't you, Stoo? Ireen's got hers in the shed. Bring your bike next time. Yurse, you can trust these two together all right, Mother.'

'Well, as long as she's back in time for tea and evening service, I suppose it's all right.'

'I'll bring her back,' I said gallantly.

'Thet's right,' Mr. Wayburn encouraged. 'I know they're to be 'oly trusted. So let 'em both enjoy theirselves.'

But, as a matter of fact, we were not to be wholly trusted. We took more than a walk. Hands linked, we walked into Kensington Gardens and, while we talked together, I led her over the Long Water into Hyde Park and towards a bird sanctuary where the great chestnut trees, gathered together, cast beneath them a broad floor of strangely dark shadow. Here the grass, elsewhere so closely trimmed, was allowed free growth and, feathering with seeds, it stood several feet high. Since this was a wild place, with the golden ragwort branching among the tall grasses, the rosebay willow-herb lifting its mauve and pink spires to the height of a man, and the purple thistles striving to compete with them, it was unvisited and undesired by the Sunday strollers, or by the lazily seated who preferred trim lawns within low iron railings; nor did the sun visit it, save with a few speckles, dropped through the entangling branches. No one came near us, so Raney and I sat in it side by side among some dense bracken; sat at first and then lay down, happily talking, till at last I drew her, unresisting, into my arms. Then we lay there, with me pressing kisses on her brow, lips, and throat, while her eyes lit up with happiness and her hands fondled my hair. This must have been far beyond what her mother was dreaming about as she nodded over her book; and perhaps rather more than her husband had foreseen— though I never felt sure of him. Even so, I felt no guilt; I could only believe, as I kissed her lips or lifted her fingers to kiss them almost reverently, that this was what God had in mind for the young.

And therefore I continued the process, only interrupting it to murmur appropriate words in little more than a whisper. Looking down upon her face beneath me, I whispered, 'Your eyes are so lovely. So lovely. Brown like your amber hair. God, I'm lucky! And your mouth. I could kiss and kiss it for ever.'

Which I proceeded to do, if not for ever, then for an hour that seemed nearer to the stillness of the infinite than to hurrying and transitory hours of poor busy earthbound men.

When we had wearied of loving and were sitting up again, pulling at the bracken fronds and raising their acrid scent around us, I resumed, for the fun of it, the 'Education of Raney', which had now been in hand, to our mutual delight, for more than a year. Though London born and living all my youth among the bricks and the pavements, where only the sparrows and the starlings, and here and there the pigeons, cared, as it seemed, to be the associates of men, I had lately acquired a love of birds and whenever on some journalistic assignment I visited the country and left the pavements behind I always took with me my bird book that I might identify any and every bird by sight or song. So now —not without vanity in my new knowledge—I taught her as we sat there the chaffinch's ditty, 'I'll bring my pretty love to meet you here'—there it was on a branch above us—and then the thrush's 'Cherry dew, cherry dew', and, best of all, the blackbird's flute, which

L

enabled me to introduce her to a new poet, Henley, and to quote:

> The nightingale has a lyre of gold,
> The lark's is a clarion call;
> And the blackbird plays but a box-wood flute,
> But I love him the best of all.

How she loved it, insisting on hearing words and rhythm again and again till she had them by heart. As I have said, never a pupil more ardent than Raney.

But soon, resolving, whatever might be God's design for the saplings in his vineyard, that I must be more loyal to Mr. Wayburn's trust in me, I pronounced, 'Well, chick, time, alas, to wander back to tea and to holy church.'

'Oh, *no*!' she expostulated. 'I don't want any tea or'—but here she stopped herself and promptly rose in silence as if ashamed, so that I began to be troubled lest I was winning her too fast and too far from her old fidelities. Here was she, 'given by her parents to the Lord', and on the Lord's Day, preferring under the shadow of the trees, and within the screens of the rosebay, a little human loving to any communion with the Divine.

13

The Return Call

As the days went by after this welcome into the Wayburns'
home I grew more and more to think—with some dismay at the
prospect—that it was Father's duty to invite them into *his*
home. And give them tea. One tea at least, since I'd had
two teas with them and a dinner. Also I was beginning to fear
lest Raney would be hurt by any apparent disinclination on
my part to show her to my parent. And I was certainly enough
in love with her to choose discomfort for myself rather than see
her hurt. So one Saturday afternoon I strengthened my will
and climbed the stairs to my father's study, carrying with me
my alarming suggestion. And walked apprehensively in.

Lonely as ever, he was deep in his easy chair with Hamish at
his side, enjoying Father's affectionate stroking of his silky
black ears so much so that he beat his paws on the carpet for an
encore whenever Father stopped. One hasty glance revealed to
me the book Father was reading, because I knew it well. It was
Ronsard's *Lyrics*; and in my mind's eye I could see its antique
sub-title, 'Les Oeuvres de Pierre de Ronsard, Gentilhomme,
Prince des Poètes François.'

Gentilhomme. Prince. The words seemed to make the proposal
with which I was burdened even more shocking.

'Yes?' he inquired, as I came in, giving me one upturned
look which suggested a desire to return to the book as soon as
possible.

'I want to ask you something.'

'Yes?'

'It's about Raney.'

'Raney?'

'Irene Wayburn. My . . . er . . . girl.' The word 'girl-friend'
was not available then or I would probably have used it, and he
would probably have been disturbed by it.

'Oh, I remember. You were telling me about her. The girl in the stationer's shop. In the Dene.'

These words carried enough of his original shock and disapproval to annoy me. 'Yes, she lives in the Dene and her father's a stationer in a very small way.'

'And she'd been a laundry-maid, didn't you say?'

'A laundry-maid certainly. At Patterson and Morley's, Lithos Street, Hollen Dene.' We were beginning badly. In my immediate resentment at his tone I felt driven to act on the sound principle of defence, 'If they advance to the attack, let them have it all. In the face. When you see the whites of their eyes.'

He nodded, as one who was hearing the worst. 'I see.'

'And I've been twice to their highly respectable home. Once for a whole day. I've been to Meeting with them. As I told you, they are deeply religious people. *Really* religious.' That 'really' might have borne any meaning.

'Brethren of some sort, aren't they?'

'Plymouth.'

'Plymouth.' A heavy sigh. 'A form of religion that is anathema to me. And this in the Dene!'

'Just so. That's what makes them so interesting.'

'Why?'

'Well . . . you know the Dene . . . and they go to their Meeting House twice every Sunday, and have family prayers every day. Which is rather more than we do. Don't you think we ought to start?'

Father threw this interesting proposition aside with a toss of his head, and felt for Hamish's ears, rather as if the companionship of this silkily obedient and unargumentative creature was more to his taste than dealing with a son now adult, egotistically independent, and with a big meerschaum pipe lifting its smoke aloft to proclaim this independence.

'But, religious or not, I suppose they're quite common?'

This thoroughly annoyed me, so that I said 'Common? Oh, yes. Not 'arf.'

'Please don't use phrases like that. Not in my hearing. We're not Cockneys, are we?'

'No. Very well. Let's say "Common as you like". Thoroughly common. Not a doubt about it.'

'And what is it you wanted to ask me about them?'

'I was wondering . . . rather . . . if you'd care to invite them to tea.'

'Oh, *no*. Have I got to do that?'

'You haven't *got* to. I just thought you might like to. They've been frightfully nice to me, and——'

'You're not suggesting, I sincerely hope, that you're regarding yourself as engaged to her?'

'I'm not considering myself engaged to her. With people of their class it needs quite long time after they've asked you to tea before they consider you engaged. You have to go on for a long time walking out—I mean, seeing one another and . . . and so on.'

'Then if it's got no further than this—and I pray it will get no further—I don't see that I'm under any obligation to——'

'There's no obligation on you at all. It was just my hope. But if'—and at this point I was inspired. I saw that I held a trump card in my hand. 'Not if you'd rather not. But I'm sure I ought to do something courteous in return. Besides, I happen to be in love with Raney. And I'm wondering if it wouldn't be better for me to leave here and find digs somewhere else so that I could invite her and her parents into my home without disturbing you. I'm earning fair money now and could afford to do this.'

It was an ace of trumps because Father needed my contribution for bed and board if he was to keep possession of this house on which he'd lavished through the years so much love; so much paint, distemper and plaster; so many shelves and furnishings that he'd carpentered himself with the tools that were as dear to him as children—or perhaps, if we are to speak truth, somewhat dearer.

Dry and difficult as our companionship may have become, he would rather have had me than some stranger in my chair at his table or anywhere else in his home, seen or unseen. He had neither the desire nor the talent to live with strangers. For a member of his family he had at least a sense of property and the easy feeling that he was free to correct and reprove them as occasions demanded.

I pushed this ace further into his view. 'I might go and live in the Dene itself. Digs would be cheap there, and I could feed cheaply at their Lockhart's.'

'No, I don't want you to feel you have to do that. This has always been your home. If you really think I ought to do this, I will do it—though, as you know, I can't approve of your affair with this girl.'

'It's more than an affair. I love her.'

'So you think.'

'So I know.'

'Very well; let's not argue about it. I've said I will do what you ask, but I must say I doubt if they're the sort of people I shall really feel at ease with.'

'I doubt it too. Enormously.' I said this with a friendly laugh, because I was grateful to him. 'But if we could just do it *once*. And perhaps not for a long time again. Just a tea and a talk . . . and all of it soon over.'

'I can't imagine what I shall talk about.'

'Neither can I.'

'But there it is. I certainly don't want a son of mine living in the Dene.'

'It's awfully decent of you,' I said, feeling some pity for him. 'I'm afraid it'll have to be a Sunday when their shop is shut. But that's all to the good because they'll leave early for their evening service. So could we say the Sunday after next?'

'We could and had better, I suppose. And I'll—I'll do my best. But I can't pretend I'm happy about it. Still, I think I've courtesy enough not to let them see that.'

'Thanks,' I said. 'Thanks most awfully.'

§

Long before this I had taken Elsa and Josef into my confidence about my love for Raney. And Elsa's shock at the news had been much the same as Uncle Douglas's and Aldith's when I first told them; but it took much longer to heal because, unlike them, she got no balm from delighting in the shock it would be to the Bonny Earl o' Murray. In Elsa there was no hostility to Father; she was fond of 'The Master' and admired him, so big and handsome as he was, and 'always the gentleman' to her. ('I always get on well with the working classes.') Father never corrected or rebuked her; he never corrected or rebuked anyone whose service was indispensable to him. Children were different; that was what they were for. Elsa was shocked at first because, like many of her class, she could not think it at all right that a real young gentleman should walk out and keep company with a girl from the streets of the poor—still less from a street in the Dene.

But with the passing of time she experienced a complete change of heart. Uncle Douglas's shock had taken twenty minutes to heal; Aldith's had taken perhaps twice or three times as long; Elsa's required several days. But when the change of heart came it was like a religious conversion; one might almost compare it with the hour when Mrs. Wayburn escaped from her misguided Anglicanism and saw the True Light. It had the same characteristic symptoms of sudden and immediate illumination. What yesterday had seemed impossible to believe—namely that the young master should have fallen in love with a poor girl from shameful streets—was now a brilliant joy to her romantic heart. In this sudden and exciting conversion there was even a touch of Tertullian's *Credo quia impossibile est*.

So it was a joy to me, after this talk with Father, to rush down to her kitchen, sit triumphantly on a kitchen chair, announce that the Wayburns were to be admitted into the house for tea, and say laughingly that I hoped she'd prepare a real spread for them. 'Do them proud, won't you, Elsa?'

'You bet I will,' she said, as she stood at the table peeling onions for our supper.

'You pet she vill,' Josef echoed from his special chair where he was smoking the long drooping German pipe. 'She do zat for your sake, *nicht wahr*.'

'But look, Elsa. Spread it all on the dining-room table, and not on that damned Damascus stool and cake-stand in the drawing-room. They wouldn't know how to balance their cups on their knees or where to put the cakes.'

'Of course they wouldn't. And quite right too. It's a stupid way to have a real good tea, I always say. I like a tea properly spread on a table where one can eat in comfort and have a bit of lettuce and celery or something.'

'That's right. Lettuce and celery are the thing. And dough-nuts, perhaps. They gave me cockles and vinegar, but on the whole, I don't think I should provide those. I don't feel some-how that Father would understand.'

Elsa was enthusiastic. 'Oh, I'm so glad the Master's agreed to this. I never thought he would. You know what he is, don't you?'

'I have some idea.'

'So much the true gentleman, I felt sure as houses is houses that he wouldn't think her good enough for you. I mean, that's only natural, in't it? But what I say is, if *you* do, that's good enough for me. And Josef agrees.'

'*Ja, ja, mein Herr.*' Josef had recently been teaching me German. '*Es steht bei Ihnen.*'

'Josef agrees that what matters is what *you* think; not what no one else thinks. And from what you tell us, she's a good religious girl, and you're much safer with one of them than with some I could mention who may be gentry but I'm not sure I'd trust 'em much further than I could see 'em. May I say me and Josef admire the way you've stuck to her, in spite of the Master. She's not a lady of course, but what's that? What's that if she's as pretty as you say, and is good and kind, and ree'ly loves you—and learns quick as lightning all the things you're trying to learn her. It at least means that she won't put on no side, dunnit? She won't have no high and mighty ideas you couldn't very well pay for, now that you and the Master ain't as well off as you used to be. I'm for a good religious girl any day. And I'm jest longing to see her, bless her.'

'Father doesn't approve of her religion.'

'Don't he now? Well, every man to his taste, I say, whether it's religion or pease-puddin' or a wife or anything else. What I say is, whether like Miss Augusta we're practically Romer

Catholic, or like the Master jest Church of England, or like Josef here a Lootheran, whatever that is, or like me who's Heaven knows what, we're all children of Gawd.'

'And dat's vot I zay too,' said Josef from behind his smoke.

'And another thing I say is, I wish to goodness you wouldn't all smoke in my kitchen when I'm cooking. Two of you make the atmosphere something chronic. You and your great pipes.'

I removed my pipe from my mouth. 'I'll willingly desist for your sake, Elsa dear.'

'No, no, Master Stewart. It was only Mr. Stauffen—I mean, "Josef"—I was gettin' at. He never stops smoking that ridiculous-lookin' pipe for one minute of the day.'

'Is it any more ridiculous-looking than mine?'

'"Course it is. Yours and the Master's are Christian-looking things. Not a nasty foreign-looking thing like his. Who ever heard of a pipe made of china? But never mind him. When is it they're coming?'

'Sunday after next. As ever was.'

'Well, you leave it to me. I'll see there's a proper welcome for 'em on the dining-room table. With some hot buns in case the Master's a bit on the cold side—eh, Josef, ha, ha?'

'It's going to be a great occasion,' I said for her encouragement, though in my heart there was plenty of misgiving.

§

It was Elsa who, when the bell rang at four o'clock that Sunday afternoon, opened to them. But, alas, not only had the bell rung, but one of them, Mr. Wayburn probably, had let the knocker fall with a single bang. That bang banged on my heart as I waited in the drawing-room because I guessed Father was thinking, 'There you are! The knock of a green-grocer's boy.' It was understood in those days that a gentleman or a lady knocked ratta-tat-tat; not bang. I had run half-way down the stairs to let them in before anything like a maid or a servant could appear, but Elsa was quicker on the target than I, racing up her kitchen stairs because she was both eager to see Raney and eager to welcome them warmly lest the air higher up should be a trifle draughty. I had tried to make our big house seem less grand to them by saying that we were rather poor now and had let off the basement to Elsa and her husband, but, as I quickly turned back from the stairs to regain the drawing-room I heard Elsa say in her grandest manner, '*Do* come in. Both the Master and the young Master are expecting you. The Master is in his study but the young Master's in the drorin'-room.'

Disturbed by these aristocratic-sounding words, I set about making the drawing-room as untidy and commonplace as possible, knocking the cushions here and there and hiding some fine Indian silver (sent by Brother Abel) in the cupboard of the rosewood bureau. I wished I had instructed Elsa not to call me 'Master Stewart'; but it was too late now. Here she was— bringing them up the stairs. 'Step this way. I know Master Stewart's in the drorin'-room. Come along, Miss Raney.' With that 'Miss Raney' (my name for her) I knew that all Elsa's good heart had gone out to the girl of my choice, and I loved her for this, however worried I might be by the 'Master Stewart' and the 'drorin'-room'. And now she was presenting them to me in the full and proper style of our more dignified days—simply, I am sure, because she wanted to welcome them as ladies and a gentleman and accord them the proper honours. 'Mr. and Mrs. Wayburn, Master Stewart. And Miss Raney.' And with a welcoming smile to all three, she said, 'I'll tell the Master you've arrived. He'll be down in a minute. Of course he's mostly upstairs in his study working, but he's expecting you and looking forward to your comin'.'

Her smile for them all as she went out was the little sister of a general benediction.

I had just got them all on to sofa or chairs when Father entered, followed by his companion, Hamish; and immediately all three of them rose to their feet like privates at the entry of the colonel. I rose after them, belatedly; he was not my colonel. I don't wonder that they rose in respect like this; he looked magnificent, six-foot-five and dressed for company. I felt touched that, though just now he must be a vessel charged to the brim with distaste for this occasion, he had creamed his hair into place, arranged his mandarin moustaches and put on his best suit for them. (He had not been to church that morning, so he must have donned it especially for these visitors from the Dene.)

Mr. Wayburn, unversed in the etiquette of our Crescents, advanced ahead of his lady and proffered a hand. 'Pleased to meet yer,' he said. It was an expression which Father always called 'one of his pet abominations'.

Father shook the hand with some show of warmth, and then Mrs. Wayburn's, though she, according to the etiquette, should not have risen from the sofa at all. But there she stood, almost at attention with her hands hanging at her side till she could offer one to Father.

'I'm delighted you've been able to come,' he said, lying generously as he took the extended hand.

'Not at all,' she said: and what a meaningless answer! 'We're so pleased to meet you. It's so kind of you to ask us.'

It was now I noticed a remarkable fact: Mrs. Wayburn, who was such a power in the Brethren's Room, stood emptied of power in this large and (to her) richly furnished drawing-room. Here her guns were unprimed; her sword was blunted. She was without ease. Had she not once been a lady's maid and known her place?

While all this was happening, Hamish left his master's side and most pointedly chose Raney as the visitor who had captured most of his interest. He leapt up at her, crouched before her, barked at her, and leapt up again almost to her shoulders and nearly knocking her down, much to her delight. Was it that he perceived she was the youngest and the one most likely to frolic and have fun with him?

'But I understood from Stewart,' Father was saying, having perceived Mrs. Wayburn's unease and magnanimously trying to disburden her of it, 'Down, Hamish!—I understood you were tremendously occupied on Sundays with your religious work.'

'Not on Sunday afternoons,' her husband put in, determined, for his part, to be overawed by no man. 'That's the one afternoon when we're able sometimes to have a bit of kip.'

I was sure Father did not know this word; I had only just

learned it on my visits to the Dene; but Father was considerate enough not to ask what in heaven it meant.

'And you're Raney?' he said, turning to her with the kindest smile yet.

I don't know that from the earliest day to the last I ever loved Father, but I did now feel a liking flushed through with emotion as I saw him striving, against all his real feelings, to do his best for my sake and not to disappoint me on this extremely difficult occasion. And he had deliberately called her 'Raney'. He must have rehearsed it upstairs. And he was holding her hand a little longer than usual that she might feel his goodwill.

In theory he had always loved youth, though with his pride and his hypertrophied sense of physical, social, intellectual, even spiritual—and certainly grammatical—superiority, he had never succeeded in making a young thing love him—unless it was one of his dogs in its puppyhood (here he never failed). Also he loved beauty in all its forms, from the self-applied paint on his walls to the roses in his garden or the faces of women; he had also been, I think, fully sexed, so perhaps it was not difficult for him to bestow this admiring smile on Raney.

Raney, for her part, couldn't say a word. She could only respond with an embarrassed but grateful smile.

'Sit down, Raney,' he said, with the same admiration in his voice. 'Do all sit down. Mrs. Stauffen will bring the tea in one minute. Raney, this was your chair, I think.'

'Elsa's laid it downstairs in the dining-room,' I interrupted.

'Dining-room? Why on earth'—he began, for he had a firmly rooted idea as to how ladies and gentlemen took afternoon tea. 'Downstairs? Dining-room?'

I didn't like to say, 'I think it's because she wants to make a fine spread of it'; but Father had sense enough to suspect something of the sort, and made haste to get himself off this marshy ground. 'Well, Raney, I gather you've been to some shows with my son.'

Mr. Wayburn, anxious to talk like a man untroubled, was prompt with a correction of Father. 'At-cherly we call her Ireen. Her real name's Ireen. She's only called "Raney" by Stoo.'

None but I could have noticed the very slight contraction of Father's eyebrows at this abbreviation of his son's name; and at the Cockney rendering of the vowel sound 'ew' as 'oo'. 'Stew' would have been bad enough, but 'Stoo' was the ultimate end. I, and I alone, saw with some sympathy that he was suffering.

When we were all seated, Mr. Wayburn, pursuing his resolve to show no social discomfort, began (and he couldn't have begun worse), 'I understand, Mr. O'Murry, that you're a teacher.'

'A what?' asked Father.

'A teacher. In a London school somewhere.'

'Yes, I'm a master at a school.' Considerately he had not described it as a school for the sons of gentlemen, but he had to offer some resistance to the word 'teacher'. 'But I haven't been there long. A year or so. I used to be a publisher.'

'I meet publishers in my job sometimes,' said Mr. Wayburn, probably meaning publishers' representatives from houses that produced his cheap magazines. 'And what standard do you take in this 'ere school?'

'Standard?' Father gazed at him, confused.

'Yepp. I mean which standard do you teach in?'

Somehow I slipped in, 'Mr. Wayburn means "what form?"'

'I take the top form in French, and other forms in English and Classics.'

'Blimey, you must be clever.' Mr. Wayburn turned to me. 'You didn't tell me your dad was all that clever, Stoo.'

At which point Elsa came in with her grand manner still around her. 'Tea is served, sir.' Ours might have been a ducal hall with His Grace entertaining a house party for the shooting season. Still, her entry, on the whole, was a relief.

'Thank you, Elsa. Well, Mr. and Mrs.'—unfortunately Father had now forgotten their name—'well, shall we all go down to the dining-room?'

I followed the three parents down, some way behind them, with my hand lying along Raney's shoulder, while she whispered, 'I've never been so frightened in my life.'

I squeezed the shoulder. 'Nothing to be frightened about.

You were an instant success. Not that this was any credit to you. Because God did all.'

She left this piece of flattery unrebuked, since she had other things to say. 'And, golly, I do think your father's magnificent to look at.'

'To look at, yes,' I agreed.

'He's just about the handsomest man I've ever seen.'

'There are less handsome men, certainly. I give you that.'

'He's a lot handsomer than you.'

'Thank you. But it's granted.'

'Mind you, you're quite handsome too, darling. As far as you go.'

'But a long way short of the masterpiece. I accept the position.'

'Hamish of course is absolutely adorable. And doesn't he love your father?'

'He does. He's the one who does.'

'Me too. I love your father. I think he's sweet.'

'*Sweet?* Good lord! Well . . .' but we were now in the dining-room.

Here I saw that Elsa had really made a spread of it. There was a big cake in the centre which she'd cooked and iced for the occasion, a covered dish of hot scones, jam sandwiches, cucumber sandwiches, fancy cakes, and neat slices of bread-and-butter for those who preferred the 'Gentleman's Relish' in its round china jar. Tall chairs were set for five. I was glad for Father's sake that there was no lettuce or celery.

I saw Father's uninformed surprise at this festal display and wondered what thoughts were astir behind his discreet silence.

'Well, you sit here,' he said to Mrs. Wayburn, though still unpossessed of her name, and, as a gentleman should, he drew out for her the chair on his right. 'And you here, sir,' probably thanking Heaven for the word 'sir' when you lacked a party's name. 'You there, perhaps, Raney dear.'

This unexpected, uncharacteristic 'dear', gentle and even affectionate, drew me a few steps nearer my father than I'd ever been. I perceived again that he'd been moved, perhaps to his surprise, by the charm of her youth, but also that he was

struggling to play the part I'd written for him in this strange
and unnatural scene.

With the two parents, one on either side of him, he pushed
the tea-tray towards Mrs. Wayburn. 'I always ask the ladies to
pour out. They do it so much better than we do. I think it's
because tea and a good talk means so much more to them;
that's it, isn't it, ha, ha?'

He was really making a splendid effort.

Mrs. Wayburn began to pour out the tea. I have told you
how, as a lady's maid, she had set herself to acquire an accent
and a correctness of speech far above her husband's; but unfortunately, like many would-be genteel people, she had come to
believe that the socially correct pronoun for the first person
singular was always 'I' and never 'me' which tended to be
low; so now, handing a cup to Father, she said in her most
refined tones, 'I must say this is giving great pleasure to Mr.
Wayburn and I.'

Now, in all Father's long list of solecisms and syntactical
errors none would draw upon us children such a shivering
rebuke as this genteel failure to put the first-person-singular,
when necessary, in the objective case. I remember the gale that
blew around me once, when I said carelessly, 'Oh, look, Daddy,
at what Uncle Douglas has given to Augusta and I.' He demanded, 'How could Uncle Douglas give I anything? Turn it
round, you little silly, and say "Look at what Uncle has given
to I and Augusta", and then perhaps you'll see how ludicrous is
the mistake.' But today there was nothing he could say to Mrs.
Wayburn which would ease his distress. Far less serious had
been her social inaccuracy in referring to her husband as
'Mr. Wayburn' instead of using his Christian name; indeed it
had had the advantage of restoring to his memory their surname, which he immediately exhibited, as one who had never
forgotten it. 'The pleasure is ours, Mrs. Wayburn. That's so,
isn't it, Stewart?' ('Stewart' for Mr. Wayburn's correction.)

There was not, at first, much opportunity for Mrs. Wayburn
to show how genteel were her language and grammar compared with her husband's, because Mr. Wayburn's determination to appear wholly at ease involved a determination to talk

frequently and at some length. He now expounded, speaking often with his mouth full, as he ate heartily, tea being a big meal in the Dene, the origins of his newsagent's business in Mortress Lane. 'It was all my ole man's doin', ree'ly. We'd had a larger business in Shepherd's Bush, but he was red-hot for the Brethren, and when the goodwill of this little business in the Dene was for sale, he became convinced that he'd had a guid-ance from the Lord that he ought to take it and see what he could do to help people in the Dene, startin' a Meeting there, because, as you probably know, 'Ollen Dene had an even worse name then than it 'as now. I'm not so sure about the message from the Lord meself but the more and more he prayed about it, the more sure he was. He was a real good man, but once he'd decided he was right he always got, as you might say, the endorsement of the Lord, after long prayin'. As I've often said to Mrs. Wayburn—though she don't altogether think I ought to, in case it's profane, like—I say I can't remember once when the Lord disagreed with him, ha, ha. So away we 'ad to go to Mortress Lane, and soon we 'ad a small Meeting going. I was only a nipper at the time, helping the dad; it was all long before I married Mrs. Wayburn. I met her at a party in Paddington and got her to come along to Meeting. She did, and by gum, she was converted—in two hoots as you might say. And she's been a tower 'a strength at the Meeting ever since. You know that, don't you, Stoo?'

Father, eating but little, because he was as empty of ease as Mr. Wayburn was full of it—or striving to appear so—feigned a polite attention to his guest's protracted memoir, but I had no doubt that he was more than bored by it. He nodded suitably at times, or said, 'I see', or provided a rather inadequate smile at the parts that were meant to be funny. Once or twice, it seemed to me, he ministered to the boredom by giving a tit-bit to Hamish, padding impatient paws at his side. Thus he intro-duced a little variety into the drear proceedings.

Perhaps to escape Mr. Wayburn, or more probably in his honourable effort to be a good host for my sake, he turned to Mrs. Wayburn on his right and lied handsomely. 'I'm much interested in your religion, Mrs. Wayburn. I've been so interested in all that Stewart's told me about it. Do tell me more.'

This was polite but unwise. Mrs. Wayburn ('in season and out of season') was not likely to let such an opportunity slip. It is probable that she saw it as a gateway thrown open to her by the Lord. Furthermore it was the subject on which she could speak with knowledge and authority, and so, for the moment, stand not only on the same level as Father but on an eminence above him. She provided exactly what he asked: a long, ardent, unwearying, unsparing exposition of the Brethren's true faith. She lectured Father on the ways of the Lord which must not be questioned by such as he; she shewed him where he was seriously wrong; she dismissed some of his contentions as the words of one who was still in ignorance; and he bore it all—he, Father, the father of Aldith, Augusta and Stewart—he bore it all with never a hint of displeasure, never an indignant shifting in his chair, never an impatient toss of his head; he sat there enduring it all for Raney's sake and mine.

As far as I remember, Mrs. Wayburn began from the beginning. She told how, some eighty years ago, John Nelson Darby —'Mr. Wayburn is named after him'—had seceded from the Church of Ireland in which he was a minister, and together with a Mr. Cronin who was a Roman Catholic, but as disgusted with the total absence of the Spirit in his Church as Mr. Darby was in his Anglican communion, started in Dublin a Meeting of those who were ready to be done with all the Churches and derive their faith solely from the written Word. They finally settled in Plymouth.

'Plymouth, yes,' said Father, like a man pleased to recognize the one thing he's been clear in his mind about, so far; and pleased to show his recognition. 'Plymouth.' So gratified was he by this moment of clarity that he ventured here with a small smile, 'But "Total absence of the Spirit" is saying rather a lot, isn't it?'

'I think not.' Mrs. Wayburn firmly put him right. 'It was a terrible state of things at the time, and I'm not sure they're all that better now. It was like John Calvin over again. Calvin had been a Catholic, as of course you know.'

M

Father saw no need to say he didn't know this; and he merely nodded his acceptance of the fact.

'Both Mr. Darby and Mr. Cronin left their Churches, rightly deeming them apostate and corrupt. They insisted—and everything in the Word shows them to have been right—that God's method is to speak directly with each individual soul—with you and me and Nelson and Ireen. So we have no ministers—only a few whom we call elders, and they are only so called when they have proved themselves before the faithful by their life and works.'

'I am an elder,' Mr. Wayburn reminded us.

Father bowed to him.

'Not that works can do anything for a man's salvation,' pursued Mrs. Wayburn, in full flow. 'They can only show that he has found it and is in possession of it. As Isaiah says, we are all as an unclean thing, and our supposed righteousness is as filthy rags.'

I sat there wondering how Father liked this suggestion that his form of righteousness was filthy rags. I was beginning to feel some guilt at having subjected him like this to the tormentors.

Mrs. Wayburn did not pause to consider his feelings; she hurried on, 'There is no other way under Heaven whereby we can be saved except by a simple faith in the sacrifice of the Lord Jesus. And that only comes to the elect, those chosen by the Lord for salvation.'

'So you believe in predestination?' Father gently intruded, with no more than a query in his voice.

'Certainly,' said Mrs. Wayburn, answering with conviction and no mercy.

'And all the millions who are not of the elect are just damned . . . ?'

'So it would appear, but we can know nothing of God's uncovenanted mercies. It is surely best not to put one's faith in them.'

Clearly Father felt compelled to speak his mind—or some of it—at this stage. 'Predestination seems to me a terrible doctrine. Just consider the deathly despair of those who believe in it but cannot believe they are of the elect.'

Mrs. Wayburn's answer was accompanied by a pitiless shrug. 'We have the words of Holy Scripture, of the Saviour himself, "Many are called, but few chosen". Just consider, on the other hand, how Cromwell's Ironsides and the Scottish Covenanters derived an unconquerable courage, and an all-conquering power, from their belief that they were of the elect.'

Father, after all this, must have been feeling anything but one of the elect. Apparently his total rejection of her doctrine, and his hidden but hot impatience that a woman from the Dene should be lecturing *him*, would have numbered him, in her view, among the damned; but he said only, 'If I may say so, Mrs.——' but here again, in the course of this warm argumentation, he had forgotten her name and was in no mood to go digging for it, so left it wherever it lay—'If I may say so, the fact that the few chosen derive some virtue from this doctrine seems only to suggest to me that it is bought at too great a price, namely the damnation of millions of their fellow men'—and for once in my life I was in eager agreement with my father and longing to say so. I would have liked to shout, 'Hear, hear! Oh, hear, hear!' but I had to keep quiet, deciding to tell him of my full support in the evening.

Mrs. Wayburn didn't support him at all. She said, 'It's not for you to decide. It's for God.' She dared to say this to Father.

I can't remember that Raney or I contributed one word to the debate. Raney, from the other side of the table, just looked at me once or twice with a tight smile as of sympathy; which pleased me because I thought it meant she would be more on my side than her mother's. I was beginning to know that, though strict parents had built in her the habits of a dutiful daughter, henceforth it was I who would come first. As for Mr. Wayburn, he followed his usual custom which, in his words, was to 'leave it to Mother when the mood is on her'. And the mood was certainly on her now. She was still in spate when we returned up the stairs to the drawing-room. One of Father's punctilios was that a man must always precede a woman up the stairs or down the stairs (presumably lest she fell up them or down them) so now he went ahead and she came behind, casting around him like an enveloping cloud a further state-ment of the things that belonged to his salvation—or damnation.

When we were all sitting down again in the drawing-room, the talk drifted to smaller matters but I could see that these were not less boring to Father and that he was aching for his guests to go, so that he could escape with Hamish to his study and find peace again in a book. Had it been today, he would have snatched furtive glances at a wrist-watch, but he had only a big hunter-watch in a vest pocket at the end of two festoons of heavy gold chain, and miserable though he was, his politeness would not allow him to bring this massively suggestive chrono-meter out of its depths and into the light. ('I hope I know how to behave like a gentleman.')

But when at last Mr. Wayburn said, 'Well, Mother, I'm afraid we must be going if we're to be in time for Evening Prayer; I'm afraid we'll 'ave to make ourselves scarce now, Mr. O'Murry,' I have never seen Father get up so quickly. Nonetheless he told the last of his lies courteously. 'Oh, I'm sorry. I wish you could have stayed a little longer. But I won't keep you if you have to get away.'

Having seen the family off his doorsteps and out of his garden he went quickly back to his study; and when I dashed up to tell him that I would be walking home with the Way-burns, he was already deep in the consolation of his arm-chair. He just looked up at me and sighed, 'Oh, my God!'

§

Poor Mrs. Wayburn further destroyed herself in Father's eyes, socially at least, by a kindly meant action. The very day after this 'ghastly theological tea', as I called it, she wrote a letter to him thanking him (perhaps with some sense of his social super-iority) for 'letting dear Stewart bring Mr. Wayburn and I and Ireen to tea with you and for giving us such a truly pleasant time'. Whether it was socially correct to write a letter of thanks after so small an occasion as a drinking of tea is not the point; the point is that she not only got his name wrong on the envelope (which no man likes) but addressed it to a 'Mr.

O'Murray' instead of to 'Augustus O'Murry, Esq.' or at least to 'A. O'Murry, Esq.'

Father looked at that 'Mr. O'Murry' and said, 'That's the way you address a letter to your grocer.' Then, for fear of hurting me, he added helplessly, 'I suppose she means well.'

14

Hadley Wood
and Aldith's Garden

On that Sunday when I spent a whole godly Sabbath in
Raney's home, Mr. Wayburn had said, 'If only Mr. O'Murry
—I mean Stoo'art—had brought his bike I'd suggest their
going to Kew Gardens or somewhere. Bring your bike next
time, Stoo.' I had seized on this invitation, and many afternoons we had cycled together to green places—to Kew Gardens
and the Old Deer Park; to Wimbledon Common and Richmond Park, there to lie together under great trees by a water's
side or deep in a feathery slope of bracken.

Usually this was on a Sunday afternoon because Raney
helped her father in the shop on Saturdays, but gradually Mr.
Wayburn, whose heart had grown warm 'to them two', decided to set her free sometimes on a Saturday afternoon so that
we could go farther afield. 'You can trust 'er to 'im, Mother.'

Among the things with which I'd loved to indoctrinate
Raney, such as the love of favourite poems or a sense of history
where it brooded over the Thames or an interest in birds other
than our London sparrows—among the things which she
caught like a happy fever from me was the craving of a
London-born and London-bound child (as we both were) for the
real green country, for truly rustic and pastoral fields that knew
nothing of the asphalt paths, iron railings, and flower-beds—
however well drilled and paraded they might be—in our London parks.

So sometimes I would spend a few shillings on fares from
Victoria or King's Cross to the nearest pastoral places where
we could see cows, smell cow-dung, and learn the flowers that
ran wild along the hedgerows. In some cottage that offered
'Teas' we would sit in parlour or garden eating thick slices of

bread thickly buttered, doughnuts whose hearts we would always enlarge with additional jam, and home-made cakes with local cream, while we smelt the honeysuckle in the garden or the heavy scent of lime-trees falling like an invisible blessing on the afternoon. One such place to which we returned more than once was a cottage at Ditchling under the Sussex Downs. After tea we would wander up on to Ditchling Beacon.

But usually we had not the time for so long an 'outing' as this, and at last, on the advice of Uncle Douglas (now loyally and jovially interested) we discovered a place of sylvan beauty to which we gave the whole of our love: Hadley Wood. Only ten miles from London, it was a wild woodland crossed by sun-spattered glades or twilit lanes under giant and over-arching trees. So it was then, and so it still is now, when I sometimes wander back to it and its memories.

Hastening there, we loved to know that our wheels were on the Great North Road. Signpost after signpost said 'To the North', 'To Hatfield and the North'; and as with a wand these words 'The North' touched the whole metalled road with romance. We picked up the Great North Road at the Angel in Islington and thence went speeding—for the traffic was as nothing compared with today—through Holloway and Highgate; through Finchley Common and Hadley Green to Monken Hadley and the woods. With my bicycle beside hers, I would remind her that Dick Whittington had heard Bow bells at 'I'git'; that Finchley Common had been the highwayman's paradise, its stretch of highway known as 'the most dangerous road in Britain', for it was here that Dick Turpin and Jack Shepherd 'touched the mails to the North'; and indeed it was here on Finchley Common, his favoured hunting ground, that poor Dick was caught at last by the Bow Street Runners. We pictured the mail coaches and the post-chaises driving fast along this ploughed-up country road, the postilions with their eyes wide open for danger, their powdered ladies gazing apprehensively through the chaise-windows, and the guards on the mail coaches with their blunderbusses at the ready, while the coachmen in their many capes urged on their horses with the whip.

This in Finchley as we wheeled through the pavements and houses of north suburban London.

§

I remember one early August day when we took the Great North Road for Monken Hadley. It must have been 1913 and we, young and happy, were still unaware, unsuspecting, of what the next August had in keeping for us. In that vigil year the road, soon after East Finchley, became a twisted and leafy lane with open country on either side and in the distance high hills wearing thick forests for their crowns. Here the white sign-posts still thrilled us with their poem, 'The North'. It might be England's premier road, later to receive the splendid accolade, 'A.1', but here it was but a narrow hedgebound affair until it drew near to High Barnet. Half-way through High Barnet we left this queen of the roads for two undistinguished sisters that led to Hadley Green and Monken Hadley. In this village we dismounted from our bicycles and wheeled them into the churchyard to 'park' them (an ancient word but unknown to the commonalty then) behind the big church and out of the quiet road's sight, sure that they would be safe in this walled and gated sanctuary. Then, hand-in-hand, we strolled the few hundred yards to our beloved Hadley Wood. So spacious was this woodland, so many the darkened aisles between old and mighty trees, so surely did each narrow avenue seem to lead to some haunt of mystery, that, even though this was a Saturday afternoon, we could often, as we wandered, be lost and alone with little sense of other wanderers around us. Strange how few people from the neighbourhood sought these tree-girt isolations for their Saturday rest. Did we pass any, or see any far off, they were usually another boy and girl with their fingers linked like ours.

For a while we just walked on together along the glades, our feet rustling the dried and powdering leaves or breaking the fallen twigs beneath our feet. Sometimes the glade was an avenue of beeches whose outreaching branches spread an awning over our heads so interwoven that it was but scantily perforated by the afternoon's sun. Every forest tree was among this congregation here—elms, and oaks and ashes, chestnuts, whitebeams and black poplars, these last with their leaves for ever twinkling, though there seemed never a breath of wind to stir them. Ever and again a glade would open out and become a small clearing which, since the sunlight could get at it, looked as we approached like a pond of bottled light.

To such a small enclosure we came at last. It seemed to be in the very heart of the wood, so deep was its silence, so lost the murmur of distant traffic or the occasional echoing of children's voices. Nor was there birdsong anywhere though, as I suggested pretentiously, we might have hoped to hear a missel thrush, a dipper or a wren. 'Or even in August a sedge-warbler.'

'What on earth's a sedge-warbler? Oh, I know nothing,' Raney bewailed. '*Nothing*. Why was I born?'

'It's only in the last year or two,' I comforted her, 'that I've learned the difference between a wren and a starling, or which birds are kind enough to sing all the year round. And which are happy to stay with us instead of going south for the winter like our bloated rich.'

'But I've never *wanted* to know till you made me. That's what's so awful.'

'We all wake up at different times,' I suggested. 'Whether to birdsong or great music or anything else. And it generally needs someone else to start us awake.'

'Still,' she objected, 'I was already nineteen before you came.'

'Chick,' I said, 'stop worrying. All the desires must have been there in you, or they'd never have come so blazingly alight at a touch.'

'Well, go on touching them,' she said. 'I want to come blazingly alight all over, please.'

Unlinking hands, we sat ourselves down on a broad bed of brown and cinnamon leaves; I spread my arms in invitation, and Rancy, as it seemed to me, threw herself into them with a breathless acceptance and desire. As I lay back on the leaves she sank against my breast as if her desire was to drown in my love.

I don't know how long we lay clasped together; it may have been an hour or more; why end an ecstasy so perfect that it seems to have passed out of time and to belong to some order that has nothing to do with 'every day'? There in that sun-speckled covert of Hadley Wood, I learned again and again through the wordless hours that at last, and beyond doubt, I did truly love someone more than myself; and it was this exultant knowledge, together with the recurring memory of her father's words, 'You can trust 'er to 'im, Mother,' that saved my unbroken caresses from adventuring too far. Twenty-four now, and still virgin (this was 1913), after too many years of merely dreaming about love, I was quickened as I lay there to a fever of passion; all the dreams lay distilled into this hour; but when at last we decided that we must rise and make for home, leaving paradise behind, I was glad that I had held the fever in check, leaning always away from her till it quietened, and so done nothing to hurt her.

Did I not love her better than myself?

§

My happiest memory in that year '13, indeed the loveliest memory in all my youth, is of a September day in Aldith's country garden.

Aldith, her first shock at my selection of Raney quickly overcome, was now, in her rebellious way—as were Uncle Douglas and, to be sure, Elsa and Josef in their kitchen—the complete ally of Raney and me. Soon after telling her about it all I had arranged a meeting for her with Raney, and Aldith throughout the meeting, probably thinking of the Dene and its disrepute, positively exuded friendliness and goodwill, all of it as easy as she could make it, with never a trace of condescension, but more as if Raney were the daughter of the local curate instead of a small shopkeeper in a suspect lane. By this time Raney's grammar was as good as—indeed rather better than Aldith's own, for Aldith would never listen to me as Raney did, and still less to Father—and Raney's accent had lost, or was losing, the affected refinement of her mother's. Afterwards, out of Raney's hearing, Aldith whispered to me, 'Stew, I think she's

rather beautiful and perfectly sweet. I suspect that, thanks to
her parents' silly religion, which may be utterly absurd but has
its points when it's a matter of bringing up a pretty daughter—
I suspect that, strange as it may seem, she's both pretty and
good. I've decided to think that it's all rather wonderful—
picking up a girl from the Dene, snatching a brand from the
burning, as it were. I'm with you in this, Stew. I think
it's delightful and must be thoroughly upsetting for the old
man.'

I lost sight of her for many months after this, but simply had
to look her up so as to tell her about the Wayburns' visit to
Dunkerry Crescent and to describe for her 'the ghastly theological tea'. She was overjoyed with the description of it,
exclaiming 'My poor, dear, darling old father. But, Stew, what
fun! Oh, I do take my hat off to the Bonny Earl o' Murray.
Who'd have believed it?'

Again it was months before she arrived one evening at Dunkerry Crescent, and after a chat with Father in his study—
and with Hamish—she came to my room and shut its door
softly with a conspiratorial air.

'Tsh . . . !' she whispered, a finger lifted. '*He* mustn't hear,
but I've an idea. You're still in love with Raney, aren't
you?'

'God, yes.'

'Well, it's ages since you've come to see us in Kent'—she and
Jack Fellbright had a week-end cottage in Kent as well as their
pleasant villa in Ealing—'ages since you've taken the least
interest in it—or in us—but that's what being in love does, I
suppose—so I'll tell you what's going to happen. You're going
to persuade her silly parents to let you bring her down to us for
the week-end. Jack'll take us all down in Grizelda'—Grizelda
was their Morris-Cowley touring car—'after he's left his office
about five, and he'll bring us back on Sunday evening. I'd like
Jack to see her: I had, I must admit, a job to convert him from
some dislike of what you were up to—the news proved rather a
shaker for the poor man—you know how it is: he's Winchester
and New College himself—and Harrow and Eton are all right
for him, and Cheltenham Ladies' College is possible, but a

board school in Scrubb Lane'—she shook her head doubtfully —'that's extremely difficult for an old Wykehamist, or whatever they call themselves, to take—you did say "Scrubb Lane", didn't you? However, he did say at last, "Well as long as they're happy, I'm satisfied"—so different from our dear father. Jack's almost totally converted to Raney now, and when he sees how pretty she is, that'll put the finishing touch on it—you know what men are. D'you think they'll let her come?'

'I doubt it. Sit down, do. And have a fag. There's their Meeting on Sunday mornings and a Gospel Service in the evening——'

'Oh, but she can pray in Kent. She can even pray in Canterbury Cathedral which is only five miles away. Jack'll take her there in Grizelda.'

'They wouldn't approve of that at all—at least the mamma wouldn't; she doesn't hold with the C. of E. or cathedrals or bishops or such things.'

'Doesn't she? Doesn't she really? I always thought everybody more or less approved of Canterbury Cathedral, even if they never went near it. I thought they thought it good for other people. Religious types.'

'Not Mrs. Wayburn. She can get quite hot about what she calls the misnamed Church of England.'

'Fancy that!'

'As far as I can see, she holds that most of its members are on the short list for damnation.'

'Oh, damn: that's a nuisance. But there's sure to be some mission house in Canterbury. In a place like Canterbury there are always heaps of religions, each one probably sillier than the last. I'll find her one and she can pray there. I'll go with her and pray too, if you like. She mustn't know that you've a disgracefully irreligious sister. Thank God there's always Abel and Augusta. I hope you work Abel and Augusta for all they're worth.'

'I do, you bet—but I keep their High Church goings-on well out of sight, and they're still C. of E. I fancy they're just saved in Mrs. Wayburn's eyes by being missionaries.'

'It all seems extremely mad to me. I mean: as long as you pray——'

'Exactly. That goes for me too. But, after all, the R.C.s have been no less exclusive. You remember: *Extra ecclesiam nulla salus.*'

'Again, please?'

'*Extra ecclesiam nulla salus.*'

'Latin, isn't it?'

'Yes. Outside the Church there is no salvation.'

'Well, did you ever? The way people go on!'

'Quite so. But such are the Wayburns in the Dene.'

'Well, tell them that we'll see she prays somewhere, and that your best-loved sister is going to pray with her.'

'I can quite imagine that Raney wouldn't at all mind a holiday from so much prayer. Public prayer, at any rate. She can say her little prayers in her room.'

'Oh, yes—and by the way, make it clear to them that we have two spare rooms. The children'll be back at school, thank God. I wouldn't want the old dears to think anything——'

I laughed and bragged, 'There's no fear of that. They've a perfect trust in me.'

'Have they really? Now fancy that. Then I'm sure they'll trust a deeply religious sister like me.'

'They'll let her come, after a few passionate demands from Raney. The odd thing about that household is that the lady is the power in the spiritual regions but her old man is the power in domestic matters. And he's easily won where Raney's happiness is concerned.'

'Well, that's fine. Look, we'll bring her back on the Sunday evening right to the door of their shop in—in whatever impossible street it is your lady-love lives in.'

'Mortress Lane,' I supplied. 'Hollen Dene, W.'

'Good God!' she exclaimed with a momentary lapse into her original shock. 'Well, try and make it soon, while the garden is still lovely.'

'And just so that everybody may be on the happiest possible terms in the garden,' I offered as a last word, 'let me tell you something. Raney's properly fallen for Father. She thinks he's sweet.'

'She does? Sweet? The Bonny Earl o' Murray? Good heavens.'

'She thinks him a lot handsomer than me.'

'Well, she could be right there.'

'And I suggest that she'll fall at once for Jack.'

'Which wouldn't surprise me. Most girls do. It's extraordinary.'

'I know Raney, and my view is that she'll think him sweet.'

'Wherein she wouldn't be altogether wrong, Stew. So he is—up to a point, though I say it myself. Anyhow, he's a marvellous gardener.'

§

And eight days later we were walking in that garden. It was a small garden deep in the country with all the low green hills of Kent heaving towards it, and never a house on one of them but only cows and sheep. Thus it seemed to lie in a hollow where the tossed hills met, but really it was on the slope of a gentle hill that had begun to climb. Out of sight along the valley road was the tiny village to which it belonged: Little Ebbing.

This was the Saturday morning after our arrival in the deepening dusk of the night before. Aldith and Jack were leading us from flower-bed to flower-bed, all tall with varied blooms, and telling us two town-bred ignoramuses the name of each flower or shrub, while Raney rhapsodized both in politeness and because she was really transported by the beauty of it all. This morning I was no longer the teacher of Raney but a mere pupil at her side; Jack was the master of the class, with some less scholarly help from Aldith.

Both were behaving splendidly. Aldith was still holding from her manner and tone any hint of awareness that her guest was a working-class girl; and as for Jack—well, Aldith had not been wrong in suggesting that Raney's face would wipe off the map with one touch all the Dene and its wickedness. The cottage too, you might say, was behaving well: small, simply furnished for week-ends only, and unserved by a maid, it could not overawe anyone, as our Dunkerry Crescent and Elsa had done.

'Jack's the gardener, Raney,' Aldith said. 'He had the enormous advantage of spending all his boyhood in the country instead of behind the pavement of a London street where the only flowers we ever saw were the scarlet geraniums, white marguerites and blue lobelias, which seemed the flowers *de rigueur* for every window-box in London—red, white and blue, in honour, I suppose of England and Victoria and King Edward. Oh yes, roses; I knew roses; and dahlias—sometimes. Our father was a devoted gardener but compared with Jack an oddly uninspired one, largely limited to roses in the summer and dahlias in the autumn.'

'He was also very good at turf-edges,' I assured the company. 'I'd say he loved them better than the roses. It was death to any of us, even Mother, if we trod on one and spoiled it.'

'My God, how true,' said Aldith.

'None of you could have been as ignorant as I was,' Raney insisted. 'There are no window-boxes in Mortress Lane. There never were. There were a few flowers in Hollen Dene Park, but nobody ever told us what they were, and I don't think any of us were ever interested enough to ask. It's like Stewart and the birds. He knows them all. I only knew a sparrow till he showed me the others.'

'And there, my dear, you're no different from me,' Aldith comforted. 'I was almost completely blind too. As for the smaller birds, I didn't know any of them till Jack put a bird-table right in front of our dining-room window, and they all came regularly to call on us.'

'Oh, I want to live in the country and do exactly that. You've absolutely converted me. Mum's always talking about conversion; I don't think I've ever experienced the one she means, but this is certainly one of a different kind. It's terrific. I think I want to live here in Little Ebbing somewhere.'

'There you are, Jack.' Aldith turned to him. 'Aren't you proud of having converted a lady? What to, I'm not quite sure. But to something.'

'I don't know about that,' said Jack, 'but I know it's a joy to show a garden to someone as enthusiastic as Raney.'

'So don't you worry, Raney dear, about only now being able

to distinguish the flowers and the birds,' said Aldith. 'Always remember it was just the same with Stewart and I'—for despite Father's many fulminations against this deplorable use of 'I' instead of 'me', she had never shaken herself free of it. Or possibly her continuous use of the abomination was an unconscious part of her lifelong rebellion against Father.

I forbore to correct her grammar (though I was my father's son), but I was hoping Raney hadn't observed the lapse because, though I often (like Father) railed at her for this error, she retained her childhood devotion to it and all too frequently reproduced it.

'These,' said Jack, able at last to get a word in, and pointing to bright orange flowers, 'are nasturtiums, in case you don't know.'

'Oh, I did just know that,' Aldith allowed.

'*I* didn't,' admitted Raney from the Dene, and I thought that the whole character of her unlovely streets was expressed in these words.

Jack moved on from tobacco plants, crimson and yellow, to rock roses, yellow too; to tansies, golden, and violas of every hue; to hollyhocks, eight-foot tall, and dahlias of all sizes, shapes, heights and colours. Over the dahlias and a massive buddleia the tortoise-shell and wood-white butterflies were loitering and drifting, while the bees slipped like sneak-thieves into every open doorway to take what was there. After a while Jack asked, 'I hope you've noticed the autumn scent in the garden?'

Alas, our London-dulled nostrils had not done so, and we had to admit this, though declaring truthfully that we were fully alive to it, now that he had drawn our attention to it.

'Well, give me the sources of it. Come now. Analyse it for me. From where and from what is it coming?'

We sniffed and sniffed at the warm air around us, but of course this exercise he'd set for his two pupils was far beyond them.

'Try again. Can't you detect that it's the very breath of the roses . . . the buddleia . . . the honeysuckle . . . the yellow broom. . .?'

184

He had only to say this for me to observe that the bees, pilfering busily from the purple flowers of the buddleia, distilled their honeyed scent into this bright and tranquil morning.

'Oh, I shall never be happy till I have a garden like this,' Raney sighed, as we left the buddleia loud with bees. 'I wonder if I ever shall. We have only a back-yard in Mortress Lane. No, of course I shan't.'

'Who can say?' Aldith laid an affectionate hand on her shoulder. 'One never knows.'

And I guessed what Aldith was wondering then.

§

I often wonder whether there is any kinship between the fascination stirred in me by streets like those of the Dene, where there are homes which may house criminals or have seen a murder done, and a similar fascination, curiously stirring and always welcome, which rises in me at the sight of any dereliction, be it an old house once lived in happily but now with windows broken and a manifest desolation behind them, or a garden once loved but now gone back to the wild, or the broken piers of a splendid gateway with the once proud drive beyond them almost buried under moss and lichen and weeds.

I don't know; but beyond the hazel hedge that bordered the north side of Aldith's garden in Little Ebbing there ran, parallel with it, a lane—or, rather, that which had once been a lane. Somehow or other, none of us knew how—possibly because of some new and better track near-by—it had been long disused and become a narrow stretch of wilderness. From its one-time opening on to the country road, and all the way between its two hedges long abandoned by hedgers and ditchers and given over to riot, its tangle of tall weeds and new undergrowths over-ran the old cart-ruts so that they could barely be seen. This narrow entangled wilderness continued to its end—which did not exist. Did not exist because the hedgerow trees and the hedges themselves stopped abruptly, and all the wild weeds seemed to have melted long since into an open field which the champing cattle kept clean and close-trimmed.

The death of the lane was stressed at both ends; literally at its opening by a four-ways signpost with three of its arms pointing north, west and south and its fourth arm, which once pointed up the lane, now removed at the shoulder; symbolically at the other end by the skeleton of a giant oak, slain on a day by Jack Lightning, which now stood on the meadow at the lane's mouth with its huge grey bole inclined and its empty grey branches spread wide as in a plea against this fate.

Inevitably all this riot and loss was laden for me with the romance of dereliction and desolation, and on the afternoon of this day in Aldith's country home I took Raney along 'the lane that had died', hoping she would share the spell it cast upon me. And besides a desire that she should feel with me the tragic poetry in dereliction, I had another and weightier reason for wanting to get her into the privacy of a dead lane. Those words of Aldith's, 'One never knows. Who can say?' had built in me a final, exciting, joyous decision.

Our walk (if an obstacle-race can be so called) along the lane was a torment of laughter and merry cursings—even blasphemies, but these from me only, Raney contenting herself with 'Oh gosh!' and 'Oh law!' and 'Oh dear, oh *dear*!' Directly we left the lane's opening where it met the public road, we entered into a half-darkness because the sycamores, limes and chestnuts mingled their branches above us and the undisciplined hedges often copied these friendly exchanges entwining their branches too, at their lower level. As these hedges were mostly bramble and thorn, they caught at us as we bent low to pass beneath the woven network. And not only the trees and the hedgerows resisted us, but the whole anarchy around our feet of grasses, weeds, ferns, and self-sown saplings, seldom less than knee-high and often waist-high. And meanwhile the hidden cart-ruts under this mad vegetation clawed at our shoes and tried to wrest them from us.

The farther we battled on, the narrower became the passageway and the greater the darkness because the hedges, as if realizing that they were now out of sight of all humans and could be as wild as they liked, had advanced their occupation of the ground below us and the air above. But at last we emerged mysteriously, suddenly, into the open day. Trees and hedges were no more, and all the disorder and riot had changed into its opposite: a clean, spacious meadow cropped into a green tidiness by the grazing cattle.

'What now?' asked Raney. 'You don't mean to say that we've got to go back through all that?'

'I certainly do.'

'But there's the cottage. I'm not afraid of cows, as long as they're not bulls, so couldn't we cross the field and climb over Aldith's fence?'

'Oh no, that wouldn't do. That would be unladylike for you. It's a high fence. Think what mamma would say. We go back the way we came.'

I had been so obsessed by our exacting and frustrated walk, so conceitedly proud as I pointed out the small flowers that peeped within the general confusion—the blue speedwell and the white bindweed working a troubled way through the entanglements like us—that I had not yet used the lane for my secret purpose. 'Come along. Back to the highroad again. Through the lane.'

'But what about my clothes? I haven't got many of them. I'm only a poor girl. And my shoes? And then there's my hair.'

'The shoes and the hair'll survive—the hair, in fact, looks rather better for a little disarray. Looks charming, to tell the truth. As for the clothes'—and here, an inveterate quoter wherever I might be with her, I could but recite '"A sweet disorder in the dress Kindles in clothes a wantonness".'

Raney could only shrug and spread her palms at her side in the traditional gestures of feminine despair at the puerilities of men. And back into the lane we went, into a temporary life of trammels and troubles and thwartings. But during this laboured journey I could not look at any flower or curse any obstacle because my heart was racing and thumping, and even my stomach was deflated by a mixture of disquiet and delight at the thought of what I was about to do. We tore onward through the nettles and docks, with the beech-mast cracking under our feet; and now we saw the sunlight again where the lane opened on to the road. It was now that I said, 'Darling, stop. Stop one minute.'

I wanted to speak before we stood on the road and in the full daylight.

She stopped three yards from the roadway. So did I.

'Raney?' I began.

She looked up at me. 'Yes?'

'Raney'—but I couldn't go on. I stood and stared at the sunlit road. I knew, as I stood there, that the greatest moment of my twenty-four years was upon me—here at the lane's end.

'Raney?'

'Yes?' Still looking up.

And I looked down at a bewilderment in her eyes. 'Please, Raney, I want you to marry me. Will you? I want you to so much. I love you very dearly.'

She only continued to look up at me with what seemed a blind bafflement in her eyes. She did not speak at once, and I could think of no further words.

Then she said only, 'Did you *mean* that?'

'Mean what?'

'Mean what you said? That you wanted to marry me.'

'I have never meant anything so surely in my life.'

'But you . . . *can't* mean it.'

'I'm sorry, my darling, but I do. With all my heart I do. I've been dreaming of asking you for days and days now. Oh no, for months and months.'

She picked up my fingers and held them. 'But . . . I'm not your class. I'm not Aldith's class. Or Jack's. They're being terribly nice to me, but we all know that.'

'*I* do not know it.'

'Yes, you do. Of course you do. You must. Just think of your father.'

'I don't know it and I won't know it. I only know that in a hundred ways you are better than I am. I know myself, you see, and I know that I'd be the lucky one if you'll only say Yes. I can't agree with your parents' religion, as you know, but I can see clearly that it's made a better thing of you than my father's has made of me. Raney, please, I want you for my wife—I want this more than anything in the world. The very thought of it is so lovely that it makes me feel almost sick with happiness. It's so tremendous I can hardly bear to think of it.'

She pressed hard on my fingers which she was holding. 'Darling, say it again. Will you say it again?'

'Say which and what?'

'What you first said. That you want me to marry you.'

'Raney, I want you for my wife. And I promise I'm going to try to be worthy of you.'

She threw herself on to my breast, and I caught her close while she sobbed and sobbed, her heart beating against mine. The sobbing was quick and convulsive; when she lifted her face to look at me, the eyes were dulled and awash with tears. 'I can't believe that this has happened. . . . I've never believed that anything like this would happen to me. I don't believe it now. Oh, my darling, if you really mean it—but you can't! You can't!'

'By God, I mean it.' As if to confirm this I stroked the amber hair.

'Of course I'd marry you. Of course, of course, of course. And I do know that if anyone has ever loved anybody in this world, I love you.' Again she looked up into my eyes. 'Please know that. Oh, I'll be a good wife to you. I promise. I promise.'

Strange that just then a car should speed along the country road, past the opening to the lane, and no one in it should know what was happening within a few feet of them. No one knew that all the world had turned to beauty, under a golden light; for two young people standing there.

I was saying triumphantly, 'It's settled. It's settled. Raney, it's settled. We marry. We marry. I feel mad with happiness.' And I drew her a little way into the lane for the embrace that would confirm a troth, and the long sealing kiss.

When we broke apart, she took my hand again and, now in control of herself, said with a smile, 'Please don't tell Aldith yet. Or Jack. I couldn't face them yet. I'm sure they're not ready for such news—naturally they're not, however kind they are—but perhaps, oh, perhaps, they'll get used to it. Prepare them for it gradually, won't you? And your father too. I want him to love me. Don't tell him for some time, will you; and I won't tell Mum and Dad at once. But it's real; it's *real*, isn't it?'

'It's real, my sweet. Nothing was ever more real for me.'

'Then may we keep it to ourselves for quite a long while? I'd rather it was like that. Oh, kiss me again. I've never believed I was going to be as happy as this. Do I believe it now? I don't think so. Kiss me again so that I can believe it. That I may know it's real.'

'It's real and our secret,' I promised. 'For as long as you like. Till you tell me that I can tell it to the world.' And this time I kissed her calmly as the affianced do. 'It'll be rather wonderful today and tomorrow, knowing what's in our hearts, but neither of them, Aldith or Jack, knowing it. Come along; back we go with our secret.'

§

So we spent the rest of those two days with neither of us showing by look or by word anything of the memory aglow and even on fire, in our hearts. Only as we sat side by side in the tiny meals-room did Raney's fingers feel for mine under the table, or mine for hers, to refresh the memory of what had happened in the lane. Once or twice when we were upstairs and out of our hostess's sight (Jack was at work in the garden) we sealed the betrothal again with a long embrace and a multiplication of kisses.

On the Saturday evening Aldith lamented to Raney, 'I'm afraid there are not half as many religions in Canterbury as I imagined, but I'll go with you tomorrow to any sort of chapel you'd like. To . . . to . . .' but just as 'Onward, Christian Soldiers' was the only hymn I could name at a pistol's point, so Aldith now could think of no other non-Anglican chapel-goers than the Baptists—'to a Baptist chapel, perhaps, if that would suit you, Raney. I'd go with you; and Stewart too, I'm sure.'

'Of course,' I endorsed. 'A Baptist chapel every time.'

'But where do you and Jack usually go?' Raney asked, as a guest should.

If a stymie is a moment when your opponent's ball blocks your approach to the comfortable hole on the putting green, then this was a real stymie for Aldith, because the true answer was 'Nowhere'. For my sake she didn't want to admit such heathenism as this and, having once in her life attended some centenary celebration in Canterbury Cathedral, she dodged around the difficulty, and away from any lies, by saying, 'Well, there's Canterbury Cathedral, of course. The top church not only of the Church of England but of the Anglican Communion all over the world. In America even.'

Then, to my delight, Raney exclaimed, 'Oh, but I'd love to go to a service in Canterbury Cathedral. Canterbury of all places! Please could we?' Coming down in the car, she had seen the Cathedral's mighty towers rising in their pride and untroubled assurance above the city's roofs and had gasped in admiration. 'Oh, do let's go to the Cathedral. Could we? Please. I'd love it of all things.' Perhaps these words expressed little more than interest and curiosity, but I saw them also as a proof of her readiness to give herself to me and to my ways. 'Yes, Canterbury. Please. If we can.'

'And it *is* the place,' Jack reminded her, coming to his wife's aid, 'to which pilgrims have been coming from all over the world for more than seven hundred years.'

'Oh, I must go there. I simply must. I'll be a pilgrim.'

On the Sunday evening Jack motored us back to London so as to be at his office in the morning, and Aldith had the grace to sit in front with him, pretending that she was less likely to be sick there when Jack, 'a completely unscrupulous driver, is grossly exceeding the speed limit and Grizelda is bumping and leaping about'; and thus giving the back seats to Raney and me where any affectionate business with our hands would be out of view. All the way to Canterbury Raney was, as she declared, 'thrilled' to know that we were on the old Dover Road— 'England's No. 2 road', said Jack—and therefore second only to our loved and adopted Great North Road. When in the late twilight we passed again the Cathedral's towers brooding over a quiet old city, she leaned towards the car's window and said, 'Good-bye, Canterbury. I love you. Good-bye,' and she watched till the towers could no longer be seen. I suspected that she was really watching the fields of Kent pass by, and saying a loving good-bye to its Little Ebbing where there was a scented garden and a wild abandoned lane.

15

'Theophrastus'

During the few months before this secret engagement in a dead
lane my career as a free-lance journalist—thanks to Uncle
Douglas's tireless training and probably to some backstairs
intriguing by him—had begun to prosper, even to flourish,
if not as remarkably as his own had done, at least in a way far
above my first expectations. Editors had begun to commission
me—actually to *commission* me—to write feature articles on
What the Rising Generation Thinks, under such titles as 'The Feet
of the Young Men' or 'Youth Knocks at the Door'. And it was
not only the editors of Portwith journals who invited these con-
tributions; gradually I had established enough of a name to be
no longer obliged to offer my pieces for acceptance or rejection but, on the contrary, able to sit back and await invitations
—though always accepting them promptly, because I could
not believe that my position, however bright just now, was
other than precarious.

At first I had signed my pieces with an uninspired 'Stewart
O'Murry' or just an 'S.M.', but now I adopted (it was Uncle
Douglas's suggestion) a single resounding and memorable
nom-de-guerre; and this, approved by my mentor, was, if you
please, 'Theophrastus'.

(For the benefit of the unlearned, and to demonstrate, after
fifty years, that there was much of a young man's classical
'showing off', not to say a spice of youthful bumptiousness, in
my choice of this pen-name, I will quote the great Lemprière
himself, from his Classical Dictionary: 'Diogenes has enumer-
ated the titles of above two hundred treatises which [Theo-
phrastus] wrote with great eloquence and copiousness. Among
these are his history of stones, his treatise on plants, on the
winds, on the signs of fair weather, and his Characters, an
excellent moral treatise begun in the ninety-ninth year of his

age. He died, loaded with years and infirmities, in the hundred-and-seventh year of his age, lamenting the shortness of life.')

The fee for my first accepted article had been three guineas; this was now enlarging steadily to ten and twelve guineas for a thousand words in the more distinguished but less popular journals and becoming considerably handsomer in the cheaper newspapers with their ever-increasing circulation. During this second year of walking out with Raney and writing at home as 'Theophrastus' I had seen articles over this arresting and, as I hoped, adhesive name in those long-forgotten papers, the *Standard*, the green *Westminster Gazette* and the old pink *Globe*. In the same year, '13, I received a letter from an agency I'd never heard of, Hamerson Brothers, offering to secure commissions for me if I was willing to be their client. Uncle Douglas recommended consent, and soon, strangely soon, the commissions came dropping through our front door, and articles or stories by 'Theophrastus' appeared in the old *Strand, Pearson's,* and *Pall Mall* magazines—good magazines long dead now. They were shown to Father, you can be sure, carried to him in my hands; and he saw them with some incredulity.

Then within less than four weeks of that betrothal in the lane, almost as if Providence wanted to bless our covenant together, there happened something which, in a single hour, transformed my whole position in the world. So much so that, when it was over, I could only pace and pace my room, unable to believe for joy. Was I now a man with a settled profession, comfortably if not, as yet, extravagantly paid? Was I a man who could dream of building his own home and—here was the thought that upset the rhythm of my heart and kept it trembling with anticipations too wonderful for ease—marrying Raney far sooner than seemed possible yesterday? Raney from the Dene—let the world gape and condemn and cry 'Fool' as it liked—Raney as my wife, in my home from morning till nightfall; in our common home together; in my arms whenever I longed to take her; in my bed. Dreaming, dreaming, there in my room, I paced back and forth from door to window, or halted to look out at Dunkerry Crescent without once seeing it.

Our home together would be in one of the old London villages whose heart at least, though encircled by Victorian London, was still beautiful: Chelsea or Richmond or Highgate (because of the Great North Road). A London village because it would be as well to be near the offices of publishers and editors and all the chatter of Fleet Street and the town. This would be necessary for a writer on topical matters (we had no dreams of a private motor-car in '13). Also I would wish to be near my club, for I was resolved to have a famous London club like Uncle Douglas, say the Savage or the Savile or the Garrick; Uncle Douglas belonged to all three of these. He *would*. But we would not be imprisoned within the London bricks, as hitherto both of us had been; we would have a week-end cottage, perhaps among Kentish hills like Aldith and Jack's, and perhaps near to them since they now loved us. And on holidays I would take Raney to Paris: I saw her walking with me in the Gardens of the Tuileries, in the Place de la Concorde, and over the bridges towards all the history and romance of the Left Bank. Or there was Greece—why not Greece one day?—with Raney, now Raney the well-informed and wise, but still my creation, because this was what she rejoiced to be; Raney standing with me on the Acropolis at Athens and gazing at the Parthenon and the Propylaea, while I expounded to her (not without some self-esteem) that here were the seeds of all subsequent architecture for another thousand years—the inspiration of St. Paul's, the Mansion House, the Banqueting House, and Wren's Greenwich Hospital which we'd passed one afternoon on the river.

So the dreams.

§

This is what had happened.

On a morning in mid-October I received an invitation to lunch from the editor of Lord Portwith's greatest paper, the *Daily World*. I supposed this was no more than the friendly meal which an editor would offer, infrequently, to one of his occasional contributors, or a publisher to one of the minor authors on his list. Certainly the invitation was to one of

London's most expensive restaurants, but this was well within the pattern of these mere courtesy luncheons.

I had never met this editor, though a few formal letters had passed between us, in one of which he had been considerate enough to tell a young writer that he had 'much liked' an article of his.

Arriving at the restaurant, I saw him drinking at a small table by the luxurious bar, a fat man plainly tall since his long legs were stretched out before him; his head nearly bald and his crisp moustache silver, so that I placed him well in his fifties. He had been pointed out to me by a cruising waiter, and as I walked towards him I learned that he was not only fat but jovial, as a fat man should be; his face crinkled into a smile when he guessed who I was, and he greeted me with, 'Aha! Enter Theophrastus.'

I did not know how to respond to this except with an answering smile, and it was he who went on with 'God, you're younger than I supposed.'

I assured him quickly that I was all of twenty-four; 'in my twenty-fifth year' were my actual words.

'Well, you look even younger,' he said, and I wasn't sure that this pleased me. 'Sit down and drink.'

We drank sherries and then went into the main restaurant, an imposing hall decked out in white and gold where we sat at a small table reserved for him.

'I've an offer to make you,' he said as we took our chairs, 'but let's enjoy our victuals first. Okay?'

'Of course, sir.'

'Yes, the victuals are good here, and it's a pity to spoil them with business talk. Work first and pleasure afterwards—I mean the other way round. I've chosen our dishes already—forgive me for this, but I think they're what you'll like.'

And indeed they should have been, because I could see they were good, but their taste was not registering on my brain so clearly as my unremitting wonder what on earth (or in the *World*) his 'offer' could be. This was a pity because I surmised, as we went on talking about anything but his paper or my articles, that the *Melon Frappé* and the *Délice de Sole Walewska* and the *Pêche Melba* were worth a more considered appreciation.

But now it was time for coffee and liqueurs and, wiping his mouth after enjoyable eating, he began. 'Well, this is it, my boy. I am prepared to offer you a column in the *World*, more or less daily, in which you can write just whatever you fancy, provided of course that it's witty and amusing, or pathetic and moving, in both of which lines you have, in my humble view, no small talent.' Casually he put a long cigar into his mouth and lit it, as if he'd said nothing remarkable, nothing to set my heart shaking where I sat. 'I suppose you inherit it from your uncle. Or can one inherit from an uncle? Perhaps it runs in the family. Is your father "witty and amusing"?'

'Hardly, sir. I should hardly call him that. I think I'd be more inclined to say he's "pathetic and moving".'

'Mercy!' He loosed a loud laugh. 'I hope my sons don't think me that. "Pathetic and moving"! Good lord! they probably do. I don't feel they're any longer inclined to think me "witty and amusing". Maybe they even think me tragic. You did a damned good tragic article on Dan Leno and the old music hall comedians who've had their day and are wanted no more. I nearly wept over it. I'd like more like that. D'you think they're beginning to see me as tragic? Could be. God, who'd be a father? Perhaps it comes from a grandfather. Did either of your grandfathers write?'

'No, it was my uncle who went out of his way to train me in the kind of writing and the sort of things that are wanted today.'

'Well, you were damned lucky. There's no finer journalist writing anywhere. Obviously there must have been a grandfather or great-grandfather to both of you.'

'But I'm not quite clear, sir. . . .' I was stammering a little in my surprise and pleasure. 'Is this an offer of permanent employment on your paper? On the *World*?'

He picked up a table-knife and set it spinning round on the cloth like a compass needle which had gone mad. Then he laughed. 'Well, I suppose we'll have to put you on approval for a week or two, but I think I can promise you that this will be only the usual formality. I feel sure that you can expect a permanent contract—say, for three years at first, and then probably, if you're happy with us, for many years after that. God, you've forty and more years ahead of you. Wish I had. You have the real stuff in you, my boy—that's obvious to me. Like father, like son. I mean, like uncle, like nephew.'

'Please sir, was it my uncle who suggested this to you?'

'Not a bit of it. I haven't seen the blighter for ages. If you want to know—and it may please you to know—the suggestion came from Lord Portwith himself. From the Chief. The Lord High Boss.'

This was certainly one of my life's big moments. It was so big that I was left dumb; and he went on, 'So it looks like a permanency, doesn't it?'

With a smile to smother any crudity in my next words, I asked, 'What would be—I don't want to sound crude—but what would the job be worth? I mean, what would the remuneration be?'

He gave me smile for smile. 'The dibs, what?—eh? The doings? Nothing crude in wanting to know that, my dear boy. Very necessary. The pay-packet. Remuneration is too pompous a word—not in your best style. I suggest that we start you off at a basic fifteen quid a week, rising perhaps to twenty later. Slightly more of course if we use four or five articles in the week. Would that suit you?'

'Suit me very well indeed, sir. And I'll try to earn it.'

'Don't worry about that. You'll do that all right. You've got the goods in you. Anyone can see that. You have the knack, it seems to me, of seeing the real truth of people—or some of it— behind the masks we all wear. You've probably got me weighed up by now, which would be a pity. Just let yourself *go* in everything you write for us. And don't worry too much if every article isn't always up to your highest standard. Nobody can always be on top of his form. If four out of six of your columns are top-class, we shall be satisfied.'

I was so grateful to this fat and kindly man for his tenderness towards a young man's nervousness and misgiving that I resolved, sitting there at this table, that I would labour to give him always of my best. This I said in a shaking voice. 'I'll try to do my best for you always, sir.'

'I'm sure you will.' He rose after leaving a sovereign and much silver on the waiter's bill. 'Well, that's settled, isn't it? May it be the beginning of a very happy relationship. I think it will.'

Fifteen pounds a week. Seven hundred and fifty a year. No, seven hundred and eighty. Home at speed to tell Elsa and Josef. To Mortress Lane to tell Raney and her parents. To Chapel Buildings, Lincoln's Inn, to find Uncle Douglas, the architect of my fortunes. Home again to my room and my desk to wait for Father, and meanwhile to contrive an excuse for writing to Aldith and Jack in Ealing, and to Abel and Augusta in India, with this news tacked on inconspicuously, unassumingly, at the letter's end. Then pacing the room, pacing the room, unable to work, unable to sit down, unable to do anything but ponder—between door and window, desk and hearth —a memory barely believable.

16

'You Can Trust Her to Him'

That October, towards its close, gave us as usual a second summer by grace of St. Luke, and possibly with the goodwill of St. Simon and St. Jude, whose day comes hard behind St. Luke's. It was on a Saturday, as October died gloriously, that we cycled again, doubtless for the last time in this year, to our quiet suburban Eden: Hadley Wood. We found the wood basking in its last autumn loveliness beneath a sun of mid-summer warmth. The great trees were splashed with their death-colours: rust-red and orange, copper-brown and yolk-yellow. Only the giant elms were still full of leaf and splendidly unconcerned with death and decay. The ashes, too, were reluctant to die. The silver birches, we agreed, were almost more beautiful in their autumn fall than in their summer pride: each had become a fountain soaring upward and sprinkling downward in a foam of pale leaves.

We came upon a place where an assembly of noble beeches with their silky olive-grey trunks stood in a kind of druid's circle around a wide space where the sun spread a lake of golden light—golden because there was a deep fitted carpet, as it were, of old-gold leaves. We thought of lying here in the sun but decided that it was too open a space for our purposes, and we walked on through an avenue of such beeches, past an undergrowth of thorns and brambles heavy with fruit, till at last we found, as we usually did, a lonely clearing in the heart of the trees which was yet large enough to admit a segment of warm sun. So warm and dry had been these last days of St. Luke that we did not fear to lie down together on the spread of brown leaves. We lay where the sun, now three hours down from its noon height, could play upon us for a while longer.

As our embracing grew tighter and more passionate the dropping leaves fell upon us unheeded at first, but when

Raney, her passion heated by my almost sadistic kissing, gasped again and again, 'Oh my darling . . . oh my darling . . . I love you so . . . my beloved . . .' the touches of the leaves began to speak to me; they said, 'This will be your last time here till the spring. You will not come again this year. With winter in possession of your London streets and its peopled parks where will you love in secret as you can love here?'

Once I looked up from her face beneath me; her eyes were closed and her amber hair lay disordered on the amber leaves; I saw that the sun, before sinking at last from view, was flinging its light on the trees' western shoulders and laying a glow on all their outspread branches; so I drew Raney yet tighter to me, thinking, 'We must go soon and we shall not come here again. Here alone we can be alone; she is now your affianced bride; you can go further than before, though always holding back the climax lest you hurt her'—and soon, unresisted by her, we were coupled together as man and wife, and Raney, after one cry of pain, having no such knowledge of a man before, was gradually rapt into cries of ecstasy—crying aloud, if unawares, to her God, 'Oh God . . . oh God . . . oh, my darling . . .' and this was too much for me in the exquisiteness of its response; it maddened me; I responded, 'Darling! Darling! *Darling!*'—and soon, when her gasps showed that she was ready for me, and craved me, and needed me for her peace—the trust of her parents was betrayed.

§

We collapsed apart, lying side by side, all embraces broken. I did not know what to say, but Raney, lapsing back in her distress to the less literate speech of the days before I found her, said sadly, 'Oh, we shouldn't've. We shouldn't've.' And when I couldn't answer, she was saying, 'I never knew it was in me to be like that. I never. We shouldn't've. We shouldn't've.'

'I know,' I admitted, 'but I love you so. It was because I love you so.' And that was all I could say.

'But we shouldn't've,' she repeated desperately. 'I never knew I could get like that, I didn't.'

'It was my——'

'Don't talk about it, *please*. I—I don't know what to think.'

'But, Raney——'

'Be quiet.' Her voice was angry. 'I asked you to be quiet. Can't you hear what I say? I don't know where I am. I don't know—I don't know anything. I dunno where I am. Leave me be.'

So I obeyed her, and we lay on the brown leaves without speaking.

It was she who rose first, uttering no more than a despairing, 'Oh, well . . .' and 'I suppose we'd better be going home.'

For the first time in our two years of courtship she seemed the one who had taken command. Perhaps this was because I was thinking of myself as the sinner rather than she, and could find no more words of excuse or contrition. I could think of nothing but her father's words, 'You can trust 'er to 'im, Mother,' and they allowed no excuses anywhere.

'Are you coming?' she asked imperiously. She seemed older than she had been one hour before: a young woman who in the last hour had sloughed off her maidenhood and left it lying there on the brown leaves.

Dumbly I rose on her instruction and after brushing from me the dust of the dead leaves, I picked up her hand.

She let me keep it, offering no word of resistance, but it lay limp and lifeless on my fingers and ready to fall away. There was no interweaving of her fingers with mine, and certainly none of the old blithe swinging of linked hands. So we walked homeward through the dense woodland, along the narrow beech avenue, and past the tangled underbrush of holly and thorn, and then of tall willow-herb which had had its summer and lost its rose-pink flowers. I did not doubt there was still love in the numbed hand she allowed me to hold, but it was a chastened love. We were two avowed lovers walking homeward with hands joined in confirmation of an avowal, but quietly, silently, and ashamed.

Only when the high fringe of the wood was in sight and the open green common beyond did I speak, for now our densely timbered paradise, scene of our fall, would soon be behind us. I said, 'Raney, sweetheart, I am sorry for what happened.

Please don't blame yourself. From beginning to end it was my fault.'

This she denied with a shake of her head and no words.

So I persisted, 'I can't bear you to be ashamed of anything. I'm simply not worthy of you—that's what it is. I'm terribly unhappy about it. Don't let it spoil our love. I simply couldn't bear that. Please let everything be the same.'

Then there came the faintest pressure of my hand but she answered only, and with a small heart-break somewhere behind her voice, 'I love you . . . I love you. . . .'

§

After that last day in Hadley Wood, and as November with its grey unkindly skies and wet gusty winds drove behind us the radiant Luke's Summer there was a heartache in me too, lest by a wildly selfish and merciless use of her I had destroyed for ever, or broken irreparably, our moment of supreme bliss in the mouth of the lane. That had been a spiritual ecstasy, and nothing less; had I thrown it away in exchange for one wild weak minute of physical ecstasy? Had I destroyed it or shattered it for Raney? All my love for her, so beyond question real, rose in anguished rebellion against this thought. Somehow I must rebuild what I had thrown down. I must give back to her, as unsoiled as possible, that exultant glory in the lane. How? How? Just as I had paced my room, living with joy after the editor's offer, so now I paced it, evening after evening, free hour after free hour, battling with this problem, 'How?' Then suddenly one evening these two things, the joy and the suffering, the gain and the loss, seemed to come together and play together, for now I had received good pay for some weeks; there was fat—or fattening—money in my bank; and I could insist that this unexpected appointment must in common decency be celebrated by a gift to Raney. Of course I would not suggest that it was a penitential gift; not a hint of that; it was just a sharing of our joy in sudden good fortune—was it not good fortune for both of us, and who was going to stop me spending some of this new 'wealth' on someone I loved? But on what sort of gift? On what? At last I had it; I hurried out; I went to the jeweller's in the High Street; I chose a small gold watch suspended from a gold bracelet shaped as a true-lover's-knot; I arranged with the jeweller for the name 'Raney' to be engraved (in a copy of my writing and in inverted commas) on the watch's back; and then I waited impatiently for three turbulent days and three sleep-broken nights till I could fetch it from the jeweller's and take it to Raney.

I gave it to her across the counter of her shop. I had waited in the street till I was sure she was in the shop with no customer near. I pushed it with a certain carelessness over the magazines on the counter, saying, 'Just a little present, my exquisite. To celebrate my recent good news—good news surely for both of us. A small gift. Nothing much. Just something.'

'Stewart, darling, *what?*' She undid the white tissue paper, gasped at the neat little leather box; opened it, and gasped again at the watch and bracelet lying on their bed of crimson silk; took them out and saw the 'Raney' on the back; then, since the shop door was well shut (I had seen to that), rushed round the corner to fling her arms about me. 'It's nothing,' I demurred. 'Just a little gift.'

'Oh, it's too wonderful.'

'You wear it here,' I explained, touching the upper left-hand pocket of my waistcoat. 'See? Just about here. But there's no compulsion on you to wear it.'

In her excitement and delight she dropped into almost the same words she had used in her dejection and self-reproach. 'Oh, but you shouldn't't've; you shouldn't't've.'

Of course neither of us spoke of Hadley Wood; and whether it rose in her mind I shall never know; but she kissed me with all the old love, and I could believe that I was forgiven.

§

There had been for a few weeks an unresting wonder in my heart lest there should come a frightening issue to that moment of love completed on that bed of dry leaves. I had said nothing of this to Raney both because of my shame and because I didn't want to dwell on any alarm in *her* heart; but behind my silence and my forced gaieties I knew that she too must be living with an unspoken dread. Her father? Her mother? What would they say? How could she ever face them?

Had the alarm sounded, and the need to speak stood menacingly before us, I had determined what to do. I would go to her father in whom, though he would be angry, even furious, clemency would be more likely to follow than in the stern and unmalleable heart of her mother. After confessing all to him I would accept his anger and ask his consent to our immediate engagement and early marriage. How I would face her mother I could not imagine. I shied away from all thought of that encounter. I shut my eyes quickly on any picture of it.

It was Raney who spoke first; Raney who, against all the austere traditions of her home which required modesty and silence on such matters from a girl; Raney who, either with the new strength and adulthood which had sprung from that harsh sowing on the dry leaves or because she wanted in her love to remove a dread she guessed to be in me—or, more probably, with both these causes at work—Raney who came and told me, when she could, that all fears were at rest.

I took her in my arms and kissed her without word spoken, for I too was a child of a home not unlike hers in its prudery and, for all my imagined rebelliousness, I could not speak aloud of such things.

Raney speaking; I silent.

But one evening—it was an evening towards the end of '13— I had arrived at the window of my room after my customary pacing, hands joined behind my back, new meerschaum pipe hanging cold, and I stood there abruptly immobilized by an idea like a pistol pointed at my breast. Why—what was I waiting for—why should I not, even if all the urgency had been removed, still go to her parents—soon—as soon as might be— and ask their consent to an engagement? I had feared that this request would be surrounded by anger and reprobation, but now, instead, it might be surrounded by happiness and benevolence. No need now to suggest the immediate marriage; if they wanted an engagement of some months, let them have it, but an official engagement let it be. Raney was now of age and could do as she wished but certainly (after that betrayal of her parents) we would both wish to do all they desired. Ask only an engagement at first; but then—the ring! Getting the ring and slipping it on to Raney's finger. No elements of guilt and amendment and recompense in *this* gift; just joy unalloyed.

Four evenings later, after a day made restless with longing so that I had been hardly able to work or to read, I hurried out when the clock said six to Mortress Lane and the Wayburns' side-door. I had left this visit till full evening so that the shop doors would be firmly shut, and daughter, father and mother all available.

Fortunately it was Raney who opened the side-door to me; and fortunately the small street was empty. I gathered her hand, pulled her over the threshold, and said, 'Greatly beloved, do you know what I've come to do?'

'No,' she said. 'But I'm not displeased. Come in.'

'Guess first.'

'You've some idea of a ridiculous long walk on this wretchedly cold night. Is that it?'

'Not quite. Walk? No. I've been thinking about you all day, odd as it may seem, and I've come to ask you to let me ask your father and mother if we can be properly engaged. Engaged before all the blinking world. Would that interest you?'

'Oh, my pet, my darling!' Her arms were around me, and she was hugging me almost painfully in the empty street. 'Oh, how absolutely terrific. How terribly engaging of you——'

'Witty child.'

'Yes. Come . . . come and do it.'

'You approve then?'

'I think I approve on the whole. In fact, I don't think I've approved of anything more for quite some time. You see, I happen to love you quite a lot. Heaven knows why.'

'Engaged then? Marry soon?'

'*Marry?*'

'Yes. Isn't that the idea? Isn't that what engagements are usually about?'

'Soon?'

'That's what I said. But not if you'd rather postpone it as long as possible.'

'Don't be too silly.' So she dragged me to the kitchen with nonsense at play around us, I saying, 'But we must hear what Mum and Dad say,' and she calling, '*Mum! Dad!*'

I just had time to add, 'We shall need a month or two to find a nice little home where I can house you properly. Then—marry, don't you think? Marry?'

'Oh, yes. *Please.*'

The kitchen was a small room. For most of the day Mr. and Mrs. Wayburn sat in the tiny office behind the shop, but after work was done they usually sat on either side of the kitchen range, on two small easy chairs drawn from the wall.

'Stewart has a small thing to ask you,' Raney explained as she drew me in.

I asked them. And for a little they both stared at me in silence. Then Mr. Wayburn said, 'This has fair taken us by surprise. We wasn't quite ready for this. Whad'you think, Mother?'

'I'm struck all of a heap,' she said. 'I don't know what to say. I think you must let me get used to the idea. Give you our Ireen? For good?'

'I'm afraid that's the idea.' I apologized for it. 'I'm sorry.'

'It's wonderful of you to want her, of course.'

'Wonderful? Nonsense. It's the most natural thing in the world. I found it enormously easy.'

'You want to be engaged *at once*?'

'Oh yes. Oh yes.' No hesitation in my voice. 'Today if you don't mind.'

Silence from her, so I suggested, 'We'll wait a bit before we marry if you wish it.'

After further thought she said, 'I feel I should like to seek the Lord's guidance first. It's a great decision.'

'Oh, no, Mum.' This was a smothered murmur from Raney which, though it implied no real hostility to God's interference in the matter, yet showed how far she had come towards me from her mother's side. She hastily amended it into, 'Yes, Mum, but if I'm certain and Stewart's certain, surely God'll be pretty certain too.'

'You know what I think, Ireen. One should submit every-thing to him. And wait for the Light.'

But here Mr. Wayburn interrupted; a business man of earthy common sense, taking command of a discussion. 'Look, Mother. They're not arstin' to marry at once. Only to be engaged. And that can always mean they'll have time to find out if they've made a mistake. Nobody's going to sue nobody for breach of promise, if it comes to it. Surely we can trust the Lord to reveal what is his will for 'em. And they'll do his will; they are good children. My reckoning is that he'll look down in his love on 'em. Ireen, you're in full agreement with what Stoo'rt has said, are you?'

'What do you think, Dad? Of course I am.'

'Then let 'em be 'appy, Mother. They can only be young once. And I think we two old people can be 'appy too. I've always had full trust in our Stoo'rt. And in our Ireen. But you mustn't run off with her at once, Stoo. We shall miss her a lot in the shop. You must give me time to make arrangements, and Mother time to get used to the idea. Shall we say: wait six months?'

I agreed instantly. 'Of course. We shall need time to make arrangements. Got to look for a home.' And within myself I was thinking, 'December now. January, February, March, April, May, June 1914.'

'Six months isn't very long,' Mrs. Wayburn objected.

Mr. Wayburn shrugged. 'Eight months then? 'Ardly fair to make 'em wait a whole year.'

June, July, August, '14.

Mrs. Wayburn's turn to shrug; and leave it to him.

'So let's say Yes, Mother. I want them to be 'appy. Look how 'appy they look. You simply can't refuse 'em.'

'I suppose we can safely say Yes,' Mrs. Wayburn agreed. 'And God bless you both, my dears. I'll pray for his blessing on you both.'

I went up and kissed her—the first time I'd done this. I promised, 'I'm going to try to make her happy.' Then straight-way I put my hand into the side-pocket of my jacket and drew out a small blue box. From this I drew a ring, a gold circlet with a large emerald framed in a square of diamond brilliants. Certain they would consent, if not this evening, then later, I'd bought the ring from the jeweller who'd sold me the watch and had it engraved. He had been much interested in the purchase, asking with a smile, 'This is for the "Raney", is it?' and offering me 'all the good wishes in the world'. I picked up Raney's hand and slid the ring on to her finger.

Overwhelmed by the sight of it, she flung herself around me, not without a moistening in her eyes. I think she said, 'I've never had anything so lovely in my life before,' but I'm not sure, because her tears were infectious and I was near to weeping myself. Mrs. Wayburn wept; and I had a fancy that Mr. Wayburn was in an emotional state, for he blew his nose and then said triumphantly—and perhaps to show that there was one person present in full command of his feelings, 'You see how 'appy they are. I like to see young people 'appy.'

§

But there was another parent whose approval had best be sought. In these days when I was excited by the prospect of a stable income, to say nothing of a small fame since the *World* had a large circulation, much of my pleasure in showing defiance of Father had fallen away. I could feel only a kindness towards all the world. Nevertheless, as I went up the stairs to his study to announce this engagement, my steps were slow, even halted here and there, because I was gripped by two conflicting emotions: one of happiness, the other of apprehension. Raney—the shop—the Dene—the laundry long ago—Stubb Lane Elementary School. It is a fact that the nearer I got to his closed study door, the slower I went, and when I was on the landing I did not immediately touch the door's handle. I just stood where I was.

Still, the step must be taken. And what would happen, would happen. I turned that handle and walked in, annoyed that my heart was pulsing faster than usual.

He was, as ever, in his large lonely chair with Hamish at his side. Hamish gave me his usual tumultuous welcome, nearly knocking me down and deafening me with barks, while Father merely looked up from his book.

I said, 'Father, I've got something to tell you. It may be rather a shock.'

'A shock?' The word was more of a bullet than I had intended. 'What on earth is it? Down, Hamish. Shut up.'

'You remember Raney, don't you?'

'Of course I remember her. There's every reason why I should since I was not a little alarmed at your liaison before, considering her class and background.'

Instantly my heart hardened, and the old defiance returned. But he softened the heart a little—not fully—by continuing, 'I remember that, for her kind and class, she seemed a charming girl. What about her? She's not ill, I hope?'

'Gracious, no. I doubt if she's ever been less ill.'

'She was certainly a pretty little creature, as far as I remember. But she had nothing to say.'

'That was only because she was terrified of you. Almost frightened out of her senses.'

This, I could see, was not displeasing to the congenital despot in him, so I followed up a small success by adding, 'And as we walked home she said that, in spite of your terrifying appearance, she really suspected that you were rather sweet.'

'Sweet! Ho, ho, ho!' But he was clearly delighted. 'Me sweet! First time I've been called that.'

'Yes,' I assented; which perhaps wasn't the politest answer. 'And she went on to say that you were magnificent to look at. Much handsomer than me.'

'"Handsomer than I" strictly. "Than" is a conjunction, and its use as a preposition is frowned on by the best grammarians.'

'Is it? I suppose it is. But may we forget that for the moment? The fact remains that she thought you handsomer than me— than I, I mean.'

Obviously he could not be other than pleased with this though he pretended not to be. 'I'm afraid that doesn't affect my feelings towards her. I'm not susceptible to flattery——'

('Oh no,' I thought. 'Not in the least.')

'So what is all this about?'

'Simply that I have made my decision. Now that I can look forward to a secure position, I have asked her to marry me——'

'Good God!'

'She has consented. And her parents have consented too.'

'Her parents have consented! I should jolly well think they have.' Strange that the shock should have trapped a magniloquent pedant into the language of his schooldays. 'I should think they're as pleased and proud as Punch. But, Stewart, you can't really be serious about this.'

'Never more serious. I love the girl, you see.'

'A shop girl from Hollen Dene?'

'A shop girl from Hollen Dene,' I repeated, my heart hardening again. 'From a tiny little shop in Mortress Lane.'

'But, good mercy, Stewart! Leaving me out of it, what do you think Aldith and Augusta will say?'

'We've had all this out before. Aldith has now met her and already loves her a lot. We've been and stayed with her in Kent.'

'I know nothing of what happens. Nobody has told me this. And Jack? Jack, a solicitor of some eminence, what does he think?'

'Jack fell for her at once. Most men do. She happens to be rather pretty.'

'He did, did he? Well, I thank Heaven I'm not at the mercy of a pretty face. I don't know what the world's coming to—I'm no snob——'

('No,' my mind agreed. 'Not at all. Not a trace of it.')

'—but it's just common sense that one should marry somebody of one's own class and education and traditions. It's useless to expect me to say I approve.'

I felt like endorsing, 'Useless. And quite unnecessary. What the hell does your consent matter?' but he almost said this for me.

'Well, you're your own master. You can do what you like without reference to me. May I ask'—his voice was satirical—'when you propose to marry?'

'Her parents said six or eight months, so I opted for the shorter. June, perhaps. When we've found a home.'

For the first time I remembered that these words must alarm him; they meant an end to my contribution to the upkeep of his much-loved home. He had consideration enough not to mention this, and I found myself wondering in what way I could help him to stay in this house which had become almost like a carapace for him. That he could accept a boarder other than one of his children whom he could correct, rebuke, and teach, exhibiting high standards, social, ethical, and grammatical, was unimaginable. But so far his only expression of disquiet was, 'Hmmm . . . and are you going to tell me that this girl's going to bring her mother's terrible religion along with her? I remember that the woman lectured me on religion for an hour at the tea-table and all the way up the stairs. She practically called me a reprobate half-way up the stairs. After taking tea at my table she consigned me in the simplest words, as far as I could make out, to perdition. . . . And she said it quite happily. That's the thing that beats me.'

'Me too,' I said. 'And I'm sure I'm damned too. You and I'll have to get into the fire together.' But I suddenly doubted if this suggestion from a son could meet with Father's instant approval, so I hurried on. 'And yet she accepts me as her daughter's young man—I mean her—her, shall we say, "gentleman friend".'

'But is this girl like her mother?'

'No. I fancy she'll accept my religion.'

'Rather like a royal engagement. You mean she'll become an agnostic?'

'Oh no. I'm only unofficially an agnostic. Officially I'm Church of England. And indeed, if it's any comfort to you, I feel a little less agnostic than I did in my youth.'

'Your youth! What age are you now?'

'Twenty-five.'

'Fully twenty-five. Well, make sure that this relapse into religion isn't senile dementia, ha, ha, ha.'

Father, as I have said, could be funny in a limited way. 'Ha, ha, ha,' I supplied for his satisfaction.

'And what about her father? As far as I remember, he hadn't an "h" in his system.'

'He has one or two.'

'Well, you've really given me something to think about. To worry about, I confess. What do you imagine the neighbours will say?'

'What the hell do they matter?' Thus at last, in a new context, I was able to express this handsome sentiment. 'So, since it's decided—*finally* decided,' I emphasized, 'may I bring Raney along to see you again—her future father-in-law?'

'For me to give her my blessing, ha, ha, ha?'

'Exactly, ha, ha, ha.'

Plainly I had softened his opposition, for he only shrugged and said, 'It's a considerable shock, I admit, and I'm not going to suggest anything else. I'm one who believes in saying exactly what he thinks. But for the girl's sake I'll do my best. If you've made up your mind, I'll do my best for both of you. But it's something I never dreamed of in all my days.'

'Thank you, Father.' This was one of the few times when, for a moment, we approached near to each other.

It was on the Saturday afternoon that, with her parents' concurrence, I brought Raney to be, in her own words, 'vetted' by Father. On our doorstep, as I fumbled for my latch-key she told me, 'Oh, I'm more than absolutely terrified. I'm in the depths. I can't see how he can possibly approve of me. Hadn't I better go home?'

'Rubbish. He said last time that you were a "charming girl".' Naturally I omitted his qualification of this opinion: 'for her kind and class.'

'But I never said a word,' she reminded me.

'No. And I explained that this was because you were terrified of him—a statement which obviously pleased him more than he'd admit.'

'Pleased him? Why?'

'Some people like to believe they're dominant types who inspire fear in lesser mortals.'

'I hope you're not going to be like that. Are you going to dominate me? I mean, I'm clearly a lesser mortal.'

'I suspect the bossiness is in me, but I don't think you need be afraid, because we children reacted too strongly against it. He also said you were a "pretty little creature".'

'I suppose we all seem little to him.'

By this time we were in the house, and the way of flight was shut against her. So we had to go up the stairs, I leading the way. Behind me I heard her sigh, 'Oh, dear . . .' and 'Don't go too fast. Have a heart.'

Before the study door her hand caught mine for a second or two of comfort, and I could feel that it was trembling. 'It's a bit like going into an enormous lion's den, isn't it?' she whispered.

'I think he'll be all right,' I comforted. 'He won't eat you'; and, putting an arm around her shoulders, I opened the door and took her in. 'Here we are, Father. Here's Raney.'

No rioting welcome or genial barking from Hamish at Father's side. He lay still and suspicious. Perhaps his identification with Father, at this dangerous moment, was so complete that he could only look with doubt on this young female companion of mine.

Father, ever punctilious about gentlemanlike behaviour, rose for a lady—even a lady from Hollen Dene. Maybe she had been transformed for him into a lady by becoming my fiancée, but, to his credit, I think he would have stood up for any woman.

He bowed to Raney and put out a hand. 'It's nice of you to come and see me.'

Raney took the hand but could say nothing. Not a word. Still, I could see in Father's eyes that, forgetting for a while his class-consciousness, he could but be charmed by her youth and beauty. I saw in those eyes that just as his statement 'I'm no snob' was seven miles this side of truth, so was his boast, 'I thank Heaven I'm not at the mercy of a pretty face.' Politely he pulled forth a chair for her. 'Do sit down, my dear. And Hamish, get out of the way. Or at least get up and welcome a lady.'

But Hamish was still suspicious. He got up and lay down again, as one who desired further knowledge before he would pronounce a decision.

We sat down and talked. There was a manifest tenderness in the way Father talked to Raney, but I could still hear the old condescension, the stooping to conquer, which was always in his voice when he spoke to labourer, plumber, crossing-sweeper or other member of the working class. His talk, all addressed to her (I might not have been in the room), enabled her to open out a little and speak with some ease, though never once showing any of her fun and mischievous gaiety. Plainly she doubted if this study, encased with heavy-looking books, was a suitable place for frivolity. Not once did he speak of our marriage or of her as his daughter-in-law. I suspected that he had not yet strengthened himself for such an achievement; or that he was hoping all such nonsense would pass. He did say— with an effort—'Of course you're going to stop and have tea with us'; but in Raney's eyes I could see a mastering desire to escape, so I intervened with a resounding lie, 'No, I'm sorry, Father, but I promised to take her home quickly.' I saw an amused trembling of Raney's lips as I provided this lie for her rescue; and as Father turned towards my voice, as if he'd remembered my presence for the first time, I saw that the relief in his eyes was just about the same as Raney's.

'Oh, what a pity. I *am* sorry,' he said, providing a lie no smaller than mine.

'Yes, I promised her parents,' I repeated, wondering where I would take her for some tea.

'Well . . . some other time . . .' he forced himself to say. And his farewell to her—and his condescending manner—were as tender as his greeting had been. A gentleman, he opened the door for her and bowed as she left him. He also waited a delicate time to let us get down four or five stairs before gently he closed his door.

When that evening, across our dinner-table, I encountered him again, he said, 'I think she got on quite well with me. I always get on well with that class. I always have, ha, ha, ha.' His 'ha, ha, ha' often followed behind a brag, like the tail of a kite; it served as a kind of submission that 'the last thing he wanted to do was to brag'.

'Yes, she said nice things about you as we went away.'

'I must confess that she was better than I feared. She speaks quite well. Quite grammatically.'

'Yes, as grammatically as any of us,' I said, thinking of Aldith.

'I hope you're not suggesting by that remark that I ever fail in my grammar.'

'Oh, no. It's only us children.'

'"Only *we* children" strictly,' he corrected. 'I must say that I flatter myself that if there's one thing I know perfectly, it's grammar.'

17

Fate Takes a Hand

Fate solved the question as to whether Father could ever leave his Dunkerry Crescent home. Fate acted almost at once. Father was now sixty-five; he had spoken to none of us about any symptoms of bodily disorder; perhaps because he prided himself on a strength and vigour that belied his years, and quite likely because his high sense of the proprieties forbade him to mention the unseemly nature of the symptoms. I had noticed a new puffiness about his fine features, and a wateriness in his eyes, both of which, with all the brutality of my own twenty-five years, I supposed to be normal in an old party of more than sixty; but only a few weeks after my presentation to him of a future bride, our doctor, who had been visiting him unknown to any of us, diagnosed his condition as acute nephritis, and came down to my room to shut the door and tell me all about it.

The year, '14, had now broken; and still in neither of our young hearts, Raney's and mine, preoccupied with first love, was there the dimmest sense of what this year, or the next, might have in store for us. Certainly ever since the death of Good King Edward the Peacemaker, and throughout the opening years of George V's reign, there had been much talk about the possibility of a German invasion, but did either of us, young and uninformed, take it seriously? Was it not rather a jolly subject for occasional chatter, quickly forgotten? I remember that in 1908 there had been a serial in a popular newspaper by the novelist, William Le Queux, picturing an invasion by the Germans, and advertised by processions of sandwich-men in the London streets. About this time, too, there came a play, *An Englishman's Home*, that was such a booming success that it occupied three London theatres simultaneously—and 'booming' was an apposite word because the guns of an invading army from a nameless nation brought down the 'Englishman's' home about his head, and on to the stage, with fire and smoke, while he was led out into his garden to be shot, properly, as a civilian who had taken up arms. I saw the play and enjoyed it hugely. So did the rest of the country, most of them thereafter putting into cold storage its stern remonstrance and call to arms. And do I correctly attribute a comic and current rhyme of those days to Captain Harry Graham, whose *Ruthless Rhymes for Heartless Homes* had long been a joy to us—do I render it correctly?

> I was playing golf one day
> When all the Germans landed,
> And all our men had run away
> And all our ships were stranded,
> The sight of England's shame
> Quite put me off my game.

But not one breath of this fashionable but ill-digested fear disturbed my heart or placed one insecure thought in my mind on the day when our doctor came into my room quietly, like an intriguer, and shut the door.

A man of much the same age as my father with a broad spade of grey beard hanging over his gladstone collar and cravat, Dr. Hillyard had been our doctor since my childhood and he now warned me with a shaking of his head that Father was suffering from acute nephritis; that the nephritis had resulted in some arterio-sclerosis; and that he was a little afraid lest this acute attack passed into the chronic disease. 'It's worrying,' he said, 'that your father has no wife to watch over his every movement and his dieting, because what he needs now is an enforced rest in bed and the lightest of foods all carefully prepared, and the careful guarding of him from any excessive activity or any danger of a chill.'

I assured him that Elsa and Josef would do all in their power, but he shook his head again and said, 'I know your father well, Stewart. I know my Augustus O'Murry, and I can't see him obeying anyone less than a wife; and I wouldn't bet on his doing even that.'

I quickly concurred. 'Nor would I. Not a penny.'

'So it'd be no good calling in Aldith, even if she could come?'

'None at all, I should say. He'd no more take orders from her than he would from me. And that's putting it as low as you can get. We're only his children, you see.'

'I see it most clearly, Stewart, and that's why, for my part, I'd like to get him into a nursing home or hospital, at least for a time, till we feel confident that the recovery is complete. But even then he ought to go easy for months, dieting himself properly and refraining from too many activities.'

'Which would mean an end to his work at his school? An end to his professional life?'

'For a time at least, and probably for a long time. And as he's sixty-five now I could wish there was an early chance of his retirement. I hinted at something like this to him, but it wasn't at all well received. He's got to learn to obey *someone* strictly, or I can't answer for the consequences. If I could have him under vows of strict obedience somewhere, and watched over by really redoubtable nurses for several weeks, I fancy we could get him as right as he'll ever be now.'

'He has very little money,' I said. 'Barely enough to live in this house as it is. And I don't see how we could afford a nursing home.'

'I know.' The good old man's voice was sympathetic. 'I know. So what are we to do?'

Suddenly and to my surprise, I heard myself saying, 'Leave me to think.'

§

I had said 'Leave me to think' because an idea, strangely pleasant, had appeared in my mind as the doctor asked his question. My two recent joys—the fine promise which was now shining upon my career and the hardly credible certainty of Raney as a wife—these had acted as a solvent to the old tough hostility to Father and melted much of it away, leaving only this extraordinarily pleasing idea that I would love to be the one who helped him in his need. I found that I could not bear the thought of an old man so pompous and self-important as Father being taken to the public ward of a hospital instead of to a private room in a nursing home. All this was long before anyone dreamed of a national health service, and public wards were then seen as charitable provision for the poor. Father might brag, 'I always get on well with that class, ha, ha, ha,' but I could not imagine him happy and 'getting on well', bedded down with the vulgar in a public ward. 'Men are what they are, and one must accept them for what they are', I thought, 'and in the depths of his proud heart Father will hold that a private nursing home is the proper place for a professional man of his standing, lately a publisher and now a classical master held in respect—and some awe—by his pupils. Then too he will have anxiety enough wondering whether this illness will mean the loss of his work and his home. Good, then: a private room he must have. I'll go and see Aldith and Jack this very evening; I'll write to Augusta now; and between us we can certainly pay for a private room.'

I'd have offered to pay half the cost since it was my (wholly jubilant) idea, but it was unlikely that Aldith and Jack would listen to this.

Aldith and Jack's answer was all that I had expected. 'Why, of course!' they said, when I came upon them at coffee after dinner that night. 'We'll share it with you now that you're such a wealthy man, and if Augusta and Abel want to come in with an offering we'll divide that with you.'

To which, however, Aldith added, 'Though perhaps it wouldn't be fair to ask anything from Abel. Missionaries don't get much in India, do they? Just a little rice or something. We three'll do it; and look: we're not asking Uncle Douglas to do any of this. He's done enough already behind the scenes. He'd probably offer to do it all, but we're not having that. Besides, I doubt if Father'd like it. A younger brother, and a shorter brother, and all. Very difficult. No, this is a job for his children. Tell the old boy that Jack'll take him to the nursing home in Grizelda—Grizelda will be delighted—and one of us'll come every day and visit him with grapes, as is proper. Between us, we'll get him well.'

'As well as he'll ever be,' I amended, remembering the doctor's words.

All else that she had said appealed to me strongly, so that I agreed. 'No, not a word to Uncle Douglas till it's too late for him to do anything. Let him discover it in his own good time. *We'll* look after Dad.'

Never had I ascended our stairs to Father's study door more happily than on that night. As I went in, he looked sick, old, and disconsolate, with his book resting on his knees as if he could not read for thinking of what the doctor had told him, and his fingers fiddling with Hamish's ears. The fine face seemed to me more puffed up and even swollen, the eyes more sunken and paled, after what I'd heard from the doctor.

I said, when I'd got rid of Hamish's boisterous greeting, 'Father, Doctor Hillyard quite rightly took me into his confidence so that I need not be too worried about your health, and he assured me that if he could get you into a hospital or nursing home for a few weeks he could get you as fit as ever.' I thought it better to omit the doctor's 'several weeks' and his 'as right as he'll ever be now'.

'I know,' Father said. 'That's more or less what he told me.'

'Well, look, Father. I've been to see Aldith and Jack, and we've all decided that we're not going to have you put in the public ward of a hospital. No, don't interrupt. Listen. Let me finish (that's what you often say to me). We're going to get you a private room in a nursing home. Aldith says that for once in a way there's to be no argument about it. You've got to let us do this for our own pleasure. We're entitled to a little pleasure sometimes, and we've set our hearts on this. It's to be our treat. Our gift to you.'

I don't know how I had expected he would take this. Vaguely I had thought there might be a proud man's refusal, and even some indignation mixed with gratitude. Or perhaps only a grateful but polite dissent. What did happen was something I could never have imagined. His lips, tight closed, shook up and down, never parting, while he struggled with a swelling in his throat; and his words when he could speak were a total astonishment to me, so little did they accord with my lifelong experience of him. Stuttering, the lips set trembling again by his own words, he said, 'Children are wonderful.'

§

Had our relations been closer I should have liked to put a hand on his shoulder and comfort him, but this, of course, was impossible. Instead I did not give him time to say further words since he was hardly able to. I just said, laughing as one who'd noticed no untoward emotion, 'We've got it all fixed up between us. Aldith and Jack are going to see the Mo—' Jack, an ex-territorial, used this word for any medical officer—'and find out which nursing home he recommends, and we're going ahead without any further reference to you. Jack's going to convey you there in Grizelda——'

'Grizelda?'

'Their car. And we're just not going to listen to anything you say. This is a revolution, no less, so you'd better get used to it. It's giving us tremendous happiness—we're up in the air about it—and I'm sure you won't want to deny us a little happiness.'

When he did speak he tried to do so with a smile. He said, 'I can only say thank you.' A pause to gulp again and get control of himself. 'Thank you all very much.'

It was enough. I knew it was not in him to utter superlatives —least of all, perhaps, to his children—but the gratitude was heavily there in the gulped words. So I accepted them with an answering smile and hurried from the room for his sake.

In the event it was not a nursing home that Doctor Hillyard recommended to us but the new Earl du Laurier's Hospital for Gentlemen, a small hospital designed to provide private rooms for professional men and retired officers at a cheaper rate than in private nursing homes or in the great London teaching hospitals. This meant that we could face the prospect of keeping him there just as long as the doctor ordered, and, as Aldith said, a name like that would be exactly right for Father.

It was a day in early March when Jack's car waited at our gate, and Father and Aldith got into its back seats while I sat myself at Jack's side. As Jack drew off for the hospital I saw Father look back at his garden where the crocuses, purple, white, and yellow, were standing up perkily under the winter-bare trees, and the forsythias were flourishing like golden conflagrations by the side of our gate and over our dwarf garden wall. The morning sun invested the house with all the golden promise of spring. Round the curve of the Crescent we lost sight of garden and house, and it was not for me to know what thoughts lay hidden in Father's heart.

At the hospital we saw him comfortably bedded in his own small room, and Aldith's last words as she kissed him were 'I'm just going down to tell the Matron that she's to be Strictness Itself, and you're to obey her in everything: there's to be no damned nonsense about this. I'm sorry for that "damned". I shall assure her that she'll have her work cut out, but the Mo says it's absolutely necessary—so there it is: we're determined to get you absolutely well.'

Father, accepting all this banter with a tired smile, lifted a hand in gratitude as we waved farewell from the door.

§

So remarkable was the pleasure worked in me by this 'giving' to Father out of my new affluence that I suddenly learned with a complete conviction the surprising truth that, as the Bible said, it was 'happier to give than to receive'. Our Canon Plumworthy in his pulpit at St. Jude's had often insisted that the Greek words were better translated 'It is happier' than 'It is more blessed', and I had heard him with no great interest; not till this hour in my life did I realize that the words were exactly true. Receiving was a delightful business, but it lacked the sharper glow of pleasure that a really expensive 'giving' flung around one's heart. I reported this remarkable discovery to Aldith, and she agreed, saying, 'Yes, I often think the Bible gets some things very right. Where does this business occur about its being happier to give? I must expound it to Jack next time I need a new dress because—well, receiving is pretty good too.'

Having discovered this new spring of joy, and wanting to experience more of it, I discussed with Aldith what we could do to help the 'old man' when he came out of hospital, fairly fit again, but unable to work as before or to remain in a large, unpractical, and costly home. Hitherto the repairs and decoration had cost him nothing; his skills and his pleasure in tools were equal to any task, whether it was plumbing or plastering or carpentering or painting the big rooms from ceiling to floor.

Aldith and I decided that while he was in hospital where he might be kept for many weeks we would search around for a small but attractive home in which, living in retirement, he could plaster and paint and plumb without undue exertion. This plan fitted well with the fact that Raney and I would also be seeking a home for ourselves. Raney would enjoy looking for two homes, one of which would be for Father whom she persisted in thinking sweet. To the agent I would say, 'Two houses, please, one small but very attractive, and the other somewhat larger—a family house—' whereat Raney would seize my arm, half in reproof and half in happy but unbelievable anticipations.

And happy the following weeks were, when she and I went from house to house to dream in empty rooms. Should we find one that captured our hearts, we dared to hope that we might be allowed to marry earlier than in June or August. During our cycling journeys to Kew Gardens in summer's April dawn, when the magnolias were breaking open and the noble trees were speckled with bright new green, or in May when the rhododendron dells were massed with every colour and the azaleas were ablaze too, we had learned such a love for these celestial fields that the top of our ambition was to acquire a Regency home on Kew Green or over the bridge at Strand-on-the-Green. Through April and May we must have inspected dozens of houses, from every one of which we came away with shaking heads because there was this or that, or both, which made them unsuitable. But at last on a shining May day, sweet with the scent of lime trees, we did come upon a little white house of much charm at Strand-on-the-Green. It had but two small rooms and a kitchen on the ground floor, and two small rooms 'and a bit' upstairs, but its front windows looked over a narrow embankment at the tidal Thames as it came ebbing or flowing, lingering or stampeding, through the wide arches of Kew Bridge. We decided it would be too small for us but all the time as we strolled through its empty rooms I was thinking, 'This could be the very house for Father. This is the very place that in his most romantic moods he has always wanted.'

And at last, standing in the front room looking out at the river, I said to Raney, 'I can't see us living here with all your brats—I mean, I shall need to work—but it would be a perfect home for the old man. He's always loved the river. He used to be a marvellous oar because he's marvellous at anything with his hands. Many a time he's taken me as a boy rowing along this very stretch but the outing was always rather spoiled for me by his impatience with my rhythm or my feathering and his exasperation when I "caught a crab", and nearly upset the boat, which was not infrequent. Then I couldn't pull anything like as powerfully as he did, so the boat went round in circles— or tried to. I was powerfully abused then. In fact, my oarsman-ship was almost as big a subject for his displeasure as my grammar. But this house, Raney my beloved, is just built for him. He could spend all day making it lovely with his paints and his tools and looking out at the river, without once over-tiring himself.'

'Oh, can't we get it for him?' she exclaimed. 'Isn't it possible? Oh, let's.'

'Why not?' I said. 'Why not?'

'But there's just one thing. It's awfully near the river. What happens when there's a flood?'

'The Thames comes in and sits on the floor with him. In this room. Rather like Hamish. But he'd be more than equal to that. I can see him handling that situation with great aplomb. He'd enjoy it so.'

'Oh, then let's get hold of the house while it's free, since he doesn't mind floods, but likes them. If he can't be persuaded to come at once, we could perhaps use it for a little.'

'Yes. Till the brats come. Perhaps the first brat wouldn't matter, but two or three——'

'Oh, do shut up. *She* might hear.' The house-agent's young

clerk who'd brought us to the house was locking a shed and bolting the back door after we'd surveyed the tiny garden. 'Your voice carries so.'

'But it's a remark that'd interest her enormously. It interests all women.'

'I don't want her to be interested in it. We were talking about getting this house for your father—not for—not for anybody else. I think it's a rather superb idea.'

'I too.'

The idea was possessing me as ardently as that first desire to secure him a private room in which he could lie and be nursed like a gentleman. Also that astounding statement that his children were wonderful was working like a power engine within me. In these first years of the century small houses could be bought at prices that sound inconceivable to us today. Aldith and I could easily find the money for this little house at Strand-on-the-Green.

Aldith, as I foresaw, was not only infected by this new eagerness of mine to 'look after' our disabled father, to be, as she said, *in loco parentis* to him, but she too fell in love with the little house at first sight; so after a surveyor's report, fairly satisfying, we bought it. Anything that the surveyor objected to, Father could see to all right. He was home from hospital now, but Doctor Hillyard insisted that he must rest quietly for at least six months with no tomfoolery about climbing up ladders to distemper high ceilings or shifting heavy furniture to paper high walls. By a welcome coincidence the doctor said to us, 'I only wish we could get him out of this vast old-fashioned house into something small that wouldn't tempt him too far.'

'That,' I said, 'is exactly what we're proposing to do.'

Our plan was to pretend I had bought the house to occupy it with Raney till we found something larger, and then, pretending we had this larger place in view, to go to Father and (taking our lives in our hands) suggest that he should have the smaller home as a gift from us all. He might refuse it at first; he might insist on paying us a rent; but I trusted that Aldith, who at times could be almost as formidable as he, would carry this campaign to a success better than I could, because Father, in spite of my recent 'good fortune' and my talk of marriage, always seemed unable to think of me as other than the young one of the family.

'I'll do it,' she said. 'It'll take time. I guess I shall have to do it in a series of gradual steps. But one thing's sure, I shall have to do it gently for my own sake, because I simply couldn't bear to see my Augustus O'Murry reduced to tears by the wonderfulness of his children. Father—Father, of all people— oh, no! Not for me. I see I must prepare with enormous care all I'm going to say the night before and have it off by heart. There are plenty of arguments. He can't possibly stay here if you've gone off to live with a woman; we simply can't have him saddled with a lodger of whom he certainly wouldn't approve in a hundred different ways. I mean, think of the lodger's manners at table, his habits, his treatment of the furniture, his daring to argue——'

'And his grammar,' I reminded her.

'Yes, of course. And his mispronunciation of words that come from the Greek or somewhere. And Augustus unable to utter one word of correction or learned instruction. No *you* sitting there at the table to receive it all and allow him to get on with his meal in peace. No, I'm not having him put through any distresses like that. Not at his age and when he isn't really well. Besides, I agree with you that he's only got to look at that little house and the river and the yachts sailing by to fall in love with it. As we all did.'

On the sly we took Elsa to see the house, and she, after walking over it, declared, 'Yurse. . . . Yurse, I feel that Josef and me could do with them two back rooms and the kitchen, because, as a matter of fact, I'm getting sick to death of that there 'uge kitchen and pantries and all. I'm getting old now, you see, and all for something smaller, like.'

'And there'll be no question,' I put in, 'of Josef paying any rent for this small accommodation, if you're looking after Father. So far as Josef can find room to move in these little rooms he'll be living rent-free.'

'Well, that'll be a consideration, natcherly.'

'And more,' said Aldith. 'We shall be paying you a wage of

227

some sort because you'll have more to do now, looking after Father.'

'Well, Miss Aldith, I dunno about that. I wouldn't expect for too much—jest doing that. Yer see, miss, I wouldn't want for anyone else to be doing for 'im; not after all these years I wouldn't. Personally I've always got on well with 'im. I believe he kind-of upsets other people sometimes, but I must say he's always been a perfect gentleman to me' (I always get on well with that sort of people) 'as the saying is.'

'Splendid, Elsa.' Aldith just touched her hand affectionately. 'We can't do without you. You're one of the family now. So's Josef. But a pity he's so big. Two of them of that size in this house. Now, Elsa: not a word, please, to Father till we've got everything arranged.'

'No, I wouldn't dream of breathin' a word of anything you don't fancy said,' Elsa promised.

Events, however, did not run exactly to plan. Raney's parents were not happy about a marriage so soon after an engagement. In their high respectability they seemed to hold that a proper engagement should last six or eight months; nothing else was quite decent. So they stood out for late July; and we were both anxious to please them. July let it be.

But Aldith saw this delay as a new and excellent avenue of approach to Father, provided she trod it carefully and equipped herself with a lie or two. As the days passed by, mounting into weeks, we saw more and more the need of getting Father out of Dunkerry Crescent. The endless stairs, said the doctor, were not too good for him; nor for poor Elsa either. The warming of these big rooms too—the doctor spoke much of his being kept warm—was a liability he could not meet. The rent also would be beyond him when I was gone.

So one afternoon Aldith arrived with their car, ostensibly to take him for a convalescent's drive, though she did admit, 'We've got something to show you.'

'What may that be?' he asked, getting into the car.

'You'll see.' And deliberately she drove us to Hammersmith Bridge, and thence to the river's side along the Lower Mall, the Upper Mall and Chiswick Mall, while he, much to our

amusement, spoke ever and again of his old love for the river.
'That's where I used to get my skiff out,' he said, as we passed
Thring's Boat House on the Lower Mall. 'I don't know how
often I've sculled along this stretch as far as Walkden's Wharf
or even Putney Pier.'

'Yes, we thought you'd enjoy a drive by the river,' said
Aldith.

And in Chiswick Mall he reminded us, 'Many's the time
I've watched the Boat Race from here. By the time they've
passed Chiswick Eyot you generally know who's going to
win.'

'Is that so?' said Aldith. 'Really now? I never knew that.'

From the Mall's end she drove quickly through the un-
inspiring built-up streets of Chiswick and Little Sutton,
stopping at the house-agent's with the apology, 'I've just got
to go in here, chaps.'

'It's all very mysterious,' said Father. 'Mystery upon
mystery.'

'Not at all. Not at all. All perfectly natural,' Aldith maintained. 'A drive by the river is universally recognized as the
right thing when one's recovering from an illness. We'll be
back by the river soon. Yes: at Strand-on-the-Green.'

She emerged from the agent's with the key concealed in her
palm; and thereafter got us quickly to Grove Park Road and
the Thames-side again. Here began Strand-on-the-Green, so
she stopped the car and commanded, 'All out, please. All
change.'

'Why?' Father asked. 'I'm very comfortable.'

'Because we're going for a walk along the tow path. Can't
drive cars along the tow path.'

'It's all extremely odd,' Father repeated; and Aldith said
again, 'Not at all. Not at all'; unable to think of anything else
to say.

On the narrow tow path we were soon among the white
Regency or Georgian houses which stood with their feet on the
brink of the river. Most were of quaint shapes and had
nautical names: Binnacle House, Capstan Villa, Ship's Cabin,
and The Cockpit. One was called Anchor House and had a

large anchor aslant on its forecourt. Another called itself humbly The Horsebarge.

It may seem incredible, or perhaps there was a telepathic explanation of it, since both Aldith's brain and mine were like two electric batteries charged with excitement, but here, only a few yards from the little house, Father said, 'This is the sort of place in which I should have liked to live.'

Aldith, after her lips had pressed upward in a secret smile and her eye swung towards me, said only, 'Is it really? Fancy that'; which must have sounded rather foolish to Father.

The tide was low; the gulls wheeled and screamed over the mud flats, and over a narrowed river so still that it seemed asleep. Lonely scullers went feathering through the still water towards the arches of Kew Bridge. One boat with a red sail was feeling for wind between this north bank and the little eyot that lay in mid-stream like a raft of green trees. The declining sun, though invisible through veils of cloud contrived to throw a patina of gleaming bronze on the widening water down-stream. And suddenly out of that lustrous water came a racing eight cleaving it with entrancing rhythm and grace.

'Oh, look at that,' exclaimed Father. 'Why didn't we live here instead of in Dunkerry Crescent, where only the milk-float goes by or the greengrocer's van?'

'Or the coal-heaver's wagon,' said Aldith, keeping him in this mood.

A few more yards, and she abruptly stopped. We were opposite the house. 'Here we are,' she said. 'This is what we want to show you.' And now came the first lie. 'This is the house that our Stewart, who's such a rich man now, has been and gone and bought. His idea at first was to live in it with Raney, but obviously they can't do that till they're married. I mean to say: obviously they couldn't. You wouldn't wish it. And we've got another idea now. At least, I mean to say, Stewart has.'

'What's the idea?'

'You'll hear. But I'm sure you'd like to look at the place. Just to look at it.'

We walked into the house. Fortunate in our day and our hour we found the small front room aglow with the falling sun, which had come forth from the clouds. The tide was near the last of its ebb; and a sudden sharp breeze from the east, responding to this new warmth, had set the width of water astir with small waves. These mirrored the sun's light, and thus the tide, going homeward through London to the sea, flung a dance of many reflections on the walls of the little white room.

These walls behind the dancing light were in no good repair, but at least they were full of a smiling invitation to one who would love nothing better than to strip and paper or paint them.

Aldith perceived this factor at once. 'Well, Father, this is the great idea. Stewart literally has this house on his hands now——'

'Not "literally", my dear. "Figuratively". It's not a large house, I know, but he'd have to be a strong man to have it "literally" on his hands, ha, ha, ha.'

'Oh, damn all that. I was just going to say something nice——'

'And you know I don't like you to swear. It sounds awful in women. In men too, for that matter.'

'Yes, I know you think that, and I oughtn't to do it in front of you, though I do it liberally at home.'

'I'm sorry to hear it.'

'I'm sure you are, but may I get on with what I was trying to say? Stew's—now don't tell me not to call him "Stew" because I want to get on, and it's an interesting subject— Stew's fully decided that he can't live here with Raney because her parents, who're even stricter than you, have insisted on a long engagement, perhaps a year—' lie number two—'so that Raney can see if she really likes him—and you can't afford any longer to live in your big cold Dunkerry Crescent—Doctor Hillyard is dead against it; he told me so only the other day—' lie number three, because he hadn't seen her at all—'and you won't be able to keep it in glossy repair as you used to love to do, because he says you mustn't, so we both, Stew and I, had the bright idea that this would make a perfect home for you and—er—this bit is embarrassing, and Stewart in his gross selfishness has left me to suffer the embarrassment; but—well— we want you to have it. See? It came as a bright idea to both of us at once.' Far from true. 'We thought that you would love it and we could see you making it absolutely beautiful. Doctor Hillyard said he wouldn't mind your messing about with paints in small rooms like this. Just think what you could make of it. No one else could do it as well as you. So there it is. Stewart wants you to have it.'

'I must break in here,' I objected. 'Aldith has told one enormous lie.' (I didn't mention the other three.) 'We bought the house between us with the idea of offering it to you. That's the idea. That's why we brought you here.'

I thought his lips trembled again; he was weak after long illness.

'It's extremely thoughtful of you both. I—I do appreciate it. And I don't think there's anywhere else where I should so like to live. And I do think I could make it into——'

'And Elsa and Josef say they'll come and look after you,' I made haste to interpose. 'In fact, Elsa said she wouldn't like anyone else to be looking after you.'

'Yes, what it is to inspire love!' said Aldith.

That trembling of the lips again and a halting before he spoke. 'I'm enormously attracted by the idea. I've always loved the river so. Curious that I said just now that I'd love to live here. But what would the rent be?'

Aldith burst in here: 'No rent, silly! No rent, no rent, no rent. That's not the idea at all. You just live here, and damn all rent.'

'But I can't let you two do that.'

'You can; and you will; and why the hell not?' Father was too shaken to deal with the collapsing of her language into all these damns and hells. 'Why should you deny us the happiness of doing this little something for you? It's a parent's business to make their children happy. The bally house wasn't dear, so where's the worry? Damn it, the house'll still be our property but yours to occupy as long as you live. That's all. Nothing much.'

'Yes, that's the idea,' I endorsed. 'Nothing very much.'

He went to the window to look out at the river from which a tug had just hooted as it towed its string of barges under Kew

Bridge. He pretended to be filling his pipe there, but probably this was to hide his face from us while he mastered the emotion within him. When he spoke, his face was still towards the river.

'It's all very wonderful of both of you. I simply don't know what to say. It's—hard to put into words. I'm sorry, but I suppose I'm not really much good at expressing my feelings.' This from Father with his face turned from us and his fingers fiddling with the tobacco in his pipe; Father admitting to his children that he was not good at something. 'It's tremendously kind, and I must say that it's a wonderful solution to many difficulties which, I confess, have been pressing on me. Where to go. Where to live. I don't know how you managed to find a place so exactly the home I should love. You must know my tastes pretty well by this time—ha, ha.'

'Oh, yes, we know your tastes all right,' said Aldith. 'We know all about you by this time. Well, that's all settled, and everybody's happy. We can go home now.'

18

June, July

Thanks to Jack whose firm was often busy with conveyances and leases, Father was able to move from Dunkerry Crescent in a few weeks and establish himself with Elsa and Josef in his little waterside village of Strand-on-the-Green. As an easement to his burden of gratitude he insisted that all the furniture he would no longer need—and there was much of it—should not be sold but go into a warehouse 'for you and your . . . Raney'.

Of course he began at once, with the doctor's consent, to plaster all the walls and ceilings of his new home, to paint all the skirtings and woodwork, and, with saw and hammer, to create new shelves and cupboards; but this daily work, though not too fatiguing, was fortunately interrupted a score of times by another spell-binding entertainment: the river's pageantry under mid-summer suns. These he must stand and watch with paint-brush or hammer in his hands and perhaps a few nails in his mouth, and Hamish at his side, not interested in the river, but looking up at him to learn when the interesting work would be resumed. Those racing fours and eights at their rhythmic practice on the lifting tide; that single sculler who knew what happiness was on the loneliness of his sliding seat between the outrigged rowlocks; the sailing craft which leaned before the breeze; the pleasure-steamers ploughing up-stream while they trailed their wash in a long fan-tracery behind them—these last, he told us, seemed to carry like an aura about them the beauty of the places they would reach or pass, places that he had once loved to pass by in his boat: Maidenhead and Wargrave, Windsor and Oxford, and all the gentle green reaches of the Upper Thames Valley beyond.

Not less fascinating to him were the steam-tugs punching up the river with their trains of blunt-faced barges; these had their special appeal because he lived with the happy notion that tugmasters and lightermen were 'magnificent types, mahogany-browned by wind and sun with mighty forearms probably tattooed, and faces just about as blunt as those of their barges. Those are the people I really admire, Stewart. I know I should get on magnificently with them.'

'But they never come ashore at Strand-on-the-Green, I imagine?'

'Oh, no, but I sometimes watch them from Kew Bridge as they pass under the arches, I love to see them. Some of the salt of the earth.'

'Yes, but what about their language sometimes, Father?'

'Well, *what* about it?'

'They have a reputation for a certain richness and fruitiness in their language.'

'They probably have, but what's wrong with that?'

'Only that I gather that they are not averse to a reasonable run of blasphemies and obscenities if the occasion demands it.'

'Well, of course I don't like blasphemies and obscenities, but I've met a few bargees in my time and they've never spoken like that with me. They've always displayed a natural courtesy. They may be rough fellows, of course, but in my view they are just natural gentlemen.'

I left him to this pleasing fancy. No doubt there was an element of truth in what he said, so I refrained from spoiling his pleasure by suggesting that some of them probably beat their wives.

Like many another man's, Father's language could approach a lyricism when he was speaking of things that really got him by the heart. High among such things were the sounds and sights and scents of the river. He loved, so he told us, to see at night-time the red and green stars of passing ships and to hear the lamenting of their sirens; and then, as he lay in bed, to listen to the full tide plopping against the tow-path wall and washing over the stair, or, when it was low, come sobbing— his own word—sobbing over the 'hard', which was the dank waste of mud left exposed by the ebb. From this shingle and mud he could smell, he declared, the salty tang of the seas from which the tides had come. This could not really be so because the sea's water did not come so far up the tideway, but who does not verge on poetry when he greatly loves?

I doubt if Father had ever been happier than in that June month which saw the first of his days in this riverside home, or Aldith, Jack and I more alight with self-congratulation at our successful removal of him from Dunkerry Crescent to Strand-on-the-Green. He had gone into the house on the third day of that June; and neither he nor we, twenty-six days later, when we read in our morning papers of two pistol shots fired by a student, little more than a schoolboy, at a place called Sarajevo in the Balkans far away, troubled greatly about them, even though they had killed the heir to the Austrian throne. Assassinations happened so easily and often in the Balkans. We did not know that those two ringing shots were the signal for our world to die.

§

From that day when we read this piece of news to the twenty-third day of the following month we lived, all of us, in a state of tranquil unconcern. I was now living in ample comfort with Uncle Douglas in his apartment at Lincoln's Inn till such time as Raney and I should have found a home and be able to marry, hardly in July, as we had once hoped, but probably in August or September. She and I spent many of these days hunting for a home, never with final success but always with laughter and gay hopes.

But then, overnight, like a collapse of fine sunny days into days of louring cloud the menace bore down upon the whole world. Day after day alarm succeeded alarm. On that twenty-third of July Austria, after weeks of lazy thought, sent a savage and intolerable ultimatum to Serbia whose countryman had dared to assassinate the heir to her throne. Two days later Serbia, not without dignity, accepted all of this ultimatum that a proud nation could bear, but Austria, having assured herself during these days of lazy deliberation that Germany would support her, refused the acceptance and on the following day declared herself at war with Serbia. At first we all—even Uncle Douglas whose ear heard all the secrets of Fleet Street in its offices and pubs—tried to make light of this bullying declaration, treating it as no more than a black, bluffing threat and maintaining that 'there were always these troubles in the Balkans'. Had not the King and Queen of Serbia been assassinated some ten years before, and nothing much had happened after that except little local Balkan wars against Turkey and Bulgaria? Even when Russia announced that if the Austrians attacked Serbia she would go to the aid of her 'little Slav brother' and to strengthen this warning, began to mobilize, we still called it another bluff designed only to frighten Austria, a perilous bluff but one that could be called, since none of these three nations could really wish for war.

But when Germany announced that she, like Russia, would stand by her weaker brother, Austria, and demanded that Russia's mobilization should stop within twelve hours or she would declare war, then Uncle Douglas, his ear hard down on Fleet Street, shook his head at me, and grimaced, and when I asked 'What now?' said only 'God knows.'

That evening, the last day of July, we were sitting together in the comfortable leather armchairs of his living-room, he with his cigar, I with my meerschaum constantly needing to be relit because my thoughts were elsewhere; and after a prolonged and loaded silence he said, 'Damned little room for complacency now, Stewart. Russia, Austria and Serbia may not really want war, but Germany's a different matter. Unlike the others she is ready. She has long been looking forward to "Der Tag" and I can see that this may well seem "The Day" for her.'

'Why?'

'Among other things because she sees that Britain has a Liberal Government in hopeless trouble with Ireland and one that would almost certainly split if there was talk of going to war in Europe; so she probably thinks we can be left out of the reckoning. In which, maybe, she is wrong.'

Blindly we knew, I suppose, as we sat in that room together, that History was sitting with us. I know that, after fifty years and more, almost every word that we spoke comes back to me vividly. And history itself might have spoken the words.

'I hope she *is* wrong,' I heard myself say defiantly. 'Dammit, we're here.'

'Yes, yes, yes—but did you know that she has given Russia twelve hours to stop mobilization, or it's war?'

'On Russia only. . . .'

'On Russia and Serbia, With Austria at her side.'

'Unless Russia backs down. . . .'

He shook his head confidently. 'Which she won't. What nation backs down before an insolent ultimatum? Even little Serbia wasn't wholly ready to do it.'

'So by this time tomorrow there'll be four nations at war?'

'Four—with a fifth coming in.'

'Fifth?'

'France. She's the sworn ally of Russia, treaty-bound to her. She might dishonour that treaty, of course, but—she can't and she won't.'

'So it's five great nations at war tomorrow or the next day?'

'Four great; one small.'

'And it'll be the first of August, the month Raney and I hoped to marry in. But at least Britain needn't join in the fighting. At least Britain can keep out? And things would be much as usual here?'

For a minute or more Uncle Douglas did not answer, but played with the cigar at his lips. Then he capped my poor 'at least's' with the warning words, 'At least there's the *Entente Cordiale*. How deep that agreement went no one really knows—except those that *do* know. Not even Fleet Street. No one.' He paused again. 'I suppose it's just possible that Britain can stand on the touch-line and keep the ring for the others. That's what our dear *Times* is advocating. Close ranks at home and limit the area of war.'

This last hope, if hope it could be called, was dead in twenty-four hours. The next day, a Bank Holiday Sunday, nearly all London's holiday week-enders, instead of escaping on cycles or excursion trains to seaside or countryside, were wandering about the capital as if to stay at the centre of things and learn there what terrible but exciting road their world might be about to take. London waited and watched in its own streets.

In the afternoon Raney and I were among these drifting crowds. All our thoughts about marriage were temporarily overshadowed by the thunder-cloud which was down over the world. We drifted with others to Buckingham Palace, as if to see what the King was doing there; to the War Office to watch important-looking people coming and going; to the Admiralty for the same purpose; to Downing Street to stare at No. 10 and wonder what was happening behind its windows; into Westminster Abbey where we saw many people, mostly women, kneeling in lonely prayer, and where an excited man, of the kind who must share his excitement with others, touched my arm, pointed to a kneeling woman and whispered that she was the Prime Minister's wife.

Throughout the day special editions of the Sunday papers were shouted by the news-boys and snatched by the people; and from these, in the early evening, we learned that Germany, after demanding a right of way through neutral Belgium had, in fact, already crossed the frontiers of Luxembourg and France.

Where was Britain now? Britain who had sworn to support the neutrality of Belgium.

On the Monday the King of the Belgians, sternly rejecting Germany's demand, appealed to the King of Britain; and Britain, responding to this appeal, sent to Germany, not an ultimatum as yet, but a warning that if Belgian neutrality were violated, Britain would not stand aside.

Tuesday, at about seven in the evening, Uncle Douglas and I were again seated together, not speaking much but just smoking. Uncle now with a pipe in his mouth; and the thin blue wreaths of smoke that leapt spasmodically from its bowl showed how troubled was his thinking. I have the clearest memory of Uncle Douglas's face on that evening whose date was to become perhaps the most memorable in our island's story. Instead of being jovial and plastic with its readiness for smiles or laughter, it was set as firm and as still as a sculptor's

239

pale cast; the lips pressed together, the eyes staring at invisible matters far away, his hands rising sometimes to finger the lips or to cover the brow like a visor. The pale face was like a studied mask of inquietude. Again and again the eyes swung to the telephone on his wall. It was an old-fashioned instrument with two bells and a ringing handle on a box, the receiver hanging from a bracket at its side. A few minutes after seven its bell rang, and Uncle Douglas, startled out of thought, hurried to it. He spoke with someone, presumably in Fleet Street, but his words were few, and the only ones I remember were, 'Just gone, has it?' and 'Well, there it is, old boy' and 'This is It. Thanks for ringing.'

Returning to his chair he said to me, 'This is It. "Der Tag". Our ultimatum has gone to Germany. Germany hasn't paid the least attention to our warning—who supposed she would? —so our ambassador has issued an ultimatum that unless before midnight tonight we receive an assurance that Belgium's neutrality will be observed, it'll be war.'

'Midnight tonight?'

'Midnight tonight. That's to say twelve-midnight by their time; eleven by ours. Four hours to go. Then we shall know. But of course we know already.'

Those four hours we sat there, sipping whisky and soda, but talking very little. Outside in the streets there was an unusual, a curious stillness; no traffic, it seemed; nor footsteps. It was as if the world were standing still. Or standing at a death-bed. Uncle's face had set again into that pale mask of apprehension. On his mantel-shelf was an expensive Sèvres set, consisting of an elaborately handsome clock ornate with coloured pictures and golden cherubim, flanked by twin goblet-shaped vases. Each of these over-decorated pieces stood on a low gilded pedestal. The clock behind its painted pictures had a striking mechanism but its bell was old and weak. We sat listening for its strokes, waiting for it to strike eleven times, knowing that in all its two hundred years of life it had never proclaimed such an hour as this. Once, just before eleven, Uncle Douglas went to the telephone again and spoke with friends in Fleet Street. He hung the receiver back on its bracket and returned to his

chair where he began, without a word to me, to resuscitate his
dead pipe.

'Well?' I asked.

'No,' he said. 'No answer. No contrite apology. Whoever
imagined there would be? On the contrary, they've crossed
the Belgian frontier and are advancing deep. Their Foreign
Secretary has expounded to our ambassador that there was
nothing else to do. War is life or death, he said, and the
obvious thing to do was to advance quickly by an undefended
route, and damn all treaties and agreements. War is war;
time is time.'

Even as he spoke our clock struck its timid and homely notes;
and our sharpened ears heard the notes of a heavier clock
somewhere out in the dark and quiet night. Eleven.

'So,' he said. 'There it is. Seven nations at war now. Nothing
like it, Stewart, in the history of the world. Poor old Britain:
she's managed to climb to the highest peak of all; and here's
an avalanche for her.' He ministered to the pipe again. 'God
knows where it will carry her, or where it will leave her.
Anyhow I hope you've noticed that we're the only nation to
declare war on Germany; all the others have let her do the
declaring—unless poor little Belgium's refusal to let them
through amounted to a declaration. It was at least a declaration that she was ready to lose all except her honour. Which
is precisely what will happen.'

I don't know whether I should be ashamed to confess—but
it is the truth—that in those hours before our clock struck its
tinny eleven my heart and mind were inflated with an excitement of suspense which was undoubtedly (though not wholly)
pleasurable, since the drama outweighed for the moment all
thoughts of the terrors, the slaughter, the human miseries and
anguishes that would set out on their march tomorrow. Or to
admit also that my emotions during the days after this opening
of the war were a blend of patriotic pride, thrilling excitement
and an almost unbounded confidence. Pride because we alone
had declared war. In defence of our pledged word and in
support of a weak little nation. I had the feeling, of which I was
slightly ashamed, that I was thrilled instead of horrified to be

alive at such a moment. No doubts as yet troubled me. My country was safe behind the walls of her Grand Fleet. It was a proud excitement to remember how, in the days just before we declared war, all the mighty ships of the Navy, four hundred vessels in all—battleships, battle cruisers, light cruisers, destroyers, flotilla leaders, gunboats—had been, accidentally or intentionally, arrayed off Portsmouth in the Solent and Spithead for the King's Review, and so had been able, before that eleven o'clock struck, to steam away, in line ahead, to action stations in the North Sea mists or elsewhere on the seven seas.

This Navy, by far the greatest in the world, could land forces anywhere—behind the German lines, perhaps, at Antwerp, Ostend, Dunkirk. And among all the generals of the nations who must direct this war, ours alone had been grilled and drilled in war—three years of it in South Africa only a dozen years ago. In Field Marshal Lord Kitchener, conqueror in the Sudan and South Africa, victor at Omdurman, Khartoum, and Vereeniging, we had surely the greatest soldier of all. That he should be making holiday in England at this moment before returning to his tasks in Egypt seemed as providential as the assembly of the Navy in Solent and Spithead. Here was 'The Man for the Moment'. All the popular press shouted this; Lord Portwith's greatest journal (and the place of my assignment) among them. The Prime Minister, accepting the clamour, halted him at Dover as he was about to embark for Egypt; whereat the people rejoiced. Next day the papers reported their triumph. He was Secretary of State for War.

I must record that Uncle Douglas, for all his highly trained shrewdness, and his avowed recoil from jingoism and sentimentality, shared at first these emotions—or most of them—with me. So great were the drama, the menace, and the hope ·in these early weeks that some of the strongest intelligences were lifted off the hard earth. All that was strongly sane in Uncle Douglas had dreaded the approach of world war, but all that was so vital and gay in him forced him to wish—and half-believe—good things for his country. I don't recall meeting anyone in the first days who was severely critical of our optimism. Certainly not Father, who found it difficult, I fancy, to believe that a country of which he—to say nothing of the splendid tugmasters and lightermen on his Thames—was a member could easily fail of victory in the end. I think Aldith and Jack held a somewhat similar view at first—though without the tugmen. Elsa was hardly less sanguine even if she had a difficulty about Josef, a German, who now, much to her indignation, had to report regularly to the police; but this was no great difficulty because basically she thought of him as having assumed her nationality by being old and having lived with her as a husband all these years.

The Germans might be advancing fast through Belgium; Liège, Namur and Brussels might have fallen, but before this we had learned that under cover of darkness one night a British Expeditionary Force had landed in France. Inevitably smaller than the French and German armies, this Force, nevertheless, was composed of highly trained regular troops, long in service, not of hastily assembled conscripts like the Germans they would oppose; and their infantrymen were famous as the finest riflemen in the world, mounting a fire-power and a marksmanship beyond anything other powers could deploy. One day I saw our Guards marching along Buckingham Palace Road obviously to take train at Victoria for the Front. Splendidly tall young men they looked in their unfamiliar khaki; and the people on the pavements watching this march-past said, '*They'll* teach 'em. Poor look-out for the Huns. One feels almost sorry for 'em.' Who could stand up against our Guards? Who had ever stood up to them? Then, far away in the East, the 'Russian steam-roller', the multitudinous Russian army, had begun to roll.

Our comfort shook when our British Force, finding its flanks exposed by a retreat of the French army, had themselves to go back from Mons—but this was the fault of the French, not of our splendid boys—who had to retreat as far as the River Marne and the very neighbourhood of Paris.

But the Marne! It was but a month and two days since our declaration of war that the British Expeditionary Force and the Fifth Army sallied forth in power from the Marne and so endangered the enemy's right flank and rear that for days he had to retreat back and back to the Aisne. Rumours and the more excitable newspapers said that his retreat was like a rout and the extravagant optimists talked of the war being comfortably over before Christmas.

Not yet had it broken upon me that I might have to turn myself into a soldier and find myself, in but a few months, one of a million fighting Britons 'over there'. Certainly enthusiastic and excited young men were volunteering in numbers greater than authority could handle; but not for a moment had I seen myself as a member of one of those packed and patient queues, shouting and singing as they waited on the pavements. The old world, just dead, still walked beside me like a ghost, and as far as I can remember now, I was loud in my admiration of these patriotic queues but thought only of them (bear in mind my dear father) as working-class chaps who alone enlisted in the 'ranks' for the King's shilling.

19

Assignment with Truth

The war, and especially the Marne days, kept my pen busy from morning till bed. I wrote 'moving' and 'exciting' articles about the war, and one I recall today with bewilderment; it was a tribute to the volunteers queuing outside the recruiting offices, and it was under a title I'd used long before when expounding the desires of Youth, but it had a new meaning now: 'The Feet of the Young Men.'

My editor had taken to sending me on 'assignments' to place after place, scene after scene, that I might report the country at war. All these reports were to be signed articles, prominently displayed on the Feature Page. This honour, for such it seemed, was another ingredient in my selfish satisfaction with these exciting days.

An evening, and the editor rang me at Uncle Douglas's to say, 'Southend tomorrow. Without fail, please. There by ten. Magnificent subject waiting for you there. Two good subjects, in fact.' And he told me what they were.

The second of these subjects sent me rushing off to Mortress Lane, where I persuaded Mr. and Mrs. Wayburn to give me Raney for the whole day so that I could take her with me to see strange things in Southend. I pretended that what these were I must not say; but was not Southend, and its great white Palace Hotel with its 'Terrace Restaurant' facing the sea, a glowing memory for both of us? They consented, and next morning off we went from Fenchurch Street Station *en route* for Southend. As a delegate from my paper I travelled first-class, Raney at my side, merrily surprised to find herself seated in such comfort and dignity; she had never travelled in a first-class compartment before. Second-class with me some-times instead of third-class—but first-class! 'A pity the journey takes only a little over the hour,' she said. 'I don't want to get out. I know it's all very sinful, but I can't help wishing some of my friends in the Dene could see me sitting here. Is that very wrong?'

'Yes, of course. But very natural. I shouldn't worry too much.'

'All right. I won't. So now tell me what it is we're going to see.'

I answered, 'In a phrase beloved of our Prime Minister, "Wait and see".'

'But there can't be anything much to see at Southend. Apart from the river and the ships, and of course the Palace Hotel, you've always said there was nothing to see at Southend except the trippers from London eating cockles and winkles. And miles of mud when the tide's out.'

'So it used to be. But there happens to be a war on now.'

'I still don't see what Southend can do about that. It's not an industrial place; it's just a seaside resort, isn't it?'

'Wait and see.'

'Well, I only hope whatever it is that, after waiting, we're going to see will be worth all this unnatural suspense.'

'It will be picturesque,' I promised her.

When we issued from the L.M.S. station into the Southend streets, the town looked little different from what it had been those two years ago. The women were shopping in the High Street; the traffic on the roads seemed much the same as ever. It was only I, as we walked down the High Street towards the sea, who noticed men loitering on the pavement as if waiting to watch something of interest pass by. A fresh and brimy air from the broad Thames greeted us when at last we were standing on Pier Hill and looking out to sea. There stood the familiar pier stretching a mile and more into the estuary so as to keep its forefeet in water even when, as today, the tide was at its lowest. After Raney had rhapsodized a little about the *Golden Eagle* tied up to the pier's head, about our journey down its long mile in an electric tram-car, and our 'marvellous dinner with the heavenly waiters' in that great white hotel, I pointed to three black blunt-bowed ships lying at anchor far out on the tideway. 'D'you see those ships?'

'Yes; what about them?'

'They are prisons.'

'Prisons. How can they be prisons?'

'They are prison hulks for German prisoners-of-war we've captured in France.'

'Do you *mean* to say we——'

'I don't mean to say anything. I know nothing. I only know that prisoners of war are going to be kept there, safely out at sea.'

'But—' a troubled look stood in Raney's eyes—'isn't that rather brutal? I don't know . . . they may be Germans . . . but I think we ought to treat them properly. Shouldn't we?'

'They're not going to be chained to the bottoms of the holds, if that's what you're afraid of. There are things called Geneva Conventions which wouldn't allow us to do that, even if we wanted to.'

'Which we wouldn't, would we?'

'No, my pet. On the contrary they'll probably have quite a healthy and interesting time, settled out there in the middle of the Estuary and watching lovely ships go by. I don't know that I'd mind changing places with them for a little. If I could have you with me as a prisoner. I fully intend to drop a hint in my article that it's our job to treat them well.'

Raney, clutching my arm, said, 'Oh, *do*. Do. They've only been fighting for their country as our boys have.'

This pleased me because from the first days of the war, even though in my simplicity I believed that our cause was as unselfish and admirable as the Germans was abominable, I could not understand that the simple truth just uttered by Raney did not stare all people in the face. But it didn't. So many people—probably the majority—preferred to be blind to it; preferred to think that every poor German conscript, forced to fight in his Government's war, was evil and worthy of hatred and punishment. I was glad that Raney was free of this ugly infection.

The ugly fever was displayed before us within a few minutes of Raney's words. We noticed that people who had been strolling between the trees or leaning on the railings had now suddenly turned to hurry towards the High Street. People in the High Street were shouting, 'They're here. They're coming.' We too crossed the road to the High Street but unhurriedly and, as we liked to think, with more dignity than these excitable persons. And soon we heard from far up the street a murmur as of boos and jeers, mingled with laughter.

We saw what was creating the excitement. Down the road-way from the station came a procession of German prisoners divested of all equipment except their field-grey uniforms. Some were without caps of any pattern; one or two were still wearing their spiked grey helmets. They marched four abreast between an escort of British soldiers who carried rifles at the slope with bayonets fixed. Fine young men they were, tall, broad, mostly blond, and all bearing themselves well; a handful picked perhaps from the finest of Germany's regular soldiers. I was disappointed to see that some of the British guarding them were shorter, narrower, less robust, and less handsome; but I took comfort in the thought that our Guards would look every inch as tall as these. Perhaps these were Prussian Guards.

'Boo ... boo ... boo-ooh!' hooted the watchers on the pavements—or many of them—as these representatives from the enemy went by.

Raney again clutched my arm. 'Oh I wish they wouldn't do that. It's not fair.'

'It's *not* fair,' I agreed loudly because angrily; and a man on my left turned to glare at me. Which, on the whole, pleased me, because I'd intended his instruction. He'd been booing.

'It's perfectly fair,' he said. 'The Germans are swine. I'm all for them knowing what we think of them.'

And a man on the other side of me offered, 'I quite agree. What the hell are you? A pro-German?'

'Oh, don't be silly,' I protested. Which didn't please him at all; his fist clenched and his teeth protruded. 'One isn't a pro-German if one refuses to hoot at every German one sees.'

'You want a lesson, you do,' he said. 'You want teaching something.'

'It's you that want the lesson, old boy.'

248

Raney pulled at my arm and shook her head in a quick rebuke. 'Don't,' she whispered. 'Oh, please . . . be quiet.'

But I didn't want to be quiet. Instead, my own fist clenching, ready for a reply to any assault, I answered her loudly, for both men to hear. 'I don't believe for a moment that all Germans are swine.'

'That's what he is.' Another voice from behind had joined in. 'A pro-German. We don't want any bloody pro-Germans. For all we know, he's a bloody German spy. There's all too many of 'em about.'

I laughed; knowing that this would hurt him most. 'Don't be quite mad.' And hotly indifferent now to what might ensue, I went on. 'Use what little sense you've got. These poor fellows may be misled, but they're not necessarily swine. I suspect many of them are quite decent chaps.'

'*Stewart*, please,' Raney begged. '*Please*. There's no sense in——'

But I held there was much sense in what I was saying, and much sense in saying it to fools like these. 'Some of them look decent enough. And I bet they've fought for their country well.'

'Good God!' exclaimed the man on my right, and his clenched fist lifted.

So did mine; ready.

I don't know what would have happened—whether or not they would have set upon me—but just then Southend was saved from a scuffle and a local sensation by a street-urchin who'd diverted everyone's attention by running up to the procession and walking beside it, in rhythmic step with the soldiers of both nations, while he pretended to be a news-boy with a news-bill. ' 'Evvy German lawses,' he shouted to all. 'Li'test news. 'Evvy German lawses.'

Cheers and laughter for this small comedian displaced, if only for a moment, the hooting and booing of the prisoners.

Pleased with his success he ran to the front of the column and, some six paces ahead of the sergeant-in-charge, led it towards the sea like a commanding officer, while still proclaiming loudly, 'Big defeat of the henemy. 'Evvy German lawses.'

R   249

I felt he had done us all a good turn by allowing a trickle of Cockney fun to infiltrate the senseless and sickening execration. 'Come along,' I said to Raney. 'We've seen that. We've something of much more importance to see now.'

As we walked away the men who had abused me glowered after us, their looks suggesting some regret at the loss of a possible victim; at this chance missed for an enjoyable punishment. The words 'Bloody pro-German' followed me. 'He wants learning a thing or two.' 'You're tellin' me!' 'A touch o' what-for'd do 'im no 'arm.'

Denying them the satisfaction of supposing I'd heard them, I put my note-book and my pencil into Raney's hand. Surprised, she demanded, 'What do you expect me to do with these? What are these for?'

'You'll see.'

I led her out of the High Street and up to the wide doors of the Palace Hotel.

'Remember?' I asked.

'Of course I remember. I remember the very table we sat at.'

'It won't be there now,' I said, as we walked into what used to be the vestibule of the hotel. The Palace was now a vast military hospital.

'Well, I could walk to the very window where the table was. Is there any chance we can see it again?'

'I don't know. I know nothing. Only keep that pencil and notebook in view.'

No polite commissionaire was there to direct us; no clerks sat waiting for us at the reception desk. Only R.A.M.C. orderlies with red-cross brassards on their arms hurried to and fro, indifferent to us; a Regular Army nurse in her caped uniform of grey and red stood talking with one of them; and here came a wheeled stretcher bearing a wounded soldier, his eyes closed, his head bandaged, and his body wrapped in a grey army blanket. The hasty, blood-stained bandage and the grey army blanket suggested that he had been brought in some make-shift vessel straight from some casualty-clearing station at the Front. Even as I halted there, wondering which way to go, a fleet of ambulances came in procession to the doors, and orderlies walked out casually to deal with them as if well accustomed to such arrivals at intervals throughout the day.

I decided we'd best get out of everyone's way; and when I noticed an officer, not young but with no more than two stars on his shoulder and therefore of no intimidating rank, I was about to go up to him and show my credentials when, far better, I saw a grey-haired chaplain standing by a door, his white dog-collar and black stock contrasting with his khaki uniform and Sam Browne belt. A black crown—actually a crown—on his shoulders denoted a major; and I knew that this was my man; a parson, even if of field rank, was not intimidating. And yet a major could carry weight.

I went up to him and told him I held a special permit, at the request of Lord Portwith, to visit the hospital and report on it for the *Daily World*. Even with a kindly-looking padre, however classless his profession and his duties, a lord, I felt, would be a good card to play.

I was not mistaken in his kindliness. 'Well, that's fine,' he said. 'The more you tell people, the better. They ought to know. They ought to know. They don't know. We're doing our best here to cope with dreadful conditions—with real heart-rending horrors—so give us a fair report.'

'I sure will, sir.'

'And . . . ?' He looked inquiringly at Raney.

'My secretary, sir. She's helping me.'

'You're very young to have a secretary.' It was said with a smile that suggested friendly flattery rather than distrust, and within his eyes the immediate pleasure of every man (be he elderly parson or youthful layman) in a pretty face.

'Part-time only, sir,' I submitted with an answering smile. 'Permanent soon, we hope.'

He caught the truth at once and, laughing, said, 'Well, my blessing on you both.' It was like a blessing out of the midst of the war's sufferings. 'And now, my dears, go your way. I don't think anyone will trouble you. Their hands are too full. We've got to vacate as many as possible today because we've hundreds coming in tonight and tomorrow. That's the men's chief ward along there and the officers' ward is in front in what used to be the Terrace Restaurant. A splendid room for them, facing the sea.'

'I know it of old, sir. So does my secretary.'

'Fine; and if anybody asks you why you're there or what you're up to, say Mr. Ensleigh sent you—no, better say "Major Ensleigh". We padres are not supposed to call ourselves by our ranks, but major's a word that can be quite useful at times. Especially with bossy busybodies.'

'Thank you very much, sir,' I said; and 'Come along, Miss Wayburn' to my secretary.

We went first into the men's ward, a spacious room which had once been—so the first orderly I spoke to told me—the Ball Room. Beds for the wounded stood so close together that there was barely a channel between them. Two parallel rows of beds, end to end, stretched down the middle of the room. Only a few orderlies wandered among the beds or stood talking with the patients. Some V.A.D.s (Voluntary Aid girls) with their veils pinned beneath their chignons, a red cross in the centre of every veil, were either standing about as if bemused, or talking to the livelier wounded who were glad to pass the time with young and pretty women.

We talked with some of the men in their beds, or, rather, I talked, Raney saying little unless I sought an answer from her. Not but what the men looked at her more often than at me. Others of the men were asleep or lying with eyes closed in sickness or pain. Some lifted their eyelids to see us go by and then dropped them again like blinds lowered against the miseries of this present world.

One man was eager to talk; and it was his spate of words that made of this visit a crucial hour in our lives. He was an old regular sergeant, with a grizzled chin as yet unshaved. A high cradle held the bedclothes off his lower limbs, and a rope with a bar-handle hung above him so that he could pull himself up or change his position. Just now he was content to lie on his back with fingers interwreathed on his breast.

To open our talk I asked 'Badly wounded?' and the spate began.

'Losing a leg, that's all, guv. But I'm a lucky one, believe you me. I can tell you: no one over here has any idea what's goin' on over there. It's utter bleedin' hell, arstin' the young lady's pardon. Blue murder, that's what it is. I was in some of the worst fighting of the Boer War, but that was toffee compared to what they're dishin' us out there. I don't know how any of us've lived through it. Most 'aven't.'

I broke in to ask in what way it was so different from the recent war.

'Guns, mister. The old Boers had bigger guns than what we ever expected, so that we had to get guns off the ships—just like us!—but the Boers' guns were twopenny pistols compared with what the Jerries have got. I seen several of my mates blown to pieces by a single shell—sorry, lady—but I mean bits and pieces; nothing left of 'em but bits and pieces all over the shop. 'Ere and there a bit o' khaki with a button on it. But this is no stuff for the young lady to hear.'

To my surprise Raney said, her voice shaken, 'But I want to hear; I do, really.'

And I, shaken too, delved for some comfort with the words, 'But aren't they on the run now? That's what we're being told.'

'On the run?—don't you believe it, mister. Tell 'em different. Tell 'em different. We got round their flank but that's all. This 'ere glorious victory is no more than the Jerries withdrawin' to a better line they got waitin'. We saved Paris—that was summat, yah; that was a bit of all-right, but that was all the victory there was. All this talk of a glorious advance is so much codswallop for you people at 'ome. Lies to keep you 'appy. If you're a gen'l'man of the Press, you tell 'em ole Kitchener's got it right. We've got a war of yurs and yurs on our 'ands. The Jerries are only gettin' back from the Marne to the Aisne' —he pronounced it 'Aisen'—'and there they'll stand. For yurs.'

'*Years?*'

'Yah. That's what I said.'

From Raney came an 'Oh, *no*', but it was little more than a breath of dismay.

'Yurs. Three or four yurs of it. They're dug down deep in

their trenches, and they can stay there for yurs. They got the machine guns, yer see.'

My heart, sickening, demanded the question: 'But do you mean we can't break through them—ever?'

'Not for yurs. We ain't got the men. More'n half the old ones are dead already, or out of it for good and all, like me. Yer see, it's not only they got far more and far heavier artillery than us; it's the machine guns.' He nodded grimly. 'That's us all over. We got two machine guns for each battalion; they seem to have one for every bloody section—pardon, lady—and a line of machine guns in nice deep gun-pits'll hold up an army for yurs.'

Despairingly, I asked, 'But couldn't we turn their flank as we did on the Marne?'

'Nah.' Never a more confident, even contemptuous, denial. 'Jerry's not going to be caught like that a second time. My officer says their line'll stretch to the sea. From Switzerland to the sea. And an outflankin' army'd get a bit wet in the sea. So'd their guns.'

Talk of the sea brought a small comforting remembrance. 'Couldn't the Navy do anything about that?'

'Oh, the Navy's all right. Thank Gawd for the Navy. She'll keep 'em out of England all right. But she'd have to land 'uge armies to outflank the Jerries, and where's the men? If you arst me ole Kitchener knows that he'll need every fit man in Britain before he's done. He knew what was what in the Boer War, and it took 'im yurs to finish it.'

Every fit man? I did not speak; I left the talking to him.

'The Jerries a' got millions o' men, and we shall need millions. In our *Comic Cuts*—that's our army newspaper—they say ole Kitchener's already got nearly a million, and I daresay that for once in a way they're telling the truth. Truth or not, he'll 'ave to 'ave them in millions—and more'n half o' that little lot'll be done in. But they'll all 'ave to come along and take their chahnst.'

I was sure he was no ̣ ̣ ̣ ̣nking of me as he said this; not essaying a rebuke ̣ ̣ ̣ ̣ ̣ing young and fit and still in a comfortable civilia ̣ ̣ ̣ ̣ ̣seemed too friendly a man for that;

but *I* was thinking of me; and a sudden touch of Raney's hand on my fingers showed that her thoughts were mine. I wished I could have dismissed my thoughts by deciding that this loquacious old fellow was an alarmist, bad news being ever better talk than good. But I didn't believe this. I thought him a sensible veteran and most of his words convincing. He had awakened me from comfortable sleep and, as on a screen, thrown the war before me. That ghost of an old dead world, which had walked into the hospital beside me, faded into nothing as he talked.

Before we left his bed he asked, 'The young lady's your wife, is she?'

'No,' I said, and attempted a smile. 'Not yet.'

'We're engaged,' Raney promptly put in; and her happiness and pride in this quick statement gave me a moment of pleasure in the midst of dark, cheerless thoughts.

'Well, lady, let an old sweat like me wish you everything.'

'Thank you awfully,' Raney responded, and with a womanly touch she laid her hand for a grateful second over his hands. Always Raney made much use of a hand to communicate emotion. 'It's very sweet of you. Thanks ever so much.' But for the first time I heard a new note in her voice; a note as of an awful doubt.

'Me wife and me've been married now for twenty-one years and it's bin a good show. I 'ope yours'll be as good, mister. I'm shore it will.'

'Thank you,' I said; but in this last hour all my thoughts of marriage had been tossed into a turmoil. I covered this chaos with a smile and the words, 'I suspect you'll be seeing your wife any moment now. That'll be something, won't it?'

'Yah. God, I'm one of the lucky ones, and I reckon she'll think she is too.'

'Well, we're both very glad for your sake, but we must go now. Good-bye, sergeant. We both wish you all the luck in the world.'

'Same to you, guv. And to you, miss.'

Raney laid again the grateful hand on his, and we went. In the passage outside she seized hold of my arm and said,

'Darling . . . darling . . . it doesn't mean you'll have to go to the war?'

'I should think it means exactly that.'

'And that we shan't be able to get married?'

'No, I'm not letting it mean that. If I have to go, I'm going to marry you first. I'm sure your mother and father'll consent; but if they don't, we'll do without anyone's consent. Agreed?'

'Oh, yes, yes—but you mustn't go; I'm sure you needn't; you mustn't.'

As she said this, I knew in the deep of my heart that she was wrong. Whatever she said, I was seeing again the war which the sergeant had depicted, and even though I had none of that eagerness to 'get to the Front' which the crowds at the recruiting offices were showing, I knew that I could no longer live with the thought that I was standing aside.

'On the contrary,' I said, 'it looks as if I must.'

'Oh, no, no.'

'Well, we can't be certain of anything yet,' I comforted her. 'Come, we'll go to the officers' ward. As you heard, it was once that big Terrace Restaurant where we had a nice meal together.'

'Oh, and things were so lovely then.'

Sadly, all the way to the officers' ward, she held my arm tight, as if somehow this could hold me near her.

We walked into the great room. It was filled with the brightness of full day because all its large windows looked out upon the Estuary, and the Estuary under the sun was a wide and glistening mirror. This being an officers' ward, the beds were not crowded together as in the ward for 'Other Ranks', and there were more orderlies, nurses and V.A.D.s to minister to the comfort of patients. Some of the older patients, no doubt, were officers of high rank.

Jokingly, or pretending to joke, we walked, each proud of our memory, straight to the window before which our dinner-table had been. It was near the farther end of the room, not far from the dais on which an orchestra had performed, and both of us remarked how strange it was to see an iron hospital bed, covered with a scarlet blanket, filling the place of our daintily ordered table. In the bed an officer of thirty or more, and probably a regular, sat upright against the back-rest and the piled pillows. Neither his head nor his body showed any bandages. He watched as we approached him, as if he would welcome us.

'I'm a fraud,' he said, when I'd asked him how he was progressing, and had laughed over the fact that we'd once eaten a memorable meal where now he lay. 'A thorough-going fraud. All the rest here are pukka casualties—some of them damned serious—but I've just gone sick. I'm only ill, and not very ill at that, though there's talk of a small operation.'

'Shall we weary you if we talk too much?'

'Anything but. I'm bored to tears lying here. Tell me all about your life, and then I'll give you a resumé of mine.' He looked at Raney. 'And I'd enormously enjoy a resumé of your companion's. Neither of you need reveal anything of which you're very properly ashamed.'

I explained my business there, but much of the time as I spoke I was looking out at the pier running its long mile into the sea and the black hulks lying sullenly off it, and the gentle hills of Kent rising like a long swaying shadow in the distant haze.

He told us that he was the staff captain of his brigade and that he was ashamed, ashamed, to have deserted them like this, but, by God, he'd get back to them as soon as he could. I snatched the chance to ask a staff officer, though without much hope, if all that the sergeant had said was somewhat exaggerated.

'Exaggerated? I'd say no. I'd say he's got it weighed up pretty exactly. Brother Bosche is going to stand on the Aisne, and it's going to take us several years and a million men to shift him. And what's more, fifty times as many guns as we've got; and some of them ten times as heavy.'

I lifted my shoulders in a pretence of surprise. 'So far we've been given a very different picture at home.'

'Dammit, what else? Why, it's only now that G.H.Q. and the Staff at home are waking up to what the war is. All that pretty talk of the cavalry charging through in all their glory

257

has become so much—' the word he was about to use he abandoned for Raney's sake— 'has become ridiculous. We all know now that this war isn't the Crimea over again or, if it is, it's the Battle of Inkerman, the "soldiers' battle", lasting years instead of a day.'

I felt that he, like the sergeant, was speaking truth. And, no more than the sergeant, did this quiet, sensible and humorous staff captain make me feel that any words of his were intended to chide me, a young man in his twenties, for standing before him in civilian dress. Probably after many years in command, or in staff management, of professional troops he was not yet fully attuned to the idea that every civilian, fit and under forty, would in the end have to be made into a soldier. Not easy for him, whatever he had said, to stomach the notion of ill-trained amateur soldiers. Our talk with him was brief, because by now I only wanted to come away and think—and think again. I took Raney's hand to lead her from the ward, imagining I'd learnt all I needed for my present purpose; but in the bed next but one to the door a big, beefy-red, sour-faced officer, watching us pass by, said to all his neighbours, deliberately loud for me to hear, for Raney to hear, for half the ward to hear, 'There goes a smart young feller who'd look well in khaki.'

My heart seemed to plunge like a dead thing within a breast deflated and sick. He had publicly snubbed me before an assembly of my countrymen, those who had done their duty and paid the price of it.

In the passage, before I had taken two steps, Raney had put both arms about me, regardless of who might pass by. 'What did he mean, that horrible man? Oh, don't let it hurt you, what he said. And it doesn't mean—Stewart darling—it doesn't mean that you'll have to go? You haven't got to listen to a man like that, have you?'

I didn't answer her. I shrugged.

'Oh don't do that,' she pleaded. 'Don't say it means Yes. You mustn't go. You mustn't.'

'If I must, I must.'

'Oh, no. You don't really think so—*please*.'

'I find it difficult to think anything else.'

'Oh, but you needn't think it. You needn't. You can do your work for the country by your wonderful articles. I'm sure that's what you're meant to do. Surely you can see that?'

'All I can see at the moment is that a fountain-pen is rather safer than a rifle and a bayonet. And my nice room at Uncle Douglas's a lot cosier than a trench. 'Specially when winter comes. I can see all that clearly. Very clearly.'

She let me go like something in which she had no rights any more. 'Then it means we shall never get married, after all. I always knew it was too good to be true. I knew something would happen to make it impossible. You were never really meant for me. It wasn't natural that you should love me. Something was bound to happen.'

'That is nonsense, my precious and best beloved. As I told you, it may only mean that we shall get married sooner than we hoped. That's to say, if you still want me.'

'As if I wanted you! As if I wanted you!' She echoed the words in ridicule. 'But we've no home to go to.'

'Listen, adorable. If I do have to go, I'm sure your parents will consent to an immediate marriage and that in these days your father'll be only too glad to have you living at home and helping him. Obviously I shouldn't have to go to France at once; I need to have months of training and could probably see much of you——'

'But it won't be the same. It won't be anything like what we'd hoped. I wanted to live with you.'

'Not quite the same. But you could go on looking for a home, and we might have one before they send me abroad.'

She had hardly heard. Her fists, clenched in a panic, were together over her breasts. 'Oh, darling, darling, my pet, my beloved, you might be . . . killed. Oh, I can't bear it. You heard what he said. "Half of them".'

I deliberately laughed. 'He exaggerated. Not all get killed. Wounded perhaps; no more.'

'Oh, don't joke like that. They talked about years. Both of them. You'd be away for years. Oh, everything has gone to pieces for us. It's like what he said: blown to pieces. And I was so happy . . . so happy. Naturally it couldn't last. It was all too wonderful to last.'

'Darling, give me a day or two to get my thoughts in order and to talk it all over with Uncle—and Father—and, come to that, with my editor who'll keep my job open for me, I'm sure; and then, if I decide I must go——'

'No, you mustn't. You needn't. You can help the war with your writing.'

'Before I go, I promise I'll marry you first. You'll be my wife. Just think of that. In a few days perhaps. The thought's so lovely I can hardly believe it. Tell them I'm coming to ask them.'

I see from an old diary that this day was the 12th September. On the 14th the Battle of the Marne was over. As our sergeant and staff captain had foretold, the German army, strongly reinforced, was entrenched along the line of the Aisne and racing to the sea-coast. Apart from that race all movement had stopped. From deep trenches, ever strengthened, the nations faced each other, exchanging death across a No-Man's-Land—probably for years. Four days of disappointment that the 'glorious victory' was arrested, and a stalemate paralysing the armies; four days in which I didn't see Raney at all; and it was Friday. On that day the war ceased to have any meaning for me. I cared nothing about it. I flung from my mind the thousands of wounded and dying and dead. I gave no thought to the tens of thousands daily stricken with anxiety or bereavement. I went to no recruiting office. I asked for no commission. I held no interest in any nation; neither in my own or any other. Nor in the world in which I must live and endure.

20

It Remains Like Yesterday

It was a Friday. And there is no one left in the world but me to remember it, for I was by many years the youngest of my family, and now I am old. My children are approaching their fifties, and though I may once, long ago, have told them something of it all, it was probably heard for a moment and soon discarded. Why should they dwell on something that happened before they were born? And as for their children, to them I am sure it has never been told. Only a few years now; and I shall not be in the world to remember it. It will have become a nothing; existing for no one.

And yet to me, as I write, it, and the nine days' agony that followed, are almost as large and real as if they belonged to yesterday.

I was standing by the Features Desk in our *World* office, delivering copy of a special Saturday article. I was proud of this article for in it, instead of pleasing my public with comfortable stuff, I had determined, after talks with Uncle Douglas and a submission of the essay to my editor, to tell much of the real truth, though, at the editor's request, in less assured terms than those of our wounded sergeant and sick staff captain. While I was at the desk a young stranger hurried towards me with the words, 'There's a telephone message for you from someone who says he's your Uncle Douglas. Is he the great Douglas O'Murry?'

'Yes, that's he.'

'Gracious! I never knew that. I didn't realize he was your uncle.'

'Well, he is, and he always has been. What's he want?'

'He just says, "Can you come quickly?"'

'Quickly? Why?'

'He didn't say. Just "Can you come quickly?" I've got the receiver off the phone, and he's waiting.'

I hurried through a vast room where a hundred typewriters and other machines were rattling away, and high on the wall before them, in huge letters, for the instruction of those who were news-writers, stood the single word, IMPACT.

In a smaller room I raised the telephone receiver to my ear. Uncle Douglas's voice. 'Can you come at once? Your future father-in-law has been ringing and ringing.' I know now that those words, 'future father-in-law' were a soft wrapping for something hard that waited to be told.

'What's he want?'

'I'll tell you. Come now.'

From the *World* building to Lincoln's Inn was no distance, and I walked there quickly, but in no disordered hurry, no heavy alarm driving me. Ever sanguine, I even hoped that there might be good news waiting for me. Uncle Douglas had so often in my life been the bringer of good news.

When I entered his study he said easily enough, 'Good. Your future father-in-law's been ringing and ringing. And as he's no telephone of his own he has to keep going out to someone else's. So I got you quickly.'

'What's it all about?'

Assuming a carelessness for my sake, he opened with a joke. 'Why you needed to be hung up at your office all the afternoon when, as far as I can gather, the war is at a standstill for a few years and nothing really exciting'll happen till God knows when, I can't imagine. It ... it seems your Raney has been taken rather ill.'

'Ill? What with?'

'He didn't tell me. He just said she'd been taken rather ill. ... I don't suppose it's terribly serious.'

'But why ring for me, if it's not serious?'

'Perhaps he thinks you can be of help in some small way.'

This well-meant performance did not deceive me. I only cried out, 'God! It must be serious. Of course it's serious.' And I dashed out of Chapel Buildings into Chancery Lane to find a taxi. After long impatient minutes I saw one cruising and hailed it.

'A shop in Mortress Lane, please. Fast as you can.'

'Where the hell's that? Never heard of it, chum.'

'In Hollen Dene.'

'Oh, I know the old Dene all right. Who doesn't?'

'Then get there as quick as you can.' And it is strange that, even from an unknown taxi-driver, I got a small relief by adding, 'It's somebody who's ill.'

'Okay, guv'nor. Then I'll do me best for you.'

And he covered the three-to-four miles across London speedily enough, turning into twenty side-roads to evade the traffic.

Stopping him by the shop in Mortress Lane, I pushed, excessively, a ten-shilling note into his hand—one of the new paper things which had just displaced the old half-sovereign and which still seemed dubious things to me; then dashed through the open door into the shop.

Mr. Wayburn was behind his counter, serving a youth with a packet of Woodbines. He saw me round the shoulder of his customer and said, 'One minute, Stoo. Glad you've come.'

The youth departed. Mr. Wayburn closed his till drawer and then, with the counter and its array of magazines between us, began to tell me all. 'Poor Ireen seems properly ill. We dunno what it can be but the night before last——'

Another customer came in for an evening paper and a tin of fifty Gold Flake, and when he was out on the pavement Mr. Wayburn said 'Oh, damn!—' the first time I'd heard this Plymouth brother swear—and irritably he slammed his shop doors upon the world. He shot their bolts and, by force of habit, returned behind his counter. 'It was the night before last; she'd complained of nothing before—seemed as right as right—but now she suddenly talks of pains in her breast—stabbing pains, she called 'em— and begins shivering like one o'clock. Her mother gets her to bed in double-quick time, and I dash off to our doctor. He's a nice young chap and he comes back along of me. Couldn't be nicer—but, Stoo, he talks in all those twelve-and-sixpenny words which neither Mother nor I can understand. We arst 'im to explain, but we didn't understand a lot more of his long words and didn't like to go on arstin'. It's something about inflammation of the heart—what can that be?—and how she ought to have a professional nurse. As if we could afford a nurse! We don't understand at all what it is, so suddenly I thinks of you. You're clever, I mean, and educated and all, and Mother and I thought that, if you'd go round and see him you'd understand. We got to know. We're properly worried.'

'Of course I'll go. At once.'

'You'll find him only a little distance away, and he'll be at home now, as it's his time. That's why we wanted you quick.'

'I'll go. But may I just see Raney first?'

'She's sleepin'. She was in pain and having palpitations so he give her something to bring down her temperacher and make her sleep.'

'Oh, my poor Raney. Does she look very ill?'

'No. Funny, but you'd think that with a temperacher like that she'd look flushed. But she looks the same as ever. A little pale, perhaps.'

'I'm going now. Tell me where.'

He gave me the address. 'You've every right to arst 'im being as how you want to marry her. Come back quick.'

I hastened round to the doctor's surgery. I too was 'properly worried' but not at first in any great panic; partly because my ever-sanguine bent has always helped me defy ill-favoured evidence and expect the best; but, more, because only days ago Raney had seemed alight with health and happiness. The doctor's surgery was a closed shop in a poor road, very like the Wayburns' shop in Mortress Lane, except that its windows instead of displaying magazines and picture postcards had brown screens across them bearing in big white letters the word 'Surgery' and the consulting hours. As I rang at the side-door, so like Raney's side-door, I thought it likely that only a junior doctor would be willing—or would have been sent by a senior partner—to practise in a neighbourhood such as this.

I heard him coming down the stairs and when he opened to

me I saw he was what I had expected: a tall young man pleasant of face, certainly under thirty and probably qualified only a few years since.

His smile was readily available and when I'd told him who I was, he said, 'Come up. I quite understand your coming. You're engaged to her, are you? Well, you've chosen a real nice girl. Come up. As you see I live over my shop.'

We ascended the narrow, steep stairway to the room immediately over the shop, the room that in the Wayburns' little house was the parlour where I'd first been accepted and entertained as her 'young man'. The room told me many things about him: that he was a bachelor, for there was but one comfortable chair, and a small oval table had lately been spread for one person's tea; that he was a young man of some taste and means because the table was Sheraton and bore porcelain of a delicate quality, and the six upright chairs were Hepplewhite—or copies; and that his qualification was recent because so many of the learned-looking medical books on a row of shelves had a fresh, even virgin, look. And if his furniture told me all this, his wondering eyes told me something else: that he recognized from my clothes, my manners, my language, that I belonged to a different background from Irene Wayburn's, and that he was surprised and interested.

He motioned me to the one easy chair, and himself stood before the fireplace, with his heels on the fender. 'Do ask me any questions you like.' He said it in friendliest fashion. We were two youths together, he perhaps twenty-eight, I twenty-five.

I said I would like to know *in the clearest possible terms*—emphasizing these words—what could explain this startlingly sudden illness of Raney. I said I was asking on behalf of her parents, simple uneducated people, who hadn't understood him at all.

His hesitation before answering frightened me; it set my heart hammering. When he spoke, it was to say, 'I've little doubt that it's a case of endocarditis resulting from some rheumatic or septic infection.'

From this first sentence I perceived a young man's pride in

learned words lately acquired. Throughout my life I have observed that this self-satisfaction in polysyllabic, medico-scholarly words can often be an occupational disease, probably unconscious, in the kindliest of doctors.

'Endo-*what*?' I demanded.

'Endocarditis.'

'I haven't the faintest idea what that means.'

'Obviously it means inflammation of the endocardium.'

'Obviously. I'd got as far as that. But if you've no idea what an endocardium is, you're not much wiser.'

'The endocardium is the membrane lining the heart and its valves. The heart has four valves, the mitral, the tricuspid, the aortic and the pulmonary.'

'I'm sure it has; and I'm sure I ought to understand what all that means, but I don't. What matters to me is—is this attack dangerous?'

Pause. 'It can be. Indeed it's always dangerous in the sense that it must be treated very seriously, but recovery is possible— very possible—though it's likely some slight damage to the structure of the heart will remain. Naturally it all depends on whether it's of the acute benign type or the malignant. It can be acute, sub-acute, or chronic.'

Each word, if giving its satisfaction to him, was a dagger-stab for me. 'What has led you to suspect this—this condition?'

'Ausculation.'

I beat my foot with impatience. 'Ausculation?'

'Ausculation is listening through the stethoscope. There was an undoubted murmur—or bruit, as we call it. A murmur does not necessarily mean endocarditis. It can have other causes, or it may mean nothing at all, but I'm afraid I've little doubt this is endocarditis.'

'Why?'

'Because of the accompanying symptoms, the breast pains, the rapidity of the pulse, the troubled breathing, the rigor, the faintness. Then there's a history of rheumatic fever in her family, so there may be an inherited tendency. And she's at a likely age. This is notably a disease that attacks young people under twenty-five; and its incidence is a seasonal thing, nearly always in the autumn of the year. We are in September now. I have decided we must get her into hospital at once. I want her under close observation; with temperature, pulse, and respiration taken frequently. Every four hours at least. With cardiac trouble only trained nurses can see that she's lying properly. Propped up is the classic position for a cardiac condition because of the breathlessness involved, but if this is what I suspect, then she must be kept supine.'

Strange that in a kindly young man this longing to 'show off' should be so manifest. An intelligent young man, he could see that I was sitting before him in an agony of suspense; and I could see that with the best of his heart he pitied me; but there it is: the heart of man is desperately exhibitionist; who can know it? And the display had to go on.

'But, doctor, a few days ago she was as fit and well as I am now. She was happy and on top of the world.'

'That's not an uncommon thing. Often there are no clear symptoms at first, but she's certainly very ill now.'

'Doctor, please, I want the truth. What are you really thinking about her?' I halted while I amassed courage to add the next words. 'Don't spare me.'

He too waited while he summoned up resolution. Then he began, averting his eyes from me, 'If pyaemia results——'

'Please—please'—my impatient foot beat again—'I don't understand these words.'

'Pyaemia is the presence of pyogenic micro-organisms in the blood which produce emboli or metastatic abscesses——'

'Emboli? *Please?*'

'Foreign bodies, clumps of bacteria—or in this case probably cardiac vegetations—which lodge in an artery and cause an obstruction, an embolus——'

I could stand no more of it. I got up and stood with my hands fumbling together. 'Doctor, all these words mean nothing to me. The truth, please? Are you, or are you not, suggesting she may die?'

'We must hope for the best——'

'The *truth*, please.' And again, with the desperate courage of one whose heart was near to dying: 'Don't spare me.'

267

'Well . . . I can only say that if it is malignant——'

'And you think it is?'

'I . . . I'm afraid so.'

'Then?'

'Recovery is rare.'

Again I had little doubt that in a well-meaning young man there was a tincture of pride that he could now stand in a position of authority and pronounce a judgment in firm, clear words.

Foolishly I could only say 'Thank you. . . . Get her to hospital quickly . . .' and hurry to his door and struggle down his stairs. I heard him coming down the stairs behind me as if aware and regretting that his words had almost slain me. I did not turn round to him or speak again. I don't know if he said good-bye. I just opened the door for myself and went out into the street. I ached to be alone and away. My walking was uncertain because of sickness in brain and heart. I staggered away hurriedly, ever repeating, 'Recovery is rare. . . . Recovery is rare. . . .'

The Wayburns' side-door was opened to me by a young but ample housewife who lived, as I knew, next door. 'Yurse. You're Mr. O'Murry, ain't yer? I seen you often and know all about yer. I live next door and come in to see if I can be of any help to them, poor lambs. My hubby made me bring 'em in a spot of whisky to brace 'em up, like, though, as you know, they're not the drinkin' sort. However, I forced 'em to take a sip or two. It does pull you round. No reason why you shouldn't take it as medicine, like. You go up to them. They're in the parlour. I'm doing a spot of clearin' up for 'em. Let them stay with their poor Ireen.'

In the parlour they were sitting in the easy chairs, one on either side of the fireplace. A square occasional table had been drawn up to them by the good woman from next door, and on it were the two glasses from which she'd made them drink. Both, barely conscious of what they were doing, rose as if a guest had entered; and both, in their anxiety remained standing. Raney was still sleeping, they told me, so they had just been sitting here, waiting for me. What had the doctor said?

All that I dared to say I told them. In softer terms than the doctor's. Both listened rather than spoke. But when I'd said all I could Mr. Wayburn did ask, after a silence, 'Then it's really serious, is it?'

'It's serious, yes . . . but all will be done for her. Everything.'

'*Very* serious?'

I decided I must not lie to her parents, and I tried to say softly, 'Well . . . yes . . . so I gathered.'

Neither said a word. Only Mr. Wayburn felt for his wife's fingers, and with their hands joined, they dropped to their knees on the far side of that little square table. I too knelt, to be their companion. It is a strange memory that neither he nor she, who was usually so eloquent in prayer, spoke one word aloud. I suppose they were in some region where words were lost. They just prayed in silence, their hands linked.

21

St. Paschal's and St. Mary's

To the north-west of the Dene, in a street that almost bridged
our highly respectable area and our highly disreputable one,
there was a little unpretentious grey brick hospital, St.
Paschal's and St. Mary's. It had once been St. Paschal's only,
and the place of work for an Anglican order, 'The Little
Sisters of St. Luke', but it had lately been taken over and
splendidly managed by Great St. Mary's, and so was now
known as St. Paschal's and St. Mary's. But to all its neighbours,
alike the virtuous and the vicious, the pious and the impious, it
was always, in my day, known as 'Paschal's', or affectionately,
especially by the sinners, as 'Pasky's'.

Forget a young doctor's self-display: he was instant and
dutiful in his ministry. He got Raney the very next morning
into Paschal's, travelling with her in the ambulance. And
there, in a small bright ward of no more than fourteen beds,
six a side and two at one end, Raney lay, and as she was on the
'Dangerously Ill' list we were allowed to visit her whenever
we wanted to, subject to the discretion of the ward sister or
the staff nurse in charge. Not that the words 'Dangerously
Ill' were ever spoken to us by sisters or nurses; in their sympathetic consideration they spoke only of 'a condition somewhat critical'.

In those few days of my life I did no work at all but wandered
most of the day along the streets around St. Paschal's, with a
rending conflict in my heart between the crying need to get
back to Raney's bedside and a young man's fear of 'being
thought a nuisance'; of being regarded with impatience and
unloved; of being severely warned that I must not weary,
excite, or worry her. The fear was unwarranted because Sister
and the nurses were good to me. That we had been on the
brink of marriage; that they knew hope was small; that Raney

was young and looked beautiful in the pallor of illness, with over-bright eyes, brown like her amber hair—all this put a fullness of pity into their hearts. They had learned that I seldom left the precincts of the hospital from early in the morning till eight at night when all visits must end, and sometimes if the rain was heavy without, and it was time to tell me gently that my visit had been 'long enough', they would say, 'If you like, you can wait in the waiting-room downstairs, and we'll see that a cup of tea is brought to you.'

Again and again it seemed that they knew I was out on the pavements wandering—perhaps a young nurse returning to duty had told them—and they agreed together, 'Oh, let him in. Let him in.' Sister had authority to allow anything.

The only good thing about those terrible days of endlessly roving around, or loitering near, St. Paschal's was the assurance every minute that I loved her far better than myself; that I loved her completely and, as far as any man can, unselfishly. As I wandered back and forth, this way and that, I was forever saying—sometimes aloud to the empty pavements or the gathering dusk, 'O God, come down and help her. . . . Let *me* die rather than her . . . I'll die, I'll die, I'll willingly die. . . . Give *me* the pain, O Lord. . . .'

I would have given all I possessed to put her into a private room, and Aldith and Jack, shocked and pitying, had offered to help, but Raney showed now that, however I might have infected her with my middle-class values, she remained, in her heart, a child of her gregarious streets who 'didn't want to be alone'. A private room had met a need of Father's; Raney's need was the friendliness, the coming and going, and all the daily pageantry of a public ward. So there she lay in a middle bed by a window, kept flat on her back with only a single pillow under her head, and so, whether I stood or sat by her bed, those over-bright eyes looked up at me, and I down at them. Generally I just held her hand, talking but little. Once it was evening, with eight o'clock coming nearer, and she said with a weak smile as if nursing memories of happy times we had enjoyed together, 'Remember the old Tivoli? And the Pav? And the Gaiety?' She even quoted weakly, 'Hadn't we the gaiety?' And after I had said, 'Do I *not* remember?', it was 'Remember the cottage at Ditchling, and the Downs? And the lovely teas?' I nodded, returning smile for smile. Then it was 'Remember the old *Golden Eagle* coming home through that glorious sunset?' and 'Remember coming to Meeting?' I could but notice that one thing she never said during this rehearsal of old joys was 'Remember Hadley Wood?' and this was a further shaft of misery for me because I had no doubt that, although we'd enjoyed many a rapturous day in the Wood, the name carried the memory of a sin which we had shared together and which still troubled her conscience. At last Staff Nurse cast a look towards me which suggested my visit must end, and Raney said as always, 'Come again, darling; come tomorrow,' unwillingly letting my hand slip slowly from hers; but this night, unexpectedly, she added the words, 'I love you so.'

'I love you so.' They were natural words. but why had she added them? Could it be—oh, could it be—that she had guessed now that the days of our love were near their end? In the years since those days of anguish I have learned that even if nurses keep the words 'Dangerously Ill' from relatives and visitors they never succeed in holding them from their patients. 'I love you so.' Firmly in my head the idea tormented me that these words were a merciful version of 'I did love you so'. This harrowing idea rooted deeper as I remembered that earlier that evening she had said in her weak voice, 'It's been so wonderful . . .' and 'More wonderful than anything I could have dreamed. . . .' Oh, could it be . . . ?

Meantime the armies of the world tore themselves to pieces across their long narrow ribbon of No-Man's-Land; and I didn't care. I opened no paper. I listened to nobody who mentioned the war; and if I caught a little of what was told I hurled it from memory; it was of no interest to me. Not that I met many who might talk of the war. After a first telephone call to my editor and the Features Editor I never went near them in Portwith Buildings or the *World* offices; and they, accepting and understanding all, stayed silent. Aldith, Jack, Uncle Douglas—Father too—had the sense and kindness to speak but little to me—and then of Raney only. And the war went on. Sometimes in quiet hours when the wind was easterly I heard it as I roamed the pavements: a throbbing in the air far away behind the autumnal dusks. And it stirred in me no emotion of any kind; only indifference. All this wide world of death and suffering had died for me; all of it except a small focus of harsh pavements and metalled streets around a small grey hospital.

A memory, not unhappy now, is that in these brief days of desperate illness, with death facing her, Raney, who had learned from me to question some of her mother's religion, and even to laugh at parts of it, lapsed the whole way back to the simple assurances given her in childhood. Lying in that bed and looking up at me, and speaking weakly with me, she was her mother's daughter again; she was the girl of nineteen to whom I'd spoken for the first time behind her shop counter: a child of simple and faithful believers. After that day she had been for three years my pupil, striving to be like me in all things; my creation, though I'd never tried to disturb her Christianity, only to blend with it some tolerance and laughter; to train her in what seemed to me an adult attitude; such had been my attempt, but her mother had her safely at the last. In a sickness so weakening to mind as well as body Raney needed and sought again her childhood faith.

And I was glad of this. Because I soon had little doubt that Raney was pretty sure death would be the issue of her illness, and that for my sake she was hiding this conviction from me. And I, of course, hid the truth that I could see all her thoughts. How could I tell her that her brave attempt to save me pain was a failure. Which of us could mention death? Nevertheless I was glad in my assurance that Raney chose to face death with all the hopes that had been given to her in her childhood. One day, sure of this and glad of it, when we talked hardly at all but just held hands, my mind ran back to that day when I went to Meeting with her and her parents and her mother had most powerfully led the prayers after the Breaking of the Bread. Then I had smiled inwardly at the prolongation and the happy intimacy of her one-sided conversation with the

Omnipotent, and at this admirable method of using prayer as a sermon to the 'saints', since preaching was forbidden to women; but now I was glad Raney must have heard her words and her teaching so often. What was it her mother had said that day? Something like 'But now they know a better country; that is, an heavenly, for thou hast prepared for them a city. Wherefore, help us all, like these thy saints, and no matter what woes overtake us, to endure always as seeing the things that are invisible, Thyself and the glorious homeland thou art keeping and guarding for us who die happily in thy faith.'

I remembered also the evening when we all sang behind her, as she strummed on the piano, a hymn with the liveliest of choruses:

> I know there's a bright and glorious land
> Away in the heavens high,
> Where all the redeemed shall with Jesus dwell;
> Will you be there, and I?

And the chorus—how she had hammered the piano for it:

> Will you be there, and I?
> Where all the redeemed with Jesus dwell;
> Will you be there, and I?

I asked myself, Was Raney finding her comfort in all this, and was she wondering—even believing—as I held her hand, 'Will you be there, and I?'

Certainly in these last days of weakness and pain there was something about her which I know not how to describe. Perhaps the best words would be 'a sad but pious radiance'. She was at peace, and I thanked God for her mother.

§

So I come to the afternoon when her parents received a telegram, 'Please come to Alice Jones Ward without delay Sister.' Sister had no need to send a telegram to me because it was one of those early afternoons when I was sitting below in the waiting-room, wondering when I could go up to the ward again 'without being a nuisance'. She came to me herself and said, 'I think you'd better come, my dear'—yes, she called me 'my dear'—'she's very ill, I'm afraid. I've sent a telegram to her parents, and I'm so glad you're here.'

'Sister?'

'Yes?'

'Is she . . . dying?'

She shook her head but not to say No; only to say, 'That, my dear, is a question I never answer; it's not for me to answer. She's very ill.'

Without another word I followed behind her. It was September's last week, and the sun, an autumnal glory around the hospital, flung cruel shafts of splendour through its windows on to the stairs and corridors. Entering the ward, I saw, in pain, that Raney's bed was not in its usual place but had been moved into one of two small single-bedded side wards that opened off this Alice Jones Ward. Sister or a nurse had often put the screens all round Raney's bed when I was with her that we might be together in privacy; today there was need for only one screen across the bed's foot, hiding it from the view of patients in the Alice Jones. Other screens stood against the wall as if waiting. On the new locker beside Raney's bed there was only one thing. It was the gold watch I had given her on its gold bracelet.

Sister, who had entered before me, announced in a cheerful voice, letting today seem no different from yesterday, 'Here he is as ever. Can't keep him away, can I?'

I didn't know how to speak. Raney just said, 'Darling . . .' attempting a smile. Surely her face was never so pale, her eyes so strangely lustred, her voice so weak.

'Sweetheart,' I said, and picked up her hand from the bedclothes.

With the same assumed cheerfulness Sister said, 'I'll leave you together. I've got plenty to do. You stay and talk a little, but don't talk too much. Just be together.'

She drew a chair from the wall for me, but I made no use of it. I just stood there, lightly holding Raney's hand. Sister opened wider the folding screen across the bed's foot and, as she went out, left a smile for us both. I said, 'Thank you,

Sister,' and she shut the door on us, shutting away the voices of the patients in the ward, and all the customary sounds: footsteps of young nurses, an orderly's laughter, trolleys rolling, screens wheeling.

'Well, how's things, beloved?' I asked at last—a feeble question, but I could think of nothing else to say, though my heart was never so charged with love.

Raney, even in her dreadful weakness, spoke more freely than I did. With the same attempted smile she asked, breathlessly, 'Can you guess . . . why they've put me in here? Away from all the others?'

I lied. 'I can only imagine it's because they want you to have more rest and quiet. It's rather nice in here, isn't it?'

'Darling, I can guess why I'm here. I know.'

'Know what, my pet?' One asked this though one knew what she knew.

Her answer was not direct, but its meaning was as clear as the shaft of sunlight that slanted into the room. 'I am ready; I am quite ready,' she said. And her next words have remained to haunt me always. They were simple and remarkable and lovely. They were, 'Stewart darling, what God wants is good enough for me.'

How could I answer anything though I longed to throw myself on my knees at her side and bury my face in her body. I did not weep; I couldn't; I was beyond tears. I could only hold her hand while I felt her fingers close on mine in an effort to grasp them tightly. That unsuccessful effort by weakened muscles was repeated again and again, and it said all that she wanted to say. And my ever-continuing response to it spoke my message to her.

Her parents entered, and she tried to greet them with a smile. She said only, 'Darlings . . .' as they passed to the side of her bed. Her mother did not hesitate to kneel by the bed and lay her arm right across her daughter's breast. Mr. Wayburn remained standing as I stood, but opposite me, the eyes of both of us striving to pour down upon her our love.

I do not know how long we remained thus, nor do I remember any words that may have passed between us, except only that

Raney repeated for their comfort her wonderful sentence which perhaps she had prepared for us all, 'Darlings . . . what God wants is good enough for me'; and that then Mrs. Wayburn did what I had wanted to do: buried her face in her child's breast. She lifted it for a moment to say only, she who could be so rich and fluent with spiritual counsel, 'We're with you, my darling. Dad and I are here.' Mr. Wayburn could only repeat her words, and that with a breaking voice. 'Yes, Mother and me's here, darling. And Stoo.'

'I know,' said Raney weakly.

I recall Raney closing her eyes at last on us all, and seeming to be in a hazed sleep. I can still see Mr. Wayburn, after a time, when he feared that she was unconscious and sinking, going out and fetching Sister in. I remember then, when the shaking of Sister's head meant that this was all, he said only, in an exclamation of intolerable loss, 'Ireen! Our Ireen, Mother.' I suspected that Mrs. Wayburn, utterly silent, her head buried in the bed-clothes, had thrown herself upon her God. And I know that, engraved on my memory, is this: in the moment of syncope and death a phenomenon old and familiar occurred. While all other muscles relaxed in death, the hand holding mine gripped it with a rigidity so firm that it was only with difficulty Sister withdrew my fingers from hers.

22

Farewells

It was but late afternoon and, barely aware what I was doing or where I was going, I went back to Chapel Buildings and Uncle Douglas. No need to wander round the hospital any more. Uncle was there in his living-room, sitting with his pipe over a manuscript, and I just said to him, 'It's all over.' My suffering would have been pure and complete had it not been for that faint pleasure which always appears when one can tell the worst.

He said nothing but laid down his pipe and, coming towards me, put a hand on my arm to urge me into a deep arm-chair. I sank myself into it. Still saying nothing, he went to the tantalus on the sideboard and took a tumbler from its cupboard. Then he spoke, but to say only, 'Have a drink.'

'Thanks.'

He poured out a portion of whisky, very large.

'Oh no; not as large as that,' I protested.

'Better a stiff one. Won't hurt you. It has only half its power when one's in pain. Sip it neat, old boy.'

I took and sipped it while he went back to his chair and relit the pipe which had gone out. He did not resume work on the manuscript. His revolving chair was now turned towards me, and he sat there and smoked, leaving it to me to speak first.

'It's all too difficult,' I said at last. 'Life's too difficult. I can't understand anything. God asks too much. Why should he make her die? I'm feeling I don't care how soon I die too. The sooner the better.'

A little drawing at his pipe; a few drifts of blue smoke from its bowl; and he answered, 'I'm no great Christian, Stewart, but I know what you feel, my dear boy, I . . . I'm with you in your suffering; please know I'm with you all the way.' Then, smoking a little longer before removing the pipe to press down the tobacco with the pencil's top, he continued, 'But I think I know how a Christian would answer you—your good brother, Abel, for instance.'

Rather than hear a Christian answer I hastened on, 'I used to brag that I was an agnostic by which I meant that God might or might not exist, but since I could never know one way or the other, I couldn't feel anything about him. I was indifferent. But, my God, I'm not indifferent now. If he exists, I hate him. Bitterly.'

Uncle's answer was unexpected. It was merely, 'I wonder.'

I didn't want anyone arguing with me, so I said hotly, 'She believed in him utterly at the end. And gave herself to him. I'll do neither.'

He pushed a silver cigarette box towards me. 'Have a cigarette.'

'No, thanks. I don't seem to want one.'

'Well, I too know nothing about God, Stew, but I'm ready to bet he'd say, "Go on feeling like that, old chap, so long as you need to. I can wait".'

'Wait? Then he'll wait for ever. I shall hate him for ever.'

So I said, but even in a depth of pain, even after this wild assertion of everlasting rebellion, I suspected, unwillingly, a wisdom in his words. So I fought against it. 'She was lovely. She was young and beautiful. And good. Why did he kill her? I shall hate him till I die too.'

Silence between us, and then Uncle murmuring again, this time with a gentle smile, 'I wonder.' And adding, 'I can imagine him saying, "I understand. I fully understand".'

It'll ever seem strange to me, this picture of Uncle Douglas, an irreligious man—or so he seemed—sitting there with his pipe and playing, as it were, the part of a ministering priest to a soul in desolation. It is as vivid a memory as Father's wholly surprising declaration in his sickness, 'Children are wonderful.' What Uncle said next, and in his own good time, has lived in my mind to echo there and console. He said, 'I don't believe what has happened to you will result in your hating anyone or anything for ever. What I do know is that it will result in your loving someone for ever.'

'What do you mean?'

'It's simple, Stewart. It's just that if there's one love that endures for ever, it's the love that was never fulfilled.'

As dimly I saw what he was striving to say, he smiled at me from behind a thin plume of smoke and proceeded, 'I think you and your Raney might have lived very happily together and loved each other to the end; I thought both of you were reaching, wonderfully quickly, towards a love that was selfless —or nearly so—and that's the one road to living happy ever after; but now you'll never have to question it or doubt it.'

I chose to answer nothing, but since he suspected there was comfort in this which I would accept one day, he stressed it in a manner that he knew would appeal to me. 'You used to love teaching her your favourite lines of poetry, didn't you?'

'Gracious, yes,' I assented angrily, remembering many a time and many a place.

'Well, there's one line ringing in my mind now.'

'Which is?'

He spoke it beautifully and softly, as it had always been his gift to do, whether on lecture platforms or in after-dinner speeches; leaving it, after his fashion, framed between brief silences. '"For ever wilt thou love and she be fair."'

§

A small seed of healing, certainly, but not at once did it steal above ground and flower. What was wholly unforeseen was that, while I held stubbornly to my angry rebellion against God, Raney's death wrought in me—almost immediately— an overthrow of previous feelings and endowed me with new ones that had far less of selfishness in them. First, my attitude to Father, so rebellious till the days of his sickness, became more than ever a tenderness. Indeed I longed to be tender with everyone. This longing to achieve tenderness stood in my mind like a last offering to Raney. Thus it was less an annulment of my rebellion against God than a part of it. How it came about I know not, but within days of Raney's death three things were in powerful possession of my heart: one was this wish to be a loving son to Father for the rest of his days; the second was a desire to be a better person independently of, and in defiance of, a merciless God, deriving some pleasure and some pride from resolving to be far gentler and kinder than God himself chose to be; the third was a complete change in my attitude to the War. Now that Raney was no more, my small nucleus of a world around her hospital broadened into the great world again, and I was free to look the War in the face. And soon I was sure where my duty lay.

Perhaps our cause was not so much a business of black and white as we young men believed it in that autumn of 1914, but I still, after fifty years of stern analysis by scholarly minds, cannot and will not deny that there was some nobility, something of *noblesse oblige*, when Britain took up the burden of that First World War. Anyhow, whatever may have been uncovered since, I affirm that the young men of my day, or the best of them, believed that we were pledged to defend the values of humanity against a dark cynicism which sought to justify dishonour and a brutal 'frightfulness' as the best and swiftest way of achieving conquests and annexations. So complete was my change that now, when I learned that the conscripted French were dying in their thousands and yet saw many young Englishmen apparently dodging their duty to volunteer, I was jealous for the honour of my country and wanted to hasten into arms as a reproachful example to all shirkers everywhere. Also in my thoughts, somehow or other, Raney's death had begun to seem of a piece with the million other deaths neighbouring the young all over the world. Somehow or other, her death seemed to compel me to put myself beside them.

It was while I was in this mood that Uncle Douglas chanced to talk one evening about the Royal Naval Division. He had a special reason for alluding to it. Long before this evening, long before Raney's death, he had introduced me to the poems of a young Cambridge scholar which had appeared, a few in a slim volume, most in journals and magazines. Those that he admired I had learned to admire too. Some of them I had quoted, or spouted, to Raney when we were together, walking the streets or lying in the grass. There was one about an old

T

vicarage in Cambridge, both sentimentally nostalgic and gaily irreverent. There was a sonnet which I declared might have been written for Raney and me, and recited to her on the down above Ditchling:

> Breathless, we flung us on the windy hill,
>   Laughed in the sun, and kissed the lovely grass.
>   You said, 'Through glory and ecstasy we pass;
> Wind, sun, and earth remain, the birds sing still,
> When we are old, are old . . .' 'And when we die
>   All's over that is ours; but life burns on
> Through other lovers, other lips,' said I,
>   'Heart of my heart, our heaven is now, is won!'

And there was a blithe and witty one about the theological vision of fishes, which would not have appealed at all to Mrs. Wayburn but delighted Raney. Entitled 'Heaven', it expounded that 'there (they trust) there swimmeth One Who swam ere rivers were begun, Immense, of fishy form and mind, Squamous, omnipotent and kind; And under that Almighty Fin, The littlest fish may enter in.'

And now on this evening in October's early days, we got talking about the Royal Naval Division, composed of old regular marines and young, barely trained volunteers, which Britain just then, having no soldiers available, had sent rashly but bravely to help the defeated Belgian army, caught in Antwerp, and he mentioned that this young poet was a sub-lieutenant in one of the volunteer brigades. (I must make it clear that this talk of ours happened many weeks before the young poet published a sonnet, 'Now, God be thanked Who has matched us with His hour', which, whatever people say about it now, expressed pretty exactly my hidden emotions then, after Raney's death.)

'There are several other brilliant young fellows with him in the Division,' said Uncle Douglas.

'But what are they?' I asked. 'Sailors or soldiers?'

'Sailors, I suppose, fighting on land like marines. With naval ranks. There are five battalions in the Division all named after our great naval captains, the Drake, the Hood, the Nelson, the Howe, the Anson. This boy's in the Anson.'

Silence between us. Uncle knew all about my resolve to volunteer. We had debated whether I should enlist in the ranks of the Artists' Rifles or the London Scottish (were we not scions, according to Father, of the Bonnie Earl o' Murray?) or perhaps the Honourable Artillery Company; or whether it would be more sensible to seek a commission. And usually, throughout these first days, Uncle had said mysteriously, 'Wait. Wait a little. The war's going on for a long time yet.' Ever acting as my putative godfather, he counselled, 'Wait.' He didn't say, 'Leave it to me,' but that was what he meant. He did once say, 'No, I'm not having you enlist just yet'; to which I replied, 'Thank you. It's nice to know.' And as it was he who, again and again in my life, had put my feet on a right road, I hesitated till he should say something more. But this evening I exclaimed, 'Oh, I wish I could be a sub-lieutenant in the R.N.D.'; and his response was 'Well, why not?'

'Do you think it would be possible?'

'Why not? Would you really like to?'

'Yes, yes.'

'Well, there'd be good company for you there. Chaps unwise enough to have fallen in love with the craft of writing. Could be I could get you gazetted to one of 'em. As you know, I have the ear of Lord Portwith and he has both ears and a lot more of the First Lord of the Admiralty. They lunch together. And old Portwith thinks well of you, for some reason or other.'

'Oh, do your damnedest with him,' I begged.

'And since the First Lord is himself in love with the craft of writing,' Uncle reminded me, 'he may be well disposed towards you. It could be he's noticed some of your work. It's featured enough, God knows.'

And gazetted I was, very soon, as a sub-lieutenant, but not, unfortunately, in the Anson which then held our admired poet; in the Hood. Still I hoped to see and associate much with him and his friends.

I went at once to Strand-on-the-Green to tell Father of this stirring development. I had written to him after Raney's death and received by return a letter beginning, 'Dear Stewart—' he was incapable of being other than formal, even after such a bereavement as this, but the compassion was there, though it must never be emotionally expressed. The letter went on: 'I simply don't know what to say except that I fully appreciate what this must have meant to you, and that my sympathy with you is very real. I know you loved her, and I am sure from what little I saw of her that she was worthy of your love. I feel I should like you to come and see me so that you could tell me everything and I could learn if there's any way that I could be of help to you. But don't trouble to come till you feel like it. I fully appreciate that you must be very troubled and occupied and sad just now. Come only when you can. I feel a desire to be of help. Yours sincerely, Augustus O'Murry.' To the end of his life Father always signed his letters to his children, in good circumstances and in bad, in joyous and in tragic, 'Yours sincerely, Augustus O'Murry.'

I went to him now, not only to tell him and Elsa and Josef of my commission, but, likely enough, to say my good-byes.

Elsa opened to me. She had not seen me since Raney's death, and she, at any rate, had no recoil from expressing the whole of her emotion. As she recognized me on the threshold, she flung her arms around me and, saying, 'Oh, Master Stewart, Master Stewart,' wept with her face pressed into my coat. Once or twice she muttered, 'She was that lovely . . . she was that lovely. . . . Oh, Master Stewart . . .' and it was I who was comforting her with pats on her back and thanking her with a 'Bless you, dear Elsa,' which set the tears aflow more abundantly. When she let me go she wiped her eyes with her apron and brushed her nose with it; then, in control of herself, opened Father's door and said 'It's Master Stewart,' which three words broke her down again, so that she had to hurry to the kitchen and to Josef. In her flurry she failed to close the door, and I heard in that small house her first words, 'Oh, the poor boy . . . the poor boy.'

I found Father in a room beautifully decorated by himself. Living only for St. Paschal's Hospital, I had not seen his room in this ultimate beauty: sea-green distemper on the walls; meadow-green paint on skirtings and window frames; frieze and ceiling dead-white to catch and spread the sunlight

284

mirrored by the river; all his books in newly carpentered shelves on either side of the chimney-breast; himself in an easy chair facing the pageants of the tideway; and a somnolent Hamish—who had barked grave doubts as he heard my approach but had now recognized me as one of the family—lying folded together again at his master's feet.

'You've really made something perfect of this room,' I said, wishing to speak first of him rather than of myself.

'I'm glad you like it. But it's thanks to you all really. You should be here at night sometimes. If it's moonlight in a cloudless sky, I just turn out my light, draw the curtains, and see the stars in the sky and the red and green stars of the ships passing by. Often the moon's silver wake seems to reach my very door.'

'Well, you've done marvels.' I kept the talk on him, as I sat down. 'You didn't overwork yourself, I hope.'

'On the contrary, the work acted as the finest tonic. But don't let's talk about me. I want to hear from you.' No easier with me than he'd ever been, he stumbled on, 'You do know, I hope how . . . how fully I sympathize. . . .'

'I know it.'

'I see it must have been pretty terrible for you.'

'Oh well . . .' was all I said, hardly knowing what I meant: probably, 'We all have to take such things sooner or later, and must bear them.'

Obviously he felt he ought to say more and was at a loss what it should be. He couldn't pretend that he'd suddenly approved of my resolve to marry a working-class girl, and it was one of his prides to tell the world that he 'believed in always saying what he thought', so now he could concede only, 'She was a charming girl.'

'She was.'

'And I do know what you must be suffering. I should like to be of help.'

'It's enough to have your sympathy.'

'You're still staying with Douglas?'

'Of course. I've nowhere else to go at present. And he's been wonderful in his sympathy.'

Hearing this, Father said something of which I should never have supposed him capable; it showed how with sickness and age his prides and egoism had softened. He said, 'Yes, Douglas is better at that sort of thing than I am. He's cleverer than me, as anyone can see by the far better show he's made of his life. What did he say?'

I turned my eyes away to look through the window. The tide was now idling up towards Kew, and a sculler on his sliding seat cutting easily through it, while sodden fragments of driftwood swept along with it at their own slow pace. As I gazed, a bossy little tug with its tow of lighters came into view, trailing a plume of black smoke from its dingy funnel. When it was through the bridge I tried to tell Father what Uncle Douglas had said. I summed it up in those words, 'If there's one love that endures for ever, it's the love that was never fulfilled.'

Father's eyes had been full on me as I repeated these words, and there was such a long contemplative pause before he said dreamily, 'Yes, I suppose there's something in that. Some truth . . .'; that I wondered of what he was dreaming. Of Mother? Of loves in his life that had grown stale and weary and fallen by the way?

When he asked, almost nervous of his son, 'I suppose you wouldn't care to come and stay here a little? Elsa did suggest this,' I thanked him, saying, 'I'd have loved to come'— which was less than the truth—'but I may be called up at any moment now, and I shall have to report to the Crystal Palace, of all places, or to the barracks at Chatham.'

'To the *Crystal Palace*?' He frowned in bewilderment, and even Hamish lifted his ears at this name and got up and shook himself before folding up again.

'Yes, the R.N.D. is based on the Palace. Or it's one of their depots.'

'You really expect to get this commission?'

At once I perceived his abiding view of me, despite my successes in the dubious world of journalism, as the young one of the family, to whom it was surely improbable that a commission from His Majesty the King could be easily granted. And, a little irritated, I said, 'I am already gazetted.'

'But how has this come about? Why?'

Not without pride I mentioned Lord Portwith and the First Lord of the Admiralty, and again I saw in his eyes a total bafflement that persons of such eminence could be interested in me. I saw also that the old and never-truly-conquered jealousy of his younger brother, so successful and so potent in high places, had lifted its old head; and I found it pathetic that he should be trying to drive it away. 'Douglas has certainly been a wonderful help to you all through your life.' Here peeped the old idea that Stewart, his youngest, had achieved his present position largely by luck. 'Gazetted as what?'

'A sub-lieutenant.'

'But that means the Navy. Are you to be a sailor?'

'A sailor-soldier. Something between the two.'

'But why choose the Royal Naval Division? Why not the Army?'

'Because Uncle Douglas knows a lot of extraordinarily interesting chaps in the R.N.D.' (Uncle Douglas again.) 'Poets and essayists and critics; quite famous, some of them, and all about my age.'

Father's expression suggested that he doubted if such as these would be healthy company or a good influence for me. Like many another teacher of literature he was ready to treat with a portentous gravity the poets and writers of our country, but only if they'd been thirty or more years dead. Matthew Arnold, Browning, Tennyson could all be treated seriously; they had died in the eighties or nineties. I don't believe he'd read any poem of later date than, say, 1884. Poets who chanced to be still alive he pictured as soft and often loose-living sawneys with long hair, flowing ties, and velvet coats.

'When exactly do you expect to be called up?'

'Any day.'

'Well, why not stay here till the day comes? It would be quiet and peaceful for you here, after all you've gone through. I and Elsa and Josef will all understand when you want to be alone.'

'There's nothing I should like better,' I said, lying again, because I was determined that he who had always hoped for

287

love from his children but had managed to destroy it, should have a showing of a son's love at the last. 'But Uncle Douglas believes things will move quickly. The R.N.D. is in real trouble. Antwerp has fallen, as you know, but what Fleet Street and Uncle Douglas also know is that a lot of the R.N.D. in a rather slipshod retreat have straggled over the border into Holland where they'll remain for the rest of the war, courteously entertained by the Dutch as internees. So Uncle suspects that the Admiralty may send for me at once.'

'I see,' said Father. And instantly I saw in his eyes some last dregs of a surprise that the Admiralty might urgently want his 'Young Stewart' as a commissioned officer and leader of men. 'I wonder if Douglas is right.'

'No doubt I shall have to do a month or two of training before they shoot me over there, so this may not be the last good-bye.'

Good-bye. A word carrying so many possibilities these days, with one of them dark and final. Father paused on it; then said, 'Perhaps you won't have to go at all. The Germans can't last out much longer, and my own view is that it'll all be over very soon.'

'Not before I get there, I hope.' So we all spoke in those first months of the war. How could it be that, even after all I'd heard from the old sergeant and the staff captain in the Southend hospital, I still, with the rest of the young men, hoped to get to the Front before it was all over? I cannot rebuild that old ambition now.

Again there was a silence, in which I knew he was thinking thoughts that his formalism and reserve would not suffer him to speak. All he could say at last was, 'If you do have to go, do take care of yourself.'

'You bet I will!'

A half-smile, designed to dilute anything like sentimentality, covered his next words. 'Remember I have only one son.'

Detecting his embarrassment at such words, I quickly changed the subject. I asked if he knew the work of the young poet in the R.N.D. whom I so hoped to meet.

'Never heard of him.' He said it proudly. 'I'm afraid I don't

288

take much interest in the poets of today. I gather they're poor stuff, most of them, making a god of obscurity, so that the more their poems turn into obstacle races, the better they think they are. I've no use for that sort of rubbish. For me the essence of great literature is the communication of lofty ideas between the poet and his readers, and the greater the clarity, the greater the success. That's what I teach my pupils.'

('Poor kids,' I thought.)

'Where are there now a Wordsworth, a Tennyson, a Matthew Arnold, or a Browning? Personally I am content with poets like these.'

Immediately I thought, 'If, good sir, you're talking about obscurity, where will you find more of it than in Browning? And your Matthew Arnold is not lacking in it here and there'; but I said none of this because I was resolved that no breath of conflict must rise between us; and anyhow Browning's obscurities were now sanctified; he'd been dead thirty years.

So I just said, 'I quite agree that there are plenty of this young man's poems you wouldn't care for at all. Especially the one about fish.'

'Fish? You can't make poetry about fish.'

'This chap can. His poem deals with the transcendental speculations of fish.'

'Transcendental *what?*'

'Speculations. Of fish.'

'I never heard such rubbish.'

'Yes, but merry rubbish. And disturbingly suggestive in its way. "In that Heaven of all their wish There shall be no more land, say fish."'

'I don't find that funny.'

'I think I do,' I said, but quickly turned away from it, that the climate of this last evening might remain at set-fair. 'He has a poem about his sheets and his blankets and the smell of old clothes. And there's a sonnet, quite good, about being sea-sick.'

'How perfectly disgusting.'

'Yes, I don't think you'd care for him at all. Besides, he's a terrible Socialist.'

'Well, that settles him for me. I've no use whatever for these half-baked young Socialists who seem to think they're the only intellectuals in the country. Do them good to realize that some of us were blessed with fairly good intellects before they were born.'

Since his words indicated that his head was warming like a pot and might approach the boil, I breathed on it gently. 'Well, at least this one joined up promptly and went to the fight at Antwerp, unlike some of his highly intellectual friends who don't approve of the war.'

'They don't, don't they? Well, I sincerely hope they'll soon be forced to go and do their duty like the French and the Germans. I'd bring in conscription tomorrow. And may I say that I shall be proud that no one had to force you.' He brooded on this before managing to overcome his reticence and add, 'It's not easy for me—for a father to see his son going out to fight and risk his life—but . . . I can have some pride in him.'

'Thank you, Father. But I don't think of it as heroic. It's only that there's nothing else to do.'

'Nothing. I'm sure you're right. I only wish I could go too. They think I'm much too old, whereas I'm pretty certain I could do a lot of things better than some of the weedy youths they seem to have collected.'

'I'm very sure you could. I'm sure you'd have made a magnificent soldier. Much better than me.' (God send he didn't interrupt with 'better than I'.) 'Though they'd have to dig all the trenches a foot or so deeper when you came along.'

These words had so clearly pleased him, both as a compliment to his height and as a tribute to his military potential, that I decided this would be a moment to rise and go.

'Well, I must be off now. I've a hell-of-a-lot of things to arrange in case my orders come quickly—' I wished I hadn't brought hell into it, but perhaps he was willing to endure loose language on an occasion so exceptional. 'Now I must go and say good-bye to Elsa and Josef.'

'Come back if you can before you get your orders. They may not want you at once.'

'If I can. But Uncle Douglas thinks the need is such that it may be a matter of only forty-eight or seventy-two hours. Some even suspect that we may be sent abroad at once.'

He had risen, as I had, and he took my hand. There was a stronger pressure in his grip than any he'd given me in twenty-five years. This made me happy because it seemed an assurance that I'd achieved the purpose of this visit: after twenty-five years of failure he was feeling at last that there was some love between him and his son.

And as I left him to visit Elsa and Josef, I found myself thinking that our settling of Father in this home, where he was so happy and where he had some assurance of our love, was at least one wholly good thing in this our present world of disasters and death.

In her kitchen, saying good-bye to Elsa, I kissed her for the first time in all the years she'd been with us; and this kiss from the young master justified her in clasping me close against her as a mother clasps a son. She begged me to be careful for all their sakes and muttered that she would pray day and night that God would keep me safe and send me back to them.

For which I kissed her again.

'This may not be the end,' I reminded her. 'I may be able to come and say another good-bye before I go. And I will, I will.'

'Oh, *ja, gut*,' came from Josef.

But Elsa, with her mouth tight and trembling, was unable to answer me. She just came to the threshold with Josef; and they waved till I was out of sight. A '*Leben Sie wohl*' and an '*Auf Wiedersehen*' from old Josef, unashamed of, or unconscious of, his German, rang in my ears as I went.

§

Uncle Douglas, as so often, was near the centre of the target. It was but three days later, days given to acquiring uniform and kit, all made and assembled for me in thirty-six hours, that I received orders to report to depot at the Crystal Palace on 'Monday next'. This was Saturday, so I had only forty-eight hours to spend with Aldith and Jack at Little Ebbing.

From the first hour after Raney's death, Aldith had suggested that I came with my bereavement into the peace and empty quiet of a countryside I'd learned to love. 'Jack and I will understand everything and leave you alone if you want to be alone. We'll just feed you at the proper times and look after you.' And both of them, living much at Little Ebbing in these first war months, were models of gentleness and understanding in those forty-eight hours. They spoke not a word about Raney; deliberately they maintained an atmosphere of warm but commonplace cheerfulness in which I could rest and bathe if I wanted to; they made no comment when I wandered alone in the garden or, without a word to them, disappeared into the empty meadows or on to the hills. A wordless sympathy; needing no voice because it was so palpably there: in the cottage; in the garden; invisible, unspoken, but waiting for me or enclosing me every moment of the day.

On that Saturday evening there had been a wonderful sunset, as I strolled alone in the garden, hand gripping hand behind my back. It had been a fiery sunset like that one over the Thames when the old *Golden Eagle* went paddling back to London. But on the Sunday morning when I was again rambling in the garden alone, the sky was nothing but one grey-white cloud and, had there been no October warmth in the air, one could have believed this was one of winter's first drab days. Most of Jack's flowers, among which Raney and I had wandered to admire and to praise, had spent their summer and gone; most of the roses were falling; only the dahlias lifted their many-coloured asterisks bravely aloft, and the michaelmas daisies too, crowding in clumps, breast-high, with the tortoise-shell butterflies busy among them.

Everything in the garden offered me its memories of Raney. The birds as they came and went recalled how I used to enjoy teaching her to distinguish and name them. I noticed a chiff-chaff, a whitethroat, a willow warbler and, high in the sky, a shapely pattern of swallows moving westward; and I longed to tell her that they were summer migrants who had probably finished with England and were heading for the south.

The tall trees that formed a border between Aldith's garden and the Dead Lane were decking themselves in their autumn hues; and inevitably they drew me at last out of the garden gate and into the lane. Was it not here in this tangled wilderness, between the unkempt and disorderly hedges, that I had first said, 'I want you for my wife; I want this more than anything in the world'; and she, when she could believe that she had heard these words, answered, 'Oh, I'll be a good wife to you; I promise; I promise.'

I felt an urge to go a little way along the lane between its rioting undergrowth and entangling branches—why, I hardly knew—perhaps in a kind of farewell because it was at least possible I might never see it again. A sailor-soldier tomorrow, it was not unlikely I might die within weeks or months; and I remember now that this strange thought held more of resignation than regret; partly because the new and totally secret desire for something like unselfishness which Raney's death had worked in me was strong enough to put a mild satisfaction in the thought of sacrificing myself for a cause that had won me; partly because there was the faint hope that if Raney's and her mother's religion was true, then all that bayonet or bullet could achieve would be to give Raney back to me.

I did not go far up the lane; the frustrations from branches and underbrush were too many; but I struggled far enough to see among the hedges the few brave truants from happier roadways: blue speedwells, yellow hawksbeards, and the pink-and-white bindweed racing and clinging along the hedgerow tops. Just before I turned about, defeated by this stumbling journey, I saw, lifting above the high grasses, a wide and jumbled spread of michaelmas daisies, probably an escape from Aldith's garden; and their display of purple asters flung into my mind the closing verse of old Omar Khayyam's *Rubaiyat* about 'the Guests Star-scattered on the Grass'. I remembered quoting to Raney many a line from that so fashionable poem, especially the haunting words, 'And if the Wine you drink, the Lip you press, End in the Nothing all Things end in. . . '.
I had given the poem to her in a tiny limp-leather volume, and she had rejoiced in every word of it, though declaring that

with its worship of wine and its spurning of all the gods in the sky it was no stuff for Mother. As I recaptured all this, the final words of the poem leapt into my mind with such a thrust of loss that I spoke aloud in the empty lane, 'Oh, Raney, Raney . . . my beloved . . .' and quoted them to myself alone there: 'Turn down an empty glass.'

§

A cold February day, with the clouds lying low, mist in the distance, and darkness already down. The Hood battalion was marching at ease, every man equipped for war, along the empty Dorset road. I, a sub-lieutenant, marched at the head of my platoon. All the men behind me or before me were singing; it was not yet eight o'clock, and who in these long country roads could be disturbed by their songs? They were singing because they were excited and delighted to be going at last to the war. It is ever strange to remember this delight, but a fighting front, for all its hail of wounds and death, was where they wanted to be. Soon they would entrain in one of those troop-trains that in these first months of war the sleepless would hear, all the nights, rolling to the ports. The Hood would travel through the night to a Bristol dock where a troopship waited to take them to an Aegean harbour at the far end of the Mediterranean. Delighted they might be but, nonetheless, it was cynically and jeeringly that they sang, 'We don't want to lose you but we think you ought to go, Your King and your Country both need you so . . .' and with a roaring gusto, 'We shall love you all the more, So come and join the forces as your fathers did before.' When they had done with burlesquing this song, they changed it for the total irrelevance of 'Hold your hand out, naughty boy . . . Last night in the pale moonlight, I saw yer, I saw yer, With a nice girl in the park. . . .' At Avonmouth Dock the great troopship against the quay was little more than a high silhouette in the darkness, pierced by a few furtive lights. I got my platoon aboard in the small and still dark hours of the morning. It was a stealthy departure from the soil of England. In the middle of that day the trooper with an escort of two destroyers sailed out into the open seas.

How long we should be in the Levant none of us knew, but all of us foresaw that this might be good-bye to England for a matter of years. As I lost my last sight of England, a ribbon of shadow along the misted horizon, I accepted, so far as my heart would allow, that an old world which had held Raney was for ever behind me.